# The Black Dragons' Chronicles II

M. R. Lucas

Copyright © 2020 M. R. Lucas

All rights reserved.

# Contents

Legal Stuff ..... i
Dedication ..... i
Acknowledgement / Special Thanks ..... ii
List of Key Characters ..... iii
Glossary ..... v
Introduction ..... vi
Death of a Legend ..... 1
A Dragon's Lament ..... 17
A Lesson in Manners ..... 22
Unforeseen Blessings ..... 29
Torondell ..... 41
Autumn Festival ..... 53
Secrets Unfold ..... 67
First Meeting ..... 87
New Sons ..... 96
Ritual of Blood: Release and Bonding ..... 103
Warnings ..... 110
Homecoming ..... 152
A Dragon's Blessing ..... 196
Meeting Death ..... 200
Gambit Answered ..... 209
Subtle Messages ..... 223
Taken ..... 241
Unrequited Love's Call ..... 266
Last Stand at Borauec Mountain ..... 272
Angel of Death ..... 284
New and Old Good Friends ..... 288

New Life and Revelations ............................................................. 293
Epilogue ............................................................................................ 310

# Legal Stuff

Copyright © M. R. Lucas, 2020

All Rights Reserved.  This book is protected by the copyright laws of the United States of America.  Any reproduction or unauthorized use of the written material or artwork contained herein is prohibited without the express written permission of M. R. Lucas.

This story is a work of fiction.  Names, characters, places, and incidents are either the product of the author's imagination and/or are used fictitiously.  Any resemblance to actual persons, living or dead, companies, events or locations is entirely coincidental.

# Dedication

This book was started long after I had transitioned into semi-retirement.  After working full-time for over forty-two years as a business management consultant, data analyst and legal project manager, I still had "extra" time and energy on my hands.  I wanted to do something more "fun;" so, I decided to tell a story, one that I would enjoy reading had someone else written this book.

This writing is dedicated first to my beloved family.  I love you all and wish you much happiness.

Next, this book is also dedicated to those readers who enjoy reading great adventures.  I do hope this book meets that criteria and you find enjoyment reading my tale.

Lastly, I dedicate this book to aspiring writers.  Have fun on your writing journey!  Your "one story" too could originate from a few random, or perhaps definite, thoughts and/or ideas you have.  Your story may be short or long, serious and/or whimsical, dark and/or light; but it is a "story" that is uniquely yours.  So, I encourage you to tell your tale!

Enjoy!!

# Acknowledgement / Special Thanks

Humble and grateful acknowledgement for this book's inspiration came from a variety of sources including some authors who tell great, transforming stories. These motivating authors include:

Dan Brown

Jim Butcher

Frank Herbert

Robert E. Howard

Christopher Paolini

R.A. Salvatore

Three very special friends also joined me on my journey during the development of this writing project. Their editing, listening, encouragement and inspiration were important and helpful. I appreciate and value our many years of close friendship. Special thanks to the following:

Jeffrey R. Lucas-Nihei

Jeremy J. Pettit

Lewis C. Rhodes

Lastly, the fantastic cover art was developed by Denise M. Vlahos. THANK YOU too!

# List of Key Characters

| \multicolumn{3}{c}{House: Je Luneefa} | | |
|---|---|---|
| **Name** | **Description** | **Age** |
| Je Buel | Great mother (First) | 580 |
| Je Taeliel | Great father (First) Husband of Je Buel | 600 |
| | | |
| Je Pagi | Great mother (Second) Daughter of Je Buel and Je Taeliel | 400 |
| Je Maron | Great father (Second) Husband of Je Pagi | 400 |
| | | |
| Je Jero | Son of Je Pagi and Je Maron | 220 |
| Je Tero | Son of Je Pagi and Je Maron | 210 |
| Je Danei | Daughter of Je Pagi and Je Maron | 200 |
| Je Kei | Son of Je Pagi and Je Maron | 180 |
| Je Leena | Daughter of Je Pagi and Je Maron | 170 |
| | | |
| Je Onyxia Ryoshi | Panther, pet of Je Danei | 3 |

| \multicolumn{3}{c}{House: Ona Feiir} | | |
|---|---|---|
| **Name** | **Description** | **Age** |
| Ona Noirar | Great father | 420 |
| Ona Drachir | Nephew of Ona Noirar | 200 |
| | | |
| Ona Kei Kuri Ryuu | Dragon of Ona Noirar | 250 |

| House: Nui Vent |||
| --- | --- | --- |
| **Name** | **Description** | **Age** |
| Nui Honei | Great mother Sister of Nui Samu | 400 |
| Nui Samu | Great father Brother of Nui Honei | 410 |

| Clan: Battle Hammer |||
| --- | --- | --- |
| **Name** | **Description** | **Age** |
| Djurdin Marta | Queen of the Blood Tears Mountains Dwarves | 500 |
| Djurdin Joerson | King of the Blood Tears Mountains Dwarves | 500 |
| Djurdin Roerson | Brother of Djurdin Joerson Commander, Mountain Wreckers | 500 |
| Brynnogaak Urtha Dal | Cousin of Djurdins Battlemage Blood-sister of Je Buel | 540 |
| Heartstone Duenor | Master Engineer and Architect Cousin of the Djurdins | 400 |

| House: Rho |||
| --- | --- | --- |
| **Name** | **Description** | **Age** |
| Rho Jiedae | Queen of Canae | 600 |
| Rho John | King of Canae | 600 |
| Rho Paul | Nephew of Queen and King Prince | 210 |
| Rho James | Nephew of Queen and King Prince | 190 |

Note: Age is expressed in "human time" and approximate at the time when character is first introduced.

# Glossary

It became evident after a while that certain "words" or specialized "terms" were being "created" in order to adequately express certain thoughts. So, this glossary was needed to document those particular words or terms used in this book:

|  |  |
|---|---|
| Belf | Young male elf; less than two hundred ten years old |
| Dragon Life Stages (Years) | Young (Birth -two hundred fifty), Adult (two hundred fifty-one – five hundred), Elder (five hundred one – seven hundred fifty) and Ancient (seven hundred fifty-one - Death) |
| Fah | Unit of measure; the "average" length of a forearm or about twelve inches |
| Felf | Adult female elf; two hundred ten years of age or older |
| Gelf | Young female elf; less than two hundred ten years old |
| Hand | Unit of measure; about eight inches |
| Melf | Adult male elf; two hundred ten years of age or older |
| Moon / Full Moon Cycle | Unit of measure; thirty days |
| Step | Unit of measure; three feet |
| Stone | Unit of measure; fourteen pounds |

It may be important to also note that to simulate the realm's spoken Dwarfish language, the words' "th" sounds are spoken as "d" sounds. Further, words normally ending with "ing" are spoken without the "g" sound effect.

# Introduction

This is a story of fantasy. More specifically, it is a sword and sorcery fantasy tale of great adventure.

This story takes place in the land of Canae, a world filled with many great wonders. In this world, many different creatures live. Both creatures of magic and those that are not inherently magical live, struggle and survive together.

Canae is ruled by a queen and king. Canae's capital city is Rhodell, founded by the ancestors of House Rho. Canae also has many powerful families of nobility called great Houses. Although there is a king who is royalty and his bloodline intends to continue to rule the kingdom for centuries to come, the true power of the kingdom, as well as the noble great Houses, is often wielded by the leading or ruling matriarchs of the families. These House great mothers are formidable and focused upon enhancing their family's status, power, and wealth through a variety of means. Most methods used are overt, such as building strong relationships or alliances through marriage. Other, covert means can sometimes lead to violent acts.

House honor and reputation are cherished and fanatically protected. One who belongs to a great noble House has an inherent duty to protect, enhance and grow the House. The well-being of one's House is prioritized higher than the individual family member. Even love can be ill-fated should it conflict with the House great mothers' strategy and direction. On the other hand, love, shared or unrequited, can be used as a weapon to achieve House goals.

This story is the continuing, great adventure saga of Houses Je Luneefa and Nui Vent. Despite the challenges they meet, the families tightly hold onto each other.

# Death of a Legend

Ona Noirar of House Ona Feiir knew his last living days could, once again, be upon him. He is a mixed-race melf of both dark and rock elf heritages. He is a bit larger, more muscular than the commonly seen woods elves. His skin is brown in color, and he has dark brown eyes and hair. His height is over six fahs, and he weighs just over fourteen stones. Being ambidextrous helps him greatly in battle. He is an elite warrior and still formidable despite his age. Ona Noirar is the former commander of the Black Dragon Knights, an elite warrior brigade of the Canae northern army. A century ago, he lost his position over a dispute with Rhodell's orders. Greatly frustrated with Rhodell, he resigned from the northern army. However, being a dragon rider has afforded Ona Noirar certain privileges. As the only dragon rider in the northern kingdom, he has been called upon from time to time to lead Canae's northern army forces into battle.

Now at four hundred twenty years of age, he is a humble teacher of the ancient elven, martial arts of hand-to-hand combat, weaponry, war, military strategy, diplomacy, history, music, culture, and life. His only student is his nephew, Ona Drachir, another mixed-race melf of both dark and rock elf bloodlines. He is a young melf of just two hundred years and the only surviving blood descendant of Ona Noirar. Like his uncle and father, this melf is also ambidextrous. Ona Drachir too is a knightly and honorable warrior like his father and uncles.

Going to battle, Ona Noirar stared at the moon recalling

many of his heroic deeds, unwise adventures (both as a belf and melf), loves lost and loves gained. He recounted the days of happiness when growing up in his warrior family as the youngest of three brothers. His family belonged to a great noble House in the northeastern part of Canae. House Ona Feiir was well established in the Canae kingdom's *Chronicles of Great Houses*. Although his life was strict, disciplined and even sometimes seemingly harsh, he braved through it all with joy for he had the unconditional love and support of his family. As he continued to grow into adulthood, Ona Noirar continued to embrace and love his knightly and warrior culture for he was a melf of great honor being born into a family who highly respected their culture, heritage, and honor.

With many successful adventures, Ona Noirar brought glory and fame to his House, as did his older brothers. During the second great war with the northern frontier Houses, he and his brothers distinguished themselves as members of the kingdom northern army's elite brigade. While serving in the army at that time, he also found the love of his life. Unlike him, this felf, Nui Honei, a four-hundred-year-old rock elf, was not a member of a noble warrior family raised in knighthood. Her House was considered "low" by elven standards, but she personified nobility, nonetheless. Nui Honei is also a fearless, practiced battlemage. She matched Ona Noirar's skills with certain melee weapons but surpassed him though with the tools and ways of an assassin. Her courage and bravery rivaled his own. Her battle-rage, when unleashed, engulfed Ona Noirar too with her mighty prowess. He truly admired her because Nui Honei was the finest warrior he knew. From that day when they first broke through the enemy's line and took the head of the enemy commander, they fought side by side thereon regardless of battle odds and personal risk. Their feats of courage and skill made them both legends and subjects of many folklore tales and songs.

However, legends they may have been and perhaps still are, they still were less in comparison to the third member of that famed party, the great black dragon Ona Kei Kuri Ryuu or Keiku. She is a nearly full-grown magical, mystical, and majestic winged creature unlike any other dragon in the kingdom. Very few dragons exist throughout the world and black dragons are valued more than any other. Like other dragons, a black dragon is highly intelligent, a fierce warrior, and bonded to his or her chosen rider till death. But black dragons somehow have more magical energy available to them and are more powerful.

Keiku feats too were the source of many bards' songs and

tales. Ona Noirar is her chosen rider, a rider she is truly proud of. When she hatched and bonded with him, he was just a young melf of two hundred twenty years. Now, Keiku is an adult female dragon.

Today, Ona Noirar, Nui Honei and Keiku are flying to yet another battle. This time, they are leading a group of northern army soldiers against the marauding House Si Moina that has been committing violent and criminal acts in the northern frontier against former Canae citizens. These emigrants journeyed to the lawless northern frontier with their hopes and dreams of starting new lives and seizing new opportunities of potential prosperity. Canae, in return, hoped to grow its kingdom geographically because of these settlers occupying the new lands.

After many outcries from the northern frontier's settlers, the king ordered his northern army to act and bring that House's leaders to justice for their crimes. House Si Moina was rumored to control dragons; hence, Ona Noirar was requested to utilize his dragon and lead the northern army forces consisting of four brigades of formidable foot soldiers, battlemages, calvary and archers. They are fierce, well trained, disciplined, and experienced. These soldiers have a well-earned reputation for their fighting prowess, much of which was earned by their highly valued battlemages, specialized warriors who utilized magic to aid soldiers in combat.

Ona Noirar, Nui Honei and Keiku flies just ahead of the northern army brigades of eight mighty hundred soldiers knowing that they may still face a much larger enemy force comprised of House soldiers, as well as war-seasoned mercenaries. The first battle they had with the House Si Moina forces took place two days earlier in the valley of Kos, a short half-day's ride away from the House Si Moina stronghold. There, the enemy employed a group of only eight hundred House soldiers and mercenaries, including two dragon riders. This enemy force proved unsuccessful in defeating this northern army war group.

The day before the battle at Kos, Ona Noirar, Nui Honei and Keiku would sometimes have a skills contest to reduce their tension before an upcoming battle. On this occasion, they chose a familiar game of accuracy, one in which they were to cast spears at distant targets. *"Ona Noirar still lost the bet, and you must pay when we return home,"* Keiku jokingly communicated mentally to both Ona Noirar and Nui Honei trying to lift the now sullen mood of her riders. Through bonding, a dragon can non-verbally communicate with its bonded rider. However, with Nui Honei, Keiku communicates with the felf through blood-magic, based on the same dragon's blood that flows through their veins. This allows Ona Noirar to also communicate mentally with Nui Honei. *"As I recall, you failed to hit the last target with your spear. Hence, you owe me a scrubbing by our lake AND dinner,"* the great dragon concluded.

"How can I possibly hit a target that you destroyed with your flame-spear moments before?" retorted Ona Noirar, obviously a bit annoyed. "You should be disqualified due to your 'cheating' since you destroyed the target! And before you comment, my dear Nui Honei, you too should be disqualified for planting those images of yourself in my mind just before I threw my spear my turn before. You both conspired against me... again. So, this contest should be voided due to technicalities; you two did not abide by our, long-standing, established contest rule: one cannot use magic to affect one's throw."

"And we did not technically 'affect your throw', as I recall. And as you know, I have studied the laws of the Canae kingdom; so, do not challenge my knowledge of rules. Afterall, I made those good rules," declared Keiku.

"No, no, no my love, you lost," said Nui Honei. "Our contest rules do not state we could not 'help' you. I just recalled that image you saw of my returning from my bath that night in the hope it would 'inspire' or 'encourage' you to do your best. So, now whining like a weak male is beneath you. Just admit to your honorable defeat. Keiku, I want fish this time. You?"

"Yes, that sounds wonderful," Keiku replied.

Ona Noirar sighed. "I do not like fish! Why do I even try..." grumbled an exasperated Ona Noirar.

Keiku finished his thought, "Because you are competitive and love us still even though you know you are outmatched and will be defeated mighty warrior. Besides, I think you truly enjoy the 'rewards' of losing sometimes!" That was her cue for Nui Honei to plant another pleasant image of her into Ona Noirar's mind knowing that Nui Honei just hugged him tighter too as they continued their flight towards the enemy stronghold.

Moments later, Ona Noirar, less frustrated, declared, "It is just not fair! You two fight much too well together, whether in love or war. Even those two dragon riders were not a fair match for you."

Keiku "smiled" (as best as a dragon could) and Nui Honei smiled too acknowledging their fierce, combined battle prowess. Although Ona Noirar was Keiku's chosen rider and bonded to him, the relationship between his dragon and Nui Honei was extremely close too, developed over many years of shared experiences.

Through her magic and blood, Keiku had even enabled Nui Honei to communicate with her mentally. This was just one of several examples of their very special and distinguished relationship.

Ona Noirar recalled that during the battle at Kos, he commanded the northern army brigades from horseback while Nui Honei and Keiku fought the enemy dragons and riders. Both enemy dragons were green, larger, adult male dragons. Both had been in battle before given their scars; but chances were they had not battled against a mighty black dragon before like the formidable Keiku. The enemy dragon riders too seemed experienced as well. Their personal weapons of choice were to use bows and arrows to kill their foes from a distance. Nui Honei also wielded a great longbow, Nui Jaei Wei, a blood-magic weapon. This bow and its companion quiver, Nui Baei Wei of ever-full arrows, were an inheritance from her grandmother, another battlemage too.

Both green dragons and their riders fought together before given their well-coordinated attacks. But Nui Honei and Keiku fought together on many other occasions too; and they were faster, fighting as one and could out-maneuver their opponents. In addition, Nui Honei's arrows were enhanced by blood-magic, both hers and Keiku. Once released from her bow, she could make the arrows disappear; so, her intended target would not see the arrows until they hit the intended mark. The black dragon's blood also frightfully increased the impact of the arrows.

Soon after the aerial battle began, two Nui Honei arrows hit the first green dragon rider. Three arrows later had penetrated the first green dragon's body armor and this dragon plummeted towards the ground. Not to be outdone, Keiku conjured and emitted a red flame-spear which she hurled from her mouth at the second green dragon rider. Upon impact the red flame-spear impaled the second dragon rider and pierced through the body of the green dragon as well. Both died instantly.

Greatly inspired, the northern army cheered, engaged the enemy forces there at Kos and defeated them.

On this day, Ona Noirar could see the Si Moina stronghold and remaining forces in the distance; so, they decided to land and wait for their troops to arrive. A short time later, the northern army brigades would engage the remaining House Si Moina forces on the plains before their castle. The enemy chose to fight outside of their castle since they no longer had any aerial dragon support. Somehow the enemy House leader knew too Ona Noirar would not take that advantage of using his dragon either for an aerial assault. Very much a creature of the air, Keiku was also more than happy to fight on the ground alongside the soldiers of the northern army.

House Si Moina first great mother Si Cairyn, adorned in her lavish bluish grey and brown armor, rode on a chariot leading her troops. The enemy force is comprised of about eight hundred soldiers. Si Cairyn even uses six great bears trained for battle. These fierce beasts stood about ten to twelve fahs high. They all appeared huge, easily weighing well over one hundred stones. Great bears were much larger than other northern territory bears, extremely dangerous, ferocious in nature, possessed extraordinary strength and seemingly feared no other beasts.

Nui Honei, as well as Ona Noirar, thought, *"Those beasts are also strengthened further by Si Cairyn's magic no doubt."* With no dragons, House Si Moina deployed these bears as a hopeful counter to the mighty black dragon Keiku.

Si Cairyn, surrounded by her armored bears and personal guard, advanced in front of her troops a short distance. She wanted, it seems, to parley.

In response, Ona Noirar and his personal guard also advanced a short distance towards this House Si Moina party, but still a safe distance away from them should Si Cairyn attempt some trickery.

"Are you here to finally propose and surrender to me? I still do love you..." Si Cairyn asked smiling devilishly. "Why aren't your two pets here with you at this parley? I see them back there hiding with your troops. Your bitch Nui Honei would still be invited to our wedding... Take my offer; for you may still live to see tomorrow's sun. Reject me again this last time and your life and great legend will be finally extinguished this day."

"Enough!" commanded Ona Noirar. "We have been ordered by the king to bring you to justice to account for your House's crimes committed in this frontier. Will you surrender to avoid more needless bloodshed?"

"I have only 'surrendered' to you once before when you were in my bed chamber long ago while we were in the Academy. I will not surrender to you here on this battlefield today. Besides, I have ordered our stronghold's gates to be closed; we will not retreat either. You are still outnumbered and weary from your recent battle at Kos. So, you should surrender to me, and I shall punish only you for your imprudence, again in my bed chamber."

With Si Cairyn's last statement, some silent command must have been given since two of her bears now charged at Ona Noirar. When they were about ten steps from him, they leapt baring their deadly claws and fangs. As quick as they were, Nui Honei was faster shooting four arrows from her great bow Nui Jaei Wei. The arrows disappeared when they left the bow because of Nui Honei's blood-magic. Si Caryn had little/no chance of countering Nui Honei's arrows too if she could not see them. The deadly arrows only reappeared after hitting their intended targets. Two arrows hit each bear piercing their armor and killing them instantly just before they fell to the ground several steps away from Ona Noirar.

Concurrently, Keiku quickly conjured and launched several red flame-spears aimed at Si Cairyn and her small entourage. The House Si Moina great mother chose not to protect her sacrificial animals. Instead, Si Cairyn countered the red flame spears with a magical protective shield placed around her group as they retreated. However, this shield weakened each time Keiku's spear hit it. In a few moments, Keiku and Nui Honei had hurled and shot enough flame-spears and arrows towards the House Si Moina troops to cover Ona Noirar's party retreat and to dissuade any further hostile attempts against Ona Noirar and his party.

Si Cairyn turned from her retreat and uttered some command. The four remining great bears all looked at Keiku, stood on their rear legs, scraped their forepaws together several times and roared loudly. They then all slowly approached Ona Kei Kuri Ryuu. This was a direct challenge for combat, beast against beast. This was also combat to the death; no mercy would be given. It was not uncommon for warring armies to have some type of prelude to their actual, forthcoming battle. These types of single battles were meant to encourage the winning combatant's army while demoralizing the losing combatant's forces.

Not dismayed, Keiku, seemingly thinking, looked at the advancing bears. She then looked at Ona Noirar and Nui Honei, bowed her head and mentally communicated, "*Avenge me should I fall.*"

"*With all our fury precious daughter of House Ona Feiir,*" both Ona Noirar and Nui Honei solemnly promised in response.

With the acceptance of this challenge, Keiku would not use her advantages of flight nor dragon's fire. Magic was not to be used either by any combatant. Thus, the unwritten rules stated. The challenged dragon turned and instinctively began approaching her adversaries. She suspected the bears' claws had been enhanced with blood-magic to make them more powerful, hoping to rip through Keiku's armor and protective wards. In kind, Keiku had called upon her magic beforehand to enhance her claws, as well. She stopped about forty steps away from the bears that now spread out in front of her. Keiku adopted a defensive stance, placing most of her weight onto her hind legs and tail, designed to minimize any exposed body areas. She felt confident that her marvelously crafted black armor and wards would protect her. However, her bare wings were still exposed along with her eyes even though she wore a protective helmet.

"What color are their claws? Do you smell anything unusual about the bears?" Nui Honei mentally asked.

"They are bluish grey in color. There is a hint of rotting deer meat in the air," replied Keiku.

"Beware! Those bears' claws have been covered with a potent poison too!" Nui Honei surmised.

The bears all suddenly attacked together - two attacked the dragon's head hoping to claw-out her eyes and the other two attacked her wings. Extremely strong and merciless, the bears raked and clawed at Keiku. Some moments passed without any substantial damage being inflicted upon any combatants. Keiku's armor proved to be strong enough to counter the bears' attacks. Keiku even moved around on just her hind legs to help protect her folded wings from danger and to keep her foreclaws at the ready. In time, she killed three bears each from a mighty slash of her foreclaws. The last bear she dispatched with her tail, hurling it into the sky and then killing it with a red flame-spear while it was helpless in the air. After the last bear fell to the ground lifeless still with her spear protruding from its body, Keiku turned and looked at the House Si Moina army with fierce defiance. With the end of her personal challenge of combat, the dragon reared back on its hind legs, bared its mighty fangs and foreclaws and emitted a terrifying roar of victory. Ona Noirar and his troops cheered long and hard.

"*Are you hurt in any way?*" a concerned Ona Noirar asked.

"*No, not at all,*" replied Keiku.

"Well done! Although a bit flamboyant at the end there though with that last kill; but I think they received your message," Nui Honei mentally communicated to Keiku. In response, the great dragon just snorted some hot steam.

"Your so-called noble dragon cheated!" screamed Si Moina's great mother Si Cairyn at Ona Noirar.

"You first cheated. She then just responded in kind to your treachery of using poison on your bears' claws!" defended Ona Noirar.

Afterwards, commands were given, and the armies charged at each other and the battle outside the Si Moina stronghold ensued. Later, after Ona Noirar and his brigade won the battle, Si Cairyn and some of her troops still managed to escape the battlefield and retreated inside their stronghold with the castle's gates closing fast behind them.

Ona Noirar ordered some of his troops to remain outside the castle while another group was to go forward and battle with any foes within the castle. He especially needed the battlemages to advance with him to detect and defeat any hidden traps. Ona Noirar, Nui Honei and Keiku first advanced towards the castle's gate. Even though the castle's wooden gates were large and reinforced with steel bindings, with one mighty blast of dragon fire, Keiku completely destroyed the castle's entrance.

As the smoke cleared, Nui Honei put away her bow and selected her fierce crescent swords as her weapons of choice for close quarters combat. Each sword has a double-edged, straight blade ending in a hook shape at the longer blade end and a point at the other, shorter end. Near the blade's shorter end is the hand grip across from which, on the other side of the straight blade, is a smaller, crescent moon shaped blade pointing outwards.

Ona Noirar dismounted from his horse, left his spear, and drew his sword, a scimitar. He also took up his shield and uttered a magical spell. His shield, another blood-magic weapon, then changed its shape from large, curved, and rectangular to round and small.

Before entering the enemy's stronghold, Nui Honei announced, "All, beware. House Si Moina is infamous for its use of poison. Be very careful."

Nui Honei, Ona Noirar, the battlemages and the select group of soldiers then entered the stronghold cautiously. These soldiers were highly skilled in close quarters combat and fought well as a unit when taking an enemy's stronghold. These soldiers were hand-picked by Ona Noirar, all members of his famed Black Dragons unit. They then began searching for any remaining Si House combatants yet unwilling to surrender. After a few more hours, the battle inside the stronghold concluded with the cornering of Si Cairyn and her last remaining, personal guard in the castle's great hall.

Si Cairyn chose not to surrender; so, she engaged in battle against Ona Noirar, Nui Honei, and the Black Dragons soldiers. Eventually, each member of this overly defiant House Si Moina party was killed; but during her last stand, Si Cairyn cast a spell of blood-magic that caused many of the weapons, spears, knives, and arrows, in the hall to be hurled at Ona Noirar simultaneously. Most of these enchanted weapons missed, but a few were successful in penetrating past his protective wards and armor, finally hitting Ona Noirar and inflicting him with a very rare, raznac poison. Raznac poison is powerful, spreads quickly throughout the victim's body, and has no known antidote.

Si Cairyn cast another deadly spell of blood-magic upon Ona Noirar just before Nui Honei took her head. Si Cairyn also knew that Nui Honei would attempt to save him, but still would watch him slowly die in the end. Si Cairyn had once been a rival of Nui Honei for the love of Ona Noirar. Si Caryn's love then was unrequited, and she slowly turned to hate Nui Honei. In her now last desperate act during her House's last battle, Si Caryn wanted Nui Honei to share the pain of watching Ona Noirar die.

Nui Honei knew that Si Cairyn's poison would not be easily undone; nor would she just kill Ona Noirar outright yet to spare him the pain and suffering... So, her love was destined to bear a slow, excruciating pain till he finally died succumbing to the poison or to her merciful hand.

Ona Noirar called out to his dragon, *"Help me."* Overwhelmed by the poison's initial pain, Ona Noirar collapsed in Nui Honei's arms and whispered to her, "Help me outside." Once outside in the burning castle's courtyard, Keiku, knowing the situation, quickly landed beside Ona Noirar and Nui Honei.

"Honei!" Keiku yelled into her mind. "Did you encapsulate the poisoned area with magic?"

"Yes, of course, as quickly as I could," Nui Honei responded angrily.

"I will now give you my blue flames. Your hands will be protected from harm; do not fear. You then know what to do next," commanded Keiku. "I will lend my magic with yours."

Keiku closed her eyes and then called upon her magic and blue flame within. She first magically strengthened Nui Honei, both body and mind. Next, Keiku brought forth three thin slivers of blue flame which were placed onto Nui Honei's protected hand. With the first sliver, Nui Honei cut away the flesh around the first large wound where Si Cairyn's poisoned knife had penetrated Ona Noirar's body. Although his body armor and magical wards had provided some protection, he still suffered a grievous wound which may prove to be fatal. Moments later, Nui Honei saw the pulsing mass of abhorrent poison surrounded by her magical bindings. As if it had life, the raznac poison contained within the mass attempted relentlessly to escape the imposed magical bonds to spread the deadly venom. Although somewhat contained, each attempted escape shot new pain throughout the victim's body. The shooting pain from the poison's escape attempts served a second purpose of also trying to inflict enough pain to still the victim's heart through torture.

Nui Honei cut the mass away with the remaining slivers of blue flame and finally threw the mass away from Ona Noirar. Keiku then with another stream of blue flame destroyed the poison mass. Lastly, she burned the wound with blue flame to cauterize the area.

Nui Honei placed the unconscious Ona Noirar into his saddle and strapped him in. She then mounted the dragon. After securing herself in the saddle, she spoke to Keiku, "*Continue to radiate his body with your healing magic and take us home.*" With one mighty beat of her wings, Keiku and her passengers lifted off the ground.

"*A few moments' delay please,*" Keiku said. Now airborne, with no northern army soldier remaining within the House Si Moina stronghold, Keiku circled the burning castle, majestically emitted a terrifying roar, and released her most destructive blue flame upon the remnants of the House Si Moina castle. Whatever was still standing, stood no more. Whatever evil may have still lingered there was now completely obliterated. Now that her revenge and fury were sated, Keiku turned towards home.

Nui Honei smiled and declared, "Well done. Well done indeed."

As always, Keiku inherently knew which way to go home and started flying quickly. With Ona Noirar dying, she knew too that her days of life were also numbered; for his death would also mark her death. Such was the sacred bond between the joined dragon and its rider. Proudly, she lived and fought by his side; and proudly, she would die knowing she had lived an honorable life. Also, Keiku and Ona Noirar absolutely loved each other. She knew his love for her was only second to the love he had for Nui Honei who had captured his heart too long ago.

During the flight home, Keiku reached out with her mind and spoke to Nui Honei, "Si Cairyn hated Ona Noirar and you so much that *we will have a small chance to completely heal him. Know that I will trade my life for his if need be. Blood-magic is at the root of this situation and your using blood-magic may be the solution to this grave problem. Afterall, you were always the better sorceress than that Si Cairyn hag. You must find a way to counter her poison.*"

"Be at peace Keiku; you know I will do all within my power to completely cure him," Nui Honei responded mentally. "Now, please reach out to Alleina and have her prepare to receive us at your lair. She is the best healer in all the kingdom, and we need her help too."

After a few moments, Keiku responded, *"She will be ready."*

A while later, they landed on Taurus Mountain, a small, isolated mountain range north of the northern kingdom and passed through Keiku's magically warded entrance. On the other side of the warded passageway, Alleina waited with other medical attendants and soldiers. They carefully removed Ona Noirar from his saddle and laid him upon a stretcher. They then moved him to a nearby table. Nui Honei first checked for any magical traps left upon him. After detecting no such harmful magic on Ona Noirar, Alleina and her attendants then began to remove all his remaining armor and clothing. Sweating, Ona Noirar had a high fever and still writhe in pain periodically; but fortunately, these episodes did not appear too severe nor lasted long.

Alleina started her meticulous and methodical examination of Ona Noirar's wound, as well as the remainder of his body. Concurrently, she was again listening to one of her attendants reading from the medical *Chronicles* about raznac poisoning.

After a while, Alleina stopped her examination, looked at Nui Honei and said, "Even though you contained and removed most of the raznac poison, there are still some traces left in his body. The poison was introduced into his body at two other areas, as well. That Si Cairyn devil knew you would focus your initial healing attempts on the obvious large wound she inflicted. But I suspect she was counting on her other small, less obvious attacks to deliver the actual, real killing blow.

"Fortunately, Keiku's healing magic radiation temporarily neutralized the poison traces. However, these traces will still try to move throughout his body via his blood. He will require a complete body blood transfusion to save him. We must draw out his contaminated blood while infusing cleansed blood into his body. This cleansed blood must also be fortified with healing magic since this procedure will place a tremendous amount of strain upon his heart too. So, we may still kill him as we try to save him."

Fiercely optimistic, Keiku mentally broadcasted to the small group around the table, *"Whatever you need of me, you can have it. What are our duties? When do we start?"*

Approvingly, Nui Honei concurred and nodded to Alleina.

Alleina then said, "Ona Noirar's condition is stable; so, let us start after a short break. Keiku, please have your armor removed. Keiku and Honei, we will need you and your magic for supplemental support. All others can leave except my healers."

Standing near the table also in the room was Ona Drachir, the young nephew of Ona Noirar. Keiku mentally reached out to Ona Drachir and said, *"Attend to me."* The belf jumped into the saddle when Keiku turned and walked away. Keiku took flight to her private lair which was higher up on the mountain. Once there, Ona Drachir removed her armor. He then faced the dragon and waited patiently for her next directive.

Keiku mentally spoke, "Listen carefully to my words and keep secret. I must reveal something very precious to me and I will only entrust this secret to you at this time. As you know, I may need to trade my life for my rider's. Should I die, you must embrace and care for my secret. Will you promise me you will do so?"

*"Yes,"* Ona Drachir responded without hesitation.

*"First, reach out your hand, for I need more of your blood."* said Keiku. With a swift swipe of her foreclaw, Keiku made a small cut on Ona Drachir's hand. She then dipped her claw into his blood and sprinkled some onto a portion of what seemed to be one of her cave's walls. She repeated the sprinkling two other times as she moved further into secret areas of her cave. As they proceeded, the dragon would utter an incantation using Ona Drachir's blood. Ona Drachir could see protective walls of magic shimmer and fade away as they passed deeper into her cave. Keiku also shared with Ona Drachir the incantations that would activate and deactivate her various deadly, protective cave wards.

Keiku then explained, "Ever since Si Cairyn sent her thieves and assassins here a few years ago, I had to erect more defenses to guard my secrets. Only you, Ona Noirar and Nui Honei now know of my secret cave compartments. Any other who would try to pass through my defense walls will be killed."

"And what else is so precious to you that you need to guard so well? I saw your treasure hoard after the second magically warded wall; but I doubt that is all you have made secret and trying to protect. No, you are not one who excessively values worldly riches," said Ona Drachir.

Keiku, in her dragon way, tilted her large head, and bared her deadly teeth as if to mimic a smile. She then said mentally, "You are astute as usual. Amongst the other worldly treasure in this innermost chamber, you will see several ordinary looking boulders and rocks. However, three of the boulders are magically crafted mirages. They are really my eggs."

The stunned look on Ona Drachir's face conveyed much; but before he could inquire further, Keiku remarked, *"We will talk later, but now..."* Keiku cut herself, dipped a claw into her blood and extended her claw to Ona Drachir. *"Take my blood, Ona Drachir," she said. After he did so, Keiku cited another incantation and explained, "I now have given you my fully blessed dragon's blood that will increase your strength, both mental and physical. You also now have dragon senses which will allow you to see clearly even in the darkest of nights, hear the faintest sound and detect the smallest odors. All these gifts will aid you when you return two nights hence."*

Keiku relayed other important secret information to Ona Drachir. She mentally transferred her magical wards' passwords, Ona Noirar's inheritance instructions and "last" rites to him rapidly. All her communications were also magically enhanced so he would not forget anything. Although honored with her trust and secrets, Ona Drachir was also deeply saddened that he may have to act upon her instructions due to her possible death. Be that as it may, he would still fulfill his promise to his kindred dragon.

Upon returning to the cavern where Ona Noirar lay still unconscious, all seemed ready to start the medical procedure. Another table was now placed next to Ona Noirar's table. Upon this new table were a variety of medical instruments, vials, beakers, and urns. Alleina, now dressed in her special medical robe (no doubt magically reinforced to protect her from any evil or harmful magic placed on and/or within the patient), spoke instructions to the assembled group, "All, forgive me, for I have never done this type of medical procedure before. I have only read about this procedure in the medical chronicles and discussed it a few times with other great healers of our kingdom. So, I may lose our dear friend in this attempt..."

Nui Honei interrupted, "Dear Alleina, we know you will do your best and we trust you. There is no need for these apologies. Please, just proceed."

Alleina then continued, "Keiku, please lay down next to the outer table. Your blood is the key component we need since it is the strongest in our world. I will need to extract some, blend it with other elf blood, dilute it, magically fortify it, and introduce it into Ona Noirar's body. Please radiate his body again with your healing magic. My two healers will remove the smaller, remaining poison traces while I focus on the blood transfusion.

"Ona Drachir lay down on this table. I need to take some of your blood since your blood is most likely the closest match and will likely not be rejected by your uncle's body. Drink this potion, close your eyes and sleep."

Alleina then nodded to her two assisting healers, each one

was quite skilled and trained for many years by Alleina. These medical assistants were responsible for removing the two remaining raznac poison traces, still contained, but still pulsating intense pain throughout Ona Noirar's body. Alleina drew blood from Ona Drachir and examined it. With Nui Honei's help, this small quantity was then magically multiplied into a larger quantity, an amount Alleina thought would be adequate for their purposes.

Alleina carefully lifted a scale from Keiku body, made an incision and inserted a tube in the incision to draw the dragon's blood. This blood was collected in an urn and mixed with the blood of Ona Drachir. Keiku also conjured several more cutting tools of blue flame which she presented to Alleina and her medical assistants after protecting their hands.

With the two remaining raznac poison sacs removed, Alleina started draining Ona Noirar's old blood while introducing the new, dragon-elf blood into the vein that facilitates the flow of blood directly into the heart. The blood transfusion was a slow process. During this time Nui Honei looked on with grave concern. Although unconscious, Ona Noirar would wince in unknown new pain from time to time as the new blood flowed into his body. There was nothing for her to do except watch and hope all would go well despite the desperate low odds of success.

After some time, Keiku reached out to Nui Honei, "Ona Noirar and I must die tonight for us to live again. Trust me, dear sister. Help me carry out my plan."

For nearly one hundred fifty years, Nui Honei placed her trust in Keiku. This unconditional faith had saved her life many times in the past; yet it was still hard for her to accept Keiku's request given whose life now was now at stake. As hard as it was to accept; and even though she did not completely understand the dragon's meaning, Nui Honei simply responded mentally, "*What do you want of me?*"

"*Let our beloved warrior die tonight,*" Keiku replied. In the next moment, Keiku cast a spell greatly slowing down the beating of Ona Noirar's heart. This decrease projected an image of death into the minds of those in attendance. Alleina made several attempts to recover Ona Noirar, but Keiku secretly countered her attempts. After some time had passed, Alleina ceased her attempts and pronounced that Ona Noirar had died. The assembly wept openly.

Keiku rose and addressed the group, "All, today marks the death of a great warrior, love and dear friend. Remember us for our kindness, loyalty, generosity, and friendship. Remember us fondly.

We will miss you all very much. Know that we both loved you all in life, as well as in death.

"I will now take Ona Noirar's body and entomb him in a secret place where he and I shall be together in death. I shall not see another sun rise; for such is the bond between rider and his dragon. Do not weep for us, for we both lived long, great lives together. We fought and won many battles. We lived with honor. We dearly loved those around us. It is now our time to pass on, onto our ancestors. May they receive us well.

*"Leave this place immediately. I must prepare our tomb before the new dawn breaks."* After her last words, Keiku took the seemingly near-dead body of Ona Noirar and took flight back to her secret lair higher on the mountain.

For a short time, one could see a red glow high on Taurus Mountain. Keiku heated the rocks so much that one could see the eerie red light from many leagues away as some molten rock even flowed down the mountain. Later, one could hear the thunderous sound of the mountain falling upon itself as the top of the mountain imploded shook the surrounding land for many leagues. This was the last act caused by a great dragon as she welcomed death honoring the bond with her dead rider. The great warrior, Ona Noirar, and his great dragon, Ona Kei Kuri Ryuu, both died that early morning.

With the new dawn two days later, there was no more red fire atop Taurus Mountain; no more lava flowed; there was just charred, smoldering rock and ground of a destroyed dragon's lair. Their mountain tomb was created as such to prevent any desecration and serve as their monument for centuries to come.

# A Dragon's Lament

Eight nights later, deep into a moonless night, Ona Drachir secretly left the stronghold and climbed high onto Toron mountain where he eventually met the great dragon, Ona Kei Kuri Ryuu. The dragon picked him up and flew even higher up the mountain where they returned to her second hidden, secret lair.

To no surprise, Ona Drachir saw his unconscious uncle being attended to by Alleina. Evidently, she too had secretly made her way there to Keiku's second, very secret lair. Alleina said, when she saw the young melf, "Your uncle still lives, but barely. I want to take more of your blood for another transfusion. He will remain unconscious for a long time it seems while his body slowly repairs itself and recovers from the poisoning. Keiku will supply him nourishment through this special harness I created. Keiku's enriched blood will also be syphoned and furnished to Ona Noirar periodically."

"How long will it take for him to recover?" asked a distraught Ona Drachir.

"Yes, how long?" asked Nui Honei who now slowly walked towards them from the darkened depths of the lair. Shrouded in black, her sadness was very deep for she still mourned the "death" of her beloved.

Alleina woefully answered, "I still do not know. It may take days, moons or even years; I cannot say. We must be patient and even thankful that he has this slim chance to perhaps live again."

After some uncomfortable silence, Keiku spoke words into

their minds, "I have something to share with all of you; something that has heavily weighed upon my heart an awfully long time. I wish to lament.

"Nui Honei, do you remember when you, Ona Noirar and some others were invited to the House Si Moina stronghold for an Academy graduation celebration given for Si Cairyn's nephew and niece?

"The year before, Ona Noirar and I had flown into the northern frontier on a routine patrol duty. There, high in the skies, were two red dragons flying. I was mesmerized by their grace and beauty. It was the first time I had seen other dragons. They were beautiful. I... was... naturally curious.

"I later learned that both dragons were adult males. At that time, I was still young and quite naïve. When I later learned about the academy graduation celebration, I was excited to know that Ona Noirar and I would be going. During the year after that first sighting of the red dragons, I believe I started to mature and entered a period of estrus. I constantly watched other animals closely as they interacted with other animals of their species, including mating. I yearned for a mate like other creatures. I wanted love like the kind I saw when Ona Noirar looked at you Nui Honei and when you looked at your beloved. Although he was still a bit confused about his true feelings for you, I believed his love for you was and is very real.

"So, he went to the graduation celebration intending to bid farewell to all his former classmates also invited to the celebration. I, of course, accompanied him hoping to find 'love' with one of the red dragons I had seen the year before. Unbeknownst to us, Si Cairyn had vastly different plans for the both of us...

"Just before we were about to depart, Ona Noirar was taken hostage. Si Cairyn also poisoned him. To keep him alive, I was forced to mate with those despicable red dragons that were just foul creatures. I learned that Si Cairyn only wanted any dragon eggs that would result from the forced 'arrangement' made. She boasted of building her own group of dragon warriors who would enforce her will upon the northern frontier initially and then beyond. Further, to make matters worse, neither of those red dragons even cared for me. Like Si Cairyn, they only wanted progeny; I was nothing more than a 'breeding' slave to them. I was greatly saddened by my first interaction with another dragon. I became terribly angry.

"My anger sustained me. I was angry at those red dragons; I was angry with House Si Moina; I was angry at Si Cairyn; but, most of all, I was angry with Ona Noirar for not protecting me from Si

Cairyn's real intentions. He should have known, or at least suspected, her evil plans. I believe that Si Cairyn only coveted three things in this life: wealth, dragons, and Ona Noirar. Underneath her outer decent being was a core of extraordinary evil and malignant hatred. Not only did she want to rule the northern frontier; she also wanted to rule the entire kingdom. Her hopes of conquest had no bounds; there was no limit to the blood she intended to spill for her to reach her goal.

"Being a skilled mage herself, she even wanted to re-bond me to her... even at the expense of sacrificing Ona Noirar's life if need be. Should her attempts fail, her alternate plan was to create dragon offspring which she intended to control.

"At one point during our captivity, I vowed to kill Ona Noirar in order to kill myself. I started by randomly killing House Si Moina soldiers and family members whenever I got a chance. In turn, Si Cairyn would punish Ona Noirar severely for my actions. However, she still would not kill him. Thus, that experience of our captivity caused my deep torturous despair. My anger gave me hope to continue to live long enough to extract revenge upon Ona Noirar and House Si Moina. With time, my anger changed to pure rage and my rage increased with each passing day of captivity.

"I did become pregnant with the spawn of Si Cairyn's dragons as Si Cairyn had hoped. With that realization, I hasten my plan to kill myself before I laid any eggs which would only be used for evil.

"One day, I noticed a familiar scent in the air. Although I did not recognize her at first, there was no denying her unique scent. You, Nui Honei had come. She had disguised herself as a House Si Moina soldier. When she saw me from a distance, she just first looked at me, trying to assess my condition perhaps. Then with pleading eyes, she simply said in an ancient elvish dialect which she chanced no one else would understand, 'Please forgive him'. For days to come, I thought about her words and found new purpose. I decided to live.

"With Nui Honei's help, she removed the chains binding me and we all escaped. Just before we escaped though, I did manage to kill one of the red dragons when it got too close to me trying to cuddle affection before he wanted to mate again... As my fangs closed around that foul dragon's neck, I knew then I was no longer a noble dragon with honor. I had become a monster consumed by my rage and bloodlust. I can still taste its foul blood from my scarred memory. I can even remember its mournful eyes staring back at me from its severed head as its life came to an end. I especially reveled in killing that tormentor. Si Cairyn just laughed at the dead beast, calling it a 'typical foolish male'. Her wicked laugh still haunts my restless dreams, reminding me of evil's powerful grasp.

"Our captivity lasted about three full moons. On our flight home, we were attacked by the other red dragon. This second dragon was filled with rage since I killed its brother. It wanted deathly revenge. That is when I realized I could summon blue flame which is powered by both my magic and rage. The second red dragon and its rider died quickly when I struck them both with my blue flame-spears.

"After finally returning home, Alleina healed Ona Noirar. When he was ready, he approached me one night and apologized for his mistakes. He knelt before me and humbled himself to receive my punishment. I cut him deeply with my claw, but I did not kill him. Alleina healed that wound too - all too quickly though. He only suffered thereafter one moon's time.

"During this same very difficult time, my relationship with Nui Honei started to grow too. We became good friends. I befriended you, Alleina, too. Through my blood-magic, they can 'hear' my thoughts; and they can share their thoughts with me. This is the same for another trusted friend, Ona Drachir. Alleina and Nui Honei both helped me release my anger and eventually accept Ona Noirar's attempt to repair our relationship. With Nui Honei's guidance, he eventually earned my forgiveness. Serving me large portions of fish for many days after his second recovery helped. My anger did subside with time too and I would share my thoughts with him again. One pact we made then is that I must endorse any of his future, potential, long-term relationships with females before he can repeat any past foolish mistakes."

Keiku barred her fangs and made a grumbling sound to perhaps mimic her laughter. After a few moments, she continued, *"I will be eternally grateful to you two for all that you have done in helping me regain my former, noble self.*

"When it was time for me to lay my eggs, you, Alleina and Nui Honei, were there to help me. Yes, some of the 'rocks' you see here are actually my eggs which I have magically hidden and guarded from any would-be thieves for over a hundred years.

"When we recently returned to House Si Moina, my old anger and rage returned too like a terrible storm flooding my being with the all-too-familiar rage. Just before we left, I meant to destroy everything that House represented. Such would be my reminder not to be the target of a dragon's wrath. Like a horrific unrelenting storm, I rained down blue flame hellfire onto that stronghold leaving nothing there but scorched ground, never to sustain any kind of life again.

"May I never feel such pain and rage again."

# A Lesson in Manners

The sun was setting and after another long day's journey, Ona Drachir welcomed the site of the inn up ahead. This young warrior looked forward to a good, hot meal and sleeping under a roof. This was the end of his several days' journey from his former, temporary home at Taurus Mountain. Five nights ago, he lost his uncle who died from poisoning. Along with his death, his uncle's dragon joined him in death as well. He was alone now; he had no other living, immediate family. Yet, his life still had purpose. He was still a young melf of just two hundred years. Although on the brink of adulthood, his uncle wanted him to continue his martial arts and weapons training with a master believed to be living in Torondell, the greatest city in the North of the Canae kingdom.

When he finally arrived at the inn, not far from his final destination, it was sunset. The inn, the Dragon's Bow, was typical in that the main room was large, warmed by two large fire blazing hearths, crowded with a wide variety of patrons, loud with many conversations spoken in different languages and with lively music being played to help the patrons drink, eat and care less about their problems for the little time they are there. As a mixed rock and dark elf, no one stopped what they were doing to pay him any attention when he walked into the inn. He quickly found an empty table near the back of the room. Most of the patrons there are either human, woods elf, gnome, or dwarf.

After ordering his evening meal, he noticed that the inn's crowd had quieted. A lone musician, a koto player, had started playing. The musician, a young lovely felf, started playing a melodic and vibrant tune, a generally known classic song depicting the heroes of the great wars. Her mastery of this stringed instrument became evident quickly. Other musicians joined her. After a while, along with some alcoholic encouragement, different patrons started to sing verses of the familiar song. Verses, old and new, were repeated often, each patron trying to out-sing the former. This merriment continued for a long time, well into the night.

After a much-needed, restful night of sleep, Ona Drachir rose at mid-morning. He is hopeful and anxious to reach his journey's end on this day. Currently, the koto musician from the night before is also there entertaining the inn's morning guests. Her music, upbeat and joyous, seemed to announce a "good day" as the bright sun shone warmly through the inn's windows. Some of the appreciative patrons even placed coins in her jar as they left the inn, no doubt thankful for such a good start to their day.

As Ona Drachir finished his late morning meal, three House soldiers arrived at the inn. They were welcomed by the innkeeper who apparently had welcomed them there before since he seemed to know their names and usual food orders. These soldiers, two melfs (male elves) and a felf (female elf), bore similar facial features too.

The soldiers all gazed around the room taking note of all the current inn's guests within the hall. After some time, one of the recently arrived House soldiers gazed at the musician as if captured by the music's haunting spell. When she stopped playing shortly thereafter, he rose from the table and started walking towards the musician. This bewitched melf seem to first introduce himself with an air of arrogance and then invited her to join him and his comrades at their table. The musician, Zhen Laehua, returned her introduction and politely declined, informing the soldier that she and her mother needed to continue their journey this morning soon. Taken aback, the soldier Je Jero was quite embarrassed with the polite rejection, especially after his comrades started laughing at him. Je Jero is the handsome woods elf, first son of House Je Luneefa, and a young two hundred twenty years old melf.

"Not every female is so charmed, it seems my handsome brother," said the felf House soldier, Je Danei. She is a two hundred years old woods elf and the first daughter of House Je Luneefa. "My thanks to you Lady Zhen for deflating my brother's ego."

Angry, Je Jero kicked the musician's coin jar scattering coins across the room. He then, still with unsated comfort for his anger, looked at Zhen Laehua's instrument. At that moment, Zhen

Laehua's eyes flashed in anger, and she declared, "You will *not* harm my koto." She then pulled a hidden long knife ready to defend and protect her precious instrument.

Further frustrated, Je Jero responded, "Then, challenge met."

As Je Jero pulled his own sword, Ona Drachir called, "Hold soldier! "Don't you think this challenge is a bit unfair? Surely, an honorable soldier, such as yourself, would not quarrel over a declined invitation, especially with uneven odds such as her knife against your sword."

"And who are you?" asked Je Jero. "Why do you wish to interfere in my affair?"

Ona Drachir responded quickly, "I am a traveler, on his way to the great city of Torondell. As to why I chose to interfere in your affair, it is my uncle's teachings to come to the aid of others when needed.

"Forgive me Lady Zhen Laehua, I do not wish to presume; but are you not in need at this moment of some assistance?" Ona Drachir asked the felf.

"Yes, I believe so," said a frightened Zhen Laehua, hesitantly.

"So, that being the case soldier of House Je Luneefa, how do you wish to resolve this matter since you owe her some hard-earned coins?" said Ona Drachir.

With a sinister grin Je Jero replied, "I drew my sword in response to Lady Zhen Laehua's first drawing her knife. My sword is at least three times the length of that knife; so, the terms of this resolution is for you to fight me and my two comrades to maintain the same odds she first established. Do you agree or wish to yield now?"

"With only three-to-one odds? I surely cannot yield now," proclaimed Ona Drachir. "Also, let us take our contest outside where we will have more room and do less damage to the inn." Now outside, Ona Drachir continued, asking his opponents, "One-blow rule? Wooden or steel weapons?"

"Yes and no," replied Je Jero. "Less time should be required in this case and I am quite hungry!" Je Jero and his comrades started to take off their capes and weapon belts, because this was to be an unarmed contest of martial skills. This contest is simple: a successful blow eliminated a fighter. The three House Je Luneefa soldiers were all fighting against the lone Ona Drachir, and they only needed to land one blow upon him to win the contest. On the other hand, Ona Drachir needed to hit each of the three soldiers before any of them managed to hit him.

"Prizes?" questioned Je Jero? "After we win, Lady Zhen Laehua will have dinner with me tonight in the city."

"Tonight, you traveler will clean and groom my horse dirtied from this last patrol duty," said the felf soldier, Je Danei. Though dirtied from her assignment, one could still see the beauty of this young, two hundred years old felf.

"My horse too," the younger brother, Je Tero, another woods elf of two hundred ten years of age, quickly added.

"What do you want traveler should you win?" Zhen Laehua asked.

The three House Je Luneefa soldiers all chuckled. Ona Drachir quietly finished removing his weapons and responded, "You soldiers are to first replace the coins Lady Zhen Laehua lost and provide her and her mother safe escort to the city. Lastly, I would like you to introduce me to the First Commander Nui Samu of the northern Canae army."

Puzzled, Je Jero remarked, "There is no 'First Commander' Nui Samu; he is now just a military advisor and headmaster of his martial arts school. And if my eyes do not deceive me, I see his banner in the distance there; so, he will be here soon to observe your lesson in manners we are about to teach you."

The four combatants now faced each other, about five steps apart. On one side stood the three House Je Luneefa soldiers apart from each other, and Ona Drachir, with confidence, faced them slowly taking his fighting position, one that was quite unfamiliar to the soldiers. As expected, Je Jero took immediate command and spoke a battle command regarding the formation he wanted his comrades to take.

"Shall we begin?" Je Jero inquired. "If everyone is ready, Lady Zhen Laehua please start this contest."

Zhen Laehua looked at the combatants and then shouted, "Begin."

As she shouted to start the contest, more House Je Luneefa soldiers rode into the inn's courtyard. A distinguished, but sinister looking, aged melf was leading this group of soldiers.

As anticipated, the three House Je Luneefa soldiers quickly advanced and attacked simultaneously with hand attacks aimed at three different parts of Ona Drachir's body. However, Ona Drachir more quickly advanced and launched a flying kick attack at the younger melf soldier who appeared more tentative about this battle. Ona Drachir's kick landed on Je Tero's shoulder knocking him over; but more importantly, this tactic propelled him past the other two

Je Luneefa combatants.

Je Jero and Je Danei now faced Ona Drachir and launched coordinated hand and foot attack combinations at him. Although Ona Drachir was fast with his feet, his hands and arms proved to be faster as he blocked the attacks from both Je Jero and Je Danei. After some time, Ona Drachir started his own series of attacks using a fighting style unfamiliar to the House Je Luneefa soldiers. His second attack combination successfully scored a hit on Je Danei while blocking a counterattack from her brother. Now facing only one adversary, Ona Drachir used another different attack combination to successfully land a blow upon Je Jero. The contest is now over.

After a yell of frustration, Je Jero sadly said to Ona Drachir, "You fought well and won; congratulations." He then reached into his bag and pulled eight silver coins from it. He presented the silver, more than enough compensation, to Zhen Laehua with an apology for his earlier bad manners.

The second Je Luneefa brother approached Ona Drachir, greeted him, and thanked him for his lesson. Je Tero then asked, "Why did you choose to attack me first?"

"You looked uncommitted to the contest; so, I chanced you would not expect my sudden attack since you claimed favorable odds. As I have learned from my House great father, 'odds do not always determine the outcome of a fight.' I was fortunate with my tactic," humbly explained Ona Drachir.

Je Danei also approached the contest winner and congratulated him. She then added, "What was that second fighting style you used? How were you able to block my brother's counterattack and still attack me? Will you teach me those attack combinations? How did..."

Ona Drachir bowed respectfully to the felf but started walking quickly towards the crowd of newly arrived House Je Luneefa soldiers. Specifically, he slowly approached the assumed Nui Samu. With great respect, Ona Drachir bowed and saluted the melf in an old, traditional manner. "Greetings and well met First Commander," said Ona Drachir.

Although this melf looked several hard centuries old, he still appeared to be powerful looking, agile, and incredibly deadly. Nui Samu responded, "Greetings. I am no longer a commander in the northern army, but now just a humble weapons master of Houses Nui Vent and House Je Luneefa. I also have the distinction of being these three soldiers' uncle, as well. Thank you for their lesson. I enjoyed watching your contest seeing that you were trained in the old ways of elven martial arts; this is still something my nephews and nieces have yet to embrace and master." Disappointedly, he voiced his comments glaring at the three House Je Luneefa soldiers. Nui Samu continued, "May I know your name and the name of your martial arts master?"

"My name is Ona Drachir of House Ona Feiir," said Ona Drachir. My weapons and martial arts master was my uncle, Ona Noirar. "My uncle wanted me to find you to ask a favor…"

Before he could continue, Nui Samu interjected, "Please join me for dinner at my stronghold tonight; we can talk further then." Nui Samu then turned away, mounted his horse, and rode away, followed thereafter by his entourage. Ona Drachir quickly left and returned with his horse ready for travel. He bid his farewell to the Je Luneefa soldiers and rode after the Nui Samu party.

Late that morning, before Je Jero and his soldiers were getting ready to depart, two more travelers arrived at the inn. Unlike other small traveling parties, this group consisted of some faces well known to him. Both his mother, Je Pagi, and adopted aunt, Nui Honei, had arrived attired and equipped for a long journey. After greeting his elders, Je Jero asked, "Where are you bound?"

His mother, a stately, good-looking, four centuries old woods elf with long, auburn hair and brown eyes responded, "We are adventure bound my son. We will travel back to Torondell, but through the great forest where several robberies have occurred over the last few fortnights. We hope to catch these bandits and bring them to justice." Then looking at her daughter, she asked "Danei, will you join us?"

Smiling, Je Danei replied, "I am now finished with my patrol duty and have earned three days' rest. Patrolling the northern territory was somewhat boring; so, catching a few thieves on the way home should indeed be more enjoyable. Therefore, 'Yes', I will join you on your little adventure. But I have no extra clothes for traveling other than my House uniform."

"Do not worry about that. We anticipated your answer and brought you something appropriate to disguise yourself as another traveler too," remarked her aunt, Nui Honei.

"By the way, where is my little Ony?" asked Je Danei.

Je Jero and Je Tero looked at each other and started to chuckle. "'Little' you say?" said Je Tero. "Your precious little pet is a nearly full-grown, twenty stone beast with long fangs and claws. She is definitely no longer 'little' dear sister."

"Again, my niece, do not worry about her either, for she is

already in the forest hunting and waiting for us," said Nui Honei.

Je Danei looked at her mother and aunt and then asked, "When do you wish to depart?"

Je Pagi said, "Shall we stay here overnight and start our journey at tomorrow's dawn?"

"Agreed," said Nui Honei approvingly.

"Thank you, my dear mother and aunt," a relieved Je Danei said.

Je Jero then said, "I have a request dear mother and aunt. Would you then please escort Lady Zhen Lae and her daughter, Lady Zhen Laehua, to our city? Tero and I will take a more direct and faster route back home." Remembering that he and his brother may still have a chance to visit with the Pi Zhou sisters tonight, he now wanted to get back to their city quickly. The two brothers could also continue a more enjoyable adventure of their own. So, the two Je Luneefa brothers departed leaving their other family members to take a longer route back to their home, Torondell.

"It would be our pleasure," said Nui Honei. With that said, the Ladies Zhen introduced themselves to Je Pagi and Nui Honei. Later that day, they all met again to share an evening meal and get further acquainted.

# Unforeseen Blessings

The next day before dawn, Ladies Zhen were also ready to depart after carefully packing their small wagon. Shortly after dawn, these females and their escort, Je Pagi, Nui Honei and Je Danei, left the inn heading to Torondell, but taking a known merchant, wagon-friendly route that goes through the great forest.

    At midday, the travelers stopped for a meal and a brief rest. They had finally arrived at the edge of the great forest. Je Pagi started to prepare a meal while the others gathered wood for a fire. During the meal, Zhen Lae asked, "Please forgive my ignorance, but I am just a simple seamstress by trade and not worldly. Why are you putting yourselves in harm's way instead of some soldiers? Even though your daughter is a soldier, is she enough protection for all of us? Are you not concerned that the thieves are all males and could possibly overpower or even harm you?"

    Nui Honei is a rock elf of four hundred years. She, a soft-spoken felf, replied, "I am of a warrior's family, born into battle, fought in many battles and most likely will die in battle. That is my proud heritage. Both my sister and niece are warriors too, despite their good looks and pretty faces. During past wartimes, females and young ones are often victims without a chance to defend themselves. All young, both females and males, in our families are taught how to wield weapons so that they, at least, will have an opportunity to defend themselves and not be hopelessly slaughtered. We are also defenders of our kingdom's northern territory. Someone needed to stop these bandits, and we volunteered given our boredom at our strongholds in Torondell."

After their midday repast, the five females packed and continued their journey. Je Danei led the group back to their city. She was followed by the felfs Zhen in their wagon. Riding side by side, Je Pagi and Nui Honei made up the rear of the small party. Travelling was easy since they were on the main road through the forest. Given the easy travel, they hope to make their destination by tomorrow morning after spending one last night in the forest. It was summer and they were in a great forest with many tall trees. Many of the trees were quite old and reached high towards the sky. Being summer though, the trees' canopy offered some relief from the sun's intense, direct heat; but it was still quite warm, as well as unusually humid, within the forest.

As the sun started to set, they found a suitable camp site by a lake, near a waterfall. The rushing water cooled the immediate area from the forest's stifling heat; so, this spot brought some welcome relief.

Well after sundown, the travelers had eaten their evening meal and are now just relaxing by the campfire. Zhen Lae looked at her daughter with the all-too-familiar expression telling her that she still needed to practice her music despite their long day's journey.

Zhen Laehua is a kind, beautiful, young felf of two hundred years old. Her spirit and mood changed often and would be expressed passionately through her music. Zhen Laehua plays the koto and is a music prodigy. With renewed high spirits, Zhen Laehua again contemplated her desired wish, *"I yearn to stop traveling and settle in a great city where I can join a great noble's or city orchestra. Then, I could hopefully earn enough money for me and Mother to live comfortably."* Even when she was much younger, Zhen Laehua's grandmother told her many stories of many great musicians and orchestras. In fact, Zhen Laehua's grandmother, another extraordinary koto player, passed on her passion for music and skills to her gifted, beloved granddaughter.

After some finger exercises, Zhen Laehua went to their wagon and retrieved her precious instrument case. It is a simple rectangular case of black hardwood. On top is engraved, "Within lies my ever-true friend, Zhen Suré." Zhen Suré is a magnificently crafted seventeen-string koto gifted to her by her grandmother and teacher, Zhen Min, arguably the greatest koto player of her time. Zhen Laehua started playing a familiar tune, providing some relaxing music.

Je Onyxia Ryoshi, Je Danei's pet panther, reached out with

her mind to mentally communicate with the young House Je Luneefa felf, *"There are three male elves approaching your campsite from the east. All are young, clumsy, and not well trained in stealth techniques at all. They do not appear to be dangerous, more hungry-looking and perhaps curious about the lovely music they have been hearing. They are about one hundred steps away from you."*

*"Hello, Ony. I saved some fish for you,"* mentally replied Je Danei. Afterwards, she flashed a very subtle hand signal to her mother and aunt to be alert since three strangers were approaching. Cautious, but not alarmed, her elders continued their normal routines.

"Thank you, but no thank you. I am no longer hungry due to my earlier hunting success. What would you like for me to do?" Ony asked.

*"Maintain constant vigilance as usual,"* Je Danei replied. She then announced to the group, "I am going for a swim. I will return shortly." She then headed towards the lake.

"Be careful, 'princess'," both her mother and aunt said in response, chuckling. The elders knew full well that Je Danei is already an accomplished warrior with a fiery spirit and could take care of herself. A typical, traditional "princess" she is not. Je Danei would much rather compete against her male counterparts on the practice field or in war games than stay inside and do so-called, traditional female activities, like sewing or cooking. But she is also the first daughter of their noble family, a noted prestigious position. This distinction attracts the attention of many nobles' sons who viewed her as a potential wife of high value and influence, just like a king's daughters.

While growing up, Je Danei would spend hours each day training to master the different blades her elders would give her. Je Danei especially loved training against or fighting with her older brothers who after some time could no longer easily defeat her in swordplay nor martial arts. A 'princess' she is definitely not.

The females of Houses Je Luneefa and Nui Vent also share an ability to communicate with each other mentally. This ability is due to their close bond with each other and through the blood-magic afforded by the great dragon, Ona Kei Kuri Ryuu, whose blood they all share.

Je Danei *told* her mother and aunt about the approaching party. Her elders knew Je Danei's tactic was truly aimed to divide the party approaching them. One member of the approaching group should and did break away and followed Je Danei as expected. Little did the two expected strangers know that potentially engaging the elder felfs would still place the intruders at an even greater disadvantage.

After a few more moments, two masked melfs emerged from the forest and walked towards the campfire where the Houses Je Luneefa and Nui Vent elders and the Ladies Zhen sat.

"Good evening," said the lead elf of medium height and build. He looks like a woods elf. This elf continued, "We are just a small gang of thieves. We would like to relieve you of any extra coin you might be carrying."

"And if you do not mind, we would also like to have some of your food too please," his companion quietly added. This second melf appears to be a rock elf due to his larger, more muscular physical features.

"Wait, you want to rob us *AND* eat our food? That is a bit extreme don't you think?" said Nui Honei. "Why do you want our food too?"

"We are hungry. We gave the spoils from our recent hunt to a poor, hungry family travelling to the city," the second thief said.

Je Pagi then interrupted and asked, "Are you the gang of thieves who target mostly wealthy travelers, rob them, eat their food and then give the money to poor families you encounter on the road?"

The two thieves then looked at each other and the first one declared, "Brother, I believe we are now famous and known across the northern kingdom perhaps. We should be proud, right? But first, before we converse further, please give us your gold."

Nui Honei looked carefully at the first, masked thief and said, with a warm, kind smile, "No."

Now irritated, the first thief issued a warning, "If you don't give us your gold quickly, we will be forced to take it."

"I think not," said Je Pagi. "In fact, we are here to actually capture you and take you to the city where you will be tried for your crimes."

"Brother, be cautious," said the second thief to the first.

"No, I think not," the first thief mockingly responded. "We are much younger than these female elves and stronger too. We will win in a struggle against you. So, please cease this unwanted discourse and hand over your coin purses."

"Sister, he did say 'please' again," remarked Je Pagi.

"And my response is still the same. A firm 'no'," responded Nui Honei.

"Must we hurt you then in order to get what we want?" asked

the first thief. "Prepare to be hurt then!" At this time, the first thief approached Je Pagi and swung his spear at her feet hoping to knock her over and quickly win any physical contest. However, the thief over-committed his balance and Je Pagi easily dodged his swing. She then quickly countered with a kick to the thief's chest sending him backwards to the ground and out of breath.

Nui Honei looked closely at the second thief and recognized he too is young, and seemingly a bit confused. She thought, "Given that he carried a single-blade axe in each hand, he appears to be ambidextrous. This melf is muscular, seems extraordinarily strong and of mixed elven blood, perhaps rock and dark elves. He height is over nine hands, and he appears to weigh less than fifteen stones. His skin color, hair and eyes are all brown."

"May I first know your name please?" inquired the second thief of Nui Honei.

"I am the great mother of House Nui Vent, Nui Honei," remarked the elder felf proudly. "Why do you ask?"

Dropping his axes and falling to his knees, the second thief replied, "Unlike my foolish brother there, I thought I recognized you. Are you not a renowned battlemage? Besides, I also assumed you two were of a noble house and likely easy prey. But you are not. So, I now surrender to you. Please forgive us; we beg for mercy."

Now walking into the campsite was the third thief with hands tied and a bruised, reddened jaw. This third thief looked at both thieves on the ground and tried to offer some solace to his comrades while staring at his captor, Je Danei, "I too surrendered brothers after being captured by this lovely angel..."

"Silence!" commanded Je Danei, apparently a bit irritated and now directing her irritation towards the first two fallen thieves, she said, "You only sent one thief, a belf at that, to try to capture me? You greatly underestimated my abilities. Or you foolishly overestimated his. Go and sit by your comrades, foolish belf. You two; remove your masks."

All three would-be thieves huddled together looking dejected.

"Are you three still hungry?" asked Je Pagi.

"Yes," all three replied quickly. Je Pagi and Zhen Lae then started preparing bowls of food for their three new guests while Zhen Laehua got them cups for water.

"Close your mouth and stop staring at my daughter, thief. It is rude." Je Pagi ordered.

The youngest thief responded, "My apologies; please forgive me. But she is the most beautiful felf I have ever seen in my life. In fact, all of you females are so very pretty. I, I..."

"Hush. What are your names and ages?" interrupted Nui Honei.

The first thief, a woods elf, seemingly the oldest, started the introductions, "I am Danka, two hundred ten years old; the big melf there is Jooba, two hundred years old; and the last member of our gang is Rei, one hundred eighty years old. We all met some time ago after our villages in the northern frontier were destroyed by some raiders from a noble house, we think. We are all orphans too. We fled from there and journeyed here by chance, guided only by fate. We decided to rob nobles, for revenge, passing through the forest, and give the spoils to the poor families, often victimized by the noble Houses. And in some cases, we will even feed these poor families with the gains from our hunting and fishing."

After eating, the thieves graciously thank their captors for their meal. Each thief also told his short, personal story version of how he made it to the great forest.

Later, Je Danei said, "I will get more wood for the fire which we should keep burning throughout the night."

"I will help you. There are packs of wolves in this forest; so, I can help protect you too," said the "smitten" Rei.

Nui Honei looked at the thief and asked, "Will you then try to escape?"

"No, House great mother Nui Honei. Lady Je Danei captured me, and I am honor-bound to abide by my captor's commands," replied a smiling Rei who seemed overly charmed by the oldest House Je Luneefa daughter.

Both Je Pagi and Nui Honei looked at Je Danei with puzzled looks on their faces. The young felf, using the silent House hand language, responded, "*I will try to explain later.*"

"Just so you know you inept, would-be thieves, escape would be futile. There is another member of our party whom you have yet to meet, said Je Danei. "Please welcome Princess Je Onyxia Ryoshi. My pet is a magnificent, twenty stone, black panther."

This panther is special in that she has some magical abilities, one of which is her telepathic bond with Je Danei. This bond allows her to mentally communicate with Je Danei. Long ago when Ony was a young cub, she scratched Je Danei drawing blood. After licking the blood, Ony started to project her thoughts and feelings to Je Danei. After the taking of the panther's blood, Je Danei, in return, could mentally communicate with and understand the panther. Later, after learning the elven and common languages,

Ony could communicate mentally with words.

Ony sat next to Je Danei upon her hind quarters, looked at the House elders and bowed her head. Je Danei continued, directing a warning to the thieves, "My Ony is a great huntress. Should you escape, she will track you, catch you and will surely kill you. You cannot outrun, out-think nor out-fight her. So, do not even try to escape. Further, if you try to harm any of us, if I do not kill you first, Ony most assuredly will."

"Stop scaring our guests, Danei" Je Pagi said with a bit of a smile knowing that the light-hearted, delivered message was the deadly truth.

Je Danei sat there scratching the head of her pet while mindlessly thinking and poking at the fire. Now, sitting with a massive, deadly beast amongst them, the thieves were no longer relaxed; so, they just sat quietly together, no longer interested in talking. They just sat there gazing at the panther and Je Danei with unasked questions on their faces.

After a while, thief Rei regained his composure, looked at Je Danei and asked if she was ready to gather more firewood.

"Yes, let's go now," she responded. She then stood and walked towards some nearby fallen trees. Rei followed her. Ony, her pet, also rose and followed Je Danei quickly. They all went into the woods and returned with more firewood. Being in a more open area near the lake, the night cooled their area. Rei built up the fire again. After a while, the Ladies Zhen retired for the night, sleeping under their wagon. The others laid down closer to the campfire.

After midnight, wolves started howling. The eerie sound indicated they were hunting. Ony was already awake and alert, given her keen animal senses. After the wolves' third howling, she woke the tired Je Danei reaching out to her mentally, *"Awake, we will have more company soon."* The panther also nudged Je Pagi and Nui Honei from their sleep.

While Je Pagi and Nui Honei woke their guests, Ony shared her story with Je Danei, "The wolves are after me. In defending my possession of a hunted and slain deer, I fought against some of this pack and killed one of them." Je Danei in turn relayed her pet's story to the others.

Je Pagi walked over to Ony and cupped the big panther's head in her hands, looked at the panther and said, "Don't even think about running away to draw the wolves away from us. You are very much a part of our family, and we stand together no matter what the odds are or how hopeless our situation might be. Your fight is now our fight too." The panther nodded her head at the great mother in gratitude.

Another wolf's howl broke the night's calm.

"How many and how far away are they?" asked Nui Honei.

Ony mentally communicated her answers back to Je Danei, relaying, "I believe there may be ten to twelve pack wolves judging from the different scents I counted. They are about two thousand steps away and closing fast. These wolves will not be easily frightened away either, for they seek blood revenge. So, prepare for battle."

Je Danei relayed Ony's message to the group, then looked at her elders and uttered, "Takai!" and walked away. That was a House battle command to prepare for a fight.

Lady Zhen and her daughter were now awake too and stood by the others. "Ladies Zhen, I would suggest you immediately go and stay under your wagon after it is moved," ordered Je Pagi. "We expect to be attacked soon by a pack of wolves." The Zhen mother and daughter obeyed without any further questions or hesitation.

Looking at Je Pagi, the excited Danka, the first thief pleaded, "Return our weapons to us so we can also help you fight against these wolves too."

"Calm yourself and turn around," Je Pagi simply said in response. There was Je Danei extending the recovered thieves' weapons to the thief. Je Pagi continued, "We now have a common enemy; so, it would make good sense for us to join forces."

Je Pagi further ordered, "Thieves, your duty in this battle is simply to protect Nui Honei. Stay close to her. Je Danei will fight alongside her panther, and I will fight alone. Should my sister, daughter or I give you an order, do it; do not question it nor hesitate in your execution. Immediate obedience is demanded. Do you understand?" She turned and walked away, returning moments later with her weapons, a shield, long and short swords by her sides. She was also adorned with a black trimmed red cape like that worn by her daughter. Emblazoned on the cape was an image of three red and black roses on a black field, the House heraldic symbol of House Je Luneefa.

Rei looked at Je Pagi with tears forming in his eyes. "Although I am no warrior yet and have little fighting skill, please let me fight by your side so you will not be alone."

Touched, Je Pagi looked sternly at the youngest thief and simply said, "No. I shall fight alone; it is better if I 'dance' all by myself. Now follow your orders and do your duty."

With assistance from Jooba, Je Danei repositioned the Zhen wagon against a wall of tough, thick thorn bushes. This tactic, Je

Danei explained to the thieves, reduced the number of fronts from which the wolves could attack. More wood was also added to the campfire. The blazing campfire was now in front of them too and this provided a well-lit battle area reducing any animal sneak attacks due to the night's darkness.

Nui Honei joined them shortly afterwards. She too wore a black trimmed red cape and a sword and long knife at her sides, but her main weapon was a bow with a quiver full of arrows. Je Danei was also ready for battle wielding a scimitar on her sides and holding a javelin. The young felf too wore a House cape like the one that adorns her mother.

Ony looked at each House Je Luneefa female and said to Je Danei, "*I want a cape too, but a small one.*"

Je Danei rubbed her panther's head and said smiling, "Of course, I will have a House cape made for you." Her elders laughed.

Danka holds a long spear and a round shield. Jooba, the second oldest thief, carries an axe in each hand. Lastly, Rei stood with two short swords, one on each of his sides and he also carries a bandolier of throwing knives.

Though a bit frightened as they waited for the wolf pack, Danka and his brothers found some comfort standing with such noble and courageous warriors. Danka also noticed that these warriors silently moved into certain positions. Instinctively, Nui Honei was in the middle in front of the Zhen wagon, no doubt having the best field of vision over the intended battlefield. She could easily provide support to either her right or left side. Je Danei and her panther moved to the left of Nui Honei while Je Pagi moved to Nui Honei's right.

Je Pagi addressed the small group, "Remember dear sister and daughter that we battle for a threatened and beloved member of our House. Fight well and do not die tonight. Take note thief brothers of a portion of the might of Houses Je Luneefa and Nui Vent."

"The wolves have arrived; they are just beyond that tree line in front of us," Je Danei relayed the mental message she had just received from her panther.

Twelve wolves then emerged from the tree line snarling announcing their presence and message of imminent danger.

Unmoved, Ony responded with a terrifying roar that made the thief brothers jump.

The wolves fanned out into a semicircle facing the elves, with fangs barred and now growling viciously. The wolves walked slowly towards the cornered elves. When the wolves reached the distance of the campfire, about thirty steps away, they attacked running at full speed towards the elves. At the same moment, Nui Honei started releasing deadly arrows into the pack killing three wolves in a few moments.

Six wolves focused on Ony and directly attacked Je Danei and her panther. Je Danei whispered a command and her javelin transformed instantly into a full-length, long spear with short blades at both ends. Within moments, Je Danei was wielding her weapon with both hands, wounding or killing wolves with deadly slashes and stabs. Whatever may have still lived from Je Danei's blows, died shortly thereafter from the claw-slash of her fighting companion, the mighty panther.

Three wolves attacked House great mother Je Pagi who was armed with her shield and long sword in hand. Unlike their typical cornered prey that is usually stationary when the wolves attack, Je Pagi presented a moving target as she moved from side to side in front of her adversaries. When one wolf got too close, it was rewarded with a fierce cut across its muzzle. After receiving this injury, one wolf ran away whimpering. The last two wolves continued their attack trying to isolate the felf away from her companions. Suddenly, one wolf attacked her high, leaping towards the felf's neck, while the other attacked her legs. Je Pagi issued a command while falling backwards in a controlled manner. Blades, like that of a large knife, emerged from all around the shield's edge; and with one jab, she killed the wolf attacking her legs. Simultaneously, as she was falling backwards, she fatally stabbed the other wolf with her sword as it passed above her.

With Je Pagi now down on the ground, five additional wolves, hidden in the forest brush and sensing a kill opportunity, rushed in. Immediately Jooba reacted and threw an axe at the first lounging wolf; and Danka jumped in front of Nui Honei to protect her, throwing his spear at the second wolf to kill it. Without hesitation, Rei instantly threw two knives killing another wolf. He then pulled his short swords and charged the remaining two wolves determined to protect the fallen House great mother. As he placed himself between the charging wolves and Je Pagi who still had not yet recovered from the dead wolf laying on top of her, he shouted some battle cry attempting to be menacing and help give himself more courage. In that same instant, he was pulled down from behind as two arrows flashed past him overhead each one hitting and killing a wolf. The battle was now over.

Rei got up from the ground, removed the dead wolf off the fallen great mother and extended his hand to help Je Pagi rise. She refused his help. She also winced in pain when he removed the wolf and had some difficulty standing thereafter.

Confused and saddened by Je Pagi's refusal for assistance, Rei walked over to his brothers looking for consolation. Danka quietly began to scold the youngest brother and informed him that he had disobeyed a battle order. Continuing, Danka told Rei, "You, in fact, disobeyed a direct order issued on a battlefield from a House great mother! That was a severe transgression and often had deadly consequences..."

Surprised, Rei thought for a few minutes, turned around and walked towards House great mother Je Pagi who was now limping, in pain, back to the campfire with the help of her daughter.

"House great mother, may I speak with you please?" asked Rei.

"What do you want?" an angry Je Pagi said, looking at the belf with cold eyes.

Rei said, "First, I wish to apologize for disobeying your direct order; I reacted instinctively in hopes of protecting you from those last two charging wolves. I saw later that was perhaps a tactic to defeat the enemy. Secondly, I now, willingly submit myself to any punishment you deem fit for my disobedience."

In response, the House great mother Je Pagi looked closely at the belf and again was touched by his honest sincerity and courage. She forgot her pain momentarily, softened her facial expression and responded with a kindly smile, "First, I understand how instincts can cause one to act contrary to given orders. In this case, your actions potentially prevented my suffering any further injury. Your act of bravery caused the wolves to stop their charge for a moment which was all the time Nui Honei needed to prepare to shoot those wolves when they restarted their charge. For that bravery, I am appreciative. Thank you. However, do not let your instincts override my orders in the future, for I shall not be lenient. Secondly, I need to give more thought to your punishment that befits your disobedience. We will discuss this matter again after reaching Torondell."

"Yes, House great mother Je Pagi. Thank you. I look forward to our next conversation," said a very relieved Rei.

Nui Honei examined her sister's leg and diagnosed that it may be fractured from the wolf falling on top of it. She set it with a splint and noticed that Rei doted on the House great mother for the rest of the evening. Whatever her sister wanted, he was glad to get it and/or do it for her. Je Pagi, using the House silent hand language remarked to her sister, "*I like these three.*"

"Yes, I do as well. They need direction, more discipline and House military training. They may be new-found blessings in disguise," reflected Nui Honei in response with her hands.

After a while when all the excitement finally left their weary bodies, the Ladies Zhen again retired. Dawn would break in a short while. Danka and Jooba went to sleep again, but the protective Rei chose to stand guard near the great mother even though the ever-vigilant panther was asleep in the group's midst.

All was quiet again at the campsite. Jooba and Danka had added more wood to the fire; so, the silence was broken occasionally by the crackling of the burning wood. Only the two House elders and younger felf were still awake around the fire.

Je Pagi and Nui Honei both noticed that Je Danei seemed lost in restless thought. "I have not forgotten either how Rei seemed completely enchanted by you earlier this evening. What happened between you two by the lake?" Je Pagi asked with her hands.

After reflecting a few moments, Je Danei answered, "I learned tonight that I also may have other capabilities too. They are what you once described as 'female powers' that apparently can captivate a male. When I emerged from the lake after my swim, I noticed he was watching me. He seemed entranced by some spell; he just looked dazed, unable to speak or move. I did not understand..."

At this point, Ony, who shared a mental connection with Je Danei, started "chuckling" as best as a panther could, for she had witnessed the same scene and communicated mentally to Je Danei, *"You are a beautiful young female, full grown in body and very desirable by males. You were naked, wet, and glistening in the moonlight as you emerged from the water. What male, the primal beasts that they are, would not be enchanted?"*

After sharing Ony's thoughts with her elders, Je Danei finally confessed, "I feel so embarrassed."

Both elders looked at each other and quietly laughed now understanding the young felf's embarrassment. Je Pagi then said, "Daughter, do not be embarrassed at all. Welcome and embrace the powers of being female. They are our blessings. In time, you will even learn just how powerful they can be."

Nui Honei added, "Also, know that that memory you created will forever be carved in Rei's mind. Hail to us females!"

# Torondell

Shortly after dawn, the travelers broke camp and first journeyed to the thieves' hideout to retrieve their few belongings including their horses. Afterwards, the group continued their journey back to Torondell, the great city of the north. Torondell was the capital city of the northern kingdom. This city was built long ago to serve as a gateway between the kingdom's southern territories and the great frontier that lies beyond the northern kingdom. This city also served as a fortress to buffer the southern territories from the yet still marauding tribes beyond in the northern frontier territory.

    As they travelled, Je Pagi started a conversation with Zhen Lae, a sun felf about four hundred years old, Je Pagi estimated. Zhen Lae shared she and her daughter were left homeless by the northern frontier House wars, one of which was the cause of her husband's death. Tired of living in fear and travelling from town to town due to the unrest of the northern frontier, Zhen Lae conveyed, "We now have dreams of rebuilding a simple, stable life in Torondell for me and my daughter. Laehua is my only child, two hundred years old and a musical prodigy. She is a master player of the seventeen-string koto. Laehua dreams of joining and performing in the Royal Orchestra of Torondell."

    Je Pagi responded warmly, "Torondell is a city of hope, dreams, and countless possibilities. For many, it was a welcome beacon where anyone could start a new life. The city's citizens are mostly comprised of elves, humans, dwarves, and goblins. Regardless of race or social status, one can find or build a home in this city. Settlers looking to farm land were given parcels. In return, a portion of their harvest is remitted to the city government for the use of the land. Je Taeliel, the first great father of House Je Luneefa, is also the appointed Warden of the North. Je Taeliel's administration is just, establishing reasonable opportunities for the farmers to purchase their lands.

"Similarly, new merchants coming to the city could easily setup and rent a shop at a reduced rate for a limited time. Whether one is a farmer, merchant, skilled craft person, soldier, or sailor, opportunities to work are abundant. Je Taeliel's vision of such a city has manifested itself in the continued growth and success of his Torondell."

Nui Honei asked Zhen Lae about her hopes for her sewing business in the city, current fashions, and the latest fabrics. Zhen Lae's response proved her knowledge is extensive and she was overjoyed with the discussions since she could now contribute something meaningful to the group.

Je Pagi promised to introduce her to Torondell's noblewomen who would be prospective customers. Further, House Je Luneefa needed more capes for its House soldiers; so, Je Pagi requested an order of capes and would advance her half of the total payment after they arrived in the city. Lastly, after joining the females' conversation, Nui Honei promised to also introduce Zhen Laehua to Torondell's leading music composer and conductor who could grant her an audition for the city's Royal Orchestra. All these promises further encouraged the Ladies Zhen that their dreams were still within their reach. Their joy of hope was rekindled as they eagerly looked forward to passing each of their journey's remaining leagues.

"Alleina also wanted to leave the city today to meet us on our journey back to Torondell. She too was bored and thought a short ride would help lift her spirits. So, we should meet her on this road sometime around midday if all goes well. She can then examine your leg and repair it better than I can," Nui Honei said to the House great mother as they returned home.

They travelled at a good pace and again stopped just before midday for a rest and a meal. It was there that Alleina, House Je Luneefa's primary healer and sometimes assistant cook, met them at their campsite. Alleina was also accompanied by an escort of eight House Je Luneefa soldiers. When she learned that Je Pagi had been injured, Alleina immediately examined the House great mother and re-bandaged her leg.

Afterwards, before the midday meal, Nui Honei introduced

the Ladies Zhen, Danka, Jooba and Rei to the House Je Luneefa party as travelers they had met the day before. She also relayed the past evening's events with the wolves as well. Since no one else was injured, Alleina turned her attention to helping with the preparation of the meal.

Alleina also noticed that Rei seemed to be "close" in proximity to Je Pagi and attended to her whenever she needed anything. But he also paid a lot of attention to Je Danei, as well. "*Another admirer?*" Alleina asked Je Danei silently with her hands.

Now wanting to deflect any further attention from her, Je Danei looked at Danka, Jooba and Rei and asked, "Are you enjoying your meal?"

All nodded vigorously in agreement while eating and Danka, their group's unofficial spokesperson, finally commented, "Very much so. This meal is unbelievably delicious. Thank you very much."

"Alleina is not only my aunt and a great cook; she is also the best healer in the northern kingdom," remarked Je Danei.

"The entire kingdom, my dear niece, the entire kingdom!" corrected Alleina.

"Yes, the *entire* kingdom," Je Danei restated with pride. "She also has another extraordinary ability. She has mastered the art of poisoning. In fact, your food could be poisoned now; but you could not even detect it. She uses poisons that can kill instantly or prolongs agonizing life till death; so, the victim dies in horrible pain. So, how do you feel right now?"

With this announcement, Danka and Jooba immediately stopped eating and maybe breathing too after dropping their bowls of food. They then just stared at Je Danei with terrorized faces of unasked questions. Rei, on the other hand, only paused for a thoughtful moment; but continued eating heartily. He looked at his Danka and Jooba and said, "Brothers, breathe. Secondly, if Je Danei wanted to kill us, she would do it herself with a blade, not poison! You should know this by now. So, enjoy your meal."

Looking at the two stunned elves' faces, the House Je soldiers just laughed at the two tormented melfs, the fated recipients of Je Danei's would-be joke.

Nui Honei just shook her head in sympathy. Je Danei scowled at Rei since her joke had not had the anticipated effect on him.

Je Pagi then said to Danka, Jooba and Rei, "Please forgive my daughter, for she misses her younger brother who is still away. He is oftentimes the target of her jokes. You were just convenient, easy victims for her. She was just teasing you."

One of the older, serious looking Je Luneefa House soldiers also added, "Alleina truly is a great healer; she has saved me and many of our soldiers from near death with her medical knowledge and skills. What Je Danei said is also true, however. She knows a great deal about poisons. In fact, I was told about one hundred years ago, several northern frontier orc tribes united intending to invade and conquer the northern kingdom. That army was twice as large as ours. Alleina disguised herself as the enemy, went into their camp three days before our intended great battle and poisoned over half their soldiers. The next day, the would-be invaders sued for peace instead of war. We lost no soldiers that fourth day due to her gallant efforts. So, always be good to Alleina; you may even need her help too one day."

The merriment was soon over, and they all resumed their journey to Torondell. By late afternoon, they could see the great city in the distance. It was, without a doubt, the most beautiful city in the northern kingdom. This city was built at the base of the great mountain, Toron. High, steep cliffs bordered the city's east side; the mighty Toronduin river is on its west side. Toron is a very tall mountain where snow laid year-round at its peak. The mountain had two waterfalls that not only supplied fresh water to the city, but these waters flowed into the upper and lower Toron rivers. The upper Toron river flowed outside the innermost wall of Torondell. The lower Toron river served the entire valley, south of the mountain. Outsides the city's outer wall, for two thousand steps, lay open land which could be recaptured for future city expansion. Beyond the two thousand steps boundary, various homesteads and farms dotted the rich land. Both upper and lower Toron rivers flowed east to west into the great Toronduin river.

Torondell, the jewel city of Canae's northern realm, is now home to the Je Luneefa family, one of the first families of woods elves who helped settled the Canae kingdom many centuries ago. Now settled in the northern part of the kingdom, this is the place where House Je Luneefa has been reestablished after their original home was first built in Rhodell, the kingdom's capital. Je Taeliel and his wife, Je Buel, wanted to leave certain painful memories and experiences of the capital far behind them.

Though House Je Luneefa flourished in Rhodell in many ways in Rhodell, including the births of five granddaughters and grandsons, the House first elders wanted something much more they would not find in the capital. So, after a long, hard military campaign to win the northern frontier, Je Taeliel, then Commander

Je Luneefa of the Canae Kuze Karkazanae army, proposed to his wife, Je Buel, that they should relocate their family to Canae's North, to the burgeoning city of Torondell.

Je Buel, the first great mother of House Je Luneefa, accepted her husband's proposal and offered her support of continuing to build their dreams in the new city of Torondell. In elven society, Houses and families are ruled by a hierarchy of powerful matriarchs. The ruling matriarch, or House first great mother, is typically the eldest female of the House and is tyrannical in guiding her House in all important matters. In many Houses, this position is held by a grandmother. The daughters of the House first great mother are the House's second great mothers. Leadership of House Je Luneefa rests mainly with Je Buel, the first great mother.

When this new House Je Luneefa stronghold was first conceived, it was originally just to be the home of the Je Luneefa family. With his appointment as Warden of Canae's northern realm, Je Taeliel knew his "home" needed to be more than just for his immediate family. So, Je Taeliel enlisted the aid of Duenor Heartstone, a then young dwarf, but an exceptional engineer and builder to design and build his stronghold and Torondell that could grow in strength and service as the surrounding city grew.

Like the mighty mountain Toron, Je Taeliel wanted his stronghold to be a subtle, but mighty fortress. Heartstone's vision then incorporated the mountain, cliffs, and river. The actual Je Luneefa home is a well disguised fortress, built into the mountain itself and was first constructed as the center of half-circles. This stronghold stands the highest above all the other structures within the city. As the city grew, a protective wall was to be constructed at certain times to further shield the expansion and the citizens of the city.

Currently, there are two great, protective stone walls in or around Torondell; Toronwalein is the innermost wall, and Toronwalzwei is the outermost wall. Toronwalein was first constructed with the sole primary purpose of protecting the Houses Je Luneefa and Nui Vent strongholds. Both walls stand tall from the ground and positioned on top of rugged inclines. Large rocks were placed in front of both walls. This deliberate construction makes it exceedingly difficult for any attackers to use war siege engines against either wall. Further, the walls' ramparts are tall providing more shielding for the wall defenders. Six and eight guard towers on the Toronwalein and Toronwalzwei, respectively, provide additional defense capabilities. The walls are thick too with centers of sand and clay. Even if an enemy were to ever defeat the outer shell of the wall, the center and inner wall would still stand strong. Both walls also have just a few gates. Toronwalein has just two gates and Toronwalzwei has only three gates. In addition to the steel reinforced wooden outer gate doors, there are two steel inner gates to further obstruct any unauthorized entrance. Opening and closing the outer and inner gates are also controlled by different controlling stations distanced from each other.

Inside the Toronwalein stands the Je Luneefa and Nui Vent strongholds along with their respective barracks for their House armies. All the land within this innermost wall belonged to the Je Luneefa family. No other family strongholds are within the Toronwalein. Je Taeliel's vision was to provide his family with a very well-protected, permanent residence location.

Further, there is no straight path from the Toronwalzwei gates to the Toronwalein gates either. Again, this design was purposely intended to make it even more difficult for an enemy to easily approach the gates of the Toronwalein. Water falling from the mountain flowed directly into the upper portion of the Toron river which surrounds the Toronwalein. This river of fast-moving water is several hundred steps in front of the Toronwalein and has steep banks. The field between the river and the Toronwalein is open; so, no enemy force can easily approach the great wall without being seen.

Outside of each Toronwalein gate, there is a drawbridge over the river and the drawbridge can be raised if need be. Archers on the Toronwalein, armed with long bows, will make any unauthorized approach to the Toronwalein gates very costly. Je Taeliel acknowledged to his family many times that "Master builder, Duenor Heartstone, is truly creative and skilled unlike any other in designing and constructing fortresses." For the first elders of House Je Luneefa, their strongholds and surrounding great walls would continue to extend their highly protective nature to many families.

Over the span of one hundred twenty years, Torondell grew into a magnificent city that it is today, protecting well over two hundred thousand citizens of various races. For over two centuries, Torondell prospered under the leadership of Je Taeliel of House Je Luneefa, the Warden of the North of the Canae kingdom. The city continues to grow due to its abilities to attract settlers, craftsmen, merchants and many others - anyone seeking a place to start anew for this was a metropolis of boundless opportunities.

Je Taeliel also administers justice fairly to all, regardless of a person's social status and political connections. The northern kingdom has been relatively peaceful under his jurisdiction. With his appointment as Warden, the king also awarded Je Taeliel several army divisions totaling three thousand troops. Housing for the active troops are generally twelve special barracks located within the protective outer wall of the city. In some cases where soldiers could no longer serve, perhaps due to severe injuries, Je Taeliel offered civilian posts to these veterans and/or housing within the city.

In addition to these actual military veterans, certain citizens can be called upon to help defend the city in times of war. This force of conscripted citizens totals another five thousand persons who are currently trained to wield various kinds of weaponry. New conscripts are identified and trained on a yearly basis. Previously conscripted citizens are retrained for potential military duty every three years. Current conscripted citizens even receive some compensation for their yearly service.

Like any other great House in the kingdom, House Je Luneefa also has a private, dedicated army of about four hundred eighty warriors. This force is solely committed to House Je Luneefa and under the command of the House's great mothers and father, Je Buel, Je Pagi and Je Maron, respectively.

Long ago, when living in Rhodell, the first elders of House Je Luneefa made the bold decision to adopt this Nui Samu, these felfs, Nui Honei and Diazae Alleina, and another outcast, Ona Noirar of House Ona Feiir, for highly personal reasons. House Je Luneefa, a family of noble woods elves, dared to adopt "low" noble rock elves, a commoner sun felf and a mixed-blood rock and dark noble melf. That decision defied certain, generally accepted, social norms, causing some outrage and discomfort amongst Canae's "high" elven noble society, dominated by woods elves. The social repercussions from other noble Houses mattered not to the first elders of House Je Luneefa.

Now, Torondell is also home to both Nui Honei and Nui Samu of House Nui Vent. Nui Samu is a rock elf of about four hundred ten years old, the great father of House Nui Vent. He is also the elder brother of Nui Honei, House Nui Vent's great mother. Being ambidextrous, Nui Samu became an elite warrior; he is also the weapons master of House Je Luneefa and Nui Vent, teaching ancient elven martial arts and the use of a variety of deadly weapons. Alone now, his wife died from war long ago; he has no young ones. Since his wife's death, Nui Samu just teaches martial arts and lives a quiet life of solitude.

Many years ago, Nui Samu left Rhodell, following his blood-brother Ona Noirar to the northern realm. Both served in the Canae Kuze Karkazanae army missioned to bring the lawless, northern frontier under Canae's rule.

While at the Rhodell Military Academy, forbidden love occurred. Canae's Princess Rho Chele first met and fell in love with Ona Noirar, the third son of House Ona Feiir. They engaged in a relationship unapproved by House Rho and the Canae's Majesties. Despite the pleas of Nui Honei, Rho Chele's closest friend at the Academy, to end her relationship with Ona Noirar, Rho Chele persisted. Nui Samu, also at the Academy at the same time, failed to dissuade Ona Noirar, his closest friend, to end his relationship with the princess. Assassins sent to kill Ona Noirar would not even change the stubborn mind of the melf, another elite warrior, who collected the severed heads of his nemeses.

When Ona Noirar joined the Kuze Karkazanae, Princess Rho Chele did so as well, hoping to escape her parents' tight control. Her actions just infuriated the Majesties more. She and Ona Noirar fled north to escape the wrath of the Canae king and queen. Even though Ona Noirar survived more assassination attempts and even many battles while in the North, Rho Chele did fall to the murderous assassin's blade.

Nui Honei is a rock elf and matriarch of House Nui Vent. With the banishment of her brother and then best friend, the queen and king's daughter, to the northern kingdom, Nui Honei followed them after first making a long, great adventurous journey to the Underworld. Like her brother, she too became an elite warrior, as well as a battlemage. She and her elder brother were raised and trained from their early years by their beloved warrior grandparents. After meeting the Je Luneefa elders in the northern kingdom, Nui Honei became fast and close friends with the second House great mother, Je Pagi. Later, she too became a beloved "adopted" aunt of the House Je Luneefa's granddaughters and grandsons. Nui Honei also became the godmother of Je Danei.

Both Nui Honei and her brother now live next to the Je Luneefa stronghold in their own stronghold, inside of the Toronwalein. With them lives the lone, mysterious Ona Drachir who had journeyed there the year before. Ona Drachir was found to be quite special when Nui Honei and Nui Samu first met him for dinner at their home. The House Nui Vent great mother and great father learned that he was orphaned a long time ago and was raised by his uncle, Ona Noirar. Ona Noirar had recently died and, before his passing, told his nephew to find the Nui Vent great father and

Ona Noirar's blood-brother. Nui Samu and Ona Noirar had lived and fought together for over a century. The House Nui Vent great father was honored to become Ona Drachir's sensei and guardian.

Ona Noirar also wanted his nephew to become a student of Nui Samu, a weapons master, and a master of the ancient elven martial arts. Although Ona Drachir had learned much from his uncle and other family elders, he is still young, being only two hundred years old; and he still had much to learn about martial arts and weapons.

During the last year after the Ladies Zhen arrived in Torondell, the Zhen Lae and Zhen Laehua became wards of House Je Luneefa; they now lived in a small home close to the Je Luneefa stronghold, just outside the Toronwalein. With the help of great mothers Je Pagi and Je Buel, Zhen Lae started a sewing business that was thriving due to her creativity and skills. After a few moons, she even opened her own tailoring shop and hired two apprentices. Her fashion designs and sewing capabilities kept Zhen Lae in high demand.

Her daughter, Zhen Laehua, had also auditioned with the city's Royal Orchestra. With a successful audition, she joined the Torondell orchestra. Shortly thereafter, Zhen Laehua became extremely popular and a featured musical artist. Both mother and daughter now had a home, stability and enjoyed the blessings of their simple lives. At long last, they felt they are finally able to live their dream. They even dared now to dream even more...

Similarly, the three former thieves, Danka, Jooba and Rei, lived well as wards of House Nui Vent. For their crimes, they all had to first serve six moons as servants of House Nui Vent where they maintained the grounds and performed menial kitchen duties. After serving, they decided to stay in Torondell and became students of sensei Nui Samu to learn ancient elven martial arts and weaponry. Through the guidance of both House Nui Vent great mother and great father, the characters and lives of the thief brothers greatly improved. They too found contentment with their simple, structured, and disciplined lives. They too found a much needed "home" in Torondell within House Nui Vent.

Danka, Jooba and Rei also decided to be the first to enlist into the House Nui Vent army. After two years of faithful and exemplary service to House Nui Vent, House great mother Nui Honei and great father approved and accepted their enlistment.

This present day is special; two new House Nui Vent soldiers are making their way to the House Je Luneefa stronghold to perform a preferred, according to them, but non-military related function. Instead of continuing their House military training, their afternoon had been committed to performing escort duties for the Lady Zhen Lae who still felt a bit uncomfortable walking around alone in the tough, bustling, chaotic market area of the big city Torondell. House great mother Nui Honei issued the request; so, the appointed House soldiers were very quick and willing to accept her request.

With purpose and dedication, they walked briskly to the home of the northern kingdom's Warden and army commander, Je Taeliel. They had to be there by noon as ordered. Zhen Lae wanted to meet with certain cloth merchants by an appointed time that afternoon; so, they could not be late. After arriving at the House Je Luneefa stronghold, the soldiers passed through the gates without difficulty and entered the main castle. House servants then ushered the House Nui Vent soldiers to the great hall. "Why are you here soldiers?" asked Je Jero who was first to meet Jooba and Rei in the House grand hall.

Jooba responded, "Well met sons of House Je Luneefa. We are here to escort Ladies Zhen to the market." Je Jero walked over to Rei and without any warning pulled a knife and thrust it at the youngest Nui Vent soldier. Rei recognized that the thrust was a feint attack to mask a blow from Je Jero's other hand. Rei, ever cautious and well trained since becoming a ward of House Nui Vent, adeptly blocked both attacks and countered with an unblocked knee to Je Jero's stomach leaving him bent over and momentarily immobilized.

Je Tero, the second oldest and son of House Je Luneefa, walked over to the escorts from his table positioned by the hall's fire. After observing his older brother's failure, he wanted to try a different tactic. "Well met escorts," he said with a stern look on his face. "You have, whether you have acknowledged it beforehand or not, accepted a duty to safely escort the wards of House Je Luneefa to and from the market. No harm must befall them whatsoever. If need be, sacrifice your lives for their safe return home; for the honor of this House is at stake. You must *not* tarnish it. Do you now fully understand this honor and sacred duty?"

Whack! This loud sound erupted across the hall as a thrown axe obliterated a wooden target. The axe was thrown by Nui Samu, their sensei, weapons master, and House Nui Vent great father. He is already an intimidating-looking melf without any formidable weapon in hand. However, when he holds any of his axes, swords, or knives, ancient or new, Nui Samu appears to be a deadly, unstoppable force unleashed from some hell. Looking at the escorts from his House, he just said, "Do not fail in this duty. Not even a tear must fall from their eyes."

The doors to the great hall opened and standing there in front were the House great mothers Je Buel and Je Pagi. House Je Luneefa great mother Je Buel is the first great mother of her House. She is the first elder matriarch of her family and essentially is the House ruling power. She shares House ruling direction and power with her beloved husband, Je Taeliel, the House first great father. House great mother Je Buel is an experienced and skilled battlemage and warrior. Her husband, of more than four centuries, is also an accomplished warrior. Despite their "ancient" ages of five hundred eighty and six hundred years old respectively, the Je Luneefa first great mother and father are still physically and mentally active and very capable in battle. Both elders are woods elves and only have one daughter, Je Pagi. She is the House Je Luneefa second great mother and wife of Je Maron, a four hundred years old woods melf.

Today, even dressed in plain, everyday attire, both House great mothers radiated "quiet" beauty, elegance, wisdom, and power. The House Je Luneefa great mothers were accompanied by the House Nui Vent great mother, Nui Honei who was the third member of Houses' powerful, elder female triumvirate. Je Danei and Je Leena of House Je Luneefa entered next followed by mother and daughter Zhen.

After greetings, Je Buel said, "I see your escorts have arrived Ladies Zhen, even a bit ahead of schedule. That is good." Looking at Jooba and Rei even more closely, she asked, "Have they been good hosts while you waited?" pointing to her grandsons.

"Yes, House great mother. They again reminded us of our duty today and why failure is not an option," responded Jooba.

Rei further added, "They even tried to test and intimidate us, but that was not necessary to get their point across. We are not afraid of them nor of any punishment they would possibly inflict upon us. These males would simply kill us and be done with us should we fail in our duty. On the other hand, we are absolutely terrified though of the wrath of the House Je Luneefa females." Rei paused after noticing that Je Leena's eyes, which are normally brown, were now like emerald-green dragon eyes, menacingly staring at him.

Jooba continued, "So, my brother and I will successfully fulfill our duty today on pain of our deaths."

With Rei's honest and sincere declaration, great mother Nui Honei smiled at them. House great mothers Je Buel and Je Pagi looked at each other and started laughing. Second House Je Luneefa daughter Je Leena looked at Nui Honei and summed up the situation by saying, "Dear Auntie, you have taught them well, very well indeed."

# Autumn Festival

It is the beginning of the autumn season; the sun is shining high in the sky and there is a slight chill in the air. The citizens of Torondell are in a festive mood for today marks the beginning of the three-day Autumn festival. Many merchants journeyed to Torondell to sell their wares, music was in the air and the outer streets were filled with all kinds of visitors from near and far away places.

For security reasons, the Warden of the North was still a bit anxious of potential serious crimes, including even attacks upon the city. Several years earlier at the same time, a group of distant frontier, orc tribe members assassinated all the Ka Kataka family elders. Unlike the Je Luneefa family, most other noble families lived inside the Toronwalzwei. So, Je Taeliel ordered that all future Autumn Festival activities shall take place outside of the Toronwalzwei wall. Access to the inner city would be strictly limited to those living in that interior and to appropriate military personnel.

The Autumn Festival is also a yearly event in which Houses could compete in games against each other. The main event is a war-like game in which two opposing teams simulate battling each other to capture the opponent's imaginary stronghold. Capturing one's stronghold is simply represented by first "killing" all the House team members and then capturing an opponent's House flag. No real, sharp weapons are used. Appointed event battlemages also place magical wards upon the combatants' weapons to prevent serious injury. Other esteemed battlemages and House weapons' masters are also posted throughout the arena to act as judges. A total of sixteen Houses could compete in this main event, the Kilecfla. Opposing Houses are randomly chosen to start the competition. Thereafter for each follow-on round, only winning House teams advanced to the next round of competition. Competing teams are randomly chosen for each round until only two teams are left.

Only two houses compete at a time. There are four designated House strongholds in the arena. A stronghold is randomly assigned to a team. Each stronghold is different and comprised of rocks, low walls, and trees. After each round, all strongholds are magically reconfigured. A team is comprised of six warriors maximum. Only one warrior can be an archer and no battlemages can be used. No magic is to be used either during battles. This event is designed to honor the ancient elven warrior ways and showcase one's mastery of weapons and martial arts.

This year's Kilecfla marked a particularly significant time for House Nui Vent. This year, Ona Drachir, Danka, Jooba and Rei, although wards of House Nui Vent, would represent the House and compete in the festival's highly competitive, main event. Joining them to complete the six-person team were the two eldest House Je Luneefa sons, Je Jero and Je Tero. For the last two years, they trained hard under the guidance of Nui Samu, arguably the finest weapons and ancient elven martial arts master in the northern kingdom.

This event was the first for all of the young melfs. The House Nui Vent team all wanted to recapture glory for their weapons master's fallen House since the Canae Majesties covertly never forgave Nui Samu of House Nui Vent for supposedly aiding Ona Noirar running away with their daughter, Rho Chele, centuries ago. The king had denounced House Nui Vent then. The plans his House second elders, his traitorous parents, had to gain noble House status were helplessly lost.

The arena's stands were packed with spectators. Nobility and common folk all were present to witness the last round of the main event. There was still some time before the event began, but there was standing room only in the stands.

Competing Houses, as well as those just spectating, occupied pavilions decorated in their House colors at choice locations within the arena. At the black and red adorned pavilion, great mothers Je Buel and Je Pagi and great fathers Je Taeliel and Je Maron hosted House first great mother and Queen Rho Jiedae, along with her nephews, the realm's two princes on this last day of the festival. Although invited to share the House Je Luneefa's pavilion, both Nui Honei and Nui Samu graciously declined knowing that the still angry queen would be the guest of House Je Luneefa.

The queen, an ageless beauty of six hundred years with a commanding presence asked, "Aren't your daughters supposed to join us too? I hear they are both lovely and are of that age to attract the attention of noteworthy suitors."

Second House great mother Je Pagi "felt" that the queen was using the festival as an opportunity to "shop" for potential princesses for her nephews. She and Je Buel also knew that any marriage of the princes to noble families in the northern realm would serve the king and queen's selfish, political ambitions more. Je Buel again thankfully contemplated, *"Fortunately, neither House Je Luneefa daughter should be a viable candidate given their strong, not demure personalities."*

Je Pagi responded, "Both our daughters would complete their assigned duties first before joining us here. They should arrive before the Kilecfla's last round starts. In fact, if I am not mistaken, I see them both making their way here to our pavilion."

A short while later, the Je Luneefa daughters, Je Danei and Je Leena, arrived at the reserved noble House pavilion level and started walking towards their reserved, assigned seating. They were escorted by four House soldiers. Both daughters were attired in their House colors of black and red. Both wore red shirts, black pants, short jackets, and black leather boots. The daughters of House Je Luneefa also wore matching House capes with a gold chain and clasp. The capes bear the House Je Luneefa heraldic sigil - three red and black roses on a black field. The air of importance and purpose clung to both. The most immediate striking feature was that both daughters had shaved heads on the sides with a middle, short, headband of black and red hair from the front to the back of their heads.

Both Je Luneefa daughters first greeted their House elders and then turned their attention to the royal guests. After a short bow, the eldest daughter began, "Greetings Your Majesty and Princes, I am the eldest House Je Luneefa daughter, Je Danei, and this is my sister, Je Leena. Welcome to our city's Autumn festival. I hope your stay here in the northern kingdom is enjoyable."

"Thank you," said the queen and House Rho first great mother. "We look forward to getting more acquainted with you at tonight's banquet." Both Je Luneefa daughters just smiled and nodded their heads in agreement.

During this brief encounter, neither prince turned his head nor looked at the House Je Luneefa daughters. The eldest, prince Rho Paul, arrogantly remarked, "You are late and that makes you a poor host. How shall we punish them dear brother?"

Je Leena quickly interjected, "Please forgive us our Princes. Our king's appointed duties of protecting the northern realm kept us a bit longer than expected."

*"Well said and nice countermove,"* Je Buel thought as she smiled at her granddaughter. Je Leena slightly nodded her head in an acknowledged "Thank you."

The younger prince, Rho James responded, "Well brother, this is a small slight and the punishment should befit their crimes. How about if they take us for food and drink after today's main event. This last match should not take long, I hope. I trust you two have no further kingdom *duties* that would keep you from being good hosts to members of the royal family?"

"Refreshments after today's final Kilecfla match would be nice and my sister and I will gladly treat you to some of our area's delicious wines, cheeses and fruits," responded Je Danei.

Horns then blared marking the beginning of the last match. This was the third day of the Kilecfla and only two teams remain to contend in the festival's main event. House Tsau Chu and House Nui Vent warriors now faced each other. With the second sounding of the tournament horns, the House combatants walked out onto the arena field and to their appointed strongholds. Fortunately, the randomly selected strongholds were directly opposite each other.

Five House Tsau Chu warriors carried spears and shields, and one warrior carried a bow with a quiver of arrows. They each had short and long swords on their sides. The House Nui Vent soldiers brandished an array of different weapons: Je Jero, Je Tero, and Danka also chose to wield spear, shield, and swords; Ona Drachir only carried his twin scimitars; Jooba carried two double-edged battleaxes; and Rei chose to wield crescent swords in this final battle.

"The Nui Vent team is already at a disadvantage, not having an archer," Rho Paul remarked. "That tactic was poorly chosen and not wise at all."

Though no reaction or response was given, all the Je Luneefa family members clearly recognized the intended disrespect shown by Prince Rho Paul by not addressing "House" Nui Vent.

Each team planted their House flag at their designated stronghold. Each team huddled together before the next horn blast signifying the start of battle. After a few more moments, the tournament horns sounded. The last and final match began.

The Tsau Chu archer immediately shot several arrows at the House Nui Vent team. This tactic was not necessarily intended to score a fatal hit as much as it was to cause the target group to disperse into smaller groups. At this point, the Tsau Chu warriors would select an opponent to attack.

Reacting quickly, Je Jero, Je Tero and Danka protected their team by raising their shields to form a "wall."

Ona Drachir broke away from the group, leaving the House Nui Vent base. It appeared he had a secret mission known only to the House Nui Vent team. Ona Drachir quickly ran to an adjacent base while either dodging or blocking additional arrows shot directly at him. In response to this tactic, two of the Tsau Chu warriors were ordered to pursue the lone House Nui Vent warrior. Under normal circumstances, the two shields and spears of the pursuing House Tsau Chu warriors would be sufficient to defeat most lone warriors. However, Ona Drachir was not a normal warrior, being quite skilled at fighting more than one opponent at a time. The remaining House Nui Vent warriors marched directly towards the House Tsau Chu base seemingly hoping to engage the remaining Tsau Chu warriors directly.

"What is that fool doing?" Prince Rho Paul wondered aloud.

Ona Drachir continued to stealthily move towards the neutral base, avoiding more Tsau Chu arrows.

Je Leena offered, "One can assume that his objective is to make his way to the enemy base to "kill" the Tsau Chu archer, thus eliminating that team's advantage."

Shortly, after arriving at the neutral base, the two Tsau Chu warriors engaged Ona Drachir. The two warriors attacked, blocked, and counterattacked relentlessly, trying to overpower Ona Drachir. After moments of brilliant swordplay, Ona Drachir finally managed to get inside his opponents spears' length. After avoiding an expected counter shield-bash, Ona Drachir parried the Tsau Chu partner's spear attack and scored a killing blow upon that warrior.

In the meantime, Je Jero, Je Tero, Danka and Jooba were moving fast on an intercept course to engage other House Tsau Chu warriors now running towards Ona Drachir. The remaining opposing team members were still a few moments closer to Ona Drachir than his House Nui Vent teammates. To further complicate matters, the House Tsau Chu archer was still continually active, shooting arrows at Ona Drachir and his teammates.

Jooba was first to engage the other House Tsau Chu warriors by running faster than his team members. Although outnumbered three to one, Jooba's use of his twin battleaxes was magnificent. Jooba's movements, both his hands and feet, were amazingly fast. He attacked, blocked, and counterattacked like a whirlwind amongst the House Tsau Chu warriors. Now inside the warriors' spear lengths, they tried devastating shield-bashing tactics to overpower Jooba; but he was too fast and too strong. Jooba eventually took advantage of his axe's capability of pulling down a shield with the edge of a blade and fatally thrusting his axe with the extended point at the center of his axe between the blades. This was a "killing" blow and another House Tsau Chu warrior fell.

While still battling his opponent, Ona Drachir noticed that Jooba's defeat of his Tsau Chu adversary left him exposed to the archer. Recognizing the moment's advantage, the House Tsau Chu archer quickly shot three arrows at Jooba in the span of two short heartbeats. Ona Drachir, as a counter, launched one of his scimitars at the archer.

Unable to counter all the attacks from House Tsau Chu warriors and arrows, Jooba suffered a fatal blow from one of the arrows and was eliminated from the competition. At the same moment, Ona Drachir's thrown scimitar hit the House Tsau Chu archer, scoring a fatal hit too. Ona Drachir momentarily hesitated as he saw Jooba fall, mimicking death in combat. In the next second, Ona Drachir's opponent scored a fatal blow against him, eliminating him from the competition.

Je Jero, Je Tero, Danka and Rei now faced the three remaining Tsau Chu warriors. Rei was ordered to retreat to their base to defend the House flag. Je Jero, the House team leader for the tournament, was now consumed with battle rage – this was the first time he had ever experienced losing a soldier, a close friend, in battle. For several moments, an incredible battle waged between the Houses Nui Vent and Tsau Chu remaining team members. However, being a more experienced and disciplined team, the House Tsau Chu warriors' long years of fighting together were beneficial. Danka was the next House Nui Vent warrior to "die" in combat and he was followed by Je Jero and finally Je Tero.

Rei is now alone. His other team members had been defeated, and he is now left to face three warriors of the House Tsau Chu. They are cunning, skillful, and worked well together. Rei knew his defeat would come soon. Like his other defeated, less skilled warriors, he expected to be physically beaten first by the House Tsau Chu team members before finally being defeated, for they specialized in humiliating their opponents just before "killing" them.

Rei took a last look at the House Nui Vent flag, the prize the opposing team would soon come to capture. Although he then knew the contest would be over soon, he yet wanted to make his older brothers and House proud of him with his last stand.

The remaining House Tsau Chu team members slowly approached him. They were across the arena and only a few hundred steps away.

Rei's heart started beating faster and faster knowing his defeat and "pretend" death was approaching. His mind raced through all his combat lessons. He gazed at Nui Honei in the stands as tears regrettably fell from his eyes. Hoping he would not disappoint her and her House, he saluted her. Moved, Nui Honei stood in the stands and saluted him. And when he saw his House great mother smiling in the stands at him, he found some lingering, inner strength she had nurtured in him for the past few years. So, instead of immediately yielding to his foes, he stabbed his weapons into the ground and began to chant his House Haka as loud as he could at the House Tsau Chu warriors. Rei found inner peace from Nui Honei's smile as he started his war dance. He then determined to protect his House flag as best as he could. As taught by his new House elders, he would "die" a warrior's death, with the blood of his enemies upon his hands!

The House Tsau Chu team stopped their approach, listened to the Haka, and looked at each other with puzzled faces. They had never witnessed this type of battle behavior before

Rei chanted loudly in ancient Elvish, "We are going to die with the blood of enemies on our hands. We die knowing we were protecting our House and our lands. May our black dragons fly me home. May our ancestors welcome me home."

From within the arena stands, House great father Nui Samu stood, filled with pride; responded with his own Haka, chanting loudly in ancient Elvish, "Yes, my sons and daughters. You die with the blood of enemies on your hands. I know this will be your final stand. Die well my sons and daughters for our black dragons to carry you home. And for our ancestors to welcome you home."

Rei again took up his arms, took a defensive position and waited for the enemy attack, no longer afraid.

No longer entranced by the Haka, the House Tsau Chu team attacked Rei shouting their rage-filled, battle cries. Rei fought skillfully and valiantly for a short time. However, after the initial attack period, the House Tsau Chu warriors reverted to their disciplined attacks and overpowered Rei, "killing" him swiftly and captured the House Nui Vent flag.

Cheers erupted throughout the arena. The Kilecfla is now over, and House Tsau Chu is the winner. This had been a glorious tournament.

While the cheering still lingered on, Je Jero gathered his teammates and they all walked to the center of the arena facing the House Tsau Chu base. Likewise, the victorious House Tsau Chu warriors walked to the arena's center and faced the House Nui Vent warriors. They all removed their helmets. Respectfully, the House Nui Vent team bowed deeply to the victors of the tournament.

Je Jero then extended his hand to the leader of the House Tsau Chu team and said after shaking his hand, "Thank you for the battle lessons you shared with us today. You and your team have taught us much."

Other members of both teams followed suit and greeted the members of the opposing team. Tsau Mei Ling, the deadly archer, approached Ona Drachir and said after introductions, "I shot twelve arrows at you and missed each time; that has never happened before. Attacking me by yourself was foolhardy. Why?"

"I wanted to get your attention," replied a smiling Ona Drachir. "When can I see you again?"

As the House Nui Vent warriors left the arena, both great mother Nui Honei and great father Nui Samu greeted them in the arena's tunnel. Proudly, the elders congratulated the team on their performance. Although defeated, they are all in high spirits. Rei, still overcome by the excitement of the day's event declared seriously, "We will still meet you tomorrow morning for training. We must start practicing for next year's tournament." All the others laughed in response.

"As expected, House Tsau Chu won the tournament," remarked the elder prince. "Now, shall we go. I now need a different type of entertainment." With a hand gesture from the prince, his escort now moved into formation in preparation to leave the arena.

"Remember to return to the House Tsau Chu before sundown, said the queen. Then rising, the queen, the House Je Luneefa elders and their combined entourage all left the arena stands.

The princes, the House Je Luneefa daughters and their escorts also rose and quickly left the arena.

"Prince Rho Paul, what did you enjoy most about the final match?" asked Je Danei as they walked to a nearby inn that had already been reserved for them.

"The Nui Vent team's lost due to their inferior experience,

skills and tactics. House Tsau Chu team's use of an elite archer gained them a significant advantage. They also fought well together as a team. It was quite foolhardy for just one warrior to leave his group just to attack the archer by himself," said the prince.

"I thought that particular House Nui Vent warrior was daring and quite brave. He also risked his own "death" by trying to save a teammate who was in dire need of assistance," responded Je Danei.

"Nonsense, they both ventured from the greater safety of the group to try to help each other and both failed," commented the younger prince. "They both foolishly sacrificed themselves and their team lost as a result."

"What was more disappointing to you: trying to neutralize the valued archer's advantages or risking oneself to help another?" inquired Je Leena. "As leader of the House Nui Vent team, my sister and I supported our brother's decision to send one warrior to "kill" the other team's archer to eliminate that advantage. Further, helping a comrade-in-arms, even at the risk of one's life, is inherent in warriors."

Taken somewhat aback, Prince Rho James said, "Are you contradicting his Majesty, the royal prince?"

"I thought my sister took an opportunity to just describe what she and I saw," explained Je Danei. "Ah, we have arrived at the famous Kyuu inn." They all went into the inn and were warmly greeted by the innkeeper, an aged dwarf, Dac Stronghammer. A table displaying a variety of fruits and cheeses had been prepared. Another table displayed several different wines. Both tables, splendidly decorated in rich fall colors, reflected the diversified and plentiful bounty of the farmland surrounding Torondell. Along with a roaring fire ablaze, minstrels began playing a lively tune.

After seating and being served the first wine, prince Rho Paul, addressing Je Danei, asked, "Why do you have an escort of just four soldiers?"

Je Danei thought momentarily and replied, "For the same reasons you travel with an escort of sixteen soldiers. However, my sister and I are not deemed important enough to warrant a larger force."

"*Good answer, Sister,*" Je Leena's hand language secretly communicated.

Prince Rho James asked, "Daughters of House Je Luneefa will you now be good hosts and serve us wine and these prepared delicacies of your region? Or do I need to order you to do so?"

"Must you always order to get what you want?" Je Leena

asked. "It is known that House Rho has great hunters and is not part of great hunting doing things to encourage your intended prey to do what you want? 'Ordering is not always needed *when* your prey actually wants to do your bidding.' Our grandmother is incredibly wise," a smiling Je Leena remarked.

A curious Prince Rho James asked Je Danei, "Why didn't you ever attend the Military Academy of Canae in Rhodell?"

"The Academy offered little more than what I already have here. We learn weaponry and martial arts from the kingdom's finest weapons masters; our grandfather teaches us military history and tactics; and the kingdom's foremost battlemages are elders of my family. Even if we wanted to study the medical arts, the kingdom's finest healer is here too. So, we have no good reason to journey to Rhodell for any education," answered Je Danei. "Although, contact with other nobles and establishing good relationships can also begin there. However, I prefer the many advantages of Torondell."

One of the inn's waiters started moving toward the prince intending to serve him wine. However, Prince Rho James simply ordered him away. Gesturing to his royal escort's commander, the soldier ordered everyone to leave. The House Je Luneefa soldiers remained in place behind the daughters of House Je Luneefa while the inn staff and minstrels left the room.

The prince continued, "Now that everyone has left, you will not be embarrassed by serving my brother and myself if there are no witnesses watching. Also, why didn't your House soldiers leave as ordered?" asked prince Rho James.

Je Danei looked at the prince and said, "Our House soldiers only take orders from our House commanders; and here, my sister and I are their commanders. Neither of us gave them an order to leave."

"I could order our guards then to just kill your escort if they will not leave," prince Rho Paul commented.

"How many of your guards would die in the process? Would that be a wise use of your valuable resources? House Je Luneefa soldiers are respected and valued. We treat them fairly and do not use them needlessly," countered Je Danei. "Besides, you and/or your brother could also die in the mayhem that would ensue. Are you willing to also take that risk?"

"I agree sister; odds are actually in our favor. I have noticed too that two of the royal guards are mages, but of low ranking. I, myself, am of the fifth rank; they would be no match for me either," Je Leena calmly remarked.

"It would be a very low risk at that; our guards outnumbered yours four to one," rebuked Prince Rho Paul. "Secondly, I suspect you and your sister would be inclined to join them given what we heard of your reputations; but you are not carrying any weapons. So, either or both of you would surely die in that same mayhem, but much more quickly."

"My prince, it seems your knowledge of the well-earned reputations of the House Je Luneefa females is still too limited. Be advised that we are *always* armed. 'Dying quickly' surely is not. Thirdly, should your guards attempt to attack ours, my sister and I most assuredly would join the fight; and I can almost guarantee that you and your brother would be the first casualties of the ensuing mayhem," defiantly proclaimed Je Danei, annoyed by the continued arrogance of the Canae princes.

"So, you do not respect royalty? You would actually try to harm us?" asked a puzzled Prince Rho James.

"Of course, we respect your position; but we also respect ourselves and our House much more. Should you try to harm me, my sister or any of our escorts, we will defend ourselves even at the cost of your lives. So, choose your fights very carefully," Je Leena said.

Prince Rho Paul, arrogant with his royal position and overconfident with the odds of his force addressed the commander of his escort, "Commander, my brother and I do not feel threatened, but only challenged. As you know, my brother and I do enjoy a good challenge. So, do not interfere with our challenge unless the Je Luneefa escort try to interfere; and at that point, kill them all."

"Gladly, Your Majesty," the royal guards commander said with an arrogant sneer.

"So, just the two of you against my sister and me?" politely questioned Je Leena. "That seems too unfair; for you two surely will lose even without our escort's aid. Even without weapons, either of us could kill you and your brother with our hands or feet since we study and practice martial arts daily and have been training for many years. Are either of you familiar with the elven ancient martial art Dragon's Flame?" Neither prince answered. "That is indeed sad. It would appear my sister and I have other advantages too over you and your brother.

"By the way, only one of you will become the *crowned* prince; the queen and king do not need both of you to continue their royal bloodline. I wonder which of you they favor most?" Both Je Luneefa sisters knew of the tension between the brothers who competed to be next in line for the royal duty of kingship. So, her remark was designed to increase that tension and hopefully reduce their ill intentions upon the Je Luneefa sisters. If not, Je Danei and Je Leena are well prepared to defend themselves even to the deaths of the princes, most likely.

The princes and the House Je Luneefa daughters are all sitting at a large, square-shaped table staring at each other with rising tension. The princes sat across and faced each other; while the sisters sat across and faced each other. With a noticed wink from Prince Rho Paul, each prince went to draw his short sword carried at their sides. In that same moment, the faster House Je Luneefa sisters pulled their concealed weapons from their capes. Each sister drew long knives placed in each of their hands. Each of their blades was now pointed at the exposed throats of the princes. Neither prince had been able to draw his blade free of its sheath before finding themselves in a lost, desperate position. Many of the royal escorts gasped in fear, placing their hands upon their weapons. In turn, the four House Je Luneefa escort soldiers had already quickly brandished their drawn swords and were crouching in an attack formation.

"Ah, the reputation of the House Je Luneefa females must indeed be true. Brother, for the first time, we've been defeated," Prince Rho Paul sadly admitted. "No doubt it was the magic of our lovely hosts who easily distracted us with their beauty." After both princes returned their blades to their sheaths and placed their hands upon the table, the House Je Luneefa sisters relaxed. All escort soldiers, royal and House Je Luneefa, sheath their weapons and returned to their relaxed, watchful positions.

Each House Je Luneefa daughter placed their knives in front of them on the table. "Thank you, your Majesty, my sister and I are both flattered by your words. By the way, Je Leena is already an accomplished battlemage for her young age. She did use her magic though; not to distract you, but to conceal another member of our escort," announced Je Danei. With that vocal signal, Je Leena removed the veil of invisibility surrounding Je Onyxia Ryoshi, Je Danei's pet panther. Ony had silently positioned herself between Je Danei and Prince Rho Paul. The panther just sat quietly on its rear haunches while Je Danei affectionately scratched its great head. Ony, however, continued to gaze at the prince with a menacing stare. Although the princes maintained their royal composure, they were both now a little frightened. "So, now you can see my prince why the odds of any possible mayhem would be in our favor. How would you and your escort possibly contend with my pet who can be rendered invisible and undetected?"

Before an irritated Prince Rho James could speak and escalate emotions and issues further, a now comfortable Je Leena remarked, "My princes, Your Majesties, let us turn our attention to more pleasant topics. What are your plans for the remainder of your stay in Torondell?"

"Brother let us leave now," a defeated and clearly irritated Prince Rho James said loudly.

The princes stood and walked out of the inn followed by their escort. The daughters of House Je Luneefa stood too when the princes rose from their seats. The felfs then bowed respectfully when the princes turned and left.

*"Finally, they are all gone. I am hungry and I smelled the deer meat you must have ordered for me when I walked in through the rear entrance. Can we now eat in peace?"* asked Ony. Both sisters laughed after Je Danei shared Ony's remarks with her sister.

Upon returning to their House stronghold, the Je Luneefa sisters sought and found their House great mothers sitting in the great hall along with their adopted aunt Nui Honei of House Nui Vent. Both sisters shared their thoughts of the afternoon's incident at the inn with the royal princes.

House great mother Je Pagi looked at her mother, Je Buel, and asked, "Will there be repercussions?"

"The royal princes had their big egos crushed. They will not complain to the queen and House Rho first great mother directly; that would make them appear weak. She abhors weakness. She will most likely counsel them to either give up their hunt now and seek weaker prey to satisfy their royal urges or to become more patient and determined hunters if they truly want revenge," said House great mother Je Buel.

"They are males. Worse, they are males with power and royal, over-inflated egos; so, they do not understand the value of patience," remarked Je Pagi. "I may know the answer to my next question, but I want to know for certain. Are either of you interested in either prince?"

Both daughters responded with a fast and emphatic "No, mother!"

"You and grandmother have both taught us to set our standards high for a potential male consort. Neither prince is qualified nor worthy of a daughter of this House!" added Je Danei.

"We may need to deflect attention away from our daughters though at tonight's grand banquet. Male egos are fragile," announced the ever-calculating Je Buel. "And I have an idea."

"By the way, how many weapons did you carry today?"

inquired a curious Nui Honei.

"I just had five, including my House cape's elegant clasp which hides my black, bladed Manriki-gusari. It is the one you gave Sister and me last year," answered Je Leena.

Je Danei thought for a moment longer and responded, "My black, bladed Manriki-gusari, two short swords, two long knives, eight throwing knives and two yawara for a total of fifteen. A bit over-prepared maybe?"

A soft growl emanated from Ony who had laid down next to Je Danei after the sisters arrived.

Je Pagi interpreted for the group, "I believe our dear Ony disagrees with your total count daughter. You indeed had one other fierce weapon."

"And they thought you two were unarmed? Foolish, foolish males indeed," remarked Nui Honei.

All the females smiled, laughing quietly.

# Secrets Unfold

"Why are you here again? Are you spying for the crown? What do you really want from my family that you are here so much? Speak truthfully former thief," an angered Je Danei demanded.

"I am here just to continue learning the dwarf language from your grandparents," answered an annoyed Jooba.

"By helping them in our kitchen and garden? You lie! After all this time, do you take me for a fool? What is your real intent?" Je Leena now asked mirroring her sister's anger.

Jooba silently continued setting the breakfast table for the Je Luneefa family while ignoring the torrent of questions from the House Je Luneefa daughters.

"I too am suspicious of your reasons for being here so often, former thieves," Je Jero stated. "For the last few years, each week you three have been here working in the kitchen, stables, garden and wherever you were assigned. You do not ever complain. Why? You have even worked outside when the weather was terrible."

Je Tero then added, "You are ever around our grandparents and parents listening to them and asking questions. Why? What do you really seek? Should you ever hurt any of them, know that you will all die that day!"

With her brother's last declaration, Je Danei pulled a knife from her boot and threw it at Jooba, aiming for his shoulder. Je Danei had noticed that he had been looking at all the daughters and sons of House Je Luneefa, but especially her, displaying anger on his face. This displeased the felf.

Jooba quickly turned his body away, snatching the thrown knife from the air by its handle. He then pivoted and threw the knife back at Je Danei aiming at the top of the high-back chair upon which she was sitting. The knife stuck deeply into the chair above her head. Rei, who happened to be standing close to the House Je Luneefa first daughter, retrieved the knife from the chair and presented it back to Je Danei handle first.

"You four clearly have misjudged us and misunderstand our intentions," Danka said, calmly trying to ease the tension in the dining hall. "You clearly have every right to be suspicious of us and should be protective, even overly protective of your grandparents and parents. They are all truly remarkable. Even more, your House elders honestly and unconditionally love you and do what they can to protect you from the harsh and evil realities of this world. My brothers and I lived, no survived, in a world with danger and evil constantly by our sides each day. Outside of our small group, *love* and *trust* were completely foreign to us or were based upon unfair or unfavorable *conditions*.

"In our past, our days and nights were filled with danger. Our next meal was not ever certain. We could never even sleep completely well in the great forest; one had to be vigilant at all times. Other refugees there may be your friends today but become your enemies before the next day's dawn.

"You can all sleep soundly, safe and secure in this stronghold. You have plenty of food to eat and clothes to wear. You even have the privileges of living a noble's life. Please do not ever take these blessings for granted. Your grandparents and parents gave you all these precious gifts at their sacrifice. You may not always appreciate or like their decisions, but always respect and honor them. I believe they always try to do what is best for the family, even at the expense of their own happiness. Appreciate your elders; show them you love them as much as they love you.

"Please forgive my brothers and myself for causing you any discomfort. Please understand that my brothers and I immensely enjoy being in the presence of such great family elders like your grandparents, parents, our House great mother Nui Honei and great father Nui Samu. There is so much we can all learn from them if we make the time to do so. Be thankful; be very thankful we have such selfless, protective, wise and wonderful House and family elders.

"Brothers, let us take our leave now; we have finished this duty and are not welcomed here." Danka, Jooba and Rei finished their early morning assignments and returned to the kitchen to continue their other duties.

The sons and daughters of House Je Luneefa sat very quietly unable to speak after Danka words made them all reflect upon themselves. They each carefully thought about the words Danka had just spoken. When the House Je Luneefa elders arrived at the hall, the daughters got up and walked quickly to their grandfather and father. The sons rose and walked quickly to their grandmother and mother. Each family elder was personally escorted to the table and seated by a House daughter or son.

"What is this that you do?" Je Maron asked.

"More importantly, what do you now want?" inquired a suspicious Je Buel.

The House Je Luneefa daughters and sons stood together in front of the family elders. A tearful Je Jero said, "Dear grandparents and parents, we first wish to sincerely apologize for not appreciating all of you more. Except for Kei, we four lacked the wisdom or trust to fully appreciate your decisions regarding our family. Your wisdom, knowledge, and experience about the world greatly exceed ours. Except Kei, we have not shown you enough appreciation for all that you have done for us. We no longer will take you, our greatest blessings, for granted. Danka, Jooba and Rei taught us all valuable lessons today."

The four House Je Luneefa daughters and sons shared with the House elders what had happened earlier in the hall. Je Leena concluded, "Papa, is that why you and Nana secretly favored Kei because he learned the lessons early?"

Later that afternoon, the House Je Luneefa first and second elders, followed by the four daughters and sons of House Je Luneefa went to the House Nui Vent stronghold. Following close to Je Danei was Je Onyxia Ryoshi, Je Danei's pet panther. The House Je Luneefa family went to the great hall where the new House Nui Vent soldiers were standing at the main table. House great mother Nui Honei and great father Nui Samu stood at the head of the table. The Houses' elders greeted each other very warmly. In turn, the daughters and sons of House Je Luneefa bowed and warmly greeted their adopted aunt and uncle. Meanwhile, the House Nui Vent soldiers bowed and warmly greeted the House Je Luneefa elders.

The Houses' elders sat at opposite ends of the long table, and the younger felfs and melfs sat in the middle of the great table but on opposite sides. Whether by chance or not, Je Danei sat directly across from Jooba; Je Leena sat directly across from Rei; and Danka sat directly across the table from the sons of House Je Luneefa.

Ona Drachir was there too and had heard what happened

earlier in the day. He chose to sit on the same side with the House Nui Vent soldiers.

Ony sat quietly on her hind legs next to Je Danei who smirked at Jooba while scratching her pet's head.

"Thank you again, House Nui Vent great mother and father, for inviting us to afternoon tea. But, before we partake of our tea and the delightful pastries, the daughters and sons of our House would like to say something to your House soldiers," Je Buel started.

Je Jero stood bowed again to the House Nui Vent elders and sincerely apologized for the behavior he and his siblings demonstrated earlier that day. He expressed their gratitude for the lessons the House Nui Vent soldiers taught them. He then looked to Je Danei to continue with her apology, but she was looking down at the table fidgeting with the tableware.

After a few moments, Je Pagi interrupted her daughter's silence, "First daughter, what do you have to say?"

Je Danei quietly cleared her throat and slowly started to raise her head. When her eyes met Jooba's, he was now smiling at her, waiting to hear her sincere apology. He also had placed two knives in front of him. Now feeling challenged, Je Danei pulled two hidden knives she carried and placed those on the table in front of her.

"Jooba, I too wish to sincerely apologize for my inappropriate behavior. Please forgive me," Je Danei said with a bit of reserved defiance for she very seldom apologized for her actions.

"Apology accepted," Jooba remarked after standing and placing two scimitars taken from the back of his chair and placing those on the table in front of him.

Feeling angry and challenged, Je Danei stood and in response, pulled two hidden short swords from her back and placed those on the table in front of her.

Smiling, Jooba pulled a mighty, fearsome looking halberd from underneath the table and placed that on the table in front of him. During all this time, Jooba continued to meet the gaze of Je Danei without ever backing away from her challenging stare.

"Well, I see those two have more to discuss. No blood is to be shed while you two continue your *peaceful* discussions. Is that understood?" House great mother Nui Honei commanded. Turning to the rest of her guests, she continued, "Since the weather is very nice today, let us leave Je Danei and Jooba here to their discussions in private while the rest of us enjoy our tea and pastries outside in the garden."

After the others left the hall quietly laughing, Je Danei remarked, "Bigger does not mean it is better."

Jooba quickly responded to her verbal challenge, "And how would you know? What experience do you have to make such a claim?"

"Ony attack!" an annoyed Je Danei commanded. In response, the great panther quickly leapt across the table at Jooba who caught the panther in his outstretched arms. The momentum of the panther knocked Jooba off his feet and he momentarily play-wrestled with the panther. He then rose, went to a chest on the side of the hall and retrieved a haunch of deer meat which he gave to Ony. Ony expressed her thanks by licking Jooba's hand. The great panther then picked up the deer haunch and also went to the garden to enjoy her fine meal.

"Why all my family elders and Ony seem to like you, I do not understand," a frustrated Je Danei said as she was leaving. Jooba quietly laughed as he watched her leave. Soon thereafter, he left the great hall to rejoin the others in the garden.

Cold blowing winds eerily howled and fearful darkness shrouded the moonless night. It was about midnight, and all is quiet within the House Nui Vent stronghold except for the quiet footfalls of the House soldiers patrolling the hallways. Over the last year, there had been several assassination attempts aimed at Nui Honei, the House Nui Vent great mother. Though all the attempts occurred around Torondell, no would-be assassin had yet ever breached the magically fortified stronghold. Despite the stronghold's many safeguards, everyone still remained vigilant.

Relatives of northern frontier's House Si Moina vowed vengeance against Nui Honei for her actions against House Si Moina. Not only did Nui Honei take the head of the renegade House Si Moina's first great mother, Si Cairyn, Nui Honei had also previously rescued Ona Noirar and his dragon, Ona Kei Kuri Ryuu, from House Si Moina's captivity. In both situations, the House Nui Vent great mother left many dead in her aftermath.

With each assassination attempt, Nui Honei took the would-be assassin's head and returned it to House Si Moina. Like her adopted nieces, the Je Luneefa daughters, Nui Honei was always armed.

As fate would have it, some of House great mother Si Cairyn's descendants survived the devastation the northern army, led by Ona Noirar, Nui Honei and Keiku, wreaked upon the House Si Moina stronghold. Although Ona Noirar and his dragon had died over a year ago, House Nui Vent remained on constant alert.

Attacks of revenge were expected.

Late that night, a melf descended from the heights of the darkest corner of Nui Honei's bedchamber and walked silently towards the sleeping felf. This intruder was cloaked with a very special cape that was enhanced with blood-magic to provide levitation capabilities and render him invisible too to plain eyes. In one hand, the intruder held a dagger made of diachrom-infused, dull black steel, a perfect assassin's blade in the darkest night. However, Nui Honei was not the usual prey of a skilled killer. When the assassin was a few steps from the base of her bed, she sat up, unveiling her naked features along with her dark-piercing, magically enhanced dragon's eyes glowing a dark emerald green. Nui Honei looked directly at the still invisible, assumed, would-be assassin.

She now gazed erotically at the fully recuperated Ona Noirar who recently returned from a fifteen-moon recovery of deadly raznac poisoning. Nui Honei whispered, "You will not need that blade to cut away my nightgown this evening."

"And how did you know it was me again and not a real assassin?" inquired a puzzled Ona Noirar.

"I still know the sound of your heartbeat beloved," whispered Nui Honei.

When dawn broke the next morning, Ona Noirar softly awakened Nui Honei who was still in a deep sleep. After a while, she awoke and asked, "Are you still hungry?"

With a devilish smile, Ona Noirar answered, "For you, yes; but we must discuss other matters with the Warden. I have news from the northern frontier."

Nui Honei responded, "I have already planned for us to meet with him and the other House Je Luneefa elders tonight during our evening meal. Arrangements have been made. You have no other commitments till midday except to do my bidding. You still owe me for the time you were gone." Seductively pausing, she continued, "Do you understand my meaning, mighty warrior?"

"Completely, House Nui Vent great mother Nui Honei. So, command me as you wish," said Ona Noirar.

"Undress and return to my arms now; for *I* am still hungry!" proclaimed Nui Honei.

Later that day, shortly after sunset, a disguised Ona Noirar secretly escorted Nui Honei to the Je Luneefa home where they had been invited for dinner. This was also a time of celebration for Ona Noirar had finally returned from death's threshold several times.

A joyous dinner had been served in the House Je Luneefa's

great hall. Other than the entire Je Luneefa family, Nui Honei and Ona Noirar, only Nui Samu, Alleina and Ona Drachir had been invited to the celebratory feast.

Je Buel magically sealed the room from any prying eyes and ears and was first to raise her glass and toast the honored guest, "Welcome back dear son and friend; it is so very good to see you alive and somewhat healthy again. I noticed you have a slight limp; are you still not fully recovered?" She then nodded at Nui Honei who removed the magical disguise from Ona Noirar's face.

"Good evening, all. I have fortunately escaped from death and did heal from the poisoning. However, I did not quite escape an unprovoked attack of the three House Nui Vent soldiers who saw me leave Nui Honei's room early this morning. One especially seemed to want to take my head," a thoughtful, but irritated Ona Noirar said. "And they were bringing you flowers again."

"Rei wanted your head?" asked House great mother Je Pagi.

"It was most likely Rei," said an assuming Nui Samu.

"Definitely, Rei," agreed Je Danei.

With these proclamations, all, except a blushing Nui Honei, started laughing over the protective actions of the House Nui Vent soldiers.

After a few moments, Ona Noirar rose from the table. The humble and grateful warrior nodded his head in thanks and addressed the assembly, saying, "I give thanks first to the best healer in all the known world, Alleina; for without her, I would not be standing here today. Secondly, Keiku too saved my life again. It was the magic of her blood that countered the deadly raznac poison and healed me. I must also thank my nephew, who with some risk, initially donated his precious blood that was successfully transfused into me too. Lastly, I must thank Nui Honei; for her love was ever the anchor that kept me planted in this world of the living and would not let me die to that poison. And thanks go to all of you too dear family for the support I needed during this ordeal."

Ona Noirar next said, "With my many thanks, I also want to bestow upon each of you a gift as a small token of my appreciation." Ona Noirar rose from his table and walked across the room to retrieve a large chest from against the far wall. He then placed the chest in front of the dais' main table and opened it. "First, I'd like to present to my healer these medical scrolls from the land of Azu which records in-depth knowledge of the body's main organs. These scrolls were supposedly created by the famous healer Mazza."

With the receipt of the precious scrolls, Alleina was surprised and with joy overwhelming, she began to cry. "How did you know? Where did you get these? Why spend a fortune for these for me?" the ever-humble Alleina asked.

Ona Noirar carefully responded, "You had mentioned you had lost your original copies of these medical scrolls during a fire accident over ten years ago. So, when I had a chance recently to get these scrolls, I seized the opportunity. Fortunately, Keiku and I had accumulated enough treasure from past adventures to pay for the scrolls. Finally, this is a small boon compared to your saving my life. Again, thank you.

"Great mothers of House Je Luneefa, I got each of you bolts of rare fabric and bottles of rare perfume. Merchants from faraway lands still trade in the northern frontier. So, I was able to purchase these which I am told reflect current fashion trends in the kingdom's capitol city." He reached into the chest and presented to Je Buel and Je Pagi two bolts each of black and red silk, a rare fabric not easily found in the Canae kingdom.

"You never cease to amaze us. You, a once nearly dead melf, have risen from death's mighty grip and now bear gifts? Thank you. Again Brother, you are very generous," said a very appreciative Je Pagi.

Ona Noirar bowed his head, reached again into the chest and remarked, "And to my beloved Nui Honei, my return from the brink of death to remain by your side till I truly die is the best gift I can give you. However, I thought this bloodstone necklace would not only grace your lovely neck; but it would also serve as a reminder of my triumphant return." He walked around the table to where Nui Honei was sitting and placed the necklace around her neck. She then stood, cupped his face in her hands and kissed him.

"Thank you, my love. I will cherish this token always. Also, please forgive our House soldiers; they can act rashly at times," Nui Honei said apologetically.

"To my brothers in arms, great fathers Je Taeliel, Je Maron and Nui Samu, I have a bottle of rare Napa brandy for each of you. You will find this brandy to be incredibly special due to how it has been enhanced with a certain secret ingredient," slyly announced Ona Noirar. Afterwards, he reached into the chest and retrieved three bottles of the liquor and presented one to each House great father. Each House great father in return thanked Ona Noirar for his gift.

"And what's the 'secret' enhancement?" asked great father Je Taeliel.

Smiling, Ona Noirar responded, "We should discuss that matter privately."

Looking at the two elder felfs, Nui Honei then remarked, "Do ensure your husbands share a glass of this remarkable, *specially enhanced* brandy with you too; you will find it very, very pleasing."

Ona Noirar closed the chest and looked at the remaining, ungifted felfs and melfs. Ona Noirar said, "I have not forgotten you either, young ones. I have decided to give each of you something special and precious to me: a full day, sunrise to sundown, of personal, one-on-one training. You can choose the training you want, be it weapons and/or martial arts."

"An entire day of your dedicated, focused attention and time would be a marvelous gift to this warrior. I still have so much to learn and would truly welcome this opportunity to learn from a master, such as yourself. Thank you very much. When can we begin?" asked an eager Je Danei.

"I would like to have your dedicated time right after Danei's session," Je Jero next remarked.

"Please let mine be the day after Jero's," Je Tero quickly requested.

Nui Samu inquired after noticing Je Leena and Ona Drachir delayed their requests, "Leena and Drachir, surely you both want to take advantage of this rare opportunity. Why delay your acceptance of this warrior's generosity?"

"Should I not make my request last since I have trained with my Uncle Noirar much longer than anyone else? However, let my private session take place the day after Je Leena's requested time," Ona Drachir responded quietly.

"Thank you Drachir; you are thoughtful and considerate. I suspect dear Uncle you will need some time to recover from the exasperating training of my elder brothers; so, please let my session start two days after Tero's session," Je Leena remarked. Je Danei quietly laughed. Both Je Jero and Je Tero aimed scornful looks at their youngest sister.

"Have you completely recovered now?" interjected Je Buel.

"Yes, Mother Je Buel; I feel perfectly fine now. Thank you," replied Ona Noirar. "So, I would like to start a normal training regimen soon. Je Danei would two days from now be soon enough?"

"Yes, thank you," a pleased Je Danei responded.

Ona Noirar continued, "Let us now turn our attention to more serious matters. As some of you know, I awoke from my healing sleep about three moons ago. Since that time, I had to re-learn many basic body movements. Thanks to the miraculous healing qualities of dragon's blood *and* Alleina's wonderful nursing care, I can now fully function as I once did.

"Since I awakened, I have been thinking a great deal about some of my life's defining events and found several mysteries that I wish to share with all of you in hope that together, we can bring more clarity to them; because I believe, some of those mysteries may forebode eminent danger.

"About twelve days ago, I decided to secretly journey back to my former secret dwelling at Taurus Mountain. Fortunately, I was completely disguised as another common woods elf thanks to Nui Honei. As expected, attempts had been made to search for any treasure left behind. There were a few dead bodies found; no doubt the remains of the would-be grave robbers who had carelessly encountered Keiku's protective, magical wards.

"One group of hopeful thieves became quite talkative after my sharing some very good wine. House Si Moina still stands. Apparently, they had another secret stronghold to which survivors fled after we destroyed their first stronghold at Nusa Rock. These grave robbers were employed by House Si Moina and were still searching for any remaining Keiku's eggs that may have survived the mountaintop's destruction.

"I also believe House Si Moina is receiving assistance from Majeejp, the Wanderer. This human has lived well beyond a human's normal life expectancy. As you know, this famed, dark mage is a human who supposedly disappeared over a century ago. Long ago, he had joined a sect of dark mages but wanted to leave them after he met a felf who became his wife. Together, they had a mixed-blood belf. His sect unsuccessfully tried to control him by capturing his family. When his sect killed his elf wife and belf, he vowed vengeance. After killing over half of his sect members, Majeejp disappeared from the capital city and started wandering around the world looking for more of what he needs to prolong his tormented life: the untainted, freely given blood of a dragon.

"Untainted, freely given dragon's blood can be the *truest blessing*; it contains wonderous powers known and unknown. Since black dragons seem to have the most powerful magical energy, it stands to reason that their blood too would be the most powerful."

Puzzled, Je Buel asked, "What do you mean by the *truest blessing*?"

"Not only must the dragon's blood be freely given, but the dragon must also *bless* the given blood to fully activate its blood's magical properties. Only the dragon can do this. That is the key.

"While captive by House Si Moina, some of Keiku's blood was taken, freely given to only keep me alive; but she did not *fully* bless it. So, that taken blood was not as powerful as it could have been. Fortunately, our enemies did not know that very secret, little-known fact of dragonosophy.

"As the Houses' elders know, Keiku's mother, Siida, was a black dragon. Her rider was a woods felf, Jaale. Siida and Jaale left behind three great tomes. The first of Siida's *Chronicles* explains that the dragon blood's power is greatly magnified by citing the Massicenae incantation, a spell named after one of the very first dragon riders. This incantation is an actual blessing cited in the ancient dragon's language. Following the ancient tradition, a full blessing, or the *truest blessing*, requires the dragon to incant the Massicenae spell fully three times after its blood is freely given.

"Secondly, Keiku believes Majeejp may have secretly stolen one of her eggs directly from her womb. Before eventually laying her eggs therein her secret, Taurus Mountain lair, she had felt the lifeforce of four dragons, not three. Keiku and I believe the dark mage used that stolen egg for his dark magic purposes to extend his life.

"We also believe Majeejp and House Si Moina will still relentlessly continue their hunt for any of Keiku's eggs. I fear once they learn that she and I are still alive, they will most likely renew their attempts to steal her eggs. Their attempts to discover any eggs will most likely resume at the destroyed mountaintop of Mountain Taurus. Keiku and I strongly feel those enemies will extend their search to Mountain Toron and even to the noble Houses Je Luneefa and Nui Vent. Si Cairyn's evil runs deep within her family. Her surviving family members continue to share and pursue the House Si Moina first great mother's vision of conquest and dominance."

"Is that remnant of House Si Moina that foolish now to provoke a potential war with House Je Luneefa?" asked Je Taeliel.

"In my opinion, 'Yes'," said Ona Noirar dryly. "House Si Moina first great mother Si Cairyn was obsessed with attaining power. She was completely overcome with the idea that she and her House should rule the entire kingdom. Her plan started with building a brigade of fierce soldiers with a core of dragon riders. Fortunately, that part of her plan did not come into fruition since we killed four of her dragons. If there are any others, we do not know. And Majeejp has very personal reasons to pursue getting any black dragon. He desperately wants it blood to prolong his life.

"Unfortunately, I failed in completely destroying House Si Moina years ago. I recently learned that some members of that family did escape to a hidden secondary stronghold further west in the northern frontier.

"Another thing I learned on my recent clandestine trip is that those would-be grave robbers had been advanced some payment which was paid with the king's rare gold coins, not the kingdom's regular gold coins. How did those lowly robbers get those? If the coins came from House Si Moina, why did that House even have them?

"Also, they were told should they ever find my body, they are to take my head back to House Si Moina for a big reward. Why would anyone want my head?" After some quiet reflection, Ona Noirar continued, "There is only one felf who would want my head that badly... I strongly suspect the queen still holds a grudge against me for what happened centuries ago. She may still hate me and hold me accountable for her daughter's death."

"I wish to also add another mystery we can solve too perhaps. Who or what is the *red falcon*?" interjected Nui Honei during the group's silent contemplation.

Je Buel said, "The king's heraldic sigil is a white falcon on an azure background. It is the symbol for House Rho. A red falcon on an azure background represents the Queen; those colors are only worn by her and her honor guard. Why do you ask?"

"As Si Cairyn was dying, just before I finally took her head, she told me that our fight was not over and that the 'red falcon will still come to devour us,'" a disturbed Nui Honei remarked.

House first great mother, Je Buel, said, "Long ago, when Queen Rho Jiedae taught at the academy, there was a rumor that Si Cairyn and Rho Jiedae were once secret lovers. It was a brief, dragon flame-hot affair that turned cold like a winter's storm after Rho Jiedae eventually rejected Si Cairyn. She then eventually recognized her long, sought-after path to the Canae throne and power did not lie with another felf."

Je Buel then turned towards Je Taeliel and remarked, "And let us not forget why dear husband you were 'rewarded' with the appointment of Warden of the North. Although you are quite capable as a leader, you are popular with your troops and the Torondell commoners who love you for your unbiased justice and fairness. The king was jealous of you for that and more. And if I remember correctly, he was not the queen's first true love; you were. Also, Rho Jiedae's unrequited love angered her greatly. So, your reward for your accomplishments and success in the kingdom's capital and northern frontier was really a banishment here, I believe. Afterall, the king still saw you as competition perhaps? He was ever a poor loser and an even more foolish, petty male.

"However, we were very pleased to leave Rhodell, that festering cesspool of evil and political mayhem, and to start rebuilding our House here. We had hoped to leave all the political maneuvering there. The king probably hoped that our House would be destroyed here given the lawlessness of the region back then. But Je Taeliel brought order here. With time, we started to flourish here. This land was barren and rugged when we first got here; your vision and Duenor Heartstone's skills transformed this land into what it is today, the best province in the entire kingdom."

An austere Nui Honei added, "Ona Noirar and Rho Chele fled north to escape the harsh controls of her family who did not approve of their relationship since it did not yield any increased political or financial advantage for House Rho. Love apparently was not reason enough to bless their wanted union. Rho Chele was my best friend and blood-sister. Ona Noirar is blood-brother to Nui Samu. My brother and I were not happy living in Rhodell and decided to follow Ona Noirar and Rho Chele on their journey north, albeit at different times. We all joined the northern army ranks. We all became distinguished soldiers and even Ona Noirar became a famed commander in your northern army.

"After Rho Chele died and his military commitments concluded, Ona Noirar left the army and went to the mountains of Taurus to grieve. There is where you discovered the egg of your famed dragon, Ona Kei Kuri Ryuu. With the birth of Keiku, you bonded with her; and your life began to improve again. Attempts against your life resumed at the same time the crown started collecting or taking any dragon eggs they encountered. Rewards were even offered for dragon eggs to encourage all to find them and turn them in."

Je Pagi continued, "After some time, Nui Honei, Nui Samu, Alleina and Ona Noirar joined our House through adoption. Nui Honei and Ona Noirar became more famous as soldiers and eventually lovers. So, now the king and queen had more reasons to hate this House. One: Father, you turned this once wasteland into a valuable thriving land. You made this province the jewel of the kingdom; the king failed in his attempt to make Rhodell such. Torondell is more precious than the king's capitol city. Your appointment here was not your downfall, but an exceptionally beautiful, unexpected success. Two: there is order here for all unlike Rhodell. Many citizens who once lived in the capital city are moving here in hopes of finding a better life. Subsequently, Rhodell slowly declines while Torondell continues to flourish. Three: your popularity, due to your successes, continues to grow. You outshine the king! Four: there is still an unfounded rumor that House Je Luneefa has significantly more wealth than House Rho. Five: Ona Noirar, the Crown's secret enemy supposedly, is directly aligned to our House through his adoption. Without question, you have been and continue to be his nemesis."

"Our Houses also have an ally the Crown still cannot ever match nor easily eliminate. The mighty black dragon, Ona Kei Kuri Ryuu, is ours!" Nui Honei exclaimed, proudly. House Rho surely fears the day when Keiku may wreak havoc and utter devastation upon them."

"And let us not forget that our Houses have very close relationships with formidable, very strong allies – the Dwarven clans of Blood Tears Mountains and the five united orc tribes of the North," Alleina stoically remarked. "I suspect the Crown is very concerned about our Houses, especially since they know very little or nothing about our secrets."

"Surely, the Crown may be uncomfortable with the fact that Father Je Taeliel and Je Maron accomplished what many consider to be impossible feats in the North; and somehow, I feel that was not the Crown's expected or desired outcomes," a stoic Nui Honei offered.

Alleina contributed additional somber thoughts, saying, "Did the Canae Majesties truly want you to fail and even die there? Canae's history records that this had occurred to all the kingdom's first assigned Wardens of new conquered lands."

Je Buel stood and started slowly pacing the floor while she thought. All others remained silent, entrapped in their own deep contemplations. Most grappled with unanswered questions. All were somewhat confused and very concerned.

After a short while, Je Buel stopped her silent pacing; she then remarked, "Know too I believe the Canae Crown or House Rho maintains detailed information about certain noble Houses within and outside this realm. This information helps House Rho leaders develop and execute their overt and covert machinations. One certain piece of critical information they seek and maintain is a current understanding of each noble House's estimated financial resources, direct and indirect. Is House Je Luneefa that much of an enigma or even a significant concern that the Crown would test our financial well-being?"

"I have even wondered if some of the past century's House wars were even covertly instigated by the ever-jealous House Rho to weaken certain targeted, strong, wealthy noble Houses," Je

Taeliel stated.

"Especially if House Rho also benefited with the sharing of the spoils recovered from the defeated House. That would not surprise me at all. Such was the case with the defeat of House Nui Vent in our House war against House Pyr Jura," Nui Samu scornfully added. A few of the other House elders nodded their heads, concurring with Nui Samu's conjecture.

Ona Noirar remarked, "A few of the miners I shared wine with also worked on the construction of several different strongholds within the realm. All of these miners shared that they were each questioned about the structural design details of those noble Houses' stronghold. I suspect that House Rho also has and maintains each noble House's architectural and construction designs, as well as any of the House's stronghold secrets that could be stolen, purchased or even surreptitiously taken. Such plans would be very helpful should House Rho or the Crown ever needed to attack that stronghold."

"Fortunately, the wealth of Houses Je Luneefa, Nui Vent and Ona Feiir are closely guarded secrets known only by the elders here. Such highly confidential information would not ever be divulged to anyone outside of our families. Furthermore, it is insignificant; so, we should, hopefully, remain outside of House Rho's jealousy, insecurities and vehement concerns in that regard," Je Buel said.

"I have also expressed, directly to Queen Rho Jiedae, that our Houses are loyal to the Crown, and we just want our families to flourish and live in peace. We have even demonstrated such exemplary, loyal commitments by helping and serving Canae."

"Yes, and yet, the Canae Crown, I believe, *enjoys* assigning the Black Knights Brigade difficult and perilous missions in distant lands, to support Canae allies in their efforts to defeat enemies utilizing dragon forces. Somehow, I do not believe the Crown would ever mourn the death of Ona Kei Kuri Ryuu, Ona Noirar or myself. Is the Crown truly trying to assuage their fears and possibly mitigate their concerns of another Canae noble House controlling a mighty, unequalled dragon?" Nui Honei inquired. "We can never trust the Crown's or House Rho's intentions."

Alleina next remarked, "Mother Je Buel, I do pray and hope you are correct. Still, I received generous offers from Rhodell's Medical Academy to accept a full-time position there after I rejected the initial offer. I have also heard rumors that certain high-ranking officials at Rhodell's Sciences and Arts Academy were 'very disappointed' that Kei chose not to study there. Lastly, the Crown has even recently shown *interest* in the daughters of House Je Luneefa. Though we have proven our loyalty to the Crown repeatedly, they continue failing in their attempts to completely *separate* us from your and Father Je Taeliel's control. Is House Rho still unfortunately paranoid of our Houses?"

Je Buel retorted, "Though any details of our strongholds' secrets have already been magically removed from the minds of our dwarven labor force, House Rho would find it very difficult to get such information. Again, House Rho should not be concerned with the secrets of our strongholds since no other noble House or even the Crown, has any legitimate reason to attack us."

Je Taeliel then added, "Yet, our Houses have a mighty dragon through our son Ona Noirar. The king and queen have no dragons that we know of, and both king and queen are quite concerned with any House that has dragons and seemingly more power than theirs. They constantly fear rebellion or any House war against House Rho."

"So, has and is House Rho secretly encouraging war amongst other Houses to weaken various Houses? Has the queen or king secretly supported House Si Moina's threats against Ona Noirar and Keiku? Is either the queen or king plotting against this House due to our growing strength over the years?" concluded Je Buel.

"Rhodell probably knows the least about our strongholds, well protected behind our Toronwalein. We even purposely started rumors that the Clan Battle Hammer's gold financed the construction of our first wall and our strongholds. Rhodell should realize our perceived wealth is inconsequential since we incurred great debt to Clan Battle Hammer. Further, know too that the architectural details and secrets of our strongholds are not known by anyone outside of this hall. Again, the confidential design and construction information was magically erased from the workforce and even Duenor Heartstone, the master architect.

"That information and all our family secrets must not ever be shared. Our accumulated wealth, generated from our financial holdings, is most likely known by Rhodell. Our spending is modest. Rhodell should harbor no concerns regarding our perceived, estimated wealth being greater than theirs. Yet, our wealth, considering our Houses have a mighty dragon, makes us extraordinarily *wealthy*, far wealthier than House Rho.

"Regardless of our repeatedly performed, exemplary services to the Crown and our willingness to remain a family enjoying our peace and not wanting more, the Crown may certainly be lurking in the deep shadows and an ever-looming threat to our Houses."

A deadly silence fell across the entire group as they all pondered over the last, unanswered questions. They all wanted more Crown and House Rho secrets to be revealed.

Later, after midnight, Nui Honei secretly left her stronghold and started making her way silently up the side of mount Toron to a designated meeting place. Although the night was cold, she was quite comfortable since she was wearing her House cape which kept her warm, as well as invisible. Even on this moonless night, her steps are sure for she is aided by the magic of dragon eyes which allows her to see clearly as if it was a bright sunny day. After arriving at the rendezvous point, a small clearing on the rugged mountainside, she could sense that her party, also cloaked in invisibility, is close by.

After a few moments, Nui Honei mentally greeted Ona Kei Kuri Ryuu, *"Well met, Keiku."*

*"Greetings, dear Honei. Shall we now go to my lair?"* inquired Keiku. Nui Honei mounted the dragon and Keiku took flight. With each beat of her mighty wings, the dragon took them higher up the mountain where the air is frightfully cold, an unwelcoming coldness with blistering, frightfully swirling, harsh winds that will kill mercilessly. The frigid temperature nor the thin air bothered either dragon or rider for they were warmed through their magic. A short while later, Keiku landed at the magically warded entrance of her secret lair. After passing through several magic-reinforced, protective walls, they arrived at the dragon's main quarters.

This inner chamber was comfortably warm despite the outside, dangerously cold weather. Keiku maintained a pit of fire stones heated by her dragon's fire. These stones would retain and radiate heat indefinitely for the comfort of her non-dragon guests who visited her occasionally.

*"What troubles you this night, my sister?"* Keiku mentally asked Nui Honei after both settled down. The House Nui Vent great mother had been sitting quietly for a long time, lost in thought as she nestled close to the great dragon. After so many years, Nui Honei still marveled at the dragon's radiating warmth and power, for this dragon is magic personified, raw, pure, and powerful. It is no surprise that all the two-legged creatures, humans, elves, dwarfs, orcs, goblins, giants, and gnomes coveted these magnificent creatures. The closeness Nui Honei has with Keiku is a special bond too, grounded in battle, friendship, and love.

Nui Honei replied mentally, "I learned today that Alleina helped deliver another baby elf and baby human into this world. I was saddened when I heard this news; because, as you know, that jealous hag Si Cairyn closed my womb many years ago with her poisonous magic so that I could not bear my beloved Ona Noirar's elves."

Moments later, with somber, tear-filled eyes, Nui Honei confessed, "My time of estrus will be upon me again soon. This is a time of great sadness and mourning for me. Even though every ten years I could conceive, I cannot. I will not ever know the welcomed joy and pain of bringing precious new life into this world. Although he asked me to marry him many times, I would not. If I could not bear him elves, I would not be his wife. Yet, for centuries, he continued to stand by my side faithfully like any real husband. Such is his so called 'love'.

"As a young felf, I defined my 'love' to include being 'mother' of blessed offspring with my husband. I cannot fulfill that duty; so, I grieve. But please forgive the frustration of this wretched old felf."

Not wanting to linger in her depression any longer, Nui Honei asked, "Shall I read to your unborn dragons again?" Over the years, Nui Honei stole away to secretly be alone with Keiku to record the exploits of the great dragon. Especially over the last year, Nui Honei spent many nights in Keiku's lair reading from the recorded *Chronicles* to the three eggs of this great dragon, an enormously proud, hopeful, soon-to-be mother.

Keiku replied, *"No, I think not. Nor ever apologize to me for sharing your grief with me. Afterall, we are sisters and part of my duty is to listen to you and comfort you. Even when your grief tried to turn Ona Noirar away from you, he would not leave you. I will not leave you either; or will I ever have a sister greater than you. My bond with you is immeasurable; so, you cannot leave us. Do not lose hope. Miracles still happen.*

"Instead of reading to my unborn or discussing old magic incantations, tell me about the three Nui Vent House soldiers you seem to like so much," requested Keiku who wanted to change the subject to something more pleasant for Nui Honei.

After some thought, Nui Honei, with a small smile, again described Danka, Jooba and Rei in detail, quietly saying, "Danka is the oldest of the three; he is about two hundred ten years old. He is just over nine hands tall. Like many woods elves, he has blond hair and deep blue eyes. His smile is warm and infectious. Danka is handsome and quite charming. He likes to talk too. As you might expect, he is the self-ordained leader of this group of former thieves.

"Jooba is about two hundred years old. Unlike Danka, Jooba is of rock elf heritage. He is big, over nine hands tall, muscular, and extraordinarily strong. This young melf will be a great warrior. He is ambidextrous and chooses to wield battleaxes which compliments his strength and dexterity. Jooba is shy and a quiet thinker. He is slow to anger and has a thoughtful, calming spirit. He seeks knowledge and wants to learn to better himself.

"Rei is the youngest of the three, being about one hundred eighty years old. He stands under eight hands but is still growing. He is also quite handsome. For some reason, he likes to throw knives. I believe this pastime calms him when he is troubled. He has big inquisitive eyes; yet he is quite shy. At the same time, he is brave and courageous. Rei wants to learn more as fast as he can. He is lithe. He is a good listener. Of the three, he is also the most skilled thief. Rei is very protective of the few females in his life. He still grieves over the loss of a young female friend who wanted to join his gang. This young felf was going to be sold into slavery, but Rei planned to rescue her and take her away to live with him, Danka and Jooba. On the night he was supposed to take her away, the leader of the slavery gang killed her – to teach the other orphans a lesson... Rei watched his friend die. The next night, Rei killed each member of that slavery gang and released all their captives."

Nui Honei mentally communicated that Danka, Jooba and Rei are all courageous and obedient. They take direction well. All three were orphaned at an early age due to the unrest and lawlessness of the northern territory. This led to them having to survive as best they could on the streets of several different towns. All three chose to steal to survive their life's day-to-day struggles. Danka, Jooba and Rei met by chance one night after a successful night of stealing their dinner which they shared amongst themselves and other orphans. They decided to leave their town and journey to the great forest where they intended to live by stealing from the rich travelers.

After some time, Nui Honei's mood even improved and brightened some as she exchanged more details about each of the new House soldiers. She concluded, adding, *"The three former thieves I met years ago and are now House Nui Vent soldiers and have become special to me. They all are proving themselves worthy of being members of my House. Although I have not enjoyed the birth and early years of these melfs, these once orphans are now my blessings, like my 'young ones'. I love them as if they were truly my birth sons."*

"Then why not adopt them as your own?" asked Keiku.

With that suggestion, Nui Honei sat straight up, smiled, and pondered that possibility and its positive impact. *"Would you like to meet them?"* asked Nui Honei. *"I would like your opinion first since you are a good judge of character."*

"Yes, very much so. When?" an excited Keiku asked.

"Tomorrow midafternoon?" asked Nui Honei.

*"Tomorrow midafternoon then!"* responded a pleased Keiku who returned slowly to a peaceful sleep.

Nui Honei again became noticeably quiet too and thought to herself. *"When the right time comes, maybe I will adopt them,"* Nui Honei said quietly. As the early sun's rays started to pierce through the distant mountains, Nui Honei greeted the dawn smiling for the first time in many days while contemplating her new secret.

# First Meeting

The next morning the sun rose brightly greeting the kingdom with its unseasonal warmth and radiance. It appears the sun is announcing that the day is going to be "very good."

That early morning, like so many others, Ona Drachir, Danka, Jooba and Rei were already at the House Nui Vent training ground preparing for their daily instruction from either House great mother Nui Honei or great father Nui Samu. All were clad in their heavy leather training clothes. Today's lesson is to be a continuation of one-on-many combat. House great mother Nui Honei had instructed the young melfs in the use of axes, swords, knives, spear, spear and shield, and sword and shield tactics. House great father Nui Samu reinforced their learning with a variety of daily and nightly exercises. Being a battlemage, Nui Honei also instructed them in how to fight against enemy battlemages with their minds and weapons. Each melf continued to develop his fighting skills to deadly proficiency. They also learned tactics and secrets of fighting as a two-, three- and even four-warrior group.

From a distance, the young melfs could see House great mother Nui Honei and great father Nui Samu approaching them. With their House elders was another unfamiliar melf whom three of the young melfs did not recognize.

Nui Honei greeted the House Nui Vent soldiers warmly, "Well met, soldiers of House Nui Vent. Mark this day; it will be quite special for you. First, meet Ona Noirar, another weapons master, former commander of the northern army and an old friend of both Houses Je Luneefa and Nui Vent. He is also the blood-brother of House great father Nui Samu and my beloved."

"Wait! Beloved? What does that mean? How can this be? We are just meeting him for the first time," exclaimed a puzzled Rei.

While the other melfs greeted Ona Noirar, Rei stepped away, just became quiet and remained aloof. Rei, the youngest melf, was saddened with the news. He knew then he could no longer hope to be his House great mother's unofficial *favorite*. He also feared losing the love of the only true *mother* he had ever known.

Training that day began as usual with exercises to improve a warrior's flexibility and strength. Afterwards, Nui Samu led the group through a series of attack and defensive maneuvers. Today's lessons focused on using spear and shield formations. Later that morning, each melf fought alone against a group of two or three attackers. Although he *died* several times, Rei especially enjoyed fighting against his new competition, Ona Noirar. Training continued the entire morning.

"Soldiers of House Nui Vent, I have a story to tell you and another announcement," addressed Nui Honei. She then shared with the melfs recent events involving Ona Noirar, his dragon and herself. "With the public resurrection of Ona Noirar and Ona Kei Kuri Ryuu, their House would most likely encounter new threats again; so, they always needed to be wary. Constant vigilance must be maintained. Lastly, who would like to meet Ona Kei Kuri Ryuu, the most noble and famed dragon of Ona Noirar?" Nui Honei asked. All three House Nui Vent soldiers responded enthusiastically to such a rare opportunity.

Before midafternoon, Danka, Jooba and Rei met at the enclosed courtyard behind the House Nui Vent stronghold. This was the appointed place where they would meet Ona Kei Kuri Ryuu, the most famous dragon in the kingdom. Just moments before, a wagon had arrived carrying a gift they planned to give to the dragon. Although they were not worldly at all, they did learn while they were homeless, fending for their meals daily, it is considered good manners to give honored guests a gift as a small token of appreciation. They had also cleaned themselves and were now dressed in their finest clothes. The two older melfs waited quietly sitting at the table that the House servants had prepared with refreshments for the elves and other guests invited to this important event.

Rei, on the other hand, paced the ground asking himself questions, "How should we even formally address this dragon? Is she an elder too? Will she understand our words? How will we understand her when she talks? Do dragons even talk?" He felt completely unprepared to meet such an important creature, the *most* important creature in all the kingdom. Further, this dragon belongs to his new rival, Ona Noirar, who had supplanted him as his House mother's favorite. That news already made him quite uncomfortable knowing this forthcoming meeting was with the dragon of his rival.

After more thought, Rei finally reasoned that the House Nui Vent great mother deserved to be happy. He begrudgingly accepted that if she chose Ona Noirar, she surely chose wisely. So, he decided to guard his true feelings of jealousy.

Zhen Lae and her daughter Zhen Laehua also attended this event. Both felfs are wards of House Je Luneefa and enjoyed the advantages of being associated with a great noble House. The misery of their former lives was far behind them now. They now enjoyed the peace and security they found in their new home of Torondell with House Je Luneefa. Zhen Laehua, a koto prodigy, entertained the guests with a variety of fanciful musical selections for this joyous occasion.

Later, other meeting guests arrived. Alleina, the healer, came along with Ona Drachir. House great father Nui Samu personally escorted the elders of House Je Luneefa to the gathering. The elders were followed by Je Jero, Je Tero, Je Danei and Je Leena. All the northern army and House Je Luneefa armies' commanders were in attendance. All seemed excited to meet the famed dragon. Although this meeting would be the first for most; a select privileged few would be meeting Keiku again.

After a short while, Ona Noirar joined the group. He was alone. After greeting everyone, he began to formally welcome them all, "Dear friends, thank you for joining us here at this first meeting of our new House Nui Vent soldiers and Ona Kei Kuri Ryuu, the most famous dragon in the kingdom."

"Lord Ona Noirar, where is the guest of honor? It is now past the appointed meeting time, is it not?" asked Danka.

"Why would you think our last two guests are late? Open your eyes and look around very carefully," responded Ona Noirar.

Looking at Rei, Ona Noirar then said smiling, "I do hope my dragon is still hungry and crave young, melf flesh. Do not fear, I will not let my dragon eat you… maybe."

In response, Rei straightened himself and responded while moving away from the dragon rider, "I will not fear," Rei said quietly to himself.

Moments later, the veil of invisibility was lifted; and sitting in the far corner of the courtyard was the great dragon, Ona Kei Kuri Ryuu. With head lifted high, the majestic dragon sat there observing the group with her keen eyes. Standing next to her was the House Nui Vent great mother, Nui Honei.

*"Shall we now greet our guests?"* Nui Honei mentally communicated to Keiku.

*"Yes, of course,"* replied the dragon. Keiku then rose and started walking towards the small group along with Nui Honei. Both felf and dragon walked with elegance and grace. Their beauty and powerful personas seemed matchless. On this occasion, Nui Honei wore a fine, semi-formal robe of red and black. She was also covered with her matching House cape. All her attire matched the radiant black scales of her companion dragon.

"Tell me again; whose dragon is she? They really look good together," quipped House great mother Je Buel, smiling at Ona Noirar.

Je Pagi then added, "I wonder had House great mother Nui Honei and Ona Noirar both encountered Keiku before she hatched, would she still have hatched for you, Ona Noirar or Nui Honei?"

"I ask myself that same question at times too. They complement each other so well. Keiku has an unusual *fondness* for my beloved it seems. One that sometimes even surpasses *my* relationship with *my* dragon. I even find myself jealous at times," declared a scowling Ona Noirar.

With his last confession, the entire group started chuckling at the famed warrior and dragon rider.

Nui Honei and Keiku stopped about twelve steps away from the group. "House Nui Vent soldiers come to attention and present yourself to the great dragon, Ona Kei Kuri Ryuu when I call each of you," announced Nui Honei. "Danka, step forward." Danka, a bit nervous, took several strides forward and presented himself to the dragon. He bowed, tried to speak, but had no voice given his proximity to the fiercest creature known in the world. Keiku "smiled" in return and bowed her head.

"Jooba, step forward," said Nui Honei. Jooba walked forward and stood next to his brother. Like Danka before, Jooba respectfully bowed to the great dragon. He too had no voice to speak, but he did smile warmly at Keiku. In return, Keiku "smiled" too and bowed her head.

Before being called forward, Rei started walking towards the dragon and his House great mother. He stopped, standing next to Jooba. "Lastly, I present to you Rei, the youngest, so impatient and apparently less fearful House Nui Vent soldier," said Nui Honei.

After bowing, Rei said, "Good afternoon great dragon Ona Kei Kuri Ryuu; I am Rei, soldier of House Nui Vent. My brothers and I would like to present you with a small gift which is a custom where we are from."

"How can you remain so calm in front of the most feared creature in the kingdom and *my* dragon who could easily devour you with one bite?" asked Ona Noirar who was still a bit annoyed with the youngest melf.

"House great mother Nui Honei loves me too much and would not want that! Not yet at least, I believe," replied Rei quickly.

*"I am beginning to like these three House soldiers; they seem honorable and have good manners. And they were thoughtful enough to bring me a gift. And it is indeed one of my favorites too!"* Keiku said to Nui Honei mentally and privately.

Danka then signaled to the House servants to present the "gift." After bringing the wagon forward, the servants started unloading two large barrels of fresh fish.

Addressing the great dragon, the nervous Danka said gesturing to the pile of fish now laying on the ground, "Our understanding is that these fish are fresh, caught this very morning and are your favorite. Please enjoy."

Keiku bent her head forward and quickly sniffed the pile of fish. She then raised her head and barred her mouthful of deadly teeth which was her way mimicking a smile. Keiku then looked at the three House Nui Vent soldiers and slightly bowed her head in gratitude.

*"Please express my thanks to them for such a thoughtful gift,"* Keiku mentally communicated to Nui Honei.

Nui Honei smiled too at her House soldiers and said, "The great dragon Ona Kei Kuri Ryuu thanks you all for her gift; it is very thoughtful she says."

"Everyone, please enjoy yourselves," announced Nui Honei to the group.

Koto music, another lively tune, again filled the air. The group started several quiet conversations and enjoyed a variety of delicacies that had been prepared. Even the great dragon Keiku took a few moments to eat some of the fish she received.

Different individuals would stride close to the dragon to get a closer view or to even converse with the dragon. At these times, Ona Noirar and/or Nui Honei would act as the translator conveying the "words" of Keiku to the other party.

After a while, Danka, Jooba and Rei again approached the

dragon. This time, however, they stood much closer to Keiku, only six steps away from her head. Nui Honei had personally escorted them this time; so, they were now a bit more comfortable given her personal proximity.

"Magnificent, isn't she?" Je Leena said as she strode past the House Nui Vent soldiers and stood next to Keiku. With both her hands, she touched the side of the great dragon. Je Leena could feel Keiku's strong heartbeat, her majestic power, and the seemingly unlimited magical power emanating from the dragon. "There is no other like her in all the kingdom!" declared the young felf. "What say you House Nui Vent soldiers?"

Danka, now having reclaimed his voice, spoke on behalf of himself and brothers, looking at the dragon, "This is our first time meeting a dragon. So, our experience is limited. We did, however, studied several *Chronicles,* in our House library last night in preparation for this meeting. We know of her history, great battles, and feats. Ona Kei Kuri Ryuu is most noble, fearless, graceful, and gloriously beautiful. Of all nature's creatures, you are indeed…"

"Perfect!" profoundly proclaimed Rei. Keiku responded with a slight raising of her head.

"*Oh my, I do like this youngest one! He has particularly good eyes and is wise beyond his years too,*" declared the proud dragon to both Nui Honei and Ona Noirar.

In response, Nui Honei chuckled quietly and asked, "You have not met nor seen other dragons before; so, how can you justify making such a declaration?"

"When she first walked towards us with you House great mother, we could all see her distinctive, royal elegance. Her scales are brilliantly radiant in this afternoon sun. Her height, length, weight, muscular features and from her horns on her head to her talons and to her tail, all are very well proportioned," said Danka. "The *Chronicles* also listed that Ona Kei Kuri Ryuu is 'flying magnificence, full of grace' too."

"In battle, she was always courageous and brave, despite the odds. This dragon even defeated four great bears without even taking flight nor using her dragon flame! That is amazing. She is indeed fearless. Ona Kei Kuri Ryuu's fighting prowess is unmatched in the world today and perhaps throughout history we know of. Je Leena's description of 'magnificence' may still be a little inadequate I believe," continued Jooba.

"She is truly a wonder of this world. So, my brothers and I agree that Ona Kei Kuri Ryuu, without any doubt, is simply perfect!" concluded Rei.

Keiku raised herself to her full height, spread her wings and bowed to the new House Nui Vent soldiers.

"*Honei,*" Keiku privately said. "*Please extend my gratitude to these three House Nui Vent soldiers again. Also, please do not tell anyone that you and I wrote about myself in your House's library tome they read. They only repeated the truth you and I both already knew, right?*"

"*Of course, dear sister, of course. It will be another secret then just between us,*" replied Nui Honei who then looked closely at Danka, Jooba and Rei and again expressed thanks on behalf of Keiku.

During the last few moments, the entire group had moved closer to Keiku and Nui Honei and had heard the conversation from the new House Nui Vent soldiers and the great dragon.

Rei took a step closer and continued, "Although we just met today, we would like to get to know you better and maybe, you would like to get to know us better. Since Ona Drachir recently hurt his hand during a training session, my brothers and I would like to volunteer to help with anything you may need such as cleaning your armor, scrubbing your scales and talons, getting more fish for you, whatever you may need."

"First you flatter my dragon and now you wish to serve her too. What treachery do you plan?" Ona Noirar asked.

"*Their praise was neither insincere nor excessive; they only spoke the truth!*" defended Keiku.

"You certainly are magnificent; there is no other dragon like you in all the world nor has there been in history. But *perfect* you are not," retorted Ona Noirar for all to hear.

"Yes, she is!" Nui Honei proclaimed immediately.

"I agree with my aunt," Je Danei said.

"Of course, I agree too with my aunt and sister," Je Leena confirmed.

Je Buel and Je Pagi looked at each other and said in unison, "We also agree that Ona Kei Kuri Ryuu is perfect!"

"Lord Ona Noirar, I witnessed this magnificent dragon's battle against those four great bears of House Si Moina," said Commander Baka of the northern army. "For any creature to battle and defeat one great bear is amazing. As many know, a great bear may well be the second most feared creature in this world. This dragon defeated four great bears without using flight nor her dragon flame; that accomplishment is nothing less than a miracle. *Perfect* suits her well."

Approving cheers and laughter now erupted throughout the

small crowd. Alleina took a few steps forward, turned and addressed Ona Noirar with a serious look on her face, "It is nothing short of three miracles that you are standing here today. Medically speaking, you should have died from the raznac poison at three different times had it not been for this miraculous wonder of both nature and magic. Keiku's blood and magic saved you several times that fateful day; her blood and magic sustained you immediately right after surgery and throughout your recovery; and her blood and magic still protected you while you recovered. A full recovery from raznac poisoning has never happened before to my knowledge. What more could you ask of her? Yes, there is no doubt in my mind either. Medically speaking, Ona Kei Kuri Ryuu is perfect. Chances are there will never be another dragon like her again. So, know my dear brother that you have truly been blessed to have such a dear friend and comrade-in-arms."

Ona Noirar looked at Keiku and then turned to the group and said, "Thank you all again for such kind words. My dragon is both humble and very appreciative. Great father Nui Samu, please discharge these three new soldiers from your service; they are quite troublesome! Also, Keiku, if you are still hungry, please eat those three soldiers, starting with the youngest first," Ona Noirar jested.

All three House Nui Vent soldiers instinctively moved closer to Nui Honei. More laughter rose from the small crowd.

"*Sister, we must also write about this day too in my Chronicles,*" the smiling dragon privately communicated to Nui Honei.

"*Oh, my dearest, vain sister, I recall little of today's many conversations. Which part of today's events or conversations do you wish to record in particular? Meeting the new House Nui Vent soldiers? Your gift? The delightful music and food? Or the glorious, sun shining day perhaps?*" questioned a curious Nui Honei who already knew her most likely answer.

"*Fortunately, we dragons do have exceptional hearing and memories; so, I can recall all that was said; so, do not worry. I will definitely help you,*" Keiku reminded.

"*Also, Danka, Jooba and Rei's first impressions are favorable; I like them too. And I observed they are quite protective of you and the House Je Luneefa females they know. Rei seems especially protective. They are all respectful, kind, and thoughtful. They genuinely love you too. I think they all would make you fine sons.*"

Nui Honei mentally replied, "*Thank you. I would be honored to call them my sons; Noirar may not though. He may still harbor some ill feelings from that chance first encounter with them. It was his fault for not being veiled invisible when he left my bedchamber that early morning and happened to meet them while they were patrolling the stronghold's hallways. I could not even fall back to sleep with all the noise they were making from the fight. Fortunately, no one was killed by mistake. Only one ego was bruised."*

Both dragon and felf laughed privately at that thought.

# New Sons

Danka, Jooba and Rei stood outside the eastern gate of the Toronwalein. The three former thieves had been just outside the gate since the early morning. Before entering through the gate, they slowly paced the ground, talking quietly amongst themselves. Danka, Jooba and Rei are somber and quite anxious, continuing to contemplate their fate. They all had been summoned by their House great mother to join her in their great hall late in the morning, before the time of the midday meal. They former thieves needed to account for their recent imprisonment. Even though the stay in prison was just a short two nights, neither Nui Honei nor Nui Samu was pleased with the actions of their wards and former thieves. Now that they were wards of House Nui Vent, the House great mother and father both had higher expectations of them than being like common rogues brawling at a local inn.

Ten years have passed since Nui Honei first met this gang of thieves. At that first encounter, these brothers were captured and taken to Torondell where they were supposed to be tried for crimes committed. However, for their acts of bravery demonstrated on the return to the city and upon the supporting words of great House mothers Je Pagi and Nui Honei, the judge was lenient and placed the former thieves into the custody of House Nui Vent. There, they were to serve the House for one year in any capacity deemed by the House great mother and father. Their duties consisted primarily of menial labor needed around the House Nui Vent stronghold. They all performed their assigned duties well without complaint. After serving the year's sentence, Danka, Jooba and Rei all requested to join the House as its first soldiers.

All three former thieves joined the House Nui Vent as recruits for the House private army. Under the supervision of Nui Samu, Danka, Jooba and Rei all trained to become well-disciplined and skilled soldiers. They also were instructed in knightly ways, elven martial arts, military tactics, and weaponry. They trained hard and eventually became skillful warriors.

So, the House great mother and father were quite displeased with them knowing they were in some so-called, meaningless brawl. The three soldiers were summoned to the House great hall to account for their "un-knightly" actions.

As the three walked into the great hall, they saw the House great mother Nui Honei and great father Nui Samu seated at the front table on the dais. Both elders were frowning and looked disappointedly at the three young melfs. Seated also at this front table were Ja Buel and Je Taeliel, first mother and father of House Je Luneefa. At a side table were the House Je Luneefa second great mother and father Je Pagi and Je Maron along with four of their four daughters and sons. Ona Noirar and Ona Drachir were seated at another side table facing the Je Luneefa family young elves. Alleina, the healer, sat next to Ona Drachir.

Ona Drachir and two of the Je Luneefa sons were also there at the inn during the time of the altercation.

Danka, Jooba and Rei quietly marched in and stood in front of the House Nui Vent serious-looking elders. They all saluted and bowed somehow knowing a severe punishment was forthcoming. All the Houses' elders had stern looks on their faces. Nui Honei spoke first, "First of all, thank you House Je Luneefa elders and family for joining our House meeting. I also wish to apologize that you are also attending a meeting to discuss the shame brought upon our House by these three House soldiers. As you all know, Danka, Jooba and Rei were all involved in a recent altercation with members of House Si Moina at the Red Horse inn. The authorities described it as a 'drunken brawl'. Twelve of their soldiers fought against these three and I believe, Ona Drachir, Je Jero and Je Tero. Extensive damage was done to the inn, and several other innocent patrons also required medical attention. Our understanding is that one of you House Nui Vent soldiers started the fight by throwing the first blow. Great father Nui Samu and I are both disappointed with your behavior, for you know we expect all of you to conduct yourselves to our House's high standards. So, explain yourselves; why did this fight occur?"

Danka, the eldest of the three House Nui Vent soldiers and still the unofficial spokesperson for the group of former thieves, attempted a defense, "We, Ona Drachir, Je Jero and Je Tero were all at the inn celebrating Rei's victory against Je Danei. That was the first time he had ever beaten her in a knife throwing contest and we were all excited for him. One of the House Si Moina soldiers had also competed and lost, not only the contest, but also some coins. The Si Moina soldiers were not pleased at all and started ranting about our poor training and martial arts school."

"So, you punched him then in response?" asked Nui Samu with a very small smile.

"No, I did not," Danka replied. "That soldier still continued his rant about our martial arts training for a short while. Given our performances in the last Autumn Festival events, he still seemed quite sour over his team's bitter defeat. We ignored his comments, sitting quietly and just talking amongst ourselves. Then another soldier started defaming you, House great father for being 'too old', 'not that skilled' and 'of peasant blood'."

Smiling, Nui Samu again asked, "Did you hit him then in response?"

"No, I did not. Rei reminded us of our House's high code of conduct. I was able to control my anger and not react to the soldier's intended bait or possible trap," Danka replied.

"So, tell me now when and how did the fight start and who started it? Be quick and to the point," inquired an agitated, impatient Nui Samu.

Silence. There was more silence for several heartbeats. Then a normally quiet Rei took a deep breath and stepped forward. Looking at the great father directly into his cold eyes, Rei said, "I actually started the fight. I threw the first punch. When another soldier called our House great mother a 'peasant whore', I stood up, walked over to him, and asked him to apologize. When he did not and started ranting again, I punched him, knocking him unconscious. The fight with the other Si Moina soldiers erupted thereafter."

In unison, House great mothers Nui Honei, Je Buel and Je Pagi and Alleina, Je Danei and Je Leena gasped quietly and said, "Ah, how sweet..."

House Luneefa great father Je Taeliel who had been seemingly indifferent started chuckling.

"Clearly, these three soldiers love you more than me House great mother Nui Honei," said a Nui Samu in a mockingly saddened voice.

"House great father, no. We love you too, but..." Rei tried to further explain, but Nui Samu's hand gesture ordered his immediate silence.

"We understand that the House Si Moina soldiers all then rose from their tables to retaliate against Rei. And you four responded in kind to protect Rei. Is that correct? questioned Nui Samu.

"Wait! House Si Moina's four slanders against me, indirectly and directly, were not enough to provoke a faster physical response? Why? But only one slander against our House great mother incited an immediate violent reaction?" a then puzzled Nui Samu asked.

Looking at Nui Honei, Nui Samu continued now pointing at Rei, "Maybe I was wrong earlier; *this* soldier apparently loves you more than me."

Now, the entire room, except for Danka, Jooba and Rei started laughing.

Smiling, Nui Honei patted her brother on his arm sympathetically and said, "Oh dear brother, they all love you too. Do not ever doubt that. But the bond between a House great mother and her soldiers is special and causes different responses from males when the House great mother is hurt, in trouble or slandered. It is just their male primal instincts. Rei is not completely at fault."

After a few more moments of laughter, Nui Honei called the meeting back to order. She granted approval to Rei to speak.

Rei said, "I apologize for not acting more wisely and I will pay for the damages done to the inn, with time... and any of the harmed patrons' medical expenses..."

Nui Honei interrupted, "Recompense has already been awarded to the inn keeper and designated patrons. You will repay me the amount of eight silver coins. This is a discounted amount knowing that you gave the House Si Moina soldiers such a good lesson in our marital arts training at no charge. By the way, which punch did you use to knock out that soldier? Was it the dragon's crossbow by chance?"

"Yes," responded Rei.

Nui Honei smiled, winked one eye at Rei and held up two fingers and silently mouthed "four silver coins, not eight," for she had recently taught the House Nui Vent soldiers that attack. She then continued, "This matter is now closed. Please be seated."

All three House Nui Vent soldiers sighed a sigh of relief now that this ordeal was finally officially over.

"We do have another important matter to discuss, but we

will do so after a meal," continued Nui Honei who thereafter signaled nearby servants to start serving the meal. After their meal, Nui Honei again called the meeting to order. "Danka, Jooba and Rei stand before our table." Danka, Jooba and Rei rose from the side table where they were sitting with Ona Drachir and Alleina. They walked back and stood in front of the head table. They all were again anxious expecting to receive punishment for possible other misbehaviors.

Nui Honei looked at the three House soldiers and said, "You three have been wards of House Nui Vent for the last eight years. From the first time we met till even now, you have demonstrated noble character, admirable skills as warriors and loyalty to this House. You make our House great father and me proud. You have continued to honor us both in your words and deeds. For that, we are very appreciative. However, I have decided to make our relationship more formal. If you will agree, I want to adopt you three as my sons."

"Yes!" exclaimed an excited Rei without any hesitation, now with tears forming in his eyes.

Laughter erupted again amongst the guests; then Je Pagi added jokingly, "I agree with you House great father Nui Samu; this melf does love House great mother Nui Honei more than you." Now turning towards Rei, she continued, "Patience, young one. You still do not know what you must do to become an adopted blood relative."

Rei immediately replied, "It does not matter what I must do. My brothers and I were orphaned long ago and have lived most of our lives without a mother, without any parental direction. House great mother Nui Honei has given us more motherly care and attention than we could ever hope for in these past few years. So, if House great mother Nui Honei wants it, then so do I. Where she leads, I obediently follow. Are we in agreement brothers?"

"Yes, most assuredly!" responded Jooba.

"Yes, of course!" concurred Danka.

"But I can still object to *your* adoption," said Nui Samu, looking sternly at Rei.

After a rejected Rei looked puzzled amongst the light laughter from the guests, he still managed to regain his composure.

Filled with great pride, Nui Honei said, "To become truly adopted into this family, you will be part of a joyful and painful blood-magic ritual in which my blood will become mixed with yours. In other words, your blood will become like mine. By doing so, you will then have access to certain secrets of House Nui Vent.

"You must also devote time to learning the history of your new family. When you become a member of this family, you will acquire new responsibilities and duties, one of which is to help grow this family. Do you still wish to become part of our House Nui Vent family?"

"Yes," all three Nui Vent soldiers responded affirmatively without hesitation.

Nui Honei then said, "Now, let us begin the adoption ceremony." At this time, Nui Honei and Nui Samu both rose from their table, walked around it, and stood in front of the about-to-be-adopted sons. Servants then brought an altar brought from the side of the room and placed it next to the House great mother. Upon this altar was a large bowl containing a fire and a ceremonial dagger suspended above the bowl. Another table was brought over and placed close to Nui Honei, as well. This second table had an ancient-looking, large, opened book on it. "Kneel and extend your hands palms up," Nui Honei said to the House soldiers.

Nui Honei, now solemn, took the floating dagger and cut the right palm of Danka, Jooba and Rei's hands. Lastly, she cut the palm of her right hand. Blood immediately flowed from the fresh wound on her hand just like the wounds of the melfs kneeling before her. Nui Honei uttered an incantation in an ancient elvish language and ended calling upon the family elders to bless the adoption of Danka. She then positioned her right hand above the right hand of Danka. Her blood from her cut fell onto Danka's hand, mixed with his blood on his cut palm and returned through his wound into his body. His and her wounds healed immediately thereafter. The same steps of cutting her hand, citing the incantation, blessing, and passing her blood onto the extended cut palm were repeated for both Jooba and Rei.

"Rise, my sons of House Nui Vent!" said Nui Honei. "Now, go and write your names in the *Family Chronicles*." Each son did so as ordered and soon realized their names were written in their blood. Looking at Nui Honei and before they could even ask, she explained, "Yes, my sons, you just experienced blood-magic again. The *Family Chronicles* and its pen only work properly for members of our House Nui Vent family."

Each new member of House Nui Vent lovingly hugged their mother and thanked her for the special honor. Each new member of House Nui Vent was also congratulated by Nui Samu and the other guests.

Nui Samu reminded his nephews that he was also now their uncle along with being their House great father and sensei. So, he would expect "more" love from them.  Nui Danka, Nui Jooba and Nui Rei just chuckled after saying "Yes, of course" in response.

Nui Honei said, "My dear brother, just stop; they will always love me just a 'bit' more.  Afterall, I am now their *mother!*"

# Ritual of Blood: Release and Bonding

Nui Danka walked slowly into the sacred and secret vast chamber of the House Nui Vent stronghold. As he walked between ornate pedestals supporting bowls of fire, he felt the sweat running down his back from the fires' heat. He was a bit frightened as well as intimidated by the room's ancient trappings. Afterall, he had a humble, poor beginning, of orphaned commoner blood. He assumed these statutes were of the House's ancestors, most of them, if not all, and most likely of noble blood.

There were also a vast array of weapons adorning the dark walls too. The weapons included various types of spears, naginatas, kusarigama, maces, long swords, short swords, and knives. There were shields, long bows and short bows too on the walls. Some he easily recognized; some he could not. Although many of the weapons were quite old, centuries perhaps, they glowed eerily red, reflecting the fire stands' light and still seemed formidable, ready to be used in battle. This chamber was a sacred museum of the House Nui Vent ancestors and weaponry dedicated to preserving the House's history.

Great mother Nui Honei and great father Nui Samu stood at the front of the room in front of a blazing altar. Both elder elves were elegantly attired in their battle armor covered by the red and black House capes. Both elves looked magnificent, yet sinister at the same time as the firelights reflected off their black armor. Neither smiled at Nui Danka but looked upon him with respect and pride. Their pride no doubt came from the fact that he, along with his brothers, was newly adopted into the House Nui Vent. During the past years, while living under the House Nui Vent, Nui Danka and his brothers distinguished themselves having become skilled warriors and extremely loyal to their House. Finally, after years of living in the great forest where there were so many unknowns from day to day, he now finally had a real home, a living parent, stability, and a bright future. In addition, he loved his adopted parent who also loved him and his brothers. Even the ever stoic and menacing-looking Nui Samu, approved of the adoption. He even smiled at them from time to time.

On either side of the altar was a table with cloths covering hidden contents underneath. Between the elder elves, Nui Danka could also see the same, floating ceremonial dagger suspended above the burning altar. At that sight, he recalled a conversation with House great mother Nui Honei regarding blood-magic and that such a dagger was often used to initially facilitate such magic spells. She had explained, "Blood-magic is an ancient and powerful form of sorcery used to lock or unlock an enchantment or spell. Unlike other enchantments or spells, one's blood, which is unique, must be used in the original casting of the enchantment, as well as each casting thereafter to effectuate the magic. In your case, your weapons can be bound to you by blood-magic; and only you can access and use their special powers through your blood and voice." She then pointed to a "blood point" on her bow near the hand grip and remarked, "There are these points on our weapons where we can cut ourselves to draw our blood which the weapon must first absorb in order to have designated weapon's capabilities magically activated thereafter. For example, I can change the size of my great bow, Nui Jaei Wei, from large to small. On a battlefield or in aerial combat, I prefer using the long bow. However, when I play the role of assassin, a small bow may be more advantageous."

Not knowing why he was summoned to this room, he was somewhat apprehensive, shaken by his surroundings and the House great elves' fear-instilling gazes and formidable warrior appearances. He stopped two steps in front of the elder elves and bowed respectfully. "On your knees," said Nui Honei. "We have asked you to come here, new son of House Nui Vent, as a next step to your adoption process. Now, receive your inheritance through blood and magic." With that proclamation, the altar's fire blazed anew, further brightening the room.

Nui Honei turned towards the table to the left of the altar and removed the cloth. Underneath the cloth were placed an elegant spear, swords, and shield. Taking the weapons, she continued speaking, "We, the great mother and father of House Nui Vent bequeath to you these weapons. Continue to serve this House with honor, always remember who you are and be brave, of great courage and follow the rules of your new heritage."

Nui Samu then retrieved the dagger from above the altar's fire, unscathed by the flame's heat. He then turned towards Nui Honei, bowed, and presented the dagger to her. The great warrior melf then stood above his adopted nephew, stared down at him and spoke, "There is an ancient tradition in our family to pass down our weapons to our young ones. I have no daughter and son; so, I want to extend this honor to you, my nephew. This night, I, Nui Samu, great father of House Nui Vent, grandson of the great warriors Nui Dreza and Nui Teru, bequeath to you, Nui Danka, this special spear, and shield, all wielded by your House ancestral great fathers and mothers. These weapons were reforged in dragon's fire and are infused with blood-magic. As long as you live, the blades will forever remain sharp, and this shaft cannot be broken. This shield will safely protect you from practically every enemy weapon's blow."

Nui Samu then took the ceremonial dagger, cut the palm of his hand, and thereafter took the spear into his bloodied hand. He then spoke the ritual incantation ending with, "Canela voi drago Nui Benoiti Wei. I release you now to my nephew, Nui Danka." Nui Samu then cut the outstretched palms of his nephew and placed the spear, Nui Benoiti Wei, upon Nui Danka's bloodied palms. The spear began to glow and magically absorbed the blood from Nui Danka's palms. Nui Samu continued by again cutting his already-healed palm and raising the shield with both hands. "Canela voi drago Nui Breici Wei. I release you now to my nephew, Nui Danka." After again cutting the palms of Nui Danka, Nui Samu handed him the shield which also began to glow, as well as absorb Nui Danka's spilled blood from his hands. Both weapons, Nui Benoti Wei, and Nui Breici Wei, ceased glowing after absorbing the blood of Nui Danka.

"These weapons are now bonded to you. This bond cannot be broken and only you can take advantage of the weapons' special capabilities. Also, now only you can further release and bond these weapons to someone else in the future. Take this scroll, go and learn how to better use your gifts," said the House great mother.

"Lastly, these fine long and short swords are not ancestral weapons of our House but are gifts from me and your uncle. Speak not of what has happened here and send in your brother, Nui Jooba." Nui Danka thanked his adopted mother and uncle and left overwhelmed with joy and pride.

After a short while, the second eldest, newly adopted son, Nui Jooba, arrived at the ceremonial room. Nui Jooba walked towards his mother and uncle and stopped a few steps from them and bowed.

"On your knees," said Nui Honei. "We have asked you to come here, new son of House Nui Vent, as the next step to your adoption process. Now, receive your inheritance through blood and magic." As before with that proclamation, the altar's fire blazed anew, further brightening the room.

Nui Honei turned towards the table to the right of the altar and removed the cloth. Underneath the cloth were placed formidable, double-bladed battleaxes and two scimitars. Taking the weapons, she continued speaking, "We, the great mother and father of House Nui Vent bequeath to you these battleaxes. Continue to serve this House with honor, always remember who you are and be brave, of great courage and follow the rules of our new heritage."

Again, like before, Nui Samu retrieved the dagger from above the altar's fire. He then turned towards Nui Honei, bowed to her and picked up the battleaxes. The great warrior melf then stood above his adopted nephew, stared down at him and spoke, "There is an ancient tradition in our family to pass down our weapons to our daughters and sons. Tonight, I, Nui Samu, great father of House Nui Vent, grandson of the great warriors Nui Dreza and Nui Teru, bequeath to you, Nui Jooba, these special battleaxes, both wielded by your House ancestral great fathers. Both weapons were reforged in dragon's fire and are infused with blood-magic. As long as you live, the blades' edges will forever remain sharp, and the shafts cannot be broken."

Nui Samu then took the ceremonial dagger, cut the palm of his hand, and took one of the battleaxes into his bloodied hand. He then spoke the ritual incantation ending with, "Canela voi drago Nui Zeinori Wei. I release you now to my nephew, Nui Jooba." Nui Samu then cut the outstretched palms of his nephew and placed the first battleaxe upon them. As before, the weapon glowed upon absorbing the blood of Nui Jooba and stopped when finished. The same ceremonial steps were repeated for the second battleaxe, Nui Teinori Wei.

"These weapons are now bonded to you. This bond cannot be broken and only you can take advantage of their special powers. Also, now only you can further release and bond these weapons to someone else in the future. Take this scroll, go and learn how to better use your gifts," said the House great mother.

"Lastly, these fine scimitars are not ancestral weapons of our House but are gifts from me and your uncle. Speak not of what has happened here and send in your brother Nui Rei." Before he left, Nui Jooba thanked his mother and uncle for his wonderful gifts.

Like his elder brothers, Nui Rei also was gifted weapons through the blood-magic ritual ceremony. He too received a special sword and shield. His short sword, Nui Rowae Wei, and shield, Nui Qui Wei, were also other examples of exquisite craftsmanship and capabilities. They too were ancestral weapons and reforged in dragon's fire. "These weapons are now bonded to you. This bond cannot be broken and only you can take advantage of their special powers. Also, now only you can further release and bond these weapons to someone else in the future. Take this scroll, go and learn how to better use your gifts," said the House great mother. "Lastly, your uncle and I wish to also gift you these four matching daggers personally. Speak not of what has happened here. Gather your brothers and meet us here again at dawn," Nui Honei remarked, concluding the gifting ceremony.

Nui Rei thanked his mother and uncle and left the room.

With uplifted spirits, the elder elves looked at each other and Nui Honei said, "We are now done gifting the new House sons with their inheritance. Let us go and prepare for tomorrow." With that declaration, Nui Honei and Nui Samu silently left the sacred room.

Early the next day, just before dawn, the new sons of House Nui Vent met again at the ritual chamber within their House stronghold. They were all still excited about their new gifts. Nui Danka said, "I read my weapons' scroll at least four times. I, at first, just could not believe the magic and power contained within my new weapons. I also felt unworthy of such gifts given my current fighting abilities; so, I must train harder and become more skillful to become worthy of such gifts. Did you read and study the scroll you received?" asked Nui Danka looking at his brothers. Both responded they had. Nui Danka then continued, "Our weapons training starts anew given our new weapons and their capabilities..."

"You are correct nephews," said Nui Samu as he had silently entered their midst unheard and unnoticed till the very last moment. "You must master your weapons' powers and capabilities. So, your training will assuredly start anew to meet this objective. Danka, tell your bothers about your weapons."

"Well met, Uncle," the brothers said calmly, no longer surprised by their uncle's unheard and unseen approaches.

Nui Danka began, "Brothers, I have been bequeathed this magnificent spear, Nui Benoiti Wei and shield, Nui Breici Wei. Both weapons can shape shift, as well as return to my outstretched hand after being thrown. My spear is full-length now but can shift to the shorter length of a javelin for close-quarters combat. Although my spear has a counterweight at one end, it can also shape-shift to another blade when needed. This shield, now small and round, can change its size and shape too. My shield can also release deadly blades along its edges upon command. Enemies will die by either hand. Further, my shield can absorb and release sunlight which can temporarily blind enemies. My shield can also absorb and release moonlight which can then detect enemies that are veiled invisible."

Nui Samu nodded at Nui Jooba. This new son of House Nui Vent declared, "Mother and uncle have given me two double-bladed battleaxes, Nui Zeinori Wei and Nui Teinori Wei. They are twin sisters of death. When either is thrown, she will return to my outstretched hand upon command. These sisters both speak devastating thunder and sinister, brilliant lightning."

Proudly displaying his weapons to his brothers, Nui Rei said, "My sword, Nui Rowae Wei, can shape-shift from long to short. Like Danka's shield, my shield can also change its size and shape. Upon command, blades can be summoned forth along my shield's edge. Lastly, my shield has secret storage areas for my daggers and two short swords. This marvelous weapon still remains light even when holding all these extra weapons."

"And here's yet another gift for each of you, my sons," said Nui Honei who had also quietly approached the group without any forewarning. "These are our House capes that each of you will receive. These capes too are infused with blood-magic. The blood contained within is mine and your uncle's, as well as that of a mighty dragon. This is another reason why dragons are so highly prized. As you suspect, the capes also have special powers. If you are covered by your House cape, you will not ever be too cold or too warm. Fire cannot destroy it. It will not wear out. It can also change colors. Your cape will give you the power to levitate above the ground for a short while. Weapons can also be hidden inside your cape. Lastly, in a very few rare cases, the cape can even conceal the one who wears it. Thus, is the great magic of dragon's blood, the most powerful blood of all." House great mother Nui Honei handed each of her sons his cape and a scroll.

"Gaze upon our family's heraldic sigil. What do you see?" asked Nui Honei.

"Several series of three red, diagonal lines going from right to left are emblazoned upon a black background," responded Nui Rei.

"What do you think it means?" the House great mother inquired further.

After a few moments, Nui Danka remarked, "I think it is a warning."

"Yes, I agree brother. It warns our enemies to 'beware the night' and that their blood will fall like rain," concluded Nui Jooba.

"My sons, you are correct. As you know, much of your training is at night or in complete darkness. You must be equally ready and able to fight in darkness or light. However, being able to fight well in darkness gives you a mental advantage which the Nui Vent warriors exploit. Afterall, you fight with your mind first and your body second," said Nui Honei. "An enemy's mind is less comfortable fighting at night than during the day."

She then said, "By the way, you will find a weighted chain in your rooms. This chain, a Manriki-gusari, is used to adorn your cape. It is also another innocent-looking, but very lethal weapon. The links are made from black steel and when you spin it, it seems invisible to the normal eye. There is a blade at one end and a weight at the other. Either end can be used to deliver death to an enemy. Read the scrolls left in your rooms. These new scrolls will provide instructions for using your cape and Manriki-gusari."

"So, I can become invisible with my cape?" asked Nui Rei.

"You, no," responded great mother Nui Honei. "Remember, I said in a 'very few rare cases.' Such is not your case, my sons, at this present time."

The brothers then looked at their uncle who also happened to be wearing his House cape. Nui Samu slightly nodded his head in acknowledgement that he was indeed one of the 'very few rare cases.'

Nui Rei looked at his mother and asked, "Are you Mother another 'very rare case' too?"

"Of course, my sons, of course," a smiling Nui Honei responded. "Your uncle and I are both incredibly good friends of a certain black dragon whom you all have met. Now go and change. Make haste and meet us at the training ground. New training starts today."

# Warnings

Nui Jooba continued to battle practice deep into the night. Although he is extraordinarily strong and could easily swing his double-bladed battleaxes with either hand with ease, he still felt uncomfortable with them in his hands. He still could not make them "sing" like he wanted, like he had often seen Nui Samu, his House weapons master, do with his battleaxes. Given his strength and agility, Nui Jooba could swing his powerful blades around him at great speeds while he moved in both attack and defensive forms across the practice floor. He imagined as a lone warrior killing his enemies with each deadly swing of his blades. His fighting dance, though graceful and perfect according to the particular martial arts form he had learned, still lacked a sense of fulfillment.

He was low-born and orphaned long ago. Many had misused him while he was growing up in the northern frontier towns. He had no formal education at all and did not regard himself very highly. He was told many times that he was a "mongrel" being of mixed dark and rock elves' blood. Since he did not ever know his birth parents, he did not know for certain what blood flows through his veins.

Like other mixed-raced creatures, he had been shunned by most. Nui Jooba's physical features mostly resemble those of rock elves – brown skin, brown eyes and brown hair. In his particular case, his hair is not tightly curled, like most rock elves; his hair is long and luxurious, like that of dark elves. Unlike most dark elves whose hair is typically straight, Nui Jooba's hair is wavy, a characteristic representative of his mixed-blood heritage. So, to maintain his true anonymity as much as possible, he would keep his hair very short in order to draw less attention to himself. A few elves, like Danka and Rei, accepted him quickly for simply being another orphan, like them, who also had to survive in a harsh northern frontier town.

Nui Jooba did learn at an early age that he could trust no one. His then so-called "friendships" were oftentimes one-sided, and usually not to mutual benefit. After years of struggle, he began to thrive given his extraordinary strength and his reserved disposition. Not wanting to ever display his limited knowledge, he was sometimes noticeably quiet and shy. He listened a great deal but said little. By doing so, he learned he could more easily gain knowledge which he craved.

The loud sound of crackling lightning jolted Nui Jooba from his deep thought. *"Tonight, it would be a good time to let my blades feast,"* he pondered. *"I have never before invoked this particular blood-magic incantation; so, I am a bit excited to witness this event."* He stopped his practice and made his way silently through the stronghold to a door that opened to the small courtyard. Nui Jooba opened the door quietly and went outside into the raging rainstorm. Within a few moments, he was completely drenched from the rain, but he did not care; he was too excited with anticipation. For tonight, for the first time, he was going to learn more about the magical capabilities of his new beloved weapons, Nui Zeinori and Teinori Wei. Since the time he had been gifted his mighty weapons, Nui Jooba practiced hard each day to master his twin-bladed battleaxes. He also devotedly studied the weapons' accompanying scrolls daily.

After reaching the center of the courtyard, lightning flashed brightly again as the storm continued to rage in its glory. Again, the booming sound of thunder followed. Nui Jooba took a deep calming breath and pricked a finger on each hand at an axe blood-point. In a calm, but strong voice, he called upon the blood-magic of his weapons, "Aummat aithorni Nui Zeinori Wei. Aummat aithorni Nui Teinori Wei." Both axes responded by immediately absorbing his spilled blood. The small wound on his fingers were also immediately healed. Filled with great expectation and excitement, he then hurled both axes upwards into the dark, night sky.

Amazed, Nui Jooba thought, *"Although the storm's winds and rain were loud, the storm must have still heard my incantation."* For when the thrown axes reached their zenith, high in the sky, the storm's lightning again illuminated the dark night's sky. This time though the jagged fingers of lightning touched both enchanted battleaxes that now seemed to float, suspended in the air.

"Feast well Nui Zeinori and Teinori Wei; feast well," Nui Jooba whispered as he watched his weapons seemingly absorb the lightning into them. He also observed that, strangely, there was no loud thunder following the last flash of lightning that touched his blades. For a few moments, Nui Zeinori and Teinori Wei remained aloft glowing warmly in the night sky till their light faded. "Entelusse!" Nui Jooba commanded. Obediently, Nui Zeinori and Teinori Wei returned to his welcoming, outstretched hands. Upon inspection of both axes, he saw no evidence of any damage from the storm. There were no char marks on his blades, and his battleaxes felt no different either. For this, he was pleased.

Nui Jooba then decided to return to his practice hall again for the last time that night. After entering the hall, he quietly closed the doors and went to a table to get cloths to dry himself and his weapons. Ever so lightly, he heard a faint whooshing sound. He reacted quickly with a feint movement to his left but rolled to his right. Nui Jooba ended his roll now with his axes at ready, crouching in a low defensive position. As he moved, he noticed that two spears had landed at his former position, deeply piercing a practice stand. Now being a disciplined warrior, he was not troubled. On the contrary, he was quite calm, waiting patiently to determine his next move against some unseen assailant. Given the angle that the spears protruded from the practice stand, he had also scanned the area of the hall from which the attack could have been launched. No figure could be seen there, still lurking in that darkness. Most likely, the attacker moved after launching the spears.

Another faint sound from his right alerted Nui Jooba that several deadly shuriken had just been thrown at him. He again reacted quickly, moving forward and deeper into the hall and avoided being hit by any of the deadly missiles. He next stepped quickly behind one of the hall's large supporting columns. After examining the assumed area from which his assailant threw the shuriken, Nui Jooba still saw no one. He also now believed the attacker was veiled, thus invisible to normal vision. Since he was not wearing any armor, he knew he could not last long against an attacker he could not see.

Nui Jooba began thinking through all the capabilities of his blades that he had read in his weapons' scrolls. After deciding upon a certain tactic, Nui Jooba pricked his fingers at a blood point on each axe and quietly uttered an incantation, 'Nui Zeinori Wei tae Nui Teinori Wei' which would allow him to magically fasten his axes together at the end of their handles. With both hands, he began spinning his blades around him while speaking another incantation, "Aiturna cala; aithorni accala." The first incantation emitted a protective shield around him; the second spell caused heat finding light to emanate from his spinning blades and flood the entire hall. This special light would line warm-blooded creatures and cling there for a short time.

There in one of the darken corners of the hall, Nui Jooba saw his assailant. The intruder appeared to be a tall male, woods elf of medium build. Several scars marked the assailant's face. His cold, dark eyes relayed a death's message. No longer able to hide under a veil of invisibility, the cloaked intruder removed the veil, his cape and drew two swords. Nui Jooba responded in kind by stopping the spinning and detaching his blades.

Nui Jooba walked slowly towards his assailant with each battleaxe level at his sides. His steps were calm and confident. He momentarily thought back to his life in the wild, northern great forest where every day his life was filled with anxiety and much uncertainty. For the most part, it was a quiet life, but filled with danger from savage beasts to other warring refugees from all parts of the kingdom. However, for the last decade, he has lived another quiet life too under a roof, in a stronghold where he had been welcomed warmly. Nui Jooba quickly thought, *"I still live a tough life, but it is a good, stable life under the roof of House Nui Vent! I am also part of a loving family too. My daily anxiety and uncertainty of the past are no more. I will make this intruder feel the full extent of trespassing and attacking a member of my beloved House. Even at the cost of my life, I will do my duty without regrets and without retreating. I will stand tall and defend his House!"* Now that he could clearly see his attacker thanks to the magic of his blades, Nui Jooba no longer harbored any concerns with engaging this intruder in combat.

The intruder too started walking slowly, with deadly purpose, towards the House Nui Vent soldier. This intruder carried a long sword in each hand.

Nui Jooba also assessed to himself that *"His blades should be much lighter than my battleaxes and should be faster to move but he may have difficulty blocking my axe strikes, especially all the combinations I have learned from House great father Nui Samu, a renowned warrior and weapons master."*

This intruder also recognized that the House Nui Vent soldier has a strong, muscular physique; he indeed looked powerful. *"A prolonged battle would not be ideal either given other House Nui Vent soldiers could arrive at any time. Victory must be taken quickly!"* the intruder thought.

When the combatants were just two steps apart from each other, Nui Jooba initiated a multi-step attack he learned from Nui Samu. With one hand, he swung his axe horizontally, and he lunged and swung his other axe vertically from a low to a high position. Both swings were fast, powerful, well disciplined, and practiced. He did not over-swing either of his blades. Nui Jooba knew that he must always be ready to defend himself after an attack. This initial tactic was intended to "power through" any attempted block by the intruder, as well as measure his opponent's skills. Still, serious damage would be inflicted by either blow should either attack land upon the intruder.

The intruder too was a skillful, quick warrior and chose not to immediately engage either of the House Nui Vent soldier's blades by just stepping backwards and to the right. The two combatants waged war against each other for the next few minutes without either gaining any advantage. Nui Jooba's opponent tried different attack combinations incorporating feints, counterattacks, parries, lunges, switching the lead attacking hand, and even tried an elbow-knee attack after a sword attack combination. The speed of their battle, as each warrior moved around the hall, was frightening fast, yet elegant.

Nui Jooba reversed the grip he had on his axes to match the hand speed of the intruder's sword movements. Even though Nui Jooba could not "cut" the intruder with his axe handle, he found by poking the intruder in the chest area, it caused the intruder enough pain to step back and utter a slight sound of agony. With that movement, Nui Jooba continued to press his opponent even more.

The intruder soon realized, thinking, *"Victory will not come fast, nor likely to be easy. A different strategy is needed."* During the next series of attacks, the intruder used a circular parry to engage both opponent's axe handles and moved them to the side. Now, with a free hand, the intruder threw the free-hand sword with an underhand throw at the House soldier; but instead of retreating, the intruder advanced forward pulling a hidden long knife from a boot. In that instance, the intruder was now inside Nui Jooba's defenses and possibly able to inflict a death blow with the long knife.

At the last moment, Nui Jooba did turn to the side so that

the thrown sword missed its intended mark. However, the intruder's knife attack was successful; it hit the left side of Nui Jooba's chest but was not a fatal wound. Nui Jooba had also advanced at the same time the intruder did; released an axe held in his innermost hand; caught it as it fell and spun around the intruder while being stabbed with the knife to bring his blade to the intruder's exposed neck.

"Hold!" commanded a familiar voice. Both combatants became deadly still. Neither could move, now locked in paralysis by magic. Now, slowly descending from the ceiling rafters were two unveiled persons, House great mother Nui Honei and great father Nui Samu.

Both House elders walked over to the combatants. After releasing the previous foes from her spell, Nui Honei quickly healed Nui Jooba's wound. She then unveiled the intruder to reveal Je Danei, the oldest daughter of House Je Luneefa. Looking at the combatants, Nui Honei said, "You both fought very well. As the last Kilecfla showed, you two fight well together and are brave warriors. Tonight, we again saw evidence of your mighty fighting prowess and skills. We are both immensely proud of you. Thank you, Je Danei, for participating in Nui Jooba's training exercise tonight."

"Gladly, I knew it would be a good contest," said Je Danei. "I enjoyed it. By the way, who won?"

Nui Samu responded, "Is that really important? You both did some things well and other things, not so well. Do not even think you should skip your next training session."

"Yes, I will be ready to train more. But I would still like to know who won had this been a real contest," Je Danei persisted.

After an irritated sigh and shaking of his head, Nui Samu said, "Je Danei scored more *hits*, but none were fatal; whereas Nui Jooba scored the only fatal blow."

Irritated and stunned, Je Danei looked at Nui Jooba. "Why do you look surprised?" Nui Jooba questioned. "After all, I had a special incentive to perform extremely well from our last encounter on the training field."

"Brother, it's time for us to leave and let these two settle their matter without our unwanted eyes and ears seeing and hearing their next contest," said Nui Honei.

Nui Samu responded, "Agreed, let us leave now."

As Nui Honei and Nui Samu started walking towards the hall's door, Nui Honei turned around and looked at Je Danei and Nui Jooba who had both retrieved their weapons and were facing each other. Nui Honei then commanded, "No more bloodshed nor serious injury!"

"Understood House great mother," Nui Jooba complied.

"Yes, understood House great mother," Je Danei agreed reluctantly. "However, I will remove that smirk from his face with my fists."

"Indeed, you can only try," Nui Jooba triumphantly remarked.

After the House Nui Vent elders left the hall and closed the door, Nui Jooba asked just as he dodged her fist aimed at his face, "Will you now honor our agreement?"

"You would still dare to want to kiss me even after I tried to kill you this night?" Je Danei defiantly questioned.

"To be *your* first kiss, most definitely. Surely, I would take such a risk," responded a smiling Nui Jooba.

"Why do you persist? Do you seek to just satisfy your lust, or do you truly wish to love me for centuries? Heed my warning foolish male. I still do not know what love is to me or even what I want from love. Attempting to *love* me for a night or for centuries may still be the death of you; why waste your time and efforts on such uncertainty?" a confused and nervous Je Danei declared.

Smiling, Nui Jooba just said, "Life is filled with uncertainties; yet we all still choose to live each day. Death awaits us all. Till then, I want to live a full life and you are now an essential part of that objective. Yes, I know you are difficult and quite annoying at times. I believe you, like me, are still a bit frightened of certain feelings. But my feelings for you have never waned. On the contrary, they have only grown ever since that first night we all met in the forest. My brothers and I all fell in love with you that very night, but they both 'fell out' shortly thereafter. I, on the other hand, could not. Though you have rejected me already a few times, I still have the courage to risk loving you. But, before we speak further, will you honor our agreement now?" Nui Jooba then dropped his axes and began walking towards Je Danei with determined purpose.

"Foolish male, I still hold blades in my hands. I still carry four more blades you have not yet seen. Do not let your lust or so-called love cloud good judgement. Is your life worth risking now over something so meaningless as my first kiss?" now questioned an angered Je Danei.

"Why are you so afraid?" the melf countered. Undisturbed, Nui Jooba walked dangerously close to Je Danei never taking his eyes from her gaze. When he was within arm's length, Je Danei dropped her swords and started to pull her long knives from sheaths on her arms. Nui Jooba caught her trembling hands before she could fully extract her weapons and slowly placed them on his pounding chest.

He quietly said with sincerity and some hesitation, "I now want you to know how I feel, but the right words will not come." Although terribly confused, not knowing what the *right* thing to say or the *right* thing to do, Nui Jooba kept his eyes locked on hers looking for some sign. He chanced not even to breathe; Nui Jooba just looked at her tenderly. He then kissed both her hands after a long moment. Next, he gently kissed her forehead. Still looking lovingly into her eyes, he kissed each of her eyes she closed. He waited a few moments drinking in her beauty and kissed her gently upon her lips. Jooba again placed her hands upon his chest over his heart and confessed, "Yes, I dare to kiss you and I dare to love you for you are so worth why my heart beats so strongly when I am near you. Now do you better understand?" the House Nui Vent second son finally said with labored breath.

For another moment, a puzzled Je Danei just looked at Nui Jooba. She then picked up her weapons, turned and walked out of the training hall.

Nui Jooba smiled to himself as he watched her leave. In this most recent battle, he had neither victory nor defeat. He was content to be able to fight on again for her heart. *"But then again, she did not try to kill me this time; so, maybe I did win a small victory?"* Nui Jooba wondered.

The next afternoon, Nui Jooba sought House great mother Nui Honei for some sage advice. "Mother, may we talk privately?" Nui Jooba asked.

"Of course, my son," Nui Honei responded, and she walked towards a small sitting room, opened the door, and walked in. Nui Jooba followed her into the room and closed the door. Like the House great hall, this sitting room was another reflection of House Nui Vent's history. On the walls were shelves of scrolls and books. A variety of paintings of ancient battles and various weapons adorned the walls.

After Nui Honei sat at a table in the room, Nui Jooba sat across from her. Looking sad, he cleared his throat and announced, "I believe I am deeply in love with the House Je Luneefa first daughter, Je Danei. I too wish to proclaim my candidacy for courtship at her upcoming Day of Adulthood celebration, her Yimibirkutla. I seek your guidance and blessing.

"As you know, I am not of noble birth; in fact, I was born into a poor family and then abandoned. I was sold away as an unwanted extra mouth to feed. I have no worldly riches to offer a noble felf such as Je Danei. My future even remains a bit uncertain for my ambition is to continue to be a soldier of House Nui Vent. Would this be enough for someone like her? I am not worldly; I am not well educated from books and scrolls; and I only speak a few languages. I feel so unworthy to even think she could even befriend, let alone love, someone like me. Am I qualified enough to profess my love in hopes of winning her heart? Would I even be given a fair chance? Would her House elders even welcome me since I am not of noble blood?"

Nui Honei asked, "What kind of love do you have for her? Is it the fleeting kind; here today, but perhaps gone tomorrow? Do you *only* want to *love* her till you satisfy the longings of your body? Afterall, she is a beautiful, desirable young felf. Many will claim to *love* her. Many more will just *want* her to fulfill their selfish desires.

"Will you fight by her side against all enemies despite the odds? Do you love her enough to want to marry her? Is your love for her strong enough to endure the challenges of raising little elves with her? Will you faithfully be by her side through life's pain? Will you love her forever and faithfully till your death?" She looked at her son with an expressionless persona waiting to listen carefully and weigh his response.

Nui Jooba reflected inwardly for a few moments and then said, "She can be unkind, difficult at times and impatient. I am understanding and have patience for what I want. She is insecure about her emotions, just like me. But, if she has enough courage to try to love me, I will more than match her courage now, as well as in the future. I will stand by her side and fight against any enemy regardless of the numbers. Through both life's pains and joys, I will love her faithfully till I draw my last breath."

After a few moments of nervous silence, Nui Jooba took a deep breath and continued, "The love I feel for her is like the love Ona Noirar has described he has for you. His temperature rises when you are near him; his passion boils from your touch, his heart beats faster and his mind and body yearn for you. His mind, body, spirit, and faith were changed after meeting you. His love for you knows no boundaries. You are his once in a lifetime, forever love. There will be no other. You are his special, only one. This is how I feel about Je Danei."

After a few moments, Nui Honei smiled at her son. She took his hands into hers, looked him in the eyes and said, "The pursuit of love can be an arduous journey of both pain and joy. Je Danei can be difficult; so, you will need to love her with patience and courage. Also, the journey of winning another's heart can be short or long; so, be truly honest with yourself always. Ask yourself each day, 'Do I still love her? Do I still want to love her? Why? Am I doing all I can to nurture this love? What more can I do? What can I do to show her how I feel?'

"Love is a journey, and you will be challenged and tested many times, sometimes every day it seems. If your love is truly blessed, you will pass those daily tests and before long, those days will turn into centuries. That is how long I have loved Ona Noirar. So, if you genuinely love Je Danei, then be off on your journey; you have my blessing. I wish you well.

"Do remember too that loving a noble felf can be complicated and have some unpleasant consequences despite the love you may have. You both still have sacred duties to your families and Houses. Those same duties can sometimes interfere with a pleasant, peaceful life. Her love alone may not be enough to ensure your happiness.

"Lastly, Je Danei is also the beloved granddaughter and daughter of very, very protective grandparents and parents. She is my beloved goddaughter and niece. She is the niece of an exceptional healer and toxicologist. Je Danei is a beloved niece of two of the realms deadliest blades. All of her elders will constantly scrutinize all your actions; any of these elders will kill you mercilessly for a transgression. So, be forewarned," reflected Nui Honei.

After a long sigh, Nui Jooba said, "I understand." Feeling relieved and greatly encouraged, Nui Jooba looked at his mother, smiled warmly and thanked her. He then hugged her lovingly in his powerful arms. After leaving the room, he knew he had a battle plan to prepare; so, he needed to find his brothers and enlist their support.

Three days later, various would-be suitors and guests started to arrive at the Warden's stronghold inside the outermost, protective wall surrounding Torondell. Here, certain Je Luneefa family events could take place without allowing the king's spies to ever see the inside of true family dwelling, which was the Je Luneefa family stronghold inside the Toronwalein, the innermost protective wall of Torondell. This continued to be a tradition the House Je Luneefa first elders established long ago and still maintained. Je Buel and Je Taeliel had always been suspicious of the king and queen's ill intent upon their family; so, protecting their loved ones is always their priority. Since Je Taeliel was the appointed Warden of the Northern realm, he took full advantage of utilizing the Warden's stronghold even for his family's social events to help maintain the secrecy of his actual family stronghold.

Unlike some nobles in the kingdom, the Je Luneefa family welcomed all members of society to their public events. They considered events such as the Day of Adulthood celebration to be an opportunity to spread goodwill from their family to the other families and citizens of Torondell.

This day is the day of the House Je Luneefa first daughter's Yimibirkutla, for Je Danei is now two hundred ten years old. In elven society, she is no longer a gelf, but a full grown felf, an adult female elf. This day marks the special occasion when suitors will formally announce their interest in pursuing a courtship with the eldest daughter of the noble Je Luneefa family. In addition to the noble melfs gathered there to announce their intentions, other guests, nobles, and commoners alike, are there too to join in the festivities. Some are there to help celebrate with the House Je Luneefa first daughter's momentous occasion; others were there to witness the event and prospect for potential suitors themselves.

The Je Luneefa family elders, as the Elven custom dictated, presided over this celebration. All family and extended members were formally attired and proudly wore House capes, bearing the House Je Luneefa family's heraldic sigil - three red and black roses on a black field.

Most of the Yimibirkutla's festivities, the music, food, and dancing, took place outside the actual Warden's castle. Inside the castle walls, in the courtyard, several tents had been erected. The largest tent covered the location where the main guests were seated. Here, there was a dais upon which several large tables were placed. Sitting at the center-most table were the House Je Luneefa first daughter flanked on either side by her grandparents, the House Je Luneefa first elders. Sitting to the right of the center table were the parents of Je Danei, the House Je Luneefa second elders, Je Pagi and Je Maron. Sitting to the left of the center table were the House Nui Vent elders, Nui Honei and Nui Samu, Je Danei's adopted aunt and uncle. Alleina sat at this table, as well. Sitting next to Je Danei is Je Onyxia Ryoshi, Je Danei's pet panther. Like other esteemed guests, Ony also wore her cape bearing the sigil of her House, House Je Luneefa.

Five suitors had come to formally announce their intentions to court the House Je Luneefa's first daughter. Prince Rho Paul, nobles Pi Rhem, Si Tadejo and Lord Gabriel, and commoner Nui Jooba stood quietly before the main table. Other Torondell noble families and dignitaries were invited to attend the main ceremony, as well. These noted guests were seated fifteen steps away but facing the front main tables.

House Je Luneefa first great mother Je Buel first addressed the guests, welcoming them all to her granddaughter's Yimibirkutla. Je Buel then introduced all of the House Je Luneefa family elders, including her adopted daughters and sons. Lastly, the House first great mother provided a summary overview of the Yimibirkutla's main activities and described the meaning underlying this House Je Luneefa's family tradition.

Je Danei next stood and addressed the would-be suitors, "Welcome all and thank you for joining me in celebrating my Day of Adulthood. As you know, this is a day in which I can learn more about each of you; and you, in turn, can learn more about me. In so doing, one of us may realize that any follow-on pursuits and/or interests would be in vain and valuable time wasted.

After sitting again, she continued, "So, to begin, let me first ask all of you, 'If my pet here, Ony, and you were both in trouble and I could only save one of you, whom would I save?' Your Highness, please respond first."

Prince Rho Paul thought for a few moments and replied, "Me, of course. For the benefit of the kingdom, we must protect and preserve our royalty."

Pi Rhem, Si Tadejo and Lord Gabriel all hesitated at first, but answered in a similar fashion stating their respective lives would be more valuable to Je Danei than her pet panther. They cited a variety of reasons ranging from companionship, their "warmth and touch" to their capability of producing progeny to further advance their Houses. Each tried to provide some clever answer that would hopefully exceed the other, previous responses to the question.

"And you, new son of House Nui Vent, how do you respond? Je Danei asked.

Without any hesitation, Nui Jooba replied, "You would save your precious Ony first for she has proven her unconditional love and loyalty to you time and time again; whereas, I have not even once."

The other four suitors started chuckling. "You are neither royalty nor of noble birth; so, your answer befits you," remarked a sneering Lord Gabriel.

"Lord Gabriel. You do think too highly of yourself. My granddaughter would most assuredly save her Ony, a precious member of our family, first before any of you. Foolish male," Je Buel rebuked. The House great mother Je Buel was an experienced, masterful statesperson. She was quite skilled at reading friends and foes alike. She also knew and loved each member of her family. This powerful matriarch wanted to send a message, perhaps even a warning, to these would-be suitors: loyalty to her family is a requirement, as well as a sacred duty. Je Buel also knew that her rebuke would deflect any potential retaliation away from her granddaughter and deflate the royal/noble egos which was a bonus she liked too.

"*Thank you,*" Je Danei communicated privately to Je Buel with their secret hand language.

"*You are most welcome, Danei,*" Je Buel replied covertly with her hand.

Je Danei could ask two additional questions in this public forum. As before, each respondent would provide his answer. At the conclusion of asking and answering the three questions, a suitor could announce his intentions to decline any future pursuit of intended courtship of the House Je Luneefa first daughter. Similarly, the Day of Adulthood honoree could announce her unwanted interest in any of the would-be suitors. Should there be lack of interest by either party, that suitor would be "excused" and exempt from any private questioning that would take place later in the day.

"For my second question, what will you gift me this day?" Je Danei asked the would-be suitors. Each suitor could give up to three gifts to the Day of Adulthood honoree. As before, they each would respond in order of their social standing or rank. Hence, Prince Rho Paul would be given the honor of first response.

"Thank you, but if I may, I would like to trade my response position with the commoner in our midst. Otherwise, this poor fellow's gift will be lost from memory should the four of us present our gifts before him," Prince Rho Paul requested. The prince was quite irritated with Je Buel's rebuke of Lord Gabriel comment, but he also realized that this was perhaps an opportunity to learn more about the secretive Je Luneefa family through someone who obviously knew them better than him. Also, Prince Rho Paul thought, *"I hope my maneuver will help me against my noble competitors by answering last. My objective is to become the foremost suitor of the House Je Luneefa first daughter and eventually wed you, Je Danei. House Rho desperately wants to join, hopefully through marriage, with House Je Luneefa, the presumed, second most powerful family in the kingdom. The dragon your House controls must be ours too!"*

Je Danei nodded, approving his request. At this time, all eyes turned towards Nui Jooba who confidently walked over to the table where all of the Day of Adulthood honoree's gifts had been placed. He picked up the large, rectangular wooden box he had brought and returned to stand in front of the dais. Nui Jooba then extended his gift to Je Danei who signaled to a servant to take the box and bring it to her table and place it in front of her.

Je Danei rose from her chair after the servant had placed the box in front of her and walked away. The House Je Luneefa first daughter opened the box and first looked puzzled at the contents. Then she smiled warmly at Nui Jooba and said, "Thank you."

The second son of House Nui Vent returned her smile and explained, "I was surprised when I learned you had never been given flowers before. So, I wanted to give you your first which is a rare orchid grown only in the southern parts of the kingdom." Je Danei raised the fragrant blue and yellow flower for all to see.

"Next, you will find something a bit more personal and to your liking, as well I hope," continued Nui Jooba. At this time, Je Danei removed a cloth covering her next gift, a pair of twin-bladed battleaxes. They were not quite the size of his battleaxes. These were smaller, designed for close quarters combat, and could be easily concealed. They were also ideal for throwing. Upon closer inspection, they even resembled a smaller version of Nui Jooba's battleaxes. They also bore an image of the House Je Luneefa's family sigil on each axe head's centerpiece.

"Since this is a very special day of your first and only Day of Adulthood, I wanted to mark this occasion with several other *firsts* for you: your first flower, battleaxes and the last gift, another first for you, I will present later this afternoon. The gift is currently not here, but on its way. I do apologize for the delay," Nui Jooba said.

"I do like blades!" Je Danei exclaimed holding up an axe in each hand. For a few moments, she spun them around to get accustomed to their weight and balance. Based upon her beaming smile and sparkling eyes, Nui Jooba knew she really liked her new weapons which would be added to her growing collection of different bladed weapons. Je Danei put her axes aside, composed herself and asked Pi Rhem to present his gifts next.

Pi Rhem, Si Tadejo, Lord Gabriel and Prince Rho Paul all presented Je Danei with jewels, lands, and/or fine horses. Although none of these gifts were unique nor personal, the prince did present a most unusual pledge, "I can offer you the throne of this kingdom," Prince Rho Paul said.

"Can you really?" Je Buel questioned. "If I am not mistaken, you are not yet the *Crowned* Prince of the kingdom; so, that gift is a bit premature is it not?"

Nui Rei entered the tent, caught his brother's eyes, and nodded. Before the prince could become angrier with embarrassment, Nui Jooba then quickly announced, "Je Danei, I would like to present my third *first* gift to you now."

"And what might that be, and will it impress my daughter?" House great mother Je Pagi asked.

Nui Jooba replied, "I do hope so. If you permit me, I would like to take you on your first dragon flight. The great dragon, Ona Kei Kuri Ryuu, awaits us."

Immediately, an incredibly surprised Je Danei responded with a huge smile. Without any further hesitation or thought regarding abandoning her elders and guests, Je Danei rose from her table, stepped quickly from around the table, grabbed Nui Jooba's hand and said, "Lead on!" Nui Rei and Nui Danka quickly formed a vanguard for their brother and Je Danei and led them to another enclosed courtyard of the Warden's castle. There waiting was the magnificent Ona Kei Kuri Ryuu basking in the afternoon sun.

When Je Danei departed from the tent, House great mother Je Buel rose and said, "Well, let us now break for our Celebration's repast. Later this afternoon, we will resume with the private questioning sessions with any remaining suitor who wishes to continue possibly pursuing courtship of the House Je Luneefa first daughter."

Any follow-on questions and answers would take place in a more private setting after refreshments were served. This light meal summoned the halfway point of the Yimibirkutla.

The assembly broke into many different conversations of surprise, shock and/or amazement. Many who had gathered there did not really know Je Danei well. Some were appalled that the noble, first daughter of House Je Luneefa would be rude enough to leave her own Yimibirkutla with a commoner no less. Some were simply awestruck that such a rare occasion had just befallen upon her. Regardless, Je Danei was not going to forgo achieving one of her life-long dreams of riding upon a dragon and soaring through the skies. Je Danei did not care about public opinion of her nor so-called "noble protocol."

Pi Rhem, Si Tadejo and Lord Gabriel looked at each other in utter disbelief. The Prince vocalized their collective, amazed looks on their faces, "Friends, I believe we have just been handedly defeated by our competitor, a simple commoner at that!"

"Je Danei is a noble; how can she be this rude and inconsiderate? This is completely unacceptable! I will not ever yield to some commoner and a former thief and rogue at that. I am not yet defeated," exclaimed Pi Rhem. Si Tadejo and Lord Gabriel's faces had already both turned red with anger. Being an esteemed military tactician, Lord Gabriel also evaluated his chances of continuing his pursuit and decided it was time for a strategic retreat. He approached the center dais to address the House Je Luneefa elders.

Je Tero saw his look and intercepted him just before he reached the table. "Lord Gabriel, a word please before you talk to my House elders. I suspect you may now wish to withdraw from pursuing my sister any further. That I completely understand; she is a bit challenging. But know that if you voice any disrespect to my elders, I will kill you immediately. Your fame, rank and prestigious noble position will not protect you," Je Tero said quietly.

Lord Gabriel looked closely at the House Je Luneefa second son, eye-to-eye, and responded, "Are you threatening a Commander of the king's army, the most senior commander of legions?"

Calmly, Je Tero replied, "I made no threat Lord Gabriel; it was a promise. You respect and demand commitment, discipline, and loyalty from the commanders and soldiers you command. You do not tolerate disobedience. You would not tolerate anyone disrespecting you or your House. But you are also arrogant at times; so, I wanted to support your *respectful* retreat should that be your intention."

Before Lord Gabriel could continue, the House Je Luneefa second great father had walked over to the Lord Gabriel and his son. "Lord Gabriel, are you trying to recruit my son for your army?" asked Je Maron who was attempting to possibly diffuse a tense moment he anticipated.

"Quite the contrary. We were just discussing tactics," replied a now calmer Lord Gabriel. "He would, no doubt, make a fine soldier and commander; but I suspect his commitments would first retain him here in Torondell for a long while.

"Please extend my sincere 'Congratulations' again to your daughter on her reaching her Day of Adulthood. I have decided to no longer pursue any courtship with her." With that last statement and after a short bow, Lord Gabriel just turned around and walked away.

Je Buel and Je Taeliel then walked over to their son-in-law and grandson.

"Lord Gabriel definitely looked unhappy when Danei left," Je Taeliel remarked.

The astute, House first great mother looked at her grandson and smiled. "Did you just save that fool's life?" she asked.

"Perhaps. I just reminded him to use good manners while addressing Je Luneefa family elders. Besides, he is too old for Danei anyways and I would not want such an arrogant fool for a brother-in-law. However, I do suspect he may become another enemy of our House after this day."

"So be it. If we stay together, the Je Luneefa family will remain strong and defeat them all," Je Taeliel said confidently.

After a short while, the great dragon, Ona Kei Kuri Ryuu, returned with her passengers to the same enclosed courtyard behind the Warden's castle. Nui Jooba dismounted first. After helping Je Danei unfasten her saddle straps, he helped the first daughter of House Je Luneefa to the ground. Despite her hair being disheveled and her face windblown, Je Danei was quite happy and still beaming with excitement from her first dragon ride. She then looked at Nui Jooba for a few moments, kissed him on the cheek and ran away into the castle to change and prepare for the next part of her Day of Adulthood celebration.

From a distance, Nui Samu, Ona Drachir, Nui Danka, and Nui Rei had all witnessed the dragon's landing and the events that took place thereafter. After Je Danei had left, they all emerged from their hiding place and hurriedly walked over to the now overwhelmed Nui Jooba who was shaking slightly from unreleased joy and excitement. Unable to contain his overflowing energy, Nui Jooba hugged each of his supporting team members. He then went to stand in front of Keiku. He looked deep into her eyes, bowed low and said panting, "Thank you most perfect gift of nature, thank you."

"I take it all went well on her first dragon flight?" asked Ona Noirar. "I am still very surprised my dragon agreed to be a part of your plan, but I suspect my beloved Nui Honei helped with your negotiations."

"That, four barrels of fish and four scrubbings," remarked Nui Rei.

"Breathe Jooba, breathe. She is only a felf," Nui Samu said as he closely watched his heavily panting adopted nephew.

"No dear Uncle; she is very much more than a felf. Fighting an enemy who would want to kill me is far easier than my meeting and talking with Je Danei. She is *the* felf who has already completely captured my heart. She is my *one*," declared a slowly recovering Nui Jooba.

"Well, she better be with all the trouble we went through to help you get this far! You are deep in our debt," Ona Drachir said.

"Congratulations, brother. You did well today," Nui Danka

said.

"Yes, congratulations, my son; you have done well indeed thus far," said Nui Honei who had silently approached the group. "But the toughest part of today's battle awaits you. So, do not fill his head with any of your male nonsense. Go and prepare yourself for the personal questioning."

Nui Jooba thanked everyone again for their support and walked away to clean himself and redress. Awaiting him would be the next part of this Yimibirkutla. He, as a remaining would-be suitor, will stand alone before the Je Luneefa family and answer three of their questions. Je Danei, as the Day of Adulthood honoree can ask another three questions.

After a short time, Je Danei returned to the main tent. She was accompanied by her sister, Je Leena. Both sisters decided to wear matching red formal dresses. They looked stunning. Both wore their formal House black capes bearing the sigil of House Je Luneefa. They each also wore their gold Manriki-gusari used to clasp their cape. When they reached the tent's main entrance, they were greeted by their brothers, Je Jero and Je Tero.

Je Tero smiled at his sisters as they approached. He said, "Brother, our family is truly blessed to have such exquisitely, good-looking females. It is no wonder these fools want to marry into our family."

"Yes, I must admit; they are both truly beautiful," concurred Je Jero.

"Danei, you look so regal. Leena, you resemble grandmother so much," Je Tero commented. Small chatter and quiet laughter ensued amongst the Je Luneefa sisters and brothers.

They all turned when they heard Prince Rho Paul and his personal guards approach.

"Greetings, daughters and sons of House Je Luneefa," the prince said.

After all bowed to the prince, Je Jero said, "Well met Your Highness. I believe you already know my sisters. I am Je Jero, first son of House Je Luneefa and this is my brother, Je Tero, the second son."

"Je Danei, your beauty befits a queen. You are indeed breathtaking," the prince said, ignoring Je Jero's greeting.

"Thank you, Your Highness; you are too kind," responded Je Danei.

"And are you well armed today too?" the prince asked.

Smiling, Je Leena responded, "We have already had this conversation before. Today is no different than when we first spoke about this. But I noticed you have another mage in your personal guard." Je Leena pointed to one of his guards in the fourth row behind the prince. "That is good, but still not enough should you try to attack my sister. The outcome would still be the same."

"Je Leena, his Highness is an honored guest here; please be courteous," Je Jero requested.

Prince Rho Paul then said, "I see you are still spirited like your older sister, but a bit scarier than you were before. Fortunately, I do not frighten easily."

"Your Highness, you have no idea how frightening she can be at times. Just the other day..." Je Tero started to remark but was interrupted.

"Shall we go in now?" Je Danei said, took the prince by the arm and walked into the main tent. They were followed by Je Leena.

Je Jero stepped in front of the prince's guards as they tried to follow him. The Je Luneefa family first son addressed them saying, "Royal guards, as you know, this is a Je Luneefa family matter and is private. I personally guarantee the prince's safety while he is inside. As such, please remain here outside. Position yourselves around this tent if need be. Just respect and honor our family tradition. Besides, should you learn of any royal secrets, the prince may have you all executed. So, staying outside protects you too."

"We will comply with your wishes since our prince had already commanded us to do so," scoffed the royal escort guards' commander who was again already disturbed by Je Leena's comments.

After entering the inner main tent, Je Danei walked to her seat behind the center table on the dais. All attendees rose and bowed to the prince when he stood in front of the main table.

First House great mother Je Buel then formally greeted the prince, "Welcome again Your Highness, first son of House Rho. During this portion of the Day of Adulthood celebration for my House's first daughter, I and the other elders will ask you three questions. Je Danei is also entitled to ask you up to three additional questions. You are honored-bound to answer all questions truthfully as best as you can. At the end of this session, we will advise Je Danei if we feel you are a worthy candidate to court our precious daughter of House Je Luneefa.

"This is another tradition to honor and glorify the family structure. Per tradition, only family members, extended family members and honored family guests are invited to participate in this portion of today's Celebration. All answers given here are confidential. Do you understand and agree to these terms?

"Yes, of course, House first great mother," the prince replied.

House great mother Je Buel continued, "Let me first start by introducing those whom you may not know. I am the first great mother of House Je Luneefa, and this is my husband, Je Taeliel. As you know, he is also the Warden of the North and First Commander of the Canae northern army. Our daughter, second great mother of House Je Luneefa, is Je Pagi and her husband, second great father of House Je Luneefa, is Je Maron." Je Buel pointed to the side table to the left of the center table and continued introductions, "Sitting to your right are Je Luneefa extended family members. First are House Nui Vent great mother and father, Nui Honei and her brother Nui Samu."

"But that house is no longer a great noble house of this kingdom," remarked Prince Rho Paul.

"Although Rhodell may not still recognize it as a House of nobility, we surely do; for we know the true character of the House great mother and father. As such, they are highly respected and honored in Torondell. Further, House great mother Nui Honei and House great father Nui Samu are the godparents of Je Danei, our adopted daughter and son, as well as my granddaughters and grandsons' aunt and uncle. So, I urge you not to let the misunderstandings of the past and Rhodell cloud your good judgement about today and the future," warned Je Buel.

Prince Rho Paul frowned slightly, thinking, *"Even though the king, my uncle, still holds a long, festering grudge against the fallen House Nui Vent, I must not conduct myself in any way that would demean House Nui Vent or even the recently deceased Ona Noirar. Surely, that will not help my chances of a successful courtship at all. So, my true feelings need to be more guarded."*

"I understand, House great mother; I meant no offense," Prince Rho Paul said, respectfully bowing first to Je Buel and then to the House Nui Vent elders.

Je Buel continued with the introductions of the Je Luneefa immediate family and the honored guests attending Je Danei's celebration. At the conclusion of the introductions, the first House great mother said, "We are now ready to begin with our personal questions. Our first question is 'Why do you wish to court the first daughter of House Je Luneefa?'"

The prince replied, "After first meeting Je Danei at the Autumn festival several years ago, I was captivated by her fiery, independent spirit. I wanted to learn more about her then and my interest has ever grown since then. I believe she would make a fine queen if and when my time comes to rule this kingdom.

"As a daughter of noble House Je Luneefa, her dowry would be given to her upon our wedding day and our combined fortunes would be a very solid foundation upon which we would build our family in Rhodell. Our combined Houses would be most powerful and unrivaled in all the kingdom."

"So, you have assumed there is some great fortune we would bequeath to her, and you would plan to take her away from her home here to live in Rhodell? That is interesting..." House great father Je Taeliel remarked coldly.

The prince looked a bit surprised and pondered to himself, *"I need to save any follow-on questions related to this matter for later. This is not the time or place to begin trying to secretly assess the House Je Luneefa family's wealth."*

"The second question from the House Je Luneefa elders is this," Nui Honei quickly started after seeing the prince's puzzled look upon his face, "Should Je Danei be engaged in battle against a large, overwhelming enemy force who had invaded your home the week after your marriage, what would you do as her husband?"

The prince reflected inwardly for a moment and then responded confidently, "I would have already commanded our guards to protect us while I, I mean we, made our escape. We would escape and our escape, unfortunately, may be at the cost of our guards' ultimate and final sacrifice. But our kingdom's royal line would be saved and preserved."

Ony growled softly. The great panther turned its head to look at Je Danei with pleading eyes, saying, *"He is not the one! This fool is a coward and does not deserve you. Dismiss him now please."*

"Hush Ony," Je Danei said gently scolding her pet. "How would you know if the prince's guards are good warriors after only being in the palace for just a week?"

"There would be no need in bringing that panther to the palace. There would be more than enough guards to protect us. Your pet could remain here in Torondell," the prince remarked. His last comments were cold, remembering, no doubt, their first frightful surprise meeting with the great panther.

Ony just narrowed her eyes while looking at the prince. *"Command me now and I will gladly end his life,"* she communicated mentally to Je Danei who just continued to scratch the great panther's head to soothe her anger.

"*Not yet, dear one, not yet,*" Je Danei calmly responded mentally.

"Do you love me?" Je Danei asked.

"Not quite yet, but I hope and want to completely one day soon," the prince responded.

"It is known that while you were at the military academy, you were interested in several females then. Do you and can you love me only?" Je Danei asked with great curiosity.

"I can and will not until you commit the same to me," the prince replied skillfully he thought with a small smile, remembering, "*Truly, my uncle and aunt, Canae's king and queen, prepared me well.*"

Je Danei continued, "My prince, as I have learned from my wise elders, 'the pursuit of love will be a series of battles with victories and defeats'. My grandparents and parents still wage war after centuries of being with each other. Is that the kind of love you want?"

The prince replied, "My limited experience and observations have shown me that love changes with time. I will do my best to communicate my love's changes and how you could best change to continue to help our love grow."

Silence.

Ony again first broke her silence, having completed her assessment of the royal suitor, "*Truly, I must say again, he is definitely not the one! His so-called 'love' is shallow, fleeting and very selfish. He would not even fight by your side in battle! He is a fool and a coward; he does not deserve you!*"

"Thank you, Prince Rho Paul for your interests and participating in my Day of Adulthood celebration. We are honored by your royal presence. Thank you," Je Danei joyfully concluded the session with an unemotional facial expression.

Je Buel took control of the session again and ended it with no further questions from the House Je Luneefa elders. She thanked the prince again on behalf of the family and asked him to leave. Everyone there rose and bowed to the prince. After the prince left, the female elders congregated around the House first daughter. Je Buel sealed the tent from outside eyes and ears.

Je Leena walked over too and hugged her sister. "How could he let you die alone in battle? Sister, please tell me again that you are not interested in that royal fool?" Je Leena asked with tear-filled eyes.

Ony growled again softly echoing her dislike for the prince too.

Je Buel just looked at her granddaughter with questioning eyes.

"Yes, grandmother, I reaffirm that the prince is still not worthy to be part of this family. I will not live in the Rhodell palace either. I most surely would not abandon my Ony for some title. My dowry, whatever it may be, would stay here; so, that fool and his family would never get their hands on it. His so-called *love* would change, probably after just a few years if not moons, and he would want to discard me. Rest assured, I am not interested in him, his title nor his family's power. I am free here in Torondell and appreciate what that freedom truly means. Why would I ever want to leave?" Je Danei said with added emphasis on her last few comments spoken loud enough for her grandfather and father to hear who both were standing nearby.

A relieved Je Taeliel just smiled to himself and nodded, appreciating that his granddaughter recognizes and acknowledges the wisdom and actions taken of her family's House first elders.

After a short break, Si Tadejo, the second son of House Si Moina was asked to come into the inner main tent for his private session of personal questions. Though formally a member of the noble House Si Moina, a dissident House in the far northern frontier and Canae's opposition, Si Tadejo claimed he has been estranged from his family for many years. His "House" is supposedly loyal to Canae, supports Canae's further expansion into the North and welcomes Canae's rule.

Je Buel thought, *"Though you appear to be completely honest, noble in character and sincere with your intentions, the elders of my House remain skeptical and wary of deceit. Elders how many blades do you carry?"*

Nui Honei first replied *"Enough to happily put a dagger in each of his eyes and two in his heart..."*

"Then, I would take his head with one of my two short swords or long knives," Nui Samu replied.

"But please command me first," Nui Honei implored, smiling evilly at the son of House Si Moina.

Nui Samu and Je Maron both hid small, near silent snickers.

"Let me start by first saying 'Thank you' for the fine horse you gifted our granddaughter; it is truly magnificent. She is a rare beauty unlike many we have seen here in Torondell," said Je Taeliel.

"You are most welcomed House great father. The horse, Starjia, is the progeny of a rare bloodline, bred for extraordinary strength, endurance, and speed. We are truly fortunate to have some of the kingdom's finest horse breeders. This is a skill my family has mastered and practiced successfully for generations," Si Tadejo remarked proudly.

Je Buel also welcomed the second son of House Si Moina and continued with introductions of her other family members and the honored guests. She next asked, "Why do you wish to court the first daughter of House Je Luneefa?"

The second son of House Si Moina took a calming breath and returned Je Buel's cold gaze replying, "After a chance meeting with her at the Autumn Festival ten years ago, I became interested given our brief conversation. She was the first to ever beat me in a knife throwing contest. I learned then she possesses a strong spirit, inner strength and confidence like no other female I have met. Like me, she is a warrior and enjoys challenges. Je Danei is also a rare beauty just like her esteemed foremothers. After we are married, we would continue to honor both great Houses by adding to our noble bloodlines through creating our own baby elves."

"The second question from the House Je Luneefa elders is this," Nui Honei remarked coldly, "Should Je Danei be engaged in battle against a large, overwhelming enemy force who had invaded your home ten years after your marriage, what would you do as her husband?"

"I would get her and our young ones to safety as best as possible. She would be my priority since we could continue making more baby elves afterwards," replied Si Tadejo.

Je Taeliel then asked the final question from the House Je Luneefa elders, "How many young ones do you have?"

"I currently have two sons," Si Tadejo replied proudly. "Their mothers are both of noble Houses too."

"*I strongly suspect this fool would just want you for breeding,*" Ony mentally communicated to Je Danei privately. In response, the House je Luneefa first daughter just continued scratching her panther's head.

"Would my pet also be welcomed in your House?" Je Danei inquired.

"Yes, of course. Your panther would be added to our collection of great bears. In fact, maybe we could even crossbreed a bear with your panther. Wouldn't that be marvelous?" replied Si Tadejo.

Ony continued to look at the second son of House Si Moina in quiet disbelief. "*He lies,*" she communicated to Je Danei. "*Great bears and panthers are natural enemies; we could not live together peacefully in the same House. And there will be no crossbreeding with me of any kind! Can I please kill this fool?"*

Je Buel concluded the personal questioning session, thanked Si Tadejo, and asked him to leave. After he left, the House first great mother magically sealed the tent again. Ony then growled loudly reflecting her immense dislike for the second son of House Si Moina.

"He lied twice," Je Taeliel announced. "Si Tadejo also has a daughter with a human. His family does not acknowledge their family's bastard children with other races at all. And Ony is a natural enemy of bears. She would have to kill them all or leave. And what was that idiot thinking when he commented about crossbreeding? Was that supposed to be a joke?" The House great father was clearly agitated and perhaps even angry.

Ony then walked over to the House great father and rubbed against his leg. She then sat next to him and growled softly.

"I believe Danei's pet just agreed with you, my husband," Je Buel interpreted. "Clearly, Si Tadejo is far from being a worthy candidate to court a daughter of this House." The House first great mother's conclusion was readily accepted by all without any doubts. "And despite your feelings, Honei and Noirar, please do not harm that fool while he is here in Torondell." Disappointedly, Nui Honei displayed the four concealed daggers she had, momentarily pouting. Nui Samu just released a long sigh, shaking his head. Je Buel then looked sternly at Alleina.

"What?" Alleina exclaimed in quiet disbelief. She sighed and then admitted, "I only secretly administered something that will disrupt his eating. His stomach discomfort will pass in a few days." Ony started mimicking laughter and was quickly joined by the House elders.

After another short break, Je Buel called the session to order to start the last and final personal questions session.

Nui Jooba returned to the main tent where the Yimibirkutla, the Day of Adulthood celebration started. Unlike before, only the House Je Luneefa family, extended family and honored guests were permitted to attend the would-be suitor's personal questioning session. Before he walked into the tent, Nui Rei told him that Pi Rhem had been asked not to continue his pursuit since Je Danei was not interested at all. House great mother Je Buel had delivered that message and the would-be suitor's response seemed to be that of 'relief'. He graciously thanked the House great mother and went to find his comrade, Lord Gabriel.

Nui Jooba was not surprised to hear the news. He thought, *"Pi Rhem is someone he felt is too old too for Je Danei. Pi Rhem is one hundred twenty years older than Je Danei and his dictatorial manner would not fit well with the spirited, independent Je Danei who would probably kill him during his first courtship visit."*

Nui Jooba also smiled to himself thinking that the first House great mother's tactic also gave Lord Gabriel someone to drink and sulk with. Lord Gabriel's being together with the fallen Pi Rhem would help soothe both their bruised egos. Nui Jooba's admiration for this felf grew as he continued his walk.

Just before he walked into the main tent, Nui Jooba saw Nui Danka and Ona Drachir standing by the entrance. Unlike before, the sides of the tent were down, and House soldiers were posted at the entrance to admit only authorized personnel.

When Nui Jooba entered the inner main tent, all the House Je Luneefa elders now sat at main center table facing him. Like before, her pet panther sat next to Je Danei piercing him with her black feline eyes. Je Danei was in the middle seat dressed in a beautiful red dress and wearing her formal, black House cape, clasped by a gold, Manriki-gusari. Nui Jooba lost his focus gazing upon Je Danei's beauty, and he wondered to himself how he would enjoy discovering all the blades she did carry...

He walked to the center of the tent in front of the center table and bowed to the House elders. The House first great mother Je Buel started, "Welcome again Nui Jooba, second son of House Nui Vent. During this portion of the Yimibirkutla celebration for my House's first daughter, I and the other elders will ask you three questions. Je Danei is also entitled to ask you up to three questions. You are honored-bound to answer all questions truthfully as best as you can. At the end of this session, we will advise Je Danei if we feel you are a worthy candidate to court our precious daughter of House Je Luneefa.

"This is another tradition to honor and glorify the family structure. Per tradition, only family members, extended family members and honored family guests are invited to participate in this portion of today's Celebration. All answers given here are confidential. Do you understand and agree to these terms?"

"Yes, House great mother," Nui Jooba replied.

Je Buel continued, "Good. You know everyone here, but House Nui Vent great mother, Nui Honei, your adopted mother, is the blood-sister of my House's great mother Je Pagi, the aunt of my granddaughters and grandsons and godmother of Je Danei. Nui Samu, your uncle, is the uncle, through adoption, of my granddaughters and grandsons and godfather of Je Danei. Alleina is an honored extended member of this family and my adopted daughter. Though not here, Ona Noirar would be another honored, extended member of House Je Luneefa; he is also an adopted son. You also know all my granddaughters and grandsons except Je Kei who is still away completing his studies at the Heartstone Architectural and Engineering Academy. My husband, House great father, Je Taeliel, will advise on Je Kei's behalf. Are you ready to begin?"

Nui Jooba again nervously replied "Yes, House first great mother."

"You have no title, no lands and no wealth. You are a former thief too. Why do you wish to court me knowing you bring little to nothing to my prestigious, noble family?" Je Danei quickly asked.

Nui Jooba felt immediate pressure from her scathing question and harsh tone. Soon beads of sweat started to form on his forehead. He took a calming deep breath and replied, "Yes, I am a former rogue, supposedly of mixed-blood, an outcast and an orphan who grew up in mean, lawless towns of the northern frontier.

"If you desire title, lands, and wealth which I believe you do not, I can acquire those in time and give them to you. I now have little to give you except my heart which I would dedicate to you only. Know also that my heart beats faster and pounds harder when I am near you. You are the only one who has ever made me feel this way.

"Like all the females of the House Je Luneefa family, you are smart, strong, courageous, independent and brave. Like you, I am a warrior, but you only fear love. You, I believe, fear that love will lessen your strength. I believe from observing our Houses' elders, love strengthens them.

"I do not know *love* like your parents and grandparents do. I also believe you do not know *love* well either. But I do know from observing your parents, your grandparents and my mother and Ona Noirar for the last many years that their *love* is incredibly special and that is what I want. You are my *one*. If you are willing to try to discover what true love is with me, I will gladly take that journey with you. I pledge my heart to only you. I pledge my loyalty, my blood and my blades to House Je Luneefa and my family. I would stand beside you in battle against any enemy and against all odds. And should I die in battle, I will do so loving you till I draw my last breath."

"Tero and I approve of this melf! He would be a good brother-in-law, son and grandson of our House!" Je Jero exclaimed. A few chuckles erupted across the tent.

"Silence!" commanded Je Taeliel.

"How many females whose pleasures have you known?" stoically asked Je Leena.

"Leena! You are not allowed to asked questions," scolded the displeased House first great mother Je Buel. Looking at Nui Jooba, she continued, "Please forgive my granddaughter's offense. You need not answer that question."

Nui Jooba glanced immediately at Je Danei after Je Leena's question was asked and noticed the House first daughter's slight hand signal. No doubt that question had been planned by the sisters he thought. "House first great mother, I am not offended, nor will I not answer the question; for I am not ashamed," Nui Jooba responded. Now looking at Je Danei, he continued, "I have no physical sexual experience. I chose and choose to wait for my *one* who will hopefully also enjoy teaching and learning how to please each other sexually."

Several quiet, private conversations commenced with that announcement. Nui Jooba could feel more sweat forming on his brow.

"Quiet please," Je Buel ordered.

"Why do you wish to join our family?" Je Maron asked.

Nui Jooba responded, "From the first day I met your wife, daughter, and my adopted mother, I was amazed by their strength, love and loyalty to each other. Je Onyxia Ryoshi was being hunted by a large pack of revengeful great wolves. Being another extended member of the House Je Luneefa family, they all chose to fight by her side regardless of the unknown odds. They would not abandon a family member who was in trouble. Till then, my experience had been that family would abandon a threatened family member in the hope of reducing the overall losses to the family. I liked and admired what I then saw as a portrayal of a real family.

"Since that time, I especially enjoyed the occasions I could help either House great mother or father prepare meals for the family. Those times were great opportunities for me to learn lessons of a dutiful son or daughter.

"Over the last ten years, I have had many conversations with House great mothers Je Buel and Je Pagi about family values and traditions. For the first two centuries of my life, I really did not have a family. The closest group I had was a gang with homeless ones, like me, who needed to survive in the northern frontier. In observing both Je Luneefa and Nui Vent families together, I saw that you all truly care for each other, laugh, cry together and support each other. At all costs, you protect each other. I found that the family elders, though strict and disciplined, absolutely love their daughters, sons, granddaughters and grandsons. In these ten years of observance, I believed in family again.

"During this same time, I also learned many things from House great fathers Je Taeliel and Je Maron. I especially enjoyed listening to the many stories they would tell of their adventures. They both willingly shared their wealth of wisdom too. I carefully watched how they interacted with the daughters and sons of the family. Like their respective wives, they too are strict and disciplined, but also love the daughters and sons of both Houses with powerful, unconditional love. All Houses' elders are extremely protective of this family and value the family's wellbeing and happiness above their own. Even Alleina, who is also an incredibly good cook, has taught me much about family while helping her in the kitchen.

"I am indeed proud to know such wonderful mothers and fathers. I have come to appreciate and greatly value the House Je Luneefa family elders' wisdom in this regard. I wholeheartedly embrace and accept these family values. I have learned much from all of you elders and wish to continue to do so whether you bless my courtship intentions or not. I am greatly appreciative of all your time and efforts."

Nui Jooba paused; tears were now forming in his eyes. He continued, saying with great sincerity, "Please know that all of you have greatly influenced me and helped make me a better melf today. Thank you all. I am still a young melf and have much more to learn from all the elders here. I want to learn and will learn more. I hope I do not burden you with too many questions or my presence. So, please be patient with me."

"*Damn you Honei; you taught him too well. He did not sweat enough,*" Je Pagi mentally communicated to her sister.

"Does any other elder have a question for Nui Jooba," asked Je Buel. "Je Danei, do you?" Her questions were only met with silence.

Ony then walked around from center table and sat on her rear legs in front of Nui Jooba. In response, Nui Jooba knelt and met the piercing gaze of the great panther. Ony, after a few moments of gazing deeply into Nui Jooba's eyes, growled lowly.

"I believe your Ony just issued a warning to me - 'that if I ever intentionally hurt Je Danei, she would kill me'," Nui Jooba interpreted for the group. "Yes, I understand completely." With that said, the great panther barred its deadly fangs in a 'smile', patted Nui Jooba on his right shoulder with her great left paw and returned to sit next to Je Danei.

Je Buel announced, "Well, then that concludes the personal questioning session. Nui Jooba, please leave now to let us discuss your candidacy in private amongst ourselves."

Nui Jooba rose, took a deep breath, and quietly released a sigh of relief. He then requested, "Before I leave, House great mother, may I say something and present tokens of my appreciation to all of you?" Je Buel nodded in approval.

Nui Jooba walked to the inner tent's entrance and asked his brothers to bring in the chest they were guarding outside. After he returned to the inner main tent, Nui Jooba opened the chest and said, "After being here for a short ten years, I care deeply for you all.

"House Je Luneefa great mothers, Mother and Alleina, I wish to give you all bouquets of these rare mountain flowers. I was told these are your favorite, first House great mother. So, I hope my informant spoke the truth." Nui Jooba next handed a bouquet of the flowers to each of the Houses' felf elders after a respectable bow. Each elder expressed her thanks in return.

"Why is Grandmother's bouquet a small bit larger than the others?" inquired an inquisitive Je Leena whose keen eyes quickly discerned the small difference. Nui Jooba cleared his throat with a small nervous cough and quickly returned to the chest to retrieve his next gift which he then presented to the House Je Luneefa second daughter.

"Je Leena, I came across this scroll of healing which I wish to give you for all your time listening to me. I was told by the scroll's renowned authors that it contains all the most important healing potions, elixirs and spells the extraordinary battlemages should know and master. It is truly rare too; for it is only the second of its kind in existence."

"And how would you know the information is genuine from a credible source? You are not experienced or knowledgeable in the areas of healing and magic," Je Leena questioned upon receiving her gift. After quickly reviewing the top portion of the scroll, she then said, "There is no need for you to answer my question. I do know that the authors are truly exceptional. Thank you, Aunties," Je Leena said bowing to Nui Honei and Alleina.

Nui Jooba reached into the chest again for more gifts to present. He next said, "And to the House Je Luneefa, Nui Vent and Ona Feiir great fathers, I give you each a bottle of Napa brandy. I intend to use all your wisdom you so graciously shared with me. Thank you all again." Nui Jooba respectfully bowed to the each melf elder followed by the gifting of the brandy. Although relieved, he was still uncertain of his chances. He turned and walked quietly out of the tent.

After he left, Je Buel again magically sealed the area from any prying eyes and ears.

Je Tero, feeling a bit cheated, said, "Why did we, his brothers in arms, not receive a gift? Afterall, did we not listen to him, as well, for these last many years? Did we not provide him with needed counseling from time to time? We also helped him a great deal..."

"Brother," Je Jero interjected. "Nui Jooba's words were sincere and honest. But, judging from the positive reactions he received from our elders, Nui Jooba is indeed spending, no investing, his coins wisely on those who can best support his intentions, don't you think?"

With an agreeing wink of an eye aimed towards her eldest grandson, Je Buel remarked, "Well said, Jero. Now, let us now expedite our ruling. Is there anyone here who would *not* approve of Nui Jooba's courtship of the first daughter of House Je Luneefa?" she asked.

A silent tent was her question's only response.

Je Danei slowly raised her hand. When she looked around the inner tent, only her hand was raised. "Ony, you can vote too. Raise your paw in agreement please," Je Danei begged. The panther only yawned in response.

"Danei, why would you object?" Je Buel asked.

"Because he is the only one, she cannot easily kill in a fight," Je Jero stated matter-of-factly. Quiet laughter across the tent erupted.

"Granddaughter, please do not fear love. Open your heart. That will not make you less strong, but more alive. Of all your would-be suitors, past and present, Nui Jooba is the worthiest. Yes, he is not wealthy with gold or land, but his wealth is rooted in his character. Nui Jooba is of humble birth and that has helped shape his noble character too.

"He will not be intimidated by you. He is kind, respects you, our family and appreciates elders. He will be patient with you on your journey of love which may end with your not loving him. That is a chance one takes. In time, if your love does grow or lessens, be honest with yourself and him. Like life, love is a journey of risks and rewards. Be brave," encouraged Je Buel.

"Also, communicate openly and honestly. Do not fear making mistakes. Honest mistakes can be forgiven; and one can learn from them. Intentional mistakes hurt. Do not hurt him intentionally; he does not deserve that. All of us elders will be watching. We can also help guide you too when you wish," Je Taeliel said with tearful eyes.

"I believe we are done here. Let us now go and continue celebrating our House daughter's Day of Adulthood with more food, drink, music and dancing!" Je Pagi declared.

House great mother Je Buel touched her husband's arm requesting his stay while everyone else left the inner main tent. "Why did you almost start to weep a few moments ago?" she asked.

Je Taeliel replied, "I love my granddaughter dearly, but she is difficult. She is a warrior; so, she presents her warrior persona *too much* at times, I believe. Her strength can be her weakness. I hope Nui Jooba truly has the patience to pursue her affections. He will need to have a great amount of inner strength to deal with Danei. I hope he does not give up too soon due to lack of progress in his *war* with our granddaughter. Frustration may discourage him."

After some reflection, Je Buel said, "Jooba seems to be quite determined. His strong will is impressive. I too love all our granddaughters and grandsons dearly. Yes, our first granddaughter is beautiful, smart, strong-willed, independent, and very capable. I also agree she will definitely *hide* behind her inner warrior in situations involving certain emotions. Jooba has been resilient when Danei intentionally hurts him with her words in the past. That was her way of dealing with her uncomfortable emotions. Time has helped her. Good armor, emotional and physical, has and will help him. Let us hope more time and good armor will help them both. Enough about her, let us now go and join the Yimibirkutla festivities. I want to dance with you again!"

The House Je Luneefa first elders rose, lovingly smiled at each other, and walked hand in hand to the other tent to join the joyous celebration.

Later, Je Buel and Je Taeliel spoke with each of the would-be suitors privately and thanked them again for their participation. The House Je Luneefa first elders informed each of them of the family elders' advice to their House first daughter. Though disappointed and even perhaps disgusted, Pi Rhem, Si Tadejo, and Lord Gabriel all thank the House elders respectfully. Prince Rho Paul became angry and just walked away thoroughly confused how any felf in the kingdom could possibly reject a potential courtship with a member of the royal family.

Late that same evening, Je Leena was escorted to a section of Torondell known for its entertainment and hospitality inns. The House Je Luneefa second daughter was treating Nui Rei and Ona

Drachir to certain rare desserts that are the specialty of the Eagle's Talon inn. The owner and main cook of this inn is Master Katsu, an ancient melf of eight hundred years with most of that time serving in the Canae army as a field cook. Whether preparing a meal for two or two thousand, Master Katsu is an exceptionally good cook with legendary cooking and logistical skills. Both Je Buel and Je Taeliel served under the cooking master early in their military careers. As punishment for their small insubordinate actions, the young House Je Luneefa great mother and father, Je Buel and Je Taeliel, were punished by working in the army's field kitchen, the place where the future House Je Luneefa elders first met.

Je Leena's reserved order of the highly demanded delicacies had to be fulfilled this night; otherwise, the desserts would be sold to other inn customers. Upon reaching the inn, they found the place crowded with many expected patrons. The inn's main room had many tables, and the crowd was joyous. The musicians also played lively tunes to keep the crowd in a festive mood, which aided their spending coins on more food and drink. After finding an empty table on the outside of the room away from the loudest groups of patrons, the three companions settled down. Je Leena ordered the fresh sweet potato pie she had reserved from a server who quickly came to their table after they sat.

"So, how are my brother's chances to successfully court your sister?" Nui Rei asked.

"Counsel him to wear his physical and emotional armor at all times when he courts my sister. As you already know, she is *challenging*. I do hope Nui Jooba is patient and does not let her emotional defense mechanisms discourage him too much. I want him to succeed too," Je Leena replied.

After eating their delicious pie, Nui Rei asked Je Leena to dance. The musicians were playing a tune to which some patrons were dancing a saltarello, a dance that incorporated skipping and hopping. Je Leena gladly accepted and the young felf and melf joined other couples already dancing. At the conclusion of the tune, both Je Leena and Nui Rei were laughing, pleased with their proficiency on the dance floor.

"Quite impressive. You two looked good together dancing," Ona Drachir remarked after Je Leena and Nui Rei returned to the table.

"Thank you, my dear friend; I owe all my dancing skills to my mother who trained my brothers and myself well in the social arts too," Nui Rei said. "and of the three of us, I am the best dancer too."

After more quiet conversations and laughter, five soldiers approached the table of the three companions. All three companions became wary of the approach and instinctively placed their hands on their weapons either ready to fight or resume peaceful conversations. Je Leena quickly recognized that two of the soldiers were battlemages she had seen earlier that day.

"Today was the second time you disrespected me; there will not be a third! I challenge you to a duel at noon. I want to know if you really can back your claims or were your words just empty. You dishonored me. The prince discharged me from his escort duty, and now I want to avenge my honor in battle and beat the arrogance out of you. I, Dariel of House Tou Ahn, battlemage of the fourth order, challenge you. What say you, insolent young bitch?" Dariel angrily challenged.

With a cold, heart-chilling stare, Je Leena replied, "Gladly. First blood or to the death? Choose wisely so you might live to see another day. You are much older than me; so, you should value your remaining days more carefully. By the way, I am ready now to battle, why wait till morrow's noon? Do you need to rest first old one? My friends and I could kill all five of you easily right here. So, why make us wait?"

"Your arrogance will be your undoing! I will not kill you, only severely humiliate you. And if I am in a good mood afterwards, I may even take you as my pleasure slave," Dariel said with a sinister smile.

"Your taking me will never happen," Je Leena responded coldly with her own sinister, evil glare. "As you wish then; let us battle to the death, at noon, at the Mesa field outside the Toronwalzwei. Now go and get your rest."

"Till noon then, my soon to-be slave," Dariel haughtily declared as he and his comrades backed away.

"Ona Drachir let us now dance too," an undisturbed Je Leena said to her friend as she took his hand and pulled him towards the dance floor. After this last dance, the three companions rode quietly back to their respective strongholds within the Toronwalein.

Although it was long past midnight, both Houses rose after learning of the upcoming duel. On their return ride to her family's stronghold, Je Leena had mentally reached out to her grandmother and aunt, Nui Honei, and informed them of the upcoming battle.

Nui Honei, Nui Samu, Ona Noirar, Ona Drachir, and the new sons of House Nui Vent made their way to the House Je Luneefa stronghold quickly. They and the Je Luneefa family congregated in the great hall where the first House elders were already there sitting quietly in front of the fire. Je Leena was there too sitting between them just staring into the depths of the fire.

After all the family and extended family members had gathered there in the hall, Je Leena apologized first and then recounted what took place at the inn. "I have but one request: under no circumstances is that fool to take me back to his House. I would rather meet my death here than to taken to his House where he would repeatedly ravaged and torture me given the rumors I have heard about his despicable House. Promise me, you will kill me first," she pleaded. "Should I fall, I want an honorable warrior's death given by the merciful hand of a loved one. Please, I implore you to grant what might be my last request."

A sad Je Jero spoke first after moments of silence, "Dearest sister, just kill that fool quickly, so we can all return home."

"Before anyone else speaks, vow to me that you will honor my request first," Je Leena tearfully replied.

"Yes, I vow I will kill you before letting you fall into the hands of House Tou Ahn," Ona Drachir pledged with a tear of sorrow running down his face.

"Yes, I too vow to kill you before letting you fall into his hands," Nui Honei solemnly pledged.

"As do I, my dear granddaughter," House Je Luneefa first great mother Je Buel sadly said.

As Je Leena looked at the others, they all nodded their heads in agreement.

The second daughter of House Je Luneefa then looked sternly at Nui Honei. "My second request is that no one here plans and executes any preemptive attack against Dariel or his House before my battle. Please, do this honor for me too. This is my first duel, and I must battle alone. I will face him bravely. Especially you Rei and Drachir, do not interfere. Do not try to kill Dariel before my battle. Promise me now," Je Leena looked at her friends and stared coldly at them waiting for their pledges.

"Wait, Danei you came late. Where is Ony? Call her back now!" Je Leena demanded. "And do not insult my intelligence by denying you already sent your pet to kill that fool."

"Damn, Sister... Forgive me," Je Danei apologetically admitted. Moments later, the House Je Luneefa first daughter said, "Ony is returning; she did not kill him."

"Dear family and friends, I have only lived a short lifetime of less than two hundred years without being in any serious battles other than training. I will not dishonor my House nor you. I will bravely face Dariel in one-on-one combat and will be victorious should fate have it so. Please understand, I must do this alone," Je Leena said.

"I will do as you wish and not kill that mage before your battle," Ona Drachir pledged.

"Nor will I either," a dejected Nui Rei confessed looking like someone who had just been caught in the act of stealing.

"Last, but not least, you, my *newly-risen-from-the-dead* uncle must pledge to me as well, please. You would be the perfect assassin now, but stay your hand," Je Leena requested looking at Ona Noirar.

"As you wish; I too pledge not to kill this battlemage before your battle," Ona Noirar quietly said. "But he and his House will be eliminated should you fall. That too I promise."

"As do I pledge all of House Tou Ahn will die horrible deaths should you fall, my beloved niece," Alleina declared.

"There is some time left before dawn. Let me spend a moment with each of you alone. After dawn, Grandmother and Auntie, please return here to help me make final preparations for my battle," Je Leena requested. "Danei, please meet with me first in our sitting room." The two sisters then quietly walked out of the hall.

After a few moments, Je Danei returned to the hall along with her panther. Je Danei then asked her brothers to go and meet with Je Leena. Nui Danka was next to meet with Je Leena followed by Nui Jooba.

When Nui Rei met with Je Leena, he walked into the room with a big smile to help encourage her and alleviate her profoundly serious mood. Before the melf could speak, she grabbed him, pushed him against the closed door, and kissed him deeply and passionately. After releasing him, Je Leena whispered smiling "Hush. Do not speak. Just kiss me again as if I might not return."

After fulfilling her wish, Nui Rei pleaded, "Please be victorious today then; so, we can both celebrate your victory tonight."

"Ha, ha, ha," Je Leena laughed. "Thank you for your encouragement and friendship. Return and ask Ona Drachir to come here." Nui Rei left a bit stunned to find Ona Drachir.

Ona Drachir silently entered the room and shut the door. When Je Leena turned around to face him, she saw the normally stoic melf welcoming her with a big smile and open arms. Like before, she walked into Ona Drachir's waiting arms kissed him deeply and passionately. "Does this mean you like melfs now, especially this melf?" he asked.

Now, Je Leena was a bit puzzled and before she could say anything, Ona Drachir continued, "We can talk again later after your victory. I will now take my leave. Whom would you like to see next?"

Afterwards, the House Je Luneefa second daughter met with each of the remaining family members to also extend her thanks and goodbyes.

Shortly after dawn, she met with her mentors House great mothers Je Buel and Nui Honei. Both elder felfs were highly skilled and experienced battlemages. The elder felfs led Je Leena through some mental and physical exercises, reviewed some useful tactics and strategies, and imparted more dueling wisdom. Lastly, Je Buel extended another special gift to her granddaughter, a vial of dragon's blood potion. After cutting her hand and letting a few drops of her blood mix with the contents of the vial, Je Buel cited an incantation to activate the magic of the potion. Je Leena then drank the entire contents of the potion.

Nui Honei then cut her palm and the palms of Je Leena's outstretched hands. The adopted aunt then performed another blood-magic ritual releasing and bonding her crescent swords to the House Je Luneefa second daughter. Nui Honei said afterwards, "Again, I will only *loan* you my prized swords today. You are to return these to me after your victory. Put all your training into practice; summon your battle-rage; and kill your enemy without hesitation and without mercy."

The elder felfs hugged Je Leena warmly. The young felf bowed to her elders and quietly left the room.

After Je Leena left the room, the elder felfs started crying quietly. "Should she fall today, I will kill everyone in House Tou Ahn and any other who stands in my way," Je Buel vehemently proclaimed.

"You and I," Nui Honei pledged too.

When Je Leena arrived at her bedchamber, she found her sister waiting there quietly. With a few hours left before noon, Je Danei wanted to personally attend to her sister. After cleaning herself in her private water room, Je Leena took a short nap. She was awakened by her sister who was now dressed in her light battle armor. Je Danei helped her sister dress and put on her light amor. Je Leena favored long knives and carried two at her sides, the two Nimru long knives gifted to her from Ona Noirar. She placed the crescent swords on her back in a special holster. Lastly, she put on her House cape adorned with her Manriki-gusari clasp.

Before leaving the Je Luneefa stronghold, Je Leena was met by all her family and extended family members. They all had shaved heads on the sides with a middle, three-fingers high, head band of black and red hair from the front to the back of their heads. Each was also wearing armor and their House cape. Je Buel stepped forward and said, "There is one more thing I need to do." The House great mother cited a magical incantation and Je Leena's hair matched the others. House Je Luneefa, House Nui Vent and Ona Feiir were united and ready for war!

Je Buel rode next to her granddaughter and led the united Houses' family members, along with half of their House army, through the western gate of the Toronwalein. At the gate and along the wall, all the remaining House soldiers came to attention and saluted the departing family members.

The united Houses' family members and soldiers arrived at the designated battleground before noon. To their surprise, a few tents had already been erected to house certain spectators. One of the interested bystanders is Prince Rho Paul. With him were Si Tadejo, Pi Rhem and Lord Gabriel. All four rejected suitors of the House Je Luneefa first daughter still seemed a bit angry with losing the privilege to formally court the House Le Luneefa first daughter. All four rejected suitors also had an accompanying entourage and combined would exceed the size of the Je Luneefa group.

After receiving an invitation from Prince Rho Paul, Je Jero rode to the prince's tent and dismounted. After greeting the prince and his guests, he wanted to apologize personally for not staying at the prince's tent to watch the duel.

"I see your family came prepared for war. Why is that when it is just a duel between two battlemages?" Si Tadejo asked.

"This should not be much of a duel. Your sister is still incredibly young; her opponent has been in many battles, skilled and at least two hundred years her senior. Today, she will fall no doubt," Pi Rhem disdainfully noted.

Je Jero replied looking at the prince, "Understand three things. One: Houses Je Luneefa, Nui Vent and Ona Feiir stand as one. We always support each other. Two: Dariel will most assuredly die today. Whether or not my sister dies is still uncertain. Three: And should my sister fall, I *will* kill everyone here in Dariel's House and anyone who stands in my way." The House Je Luneefa first son then looked at Pi Rhem and declared, "Please do not misunderstand my message. This is not a threat, but a solemn promise." After bowing to the prince, Je Jero left and returned to his family's group leaving the prince and his friends in shock with his ominous warning.

Dariel emerged from a tent flying the flag of House Si Moina. House Tou Ahn was a smaller House and closely related to House Moina through several marriages. He was wearing his bluish grey and brown full body armor and carried two short swords at his sides and a short shield on his arm. This battlemage covered his head with a helmet, also bluish grey with a plume of brown horsehair down the center. On either side of the plume is an image of a snake, most likely a replica of a poisonous viper. Four coiled snake replicas were also on his shield as the centerpiece used for bashing.

"*Granddaughter beware the snakes on his helmet and shield. Most likely he can bring them to life to strike at you,*" warned Je Buel who instinctively communicated her warning mentally and privately to Je Leena.

Dariel walked confidently to the center of the Mesa field which was just a small clearing of land before the Toronwalzwei western gate. He was accompanied by his seconds, a male and female, both clad in armor and carried weapons. These other two were most likely battlemages, as well.

Being challenged, Je Leena could enter the designated field of battle last. After dismounting her horse, she was joined on foot by her grandmother and Nui Honei. Je Leena bowed to her grandfather and then her parents. She then turned and walked to the center of the Mesa field about twenty steps away from her adversary.

"It is nice to see that your whole family came to witness your defeat, little bitch," yelled Dariel. "Your defeat will come slowly and with much pain, I assure you. I do hope your teachers taught you well. Buel and Honei, your proud Houses too will fall, just like this young one will fall this day!" He then turned to his seconds and ordered them to leave.

Je Leena bowed and smiled at her grandmother and aunt. The young felf then turned and then looked defiantly at Dariel. Je Buel and Nui Honei left the field returning to their mounts. Je Leena drew her crescent swords and assumed a defensive position waiting for her opponent to initiate the first attack.

Dariel drew his sword with his right hand and assumed a standard attacking position with shield in front and his sword in the upper right area of his shield. "Are you still a virgin by chance? I do hope so. That will make my taking you even more pleasurable. Ha, ha, ha, ha...," Dariel arrogantly yelled his inquiry.

Je Leena offered no response, choosing to concentrate on the battle at hand.

Duels between battlemages often do not include close quarters combat since spells can be cast from a distance.

"Did I tell you how I plan to take you? No? Then know that each of your limbs will be tied taut to my bedpost as you lie naked on your stomach. I will then ravage you as much as I want and as often as I please. Ha, ha, ha, ha..." Dariel continued his verbal torment as he advanced towards his opponent.

When Dariel reached a distance about ten steps from his opponent, he launched a non-verbal attack of emitting bright sunlight from his shield's centerpiece. In addition, he was able to leave his sword and shield floating in the air while he moved away from them. Both weapons continued to point at his opponent with deadly purpose. Dariel next started throwing bolts of magic at the hopefully surprised and blinded Je Leena.

When Je Leena initially detected Dariel's arm movement to perhaps release his shield, she quickly summoned her dragon eyes' vision. This magic spell would protect her eyes with its own covering like that of a dragon. She also moved instinctively to her right and blocked the thrown magic bolts with her swords, weapons designed and specially crafted for battles of magic.

"Impressive. You avoided my first attack; that is good. We must prolong this deadly game. However, I do expect much more from you!" Dariel yelled ever taunting his opponent.

Je Leena uttered a spell and patches of earth around Dariel became tar pits upon which if he stepped, he would be entrapped. As expected, her opponent avoided those areas by moving away. Dariel cast and hurled more magical bolts at Je Leena who blocked them all again with her swords. When Dariel tried to encapsulate Je Leena with a wall of magic, the felf simply cut her way through it with her crescent blades. The power of her aunt's crescent blades was also enhanced with dragon's blood and made them even more powerful. Meanwhile Je Leena was moving closer to her enemy. Je Leena thought, *"Fool! My plan will ensnare you in one of the tar pits I set earlier."*

Dariel hurled more fire bolts at Je Leena, but she was well protected by her House cape and her armor. The older melf continued to move towards his shield.

Je Leena evoked another spell and started spinning her swords. At certain points in her movement, multiple beams or darts of magic from the crescent, half-moon portions of her swords were hurled towards Dariel. He in turn quickly cast a spell of magic to shield him from the onslaught of missiles hurled at him.

The older melf continued to move towards and eventually

recovered his shield and sword. Now feeling more secure with his recovered weapons in hand, he screamed a battle cry and charged Je Leena, hoping to surprise the inexperienced battlemage. When about five steps away from the young felf, he issued a command, and all six snakes came alive and leapt at their intended target. Dariel announced loudly, "These are special serpents trained to latch onto their intended target, find a bare, unarmored part of an opponent and bite several times. The snakes' venom is either poisonous or will immobilize the intended target. Oh, I do hope I prepared the right venom; I do not wish for you to die this day. Ha, ha, ha. Such are the dark arts I practice."

In response, Je Leena immediately *vanished*. All the snakes missed her but landed in the tar pits she had set. Upon capture, the tar pits immediately started burning their hopelessly trapped victims. The snakes could not escape and were now no longer a threat to her.

Meanwhile, Dariel cast a spell trying to detect his now invisible enemy somewhere around him. He also cast another spell encircling himself with a high protective wall of magic. Fear could be heard in his voice as he again taunted Je Leena, "Where are you now hiding? I want to play with you more." But it was too late; fear no longer gripped her, and her patience had expired...

Je Leena had leapt high into the air with the aid of her House cape and descended slowly down behind her enemy, inside his protective wall undetected. She then removed both his hands with a swift, mighty swing of her swords. Dariel screamed in pain from his severed hands. His magical shield now could no longer be maintained; so, it fell immediately. When he turned around and saw his now visible nemesis, he then tried to kick the felf. Je Leena blocked his kick with her arm and countered with a powerful kick of her own to his chest that launched him off his feet and hurled him several steps away. She sheathed her swords.

All could now see the rage on Je Leena's face. Intense, powerful battle-rage had now engulfed her. Moving her hands in the deadly Engere martial arts form while citing another incantation, she raised the tortured Dariel off the ground in front of her and above her head for all to witness her merciless fury. Her magic stretched him taut by his head and four limbs. Dariel screamed uncontrollably in fury-magnified intense pain. Je Leena continued to stretch all his limbs and head as she walked away towards the House Je Luneefa party. The tortured floating Dariel followed her. She increased his pain with each of her steps until his cries of severe agony were punctuated by the sound of each limb being savagely torn away from his body. Lastly, his head was finally ripped from his dead body. The young battlemage glanced at the crowd of spectators; her evil stare sent a silent message. When Je Leena finally lowered her arm, Dariel's decapitated corpse fell hard to the ground.

Je Leena mounted her horse and rode away, back to the House Je Luneefa stronghold. She was quickly followed by her family and House soldiers.

None of the royal nor noble spectators mourned the death of Dariel. All though clearly understood the ominous message issued: *Houses Je Luneefa, Nui Vent and Ona Feiir stand united and ready and able to meet all challenges. Be warned*!

# Homecoming

House Je Luneefa great mothers Je Buel and Je Pagi, along with great father Je Maron, finally arrived at the foot of the Blood Tears Mountains range. These mountains were the stronghold and center of the dwarven lands of the Canae kingdom. Throughout these mountains various clans of dwarves, the largest of which is the Battle Hammer clan, inhabited these mountains. Other prominent dwarf clans include the Staraxe, Red Hammer, and Storm Rock. The Je Luneefa party had made the eight-days trek there in time for Je Kei's graduation two days hence from the famed dwarf Heartstone Architectural and Engineering Academy.

Je Kei is the third and youngest son of House Je Luneefa. After his first completion of the House Je Luneefa stronghold, Duenor Heartstone went back to his home in the Blood Tears Mountains. Heartstone did return to Torondell from time to time to inspect the work that had been completed and to review the current and future work plans he had designed. During those visits, Je Kei maintained his keen interest in the master dwarf's craft and often would follow him on his work inspection and review visits. When not doing his duties or studying, Je Kei was like Heartstone's shadow. He loved this dwarf as much as he loved his family. Je Kei also had a gift for engineering and construction too unlike any other elf in the kingdom. So, it came as no surprise when he met with his House elders to request their permission to pursue further studies at the famous dwarf academy of engineering and architecture in Heartstone's homeland. So, on his last inspection and review visit,

Duenor Heartstone returned to his homeland with an honored guest, Je Kei of the House Je Luneefa family.

Founded by and named after Duenor Heartstone's grandfather, Dueson Heartstone, another gifted dwarf engineering and architecture prodigy. This was indeed a particularly, momentous event for the Je Luneefa family, because Je Kei was the first non-dwarf to ever graduate from this highly acclaimed academy with highest honors. To no Je Luneefa family member's surprise, Je Kei did exceptionally well in his engineering and architectural studies. The dwarves, being masters of metal, stone, and rock, continued opening new tunnels in their beloved mountains and strengthened their stronghold. Je Kei even had opportunities to help design and build some of these additions and enhancements. This was an exceedingly rare honor for a non-dwarf. In time, he even earned respect and high praise from the tough, stubborn dwarves for his hard work and capabilities.

When the Je Luneefa party arrived at the southern gate of the Blood Tears Mountains stronghold, they were greeted by a royal honor guard and several royal dignitaries. Prince Dajald, the king's second grandson and Urtha Dal, blood-sister of Je Buel, warmly greeted the Je Luneefa entourage. Also, in the welcoming party was the Je Luneefa third son, Je Kei whose joy of seeing his family elders was quite evident on his young, one hundred ninety years old, handsome face. "Grandmother, mother and father, welcome!" he said as he hugged each of his parents affectionately.

"On behalf of me king and queen, grandfader and grandmoder, I, Prince Dajald, welcome ye to our home," greeted the prince.

The Je Luneefa family elders bowed to the prince. "Thank you, Your Highness; it is our pleasure to be here," replied House great mother Je Buel.

"Ye keep gettin' prettier, me see Sister," Urtha Dal proclaimed as she moved through the dwarf welcoming crowd towards Je Buel who walked hurriedly towards Urtha Dal, smiling with open arms too.

"It has been way too long since we last met. It is so incredibly good to see you again too, dear Sister. We have much to discuss," Je Buel said.

After the evening meal, King Djurdin Joerson and Queen Djurdin Marta led the Je Luneefa family elders to another room where they could talk privately. Joining them was also Urtha Dal. Although large, the room was cozy with a table containing decanters of wine and jugs of ale along with platters of cheese, bread, and fruit.

A roaring fire kept the room quite comfortable despite it being deep within the mountain stronghold. There were two sets of four chairs facing each other. Four chairs easily accommodated either human or elf guests comfortably while the other four chairs were designed for dwarves and other smaller folk. Shortly after settling into the room, the guards admitted two servants who carried a chest and a sack. These items were placed on the floor near the dwarves and elves. After the servants left, the guards closed the doors again.

"Queen Marta and King Joerson, we bear you gifts. We would like to give you these rocks," said Je Buel. She opened the sack and poured out several large, ordinary-looking rocks. The six rocks looked like ordinary stones of different shapes and sizes; but all were an unremarkable grey in color and seemingly had no value nor other distinguishing qualities.

"First, we be awfully close friends here in me private sittin' room; so, call me by dat *close friend* name ye gave me. Secondly, rocks eh? Nah, stop yer jokin' Bueli. What ye really got me?" asked King Joerson who now seemed a bit disappointed.

"Please, Bueli, fergive me husband. Even dough he be old and wise; he can still act like a youngin' dwarf who gets excited over gifts," Queen Marta explained apologetically. "He been eyein' dat chest ye brought wid ye, hopin' his gift be in dat."

"Then let him choose his gift," said Je Buel pointing to the chest and rocks. "Joeri, please choose then between this chest or these rocks."

"Hmmm... me dinkin' ye got me somedin' nice and shiny in dat chest. But rocks? Me live in a mountain full of rocks. Me been around rocks all me life. Gonna be entombed in a rock like me forefaders too. Me do not need any more rocks me dink. What ye dink, Dalli? Ye did dis to me once befer too. Did ye tell Bueli bout dat time dinkin' it be fun again?" questioned King Joerson.

Urtha Dal thought for a few moments then looked at her cousin and said, "Ye know cousin, Bueli be a mage and a good one too. So, do not let yerself be fooled by dose ordinary-lookin' rocks. Dey may not be only plain, ugly rocks."

"Shhh Dali; please do not spoil the surprise," Je Buel requested smiling warmly. "Actually, Your Majesties, all these rocks and the contents of this chest are for you both."

Now beaming with a huge smile from ear to ear, King Joerson is quite pleased to now know he and his wife are getting multiple gifts. "Marti, ye open de chest den," the king said enthusiastically rubbing his hands happily in anticipation.

Queen Marta walked over to the chest and opened it. On top

were two bottles; both were resting atop a bolt of rare, dragon cloth. She pulled the bottles out, one in each hand, and showed them to her husband with a big smile.

"Let me guess; dat be Napa brandy?" asked King Joerson. "One of dose bottles be fer me Marti; so, do not go dinkin' ye be drinkin' dem both!"

"Ye got yer rocks; so, play wid dem!" Queen Marta jested, grinning at her husband. Hugging both bottles, she then looked at the king with a big smile and simply said, "Mine!" She put the bottles aside and presented the precious cloth to the king.

The king, upon seeing the dragon's cloth, opened his eyes as wide as he could and sked, "Be dat what me dink it be?"

"Yes, Joeri, it is very rare dragon's cloth that has been enhanced with the blood of our dear friend, the black dragon, Ona Kei Kuri Ryuu. I have already released the cloth's bond to Dali and she will release and bind it to you and Marti through another blood-magic ritual," Je Buel said.

"So, be nice to me Cousin or me will use a spell to make ye itch instead! Ye should start by sharin' some of yer brandy wid me now, me dinkin'," announced Urtha Dal as she extended a glass to her cousin, the queen, to fill.

"Anything else in there?" asked Je Maron.

Now curious, King Joerson rose from his chair, walked over to the chest, and peaked inside. "Looks empty now," the king said. Still, he lifted the chest, shook it a few times and placed it back down on the floor. "Like me said, it be empty."

"Are you sure? Look more closely," said Je Buel. She then waved her hand and magically released two locks that then released two hidden compartments on the sides of the chest. Within each compartment was a jewel-encrusted gold chain, one for the king and one for the queen. The centerpiece of each chain was a disc of diachrom marked with the heraldic sigil of the king's Clan Battle Hammer, a double-headed battle hammer between two mountains. Attached to the gold chain on each side of the centerpiece were a variety of jewels, including diamonds, rubies, and emeralds.

Both King Joerson and Queen Marta were astonished by this last gift.

"Bueli, Pagi and Mari, me words me cannot find to express me danks for such wonderful gifts. Dank ye all," King Joerson said.

"Yes, many, many dank yous too," added the tearful queen extremely honored by the House Je Luneefa elders.

Je Buel responded, "Dear Joeri and Marti, you opened your home and your hearts to the youngest son of our family for the last eight years. And that was only for his formal education. Before that time, Kei was here for a few years to learn your Dwarven ways and customs. Taeli, I and my House cannot thank you enough for your kindness and generosity. These are just small tokens of our sincere appreciation for your very generous hospitality."

The king and queen both took a few moments to admire all their exquisite gifts.

"Wait. Now, me be a wee bit confused," said King Joerson. "After dese wonderful gifts, why also give us rocks? Wait. Are dey really rocks? Why would anyone give a mountain-dwellin' dwarf rocks? Grew up wid rocks around me all me life... Rocks still around me now. Me even be dyin' under dis here rock of a mountain too me wager. So, Bueli, ye be trickin' me again wid yer magic?"

Je Maron picked up all six "rocks" and placed them on the floor in front of the queen and king. With another wave of her hand, Je Buel removed the magical veil of disguise from the rocks to reveal their true nature. Before the king and queen were two large "rocks" of pure, unrefined diachrom, the hardest metal in the world and three large rocks of pure gold. Of all the ore in all the mountains, none was prized more than diachrom. It is known to be the strongest metal to exist. Kings and queens would boast about small jewelry pieces made from the precious ore; yet before Queen Marta and King Joerson was enough diachrom to forge at least two battle hammers or short swords. The last rock enclosed a vial that would glow alternately from a soft red to black.

"Dali, please seal the room!" ordered the king. Urtha Dal immediately complied as ordered by magically sealing the room from sight and sound; so, no one outside the room could see or hear what was about to take place or said in the room.

"We unfortunately missed your Day of Birth celebration; so, these 'rocks' are also a belated birthday gift," Je Pagi announced.

Still reeling from the shock of receiving a kings' ransom worth of precious treasure, King Joerson then asked, "Where did ye find dese here rocks? And is dat dere a vial of dragon's blood?"

Smiling, Je Buel said, "We have a story to tell you first before I answer your questions." Je Buel recalled and shared the time when Ona Noirar and his dragon left the Taurus Mountain to go to Toron Mountain where the famed warrior needed to recover from severe poisoning. She continued, saying, "Within the Taurus Mountain, they had discovered rich gold and diachrom deposits there over a century ago and they kept that discovery a well-guarded secret, only sharing that knowledge with the elders of Houses Je Luneefa and Nui Vent. Before leaving their Taurus Mountain stronghold to go to the Toron Mountain, Keiku destroyed much of the Taurus Mountain peak to further hide the precious treasures.

"With much time passing and with the dwarves of Clan Battle Hammer seeking a second stronghold, the elders of Houses Je Luneefa and Nui Vent agreed that sharing this rare opportunity would yield many advantages for all. The least of which Taeli and I thought that their share of treasure was another inheritance we could pass on to our daughters, sons, granddaughters and grandsons. Somehow all the House elders knew any treasure recovered could sustain Houses Je Luneefa, Nui Vent and Ona Feiir for centuries to come."

More discussions followed. After drinking a bottle of brandy and several tankards of the king's finest ale, the elder dwarves and elves were all in a joyous mood. Queen Marta and King Joerson both greatly enjoyed the story of the birthday rocks.

"So, to be sure, me ears heard ye right Bueli, ye want me to send an expedition party to dis Taurus Mountain where ye found dese here rocks. Dere bound to be more, maybe, even a mountain full of dem. Ye be not sure dough. And yer family only wants a small share of what we mine each year? Yer cut starts at twenty-five percent, den twenty percent de second year, fifteen percent de next year, ten percent after dat, and only five percent fer de next ninety-six years. No more cuts fer ye after de hundredth year. Be dis what me hearin' Bueli?" queried King Joerson.

Queen Marta quickly added, "Dis Taurus Mountain be in de nord nordern frontier; so, King Rho John be no claim to dem. And we be not owin' him any Canae taxes since Taurus Mountain be not in de Canae kingdom. But, he may be stirrin' up trouble dere for ye."

"Hmmm.... Dere be too many dwarves here now in our beloved stronghold of Blood Tears Mountains; so, expandin' not too far away would be good. Dese new mountains be only a six to eight-day journey away too. It would be excitin' again to explore fer anoder second stronghold. And we be closer to our dear friends here too, only two days away from dose mountains. What say ye, Bueli?" King Joerson asked.

"Joeri, 'Yes', your ears heard correctly and Marti, 'Yes', we would love to have our very dear friends closer. It is always good to have good neighbors close. We could all see each other more often," Je Buel remarked.

"So den, how big of an expedition party do ye dink we be needin' and when?" asked King Joerson.

"Perhaps three full teams of miners, one for each main shaft we know of. Could you meet us there by the next full moon which is about sixteen days from now?" asked Je Buel.

"Also, this frontier is still a bit lawless with several marauding Houses and renegade orc tribes. Your miners will need adequate protection. So, maybe one thousand warriors too should accompany them?" warned a thoughtful Je Buel.

"Hmm... dat may not be enough warriors, especially if dose marauders and renegades be not likin' us much fer bein' der new neighbors. Me dink two dousand warriors should be enough dough. How dat sound me Queen?" King Joerson pondered out loud, looking at his queen.

After some quiet thought, Queen Marta replied, "Just two dousand warriors might give our neighbors de wrong idea about der own strengths and capabilities. Some of dem orc tribes be large me hear and may want to prove demselves. Dey may even dink dey could beat and drive us away. So, me dinkin we should send dree dousand warriors, includin' a brigade of our fearsome Mountain Wreckers, to quickly remove any doubt from der minds. Dat way dey will not even try, me hopin'. We save more dwarf lives dat way too me dink," the ever-wise Queen Marta reasoned.

After a bit of more thoughtful silence, Je Maron asked raising his tankard, "Are we all in agreement then?" The others raised their tankards too and collectively responded "Aye" enthusiastically.

"Now dat de business be settled; we got a wee bit of a surprise fer ye too. But we will save ours till tomorrow night after de graduation ceremony," announced Queen Marta.

"What, more rocks?" asked Je Buel jokingly. In response, both dwarf and elf elders laughed hard as they enjoyed more wonderful ale and delicious food.

The next day, the graduation ceremony took place in the Blood Tears Mountains' Heartstone Architectural and Engineering Academy amphitheater. Of all the places within the Academy, this place is the most revered. For it was here that all the great Academy professors and each class *First* graduates were enshrined along the walls. Each honoree has a bust of marble or granite resting on a pedestal.

King Joerson and Queen Marta formally welcomed everyone to the graduation ceremony. They both proudly wore their new, royal gold chains they had received. Duenor Heartstone, clad in his professor's finest robes, spoke next. He also welcomed the guests and presided over the graduation ceremony's activities. After introducing the Academy's staff, he then called each graduate to the stage where she or he received a scroll signifying that she or he had successfully completed the architectural and engineering academy curriculum.

Forty-eight graduates completed the arduous eight-year program. Forty of the graduates were dwarves, seven were human and one, the first, was an elf. Not only was he the first elf to graduate from the prestigious Academy, but he had also earned special honors for being ranked first in his graduating class. Je Kei was the youngest son of House Je Luneefa and the first, non-military academy graduate.

When Je Kei, the last announced graduate, went to receive his graduation scroll, Duenor Heartstone kept him on stage a bit longer. To the graduating class first student, Je Kei was awarded a chain of rocks. The names of the current year's Academy' graduates, each Academy professor and the first student were inscribed on the chain. That chain was proudly presented to Je Kei by his mentor, Duenor Heartstone.

Prior to qualifying to enter the dwarf architectural and engineering academy, Je Kei had been studying under the great dwarf builder Duenor Heartstone. Duenor Heartstone was world renowned as the greatest engineer of the last few centuries. Je Kei, an aspiring young engineer and builder too, was accepted as an apprentice over ten years ago. Even before he became Duenor's apprentice, Je Kei "invested" over a year living amongst the dwarves just to earn the right to be considered for the prestigious apprenticeship. Fortunately, his grandmother has a good, close, centuries old relationship with King Joerson, of the Battle Hammer Clan, who gladly endorsed and hosted the Je Luneefa elf while he lived in the dwarf stronghold at the Blood Tears Mountains. Je Kei's successful apprenticeship also earned him Duenor Heartstone's endorsement to the highly selective Heartstone Architectural and Engineering Academy.

Though his family is very close to the Clan Battle Hammer leaders, Je Kei received no favors or special privileges. In fact, he had to work harder than any other student to earn recognition. Rightfully so, Je Kei persevered through the difficulties to earn his graduation ranking.

To no Je Luneefa family member's surprise, Je Kei did exceptionally well in his engineering and architectural studies. He has a keen mind and is gifted. Unlike his warrior siblings growing up, Je Kei spent his free time studying construction history, engineering, and architecture. He loved to build and repair things; so, it was not unusual for him to help with the construction of additions to the Je Luneefa stronghold. Further, Je Kei had often journeyed around Torondell helping others with needed repairs to their dwellings too.

At the dwarf Academy graduation ceremony, he was honored by earning the First Place in the Class award. After the ceremony, Duenor Heartstone praised him privately before his House elders when he said, "Laddy, stones be in yer blood unlike me ever seen befer in someone oder dan a dwarf! Go now, leave yer mark on dis world wid yer great buildings and engineerin' feats. Return to us when ye be ready to learn more of me craft." The proud Je Luneefa family elders were indeed incredibly pleased with Je Kei's accomplishments and thanked his mentor for all that he had done for Je Kei over the past decades.

A variety of guests also arrived to attend the graduation ceremonies and the reception. Supporting family members, both noble and commoner, were there to witness their loved ones' graduation. Representatives from each major town, near and far, in the kingdom were reflected in this graduating class. Members of the royal court, including the king's own chief commander of the army's engineering brigade, were there. This official, Rho Phillip, the king's cousin, was also there to privately recruit new members for the army's engineering brigade.

Most of the graduates had received sponsorship from their respective towns or kingdoms; so, they had commitments to first fulfill to those places. However, there were a few graduates though, like Je Kei, who had no such requirement to return to his hometown.

Rho Phillip desperately wanted Je Kei in the king's engineering brigade. "Tell me young Je Luneefa, what would it take to get you to enlist into the king's engineering brigade?" asked the commander when he was able to have a private conversation with Je Kei after the graduation ceremony.

"Commander Rho Phillip, thank you for your kind consideration. I am flattered that you would even think I am worthy of joining your elite group. You have built a highly regarded brigade, well known across the kingdom. But I must say, I have family obligations that I must first fulfill after my graduation. So, I must respectfully decline any offer that would again take me away from my family and Torondell," responded the gracious Je Kei.

At that same moment, House Je Luneefa great mother and father, Je Pagi and Je Maron, joined their son. They greeted the commander politely. "Commander, I hope our son has already told you that he has commitments in Torondell that he now needs to fulfill after his graduation. Surely, you understand," Je Pagi said.

"Of course, of course I understand. I had to at least try to lure him away. Torondell continues to grow and prosper. It still can attract and retain great talents like your son, but Rhodell is the center of our kingdom; its wonders exceed all other cities in our kingdom by three-fold at least. A talented and noble melf like Je Kei would have so many more opportunities in Rhodell, the capital, to prosper. I can also guarantee him certain advantages too by being his sponsor. Maybe one day in the not-too-distant future, he could join us," remarked Commander Rho Phillip.

"Perhaps one day. For the time being though, he has at least a half century's worth of work to do now in Torondell. The sooner Je Kei can start fulfilling these obligations, the sooner he can then travel to other parts of the kingdom," remarked Je Maron.

Now knowing his attempted lure was completely unsuccessful, Commander Rho Phillip bowed respectfully to the House Je Luneefa great mother and father and politely took his leave.

"You do know that new wing on our stronghold would only take two more years to complete and I do not recall any other commitments I have beyond that," Je Kei said to his parents privately, a bit puzzled.

"My dear Grandson, there are many other things that require your attention in our city, the least of which is spending another half century just with your grandparents who missed you very much. So, your commitments in Torondell will require you to be there at least for the next one hundred or so years," selfishly interjected House first great mother Je Buel. She had silently approached her family and heard the last portion of the commander's plea. Je Buel smiled, thinking, *"The King's attempt again, through his puppet commander, to divide my family failed, as expected."* She also wanted to again reinforce the fact that she wanted her family close, protected within the Je Luneefa stronghold and lands. Je Buel hugged her grandson very warmly, and then said, "We all sincerely missed you very much these last several years. You have grown some and you are more handsome too, perhaps even our most handsome grandson now. We are all immensely proud of you too for completing your studies and graduating first in your class. You again honor our family. But it is time now for you to return home."

Je Kei responded, "Thank you, Grandmother. My family's support throughout my years meant a great deal to me. They helped me get through many difficult times. Even the food you sent from time to time reduced my loneliness and home sickness. The thoughts of all of you and your support strengthened me during those difficult periods here. I am very appreciative. I am also very humbled too for becoming a member of an extraordinary group of architects and engineers who were first in their respective graduating classes. Those dwarves accomplished much through many spectacular wonders in this world. I hope and wish I can honor them and Duenor Heartstone with my future work, as well."

"In time, you will; we have no doubts about that," declared a proud Je Pagi. "Now, let us enjoy this feast. Afterwards, we have some family business to discuss."

Later that night, King Joerson, Queen Marta, Urtha Dal and the House Je Luneefa elders all met again in the same sitting room for another private discussion. They were later joined by Prince Dajald and Je Kei.

"Out of me way, ye sons of mountain goats or me will bash yer heads in wid me fists! De six of ye ain't enough to stop me eider!" shouted a new, late arriving guest from outside their room.

"Ah, me broder be arrived, if me ears hear right," announced King Joerson who nodded to the guards who quickly unlocked the room's heavy stone, steel-reinforced doors. With the last bolt unlocking the doors, they were immediately pushed inward, knocking over the two guards. There in the doorway stood a bulkier, meaner-looking version of King Joerson, his twin brother Roerson, the scarred commander of the famed Mountain Wreckers Brigade of Clan Battle Hammer.

"Roeri, you finally returned!" said House great mother Je Buel who stood, smiled, and opened her arms to the dwarf commander.

"After we cleared out dose would-be robbers, we marched back here as fast as we could. Me and me boys would not miss dis chance to see ye again," said Roerson as he walked over to the House Je Luneefa first great mother and gave her a mighty hug. After a few moments, he released her. "Fergive me everyone. I ferget me manners again." Addressing the king and queen, Roerson quickly said while bowing, "Yer Majesties." He then turned to Je Pagi and Je Maron and greeted them warmly with a big smile, "Honored guests, welcome to me home.

"Me apologies fer me poor manners, but whenever me see dis wonderful felf, me mind goes back one hundred fifty-eight years now, me believe, durin' dat time of famine. Not only did her party brave drough harsh weader, but she also defied dat fool king's orders by gettin' food here. Befer me and me brigade got dere; she beat de would-be raiders too. I saw her fight off four of de fools single-handedly. She was a ding of beauty to watch. Yer defiance den saved many dwarves back den includin' half of me troops! We be ferever in yer debt. Dank ye again. When do ye leave to return home?" Roerson asked lastly.

"The day after tomorrow," replied Je Buel.

"Den, please honor me and me troops by attendin' a feast tomorrow night in yer honor," said the commander. "And all of ye be invited too, except me broder who be doin' oder kingly things. Sister-in-law, of course, ye always be welcomed."

"We would be happy to do so. Thank you," Je Buel responded.

After the group settled down again enjoying the refreshments placed the on the table, Je Buel asked, "Where is that other bottle of brandy?"

"Me hid it away! It be all mine and not fer more sharin!" declared Queen Marta looking at her husband.

"Oh, we will talk later me Queen," King Joerson said devilishly.

"Well, I have come prepared then!" announce Je Maron. He then pulled two bottles of the precious brandy from inside his cape and presented it to the group.

"Such a good friend we have me King! How we love ye so," said a smiling Queen Marta.

"Bah! Ye only glad to be drinkin' somebody else's bottle me dink," King Joerson responded, laughing hard. The rest of the group just laughed and offered their glasses or goblets to Je Maron to fill with the fine brandy.

Before finishing her glass of brandy, House great mother Je Pagi rose and made a toast, "To good, dear friends; may the rest of our nights be like this!"

"Aye," was the loud, joyous response from the group.

"By the way Queen Marta, you mentioned that you have a surprise for us?" later inquired Je Buel.

Queen Marta looked at the anxious Je Kei and nodded.

Je Kei rose then and addressed his House elders, "Grandmother, mother and father, I would now like to introduce someone to you who is special to me. She, in fact, is incredibly special to me. I would like to introduce to you a felf of the Battle Hammer clan. She is the adopted daughter of Queen Marta's cousin and Urtha Dal's granddaughter." Je Kei nodded to the guards at the doors, and they opened them. In walked a young, lovely looking felf accompanied by a female dwarf and Duenor Heartstone. Je Kei walked over to the small party and took the felf by the hand and walked her back in front of his House elders.

House great mother Je Buel stood and gazed at the felf as soon as she had entered the room. "I recognize you. You brought fresh mountain flowers to our rooms each day. Thank you; that was nice of you. Please come forward," Je Buel said and stretched out her hands towards the young felf who nervously took them.

Je Kei tried to speak, but his grandmother's hand signal commanded his immediate silence. House great mother Je Buel could see that this felf has kind eyes and a warm smile. She was nicely dressed, but not elegantly attired. Je Buel surmised her simple dress may well be the felf's finest attire. Je Buel continued to examine the felf with her keen eyes. The pretty felf is tall like her grandson, had deep green eyes, auburn colored hair, strong hands, and lovely curves. Although she could feel the felf's nervousness, she did not release the House first great mother's powerful hands or strong gaze.

*"Those are good signs,"* Je Buel thought. "What is your name, young one?" Je Buel asked.

"Me be Annaei of the Clan Battle Hammer, first great mother of House Je Luneefa," replied the felf proudly.

"Please tell us why you are here," said House great mother Je Buel in a commanding voice.

"Me came to introduce meself and announce me intentions on dis here son of House Je Luneefa," responded Annaei boldly.

"She be wastin' no time on small talk," King Joerson snickered quietly resulting in a soft hit and "Shhh!" from his queen.

"Really? And what are your intentions upon my grandson, Annaei of the Clan Battle Hammer?" asked Je Buel.

"To love him..." Annaei responded.

"To court him, she means House first great mother," quickly interjected the female dwarf who had accompanied Annaei.

"Shhh Moira," Annaei continued, "Please fergive me cousin, Moira. She be just tryin' to help me since me do not really know yer customs well and me be extremely nervous now too." Annaei closed her eyes and took a deep breath to calm herself. She then opened her eyes and continued, "Me will just be honest and speak me mind. Me be in love wid yer grandson and me want to make him mine ferever or at least till me die. Where he goes, me will go. Me promise to be a faidful and dutiful wife and a dutiful daughter of yer House. In de last five years me have known yer grandson, me love for him keeps growin' even after turnin' him away a few times. Me words may not be right, but me heart be."

"Also, know that me be not of noble blood like yerselves. Me have no riches. Me only have me fine steel war hammer and shield, but not much else. Me be orphaned long ago; so, me do not even know de elves who birded me, but me do know me real family be de Battle Hammer clan of de Blood Tears Mountains. May me please have yer blessin' to court yer grandson?" Annaei earnestly requested as she continued to bravely bear the hard scrutiny of the House first great mother.

After a few more moments of more quiet scrutiny, the first House great mother Je Buel asked, "What say you, Your Majesties? Is she worthy?"

"Aye!" both king and queen heartily responded without hesitation.

"Dali, you are my blood-sister and know Taeli and I are very protective of our family. I value and trust your judgement too. She is also your granddaughter through adoption; so, you know her well. Are her intentions true? Will she be a good granddaughter and daughter of my House too? Should she court my grandson?" asked Je Buel.

Urtha Dal, a long-time, dear friend and blood-sister of Je Buel remarked, "Me watched dese two youngins closely over de last several years. She did turn him away more dan once wid her words, but not ever truly wid her heart. It took her awhile to finally git her mind in order wid her heart. But after she did, me knew, like any stubborn dwarf, she would finally go after him wid her whole heart and mind. Her intentions be true. Me do love me granddaughter; she is good and kind. She works hard too; ain't afraid of anythin'. She be a true daughter of Clan Battle Hammer; her mind be made up; and she will not be moved like dis here mountain. She loves yer grandson, and me would be proud and honored when he joins our Clan!" solemnly endorsed Urtha Dal.

Duenor Heartstone quietly added, "During an expedition, which included Je Kei, we be attacked by some gnomes. Annaei be part of de escort team assigned to protect our miners. Me saw her fight her way drough dose marauders to finally fight by Je Kei's side. She would not let him die alone should fate be so. Annaei be also remained true to him despite several prestigious traders' attempts to woo her away at different times."

"Daughter, what say you?" Je Buel asked.

"She already passed my test on the battle training field two days ago. I like Annaei and would also bless her good intentions," said House great mother Je Pagi.

"I too have been impressed by this young felf. Your blood

may not be noble, but your heart and character certainly are, and these qualities are that House Je Luneefa values most. Riches can be earned; other things you can be learned. Know that then, you have my blessings too to court my grandson," said the House great mother glowing with a warm smile. Annaei released the House great mother's hands and embraced her tightly with tears falling from her eyes.

"Dank ye, House great mother. Me will make ye proud," said the tear-filled felf. Everyone then started clapping for Annaei and Je Kei and wished them well. "Me would also like to give Je Kei somethin' now too," Annaei said. Moira walked forward with a small box and presented it to Annaei who opened it and removed a chain holding a steel centerpiece that resembled a heart. On the centerpiece was the Clan Battle Hammer sigil. "Know dat dis be a symbol of me heart dat me only will give to ye. Me would be honored if ye would accept and wear it," she said.

"Yes, of course I will. Thank you," Je Kei humbly responded. Annaei then placed her chain around the neck of Je Kei and hugged him.

"Beggin yer pardon everyone, me have somedin' to say too," said Roerson.

"No, no, no cause everydin's settled; the deal is struck and dere be more brandy to be drinkin'. Ye might mess dings up. Save it fer tomorrow night at yer feast since me be not invited! Now, let us toast to de courtship!" King Joerson commanded.

"Aye!" a resounding roar erupted from the group.

Sometime later, King Joerson required the attention of the group. "Shhh all ye," the king ordered. "Me got more good news. Dali, please seal de room." Urtha Dal again magically sealed their room so that no one outside the room could see or hear what was about to take place. The king then placed several rocks in front of the group. "Dese be gifts from Bueli's family," King Joerson said.

"Huh? Why would anyone give a mountain-dwellin' dwarf rocks? Don't we already have enough of em? Broder, ye need more to play wid?" Roerson jokingly asked.

"Me bet dese ain't just rocks. What are dey? Gold? Diamonds? Diachrom?" Duenor Heartstone inquired after looking closely at the rocks.

"Darn ye Duenor. Yer still too dern smart, even after drinkin! Ye took me fun away," responded King Joerson. "Dali, if you would please."

Urtha Dal then removed the veil of disguise to display the three large rocks of pure gold and the two rocks of pure diachrom.

All the new guests in the room became incredibly quiet as they gazed upon enough treasure before them to buy a completely furnished castle and accompanying land. The king then informed them of the previous night's discussion. "Dis be all a secret and ye all must keep it so till me tell ye otherwise," King Joerson said. "De prince here be in command of dree dousand warriors and lead an expedition to find us another stronghold in de mountains west of us, six days away. Duenor, ye of course, will lead de dree mining teams. Roeri, me need ye to lead a brigade of yer Mountain Wreckers fer extra *encouragement* fer peaceful passage wid any new neighbors ye may meet. Ye all need to be dere by fifteen days from now."

Queen Marta then added, "Me also want an escort for Bueli and her family ready to go wid her in dree days. Bueli, is dat alright wid yer stayin' an extra day waitin' fer yer escort?"

After a quick check with her daughter and son-in-law, the House great mother replied "Yes indeed. Thank you."

"Daji and Duenor, ye should be ready to go in seven days' time wid de main group," the king continued.

Roerson stepped forward, looked his brother in the eyes and requested, "Me be in charge of de escort? Me and a hundred of me boys will make sure Bueli and her family git back safely. The oder hundred be goin' wid de main party."

"Dank ye, Roeri. Done. But remember to not go startin' fights wid our future new neighbors. And do not go drinkin' all dat fine Napa brandy up eider ye find dere!" King Joerson commanded.

"Broder, ye know me do not go lookin' to start fights. But me do and will finish em!" Commander Roerson proclaimed. "And no promises regardin' savin' ye any brandy me find eider!"

Je Maron again reached into his cape and pulled out two more bottles of the exquisite liquor they have enjoyed and offered it to the group.

The king looked at the House great father and hugged him. "Mari, please git me a magic cape like yourn for me birdday next time, please!" pleaded the king. "Now dese are in-laws word havin'!" declared the king loudly.

Another loud, rowdy "Aye!" was the collective response from the group as they lifted their glasses, now filled with more brandy.

Since her earlier confession that evening, Annaei remained awfully close to Je Kei. She held his hand mostly, listening to all the elders and observing Je Kei's elders. She marveled at the closeness Je Kei's elders have with her king and queen. For someone not born in the Battle Hammer clan or even a dwarf, the House Je Luneefa elders were quite special to these hard-to-get-to-know, not-easily-trusting dwarves. She now felt confident that she had made a good choice to love Je Kei. Both families would get along and even welcome their union, she thought.

Annaei pulled Moira to the far side of the room to talk privately with her cousin. "Ye be de commander of the de prince's personal guard and be courtin' Dajald fer a while; how long be a courtship normally?" Annaei quietly asked.

"We be courtin' fer five years now. Dree of dem years were in secret dough. And Kathryn courted Stone Axe fer ten years and..." replied Moira.

"How long do ye dink me need to court Je Kei?" Annaei impatiently interjected.

Moira thought for a few moments and said, "He bein' an elf, dey live long too like us dwarves. Je Kei be a noble too; so, his family need be extra sure ye be right fer him and der family. Me dink de courtship could last twenty to dirty years easily," Moira replied seriously.

"What! Ye jokin' right?" the bewildered Annaei exclaimed. Moira just shook her head then noticed that her glass was empty. Moira excused herself and left Annaei alone to look for more brandy.

Absorbed in confusion and solitude, Annaei started pondering again and was happy that things had gone well this evening. *"Me have such strong affection for de youngest son of House Je Luneefa dat me truly love him. And now me have all de elders' blessins to court Je Kei. But, a twenty-plus year courtship be far too long,"* she thought. She knew she had to do something to better understand how a noble elf courtship worked and how to shorten the anticipated long courtship period. *"However, despite de possible, ridiculously long, courtship time, me want Je Kei and will respect and accept de decision from his House elders."*

"Father, you've been quiet most of this evening. Is anything troubling you?" Je Kei asked his father privately, stepping away with Je Maron from the group.

"No. I am again just so proud of you for all that you have accomplished here. Not only did you graduate first in your class from the toughest academy in the kingdom, but you also somehow seem to find a rare happiness in something other than scrolls or rocks. You have surprised me by finding your one true love inside this mountain. That I had not expected at all. Regardless, I am happy for you both. You know you had several options throughout the kingdom. Why choose Annaei?" Je Maron inquired.

Je Kei closed his eyes and reflected upon that special moment when he fell in love with Annaei. He then replied, "Annaei is kind, hard-working, strong-willed, spirited, smart, humble and generous. Her smile moves me like no other; she excites me just by looking at me. I have even walked into walls at times when her gaze captured me. No noble felf in our kingdom has ever done that to me.

"I believe she would want me even if I was not a son of the noble Je Luneefa family. She does not seek happiness through riches nor political status. She believes in family and wants one.

"When we were in a large cavern in one of the stronghold's adjoining mountains, we were attacked by a large party of gnomes. That was the gnomes second attack. They attacked from two different tunnels. Some of the gnomes went straight for our wounded and I went there to defend them. Even though the gnome war party had the numbers in their favor, I could not retreat like some of the miners. I was a son of House Je Luneefa and could not leave my comrades to be slaughtered.

"Bloodlust overtook me for the first time. I fought like a demon possessed. My battle rage sustained me for some time, long enough for Annaei to return with more warriors. Instead of guarding the retreat of the remaining miners, she fought her way through the gnomes to stand by me. She bashed them with her vicious hammer and shield while I slashed and stabbed them with my sword and shield. Regardless of how many enemies tried to break through to kill our wounded, we held our ground knowing at any moment, we most likely would be killed. She would not leave my side. Her rage matched mine. Our battle *dance* was like how you described fighting with Mother for the first time: fast and ferocious, each complimenting the other. Our battle *dance* was like that too; and together, we lasted long enough for more dwarf warriors to arrive and defeat the remaining gnomes. You had told me that story; how you finally knew Mother was the *one* for you. You were then old enough to know war between enemies, as well as hearts. You still dance with Mother well over two centuries now and I greatly admire that. I want that same feeling and passion too. I have found that feeling and passion with Annaei; she is my *one*".

"Then love her faithfully, honestly and to your full extent, as best as you can each day till centuries past. You too have my full support and blessings," Je Maron said. Je Kei then embraced and hugged his father warmly in thanks.

The other males in the room soon joined Je Kei and his father after being nicely sent away by Annaei who wanted to talk privately with the females in the room. "First, let me refill yer glasses wid more brandy," Annaei started saying. She then produced another bottle she got from Je Maron who had hidden it in the room earlier.

Je Pagi commented, "My husband is more an elf of actions than words. If he gave you that bottle of brandy secretly, it is a good sign; he likes you too Annaei."

"Dank ye. Dank ye. Yer tellin' me dat means a lot," a smiling and grateful Annaei said. After a few moments, with a serious look, Annaei continued, "Please, again fergive me House great mothers fer me do not know yer courtship customs. Me mean no offense. And what I am about to ask ye may not come out right. So, please just know me heart be in de right place." After taking another deep breath, Annaei continued with a serious countenance, "How long me supposed to court Je Kei before we can get married? Me hear it could be twenty to dirty years."

Moira turned away and softly snickered, unable to keep a straight face.

Urtha Dal announced, "Now, dat be a good question Granddaughter! Courtin' be war too of a different kind! Know ye be not alone in yer heart's battle wid Je Kei. Ye got some of de best female minds to help ye, except Moira; she be only two hundred years old and ain't wise enough yet." As a sign of solidarity, the elder female dwarf raised and clinked her glass with the glasses of Queen Marta and the House Je Luneefa elder felfs.

"How long did Taeli court ye befer he asked ye to marry him?" Urtha Dal asked the House Je Luneefa first great mother. "And ye too Pagi, how long befer Mari asked ye?"

Both felfs laughed quietly.

"Me knew me husband fer about two years befer me decided we would den court officially. Me decided we git married a year after dat! He had no choice but to agree if he be wantin' me," declared Je Buel who started sounding like her dwarf friends.

"Pagi, yer ma is startin' to talk like us like in de old days! More brandy Anni!" shouted Queen Marta. Annaei started refilling the glasses of the females quickly. She was most anxious to hear the response of Je Kei's mother too.

Je Pagi just smiled, knowing that her mother and she were a bit drunk. "To answer yer question, me courtship only lasted six moons. After dat, I proposed to him!" Je Pagi reflected, smiling on a distant thought. "De dern fool would have waited ten years, accordin' to his moder's wishes, if me hadn't. Der be no need to wait; he be my *one* and me knew it!

"Look at 'em over der. Ye all know males be basically foolish by nature. Der two heads confuse dem too much. Be us females who make great males into greater males!" Looking at Annaei, House great mother Je Pagi continued, "So, Anni darlin', make me son greater! When yer ready to be his wife, ye might need to help him understand why it be in his best interests to do so. He be an exceptionally good dinker, ye know. He dinks too much and too long sometimes dough, especially if it ain't engineerin' or architectural or construction dings. Ye got to help him dink yer way sometimes!"

"He be my *one* and me know it deep in me heart! Besides, de sooner we get married, de sooner we make baby elves fer ye too!" Annaei quietly announced.

"Ah, me darlin' felf, ye know me weakness den. Auntie Dali, ye taught her well!" a beaming Je Pagi declared, raising her glass and smiling warmly at the young felf.

"Anni, it be up to you den to decide how long yer courtship will be. Bah, ye only need to convince one elf in dis here room and it ain't me," House great mother Je Buel concluded hugging the young felf affectionately.

Looking at Moira, who was now laughing, Annaei just said, "Cousin, ye lied to me, jokin' around. Bah. A twenty-year courtship be just ridiculous. Ye got me good wid dat Cousin!"

The other females now joined Moira in her laughter, except the House great mother Je Buel who looked at Annaei with a beaming smile and simply said, "Go git yer elf!"

An encouraged Annaei announced to the females, "Now, me dink it be time to get startin' wid dis courtship den! Excuse me please." She then walked across the room, pulled Je Kei to the side of the room and kissed him deeply thinking no one would be watching. "Imagine yer having dat every day and much more," she teased whispering into and biting his ear. Je Kei just stood there momentarily stunned and unable to speak or move, paralyzed by her bold kiss and loving gaze.

"Hey! We all saw dat! Ye only got our blessins' to court her tonight, dat be all!" an ever-watchful Roerson yelled.

"Wait. Both families' elders blessed *her* intentions to court *me*. I am innocent; *she* kissed me first. I, I..." pleaded the blushing Je Kei.

"Shhh, me love; ye be caught charmin' me from across de room to come and kiss ye. Me knew it and ye knew it! It be yer fault and me cousin saw it and knew it," Annaei declared in her defense.

"And if dat still does not git his attention enough, use yer fists like me did to finally git yer grandpa!" Urtha Dal shouted.

"Me too to git dis young king in de makin' back den!" Queen Marta declared, raising both her fists. "And me be sure Bueli and Pagi can share some oder female *magic* wid ye too!"

"Aye!" responded the Je Luneefa female elders who laughed hard with new-found energy. The courtship celebration was loud, joyous, and continued on well into the night.

Three days past the Academy graduation, the Je Luneefa family was finally ready to return home. Preparations to return, including the assembling of their dwarven escort, took less time than the House first great mother had imagined. Roerson, commander of the Mountain Wreckers, announced at his feast honoring Je Buel and her family that an escort would be needed. Many of his troops immediately volunteered, much more than he requested in fact. Such is the respect many of the Mountain Wreckers have for the House Je Luneefa first great mother who and her House aided the Blood Tears Mountains clans in their most desperate times of need, despite the wishes of the Crown, formidable clan enemies and severe weather.

No doubt the story Roerson told his troops surely moved them, some even to the point of tears. One young dwarf, Jaso Ironfist of the Clan Ban Battle Hammer, approached the House great mother during their feast and presented her with a bouquet of fresh mountain flowers. "Excuse me, beggin yer pardon House first great mother, me be Jaso Ironfist of Clan Battle Hammer. Me be alive today because of yer bravery over a hundred years ago. Me family and me survived dat winter because of ye and yer family. Me promised me grandma befer she died dat me be givin' ye some flowers because she knew ye would like dem. Thank ye again on behalf of me family," Jaso said to her.

The entire Je Luneefa party swelled to about two hundred twenty-three including the dwarf warrior escorts and their support. The original Je Luneefa family party only consisted of forty-eight members. Although Roerson asked for one hundred volunteers, much more than that requested to join his escort group. Many cited the reason to be a blood-debt to repay. Roerson, understanding the seriousness of repaying blood-debts, gladly allowed his ranks to exceed the initial one hundred warriors. "It be more *encouragement* for peace wid de new neighbors," he reasoned. The queen and king approved and laughed at the wise reasoning of the fiercest dwarf fighter in the mountains.

That morning, Queen Marta, King Joerson, Urtha Dal, Commander Djurdin Roerson and Prince Dajald personally escorted the House Je Luneefa elders and Je Kei to the Clan stronghold's western gate from which they would depart.

After the heavy doors were opened, the group was greeted with late morning sunshine and a mild, early autumn temperature. Hugs and warm goodbyes were exchanged between the dwarf and elf elders.

"This was a very good visit; thank you again for your generous hospitality," House great mother Je Buel said bowing to the king and queen. She then addressed the prince, "Prince Dajald, we will see you again soon just over ten days from now. Please be sure to make the rendezvous point by the next full moon."

"House first great mother, ever since me king and queen told Duenor Heartstone about de expedition, he be barkin' orders like he be de king! He be ready to go himself fer two days now. He be just too excited to explore anoder, new dang mountain. Trust me, we be der befer de next full moon, especially wid Duenor makin' dis trip!" declared Prince Dajald.

"By the way, where is he? I have not seen him this morning," Je Buel commented.

"Me be comin. Me be comin me king and queen," came a shout from within the stronghold. Driving a wagon pulled by two strong, great mountain goats, Duenor Heartstone arrived at the gate. He dismounted, approached and bowed to his queen and king. "Me king and queen, me feel me should go now wid de escort party and git a jump on de surveyin' of dat new mountain. Wid yer permission, me be joinin' dem."

"Granted!" immediately exclaimed a relieved Prince Dajald.

"Was Duenor not addressin' de king and queen? Ye ain't de king yet youngin and surely not de queen. So, mind yer tongue!" scolded King Joerson. He then looked at the queen and continued, "Me dink it be in *our* best interest to permit Duenor to go early. Afterall, he will be wid his prized student who can help him. And it surely be much quieter here wid him gone," growled the king. "What say ye me Queen?"

The queen thought for a moment and said, "Me not sure if dat be right. Me would not want any harm to befall dem. Dey could git lost in dat new mountain or when dey start havin' too much fun wid de new rocks dey might find. What if der are bandits already in dat mountain? So, we should also assign dem a personal escort to protect them. Who should we assign to dat duty?" Queen Marta reflected.

"Me! Me will protect dem," came a pledge from a rushing Annaei who was behind the group and just joining them. Annaei was carrying her weapons and packed for the road. "Ye be not plannin' to leave widout me, be ye?" she whispered to Je Kei as she moved past the young melf to stand before the queen and king and then bowing afterwards.

"Dis ain't no courtship; dis be serious duty. Do ye understand?" Urtha Dal said to her granddaughter.

"Yes grandmother, me understand and will do me duty as a true daughter of Clan Battle Hammer," responded Annaei solemnly.

"Your Majesties, can I please object?" asked Je Kei. "She can be... ugh... very distracting when I work and..."

"No!" House great mothers Je Buel and Je Pagi concurrently responded.

Queen Marta said, "Ha! It be settled den. Yer elders know best! Dey know we need ye to be safe; ye be now a serious investment to both our futures. Ye got yer personal guard den. Me King?"

"Hmmm... House great father Je Maron, do ye have any concerns wid dis felf joinin' yer son as his personal guard?" King Joerson asked.

"No, I think not," replied a pleased Je Maron. "Thank you, Annaei for accepting this assignment."

"Den, me too agree. Duenor and Annaei, ye can go wid dis party here den; permission be granted," announced the king.

"Thank ye, yer Majesties," a grateful Duenor Heartstone said, excited and happy with anticipation of exploring a new mountain.

Another round of warm goodbyes and hugs took place. When Urtha Dal went to hug her granddaughter, she whispered in her ear, "A spring weddin' be de best!"

"Commander Djurdin Roerson, git the Je Luneefa family home safely or ye be answerin' to me!" Urtha Dal loudly ordered. Roerson frowned at his cousin, muttered something unpleasant in the Dwarfish language, mounted his great mountain goat and led the escorts out of the stronghold. They all started joyously singing an old Dwarfish traveling song.

Je Maron said goodbye to the party who had congregated at the gate to send them off. He purposely hugged and said goodbye to the king and queen last. Afterwards, he again reached into his cape and pulled another bottle of Napa brandy which he presented to the king. He mounted his horse and joined the other House elders at the front of their entourage. He turned one last time and saw the king looking at the bewildered Queen Marta, hugging the bottle of brandy closely to his chest and simply said, "Mine!" Je

Maron laughed to himself, grateful for so many reasons.

"Now, let us go home," Je Buel said as she spurred her horse homeward.

With the late summer's good weather, the Je Luneefa party made good time returning home. Unlike their initial journey to the Blood Tears Mountains, they returned home a different way. They first would journey directly westward for six days and then two days southward. Despite an uneventful journey to the Taurus Mountain, they were quite anxious to finish their final trek as soon as possible.

Using a special scrying bowl, Je Buel would communicate with Urtha Dal and Je Leena each night of their return journey. The House Je Luneefa first great mother would give them both updates regarding their progress on their return trip. Je Buel was pleased when she learned that Prince Dajald's group would be leaving soon and arriving at the designated rendezvous point three days ahead of the original scheduled day. Evidently, when dwarves go to war or on an expedition, preparations are made expeditiously. Both activities are considered especially important and taken very seriously; so, no time is wasted. In this case, the potential of finding a second stronghold got many excited. So, all those involved with the actual expedition or just supporting it were quite enthusiastic and filled with dedicated optimism and duty.

Selfishly, Je Buel wanted to keep a few surprises to herself and decided not to share too much information with rest of her family still in Torondell. On the third night of the return trip, Je Leena asked, "Did you bring us any presents from your trip?"

"Of course; we are returning with your beloved brother. Is not he the best gift I could bring you?" Je Buel asked.

"Yes, but his return is for everyone, especially you and Papa. Surely, you got something special just for me since I missed you, mother, and father so much," a pouting Je Leena explained.

"Never fear dear granddaughter, I bring back something very special for you," confessed Je Buel. "Please do not disclose to your brothers and sister the fact that I am bringing you a rare and valuable book of spells used primarily by dwarf mages to move under the ground or through rock. These spells aid them in their tunneling. You too may find them of great value one day; so, you should also study them."

"Thank you, Nana; I knew you would not forget me," a relieved Je Leena said.

"Please have Jero meet us at the southern base of Taurus Mountain three days from now," Je Buel added.

Je Leena replied, "Yes Nana, I will inform him."

"Is all well at home and with you?" Je Buel asked.

"Yes and yes," replied Je Leena. "Is something troubling you?"

"I am tired from the visit and this road. I long to be back home again with my entire family around me. I do miss not having all of you close by and eating together, despite the noise," reflected Je Buel, a loving grandmother who has great pride in all her daughters, sons, granddaughters and grandsons.

"Well, after you return and rest, will you and Papa prepare a meal for all of us like you use to?" Je Leena requested.

"That is a wonderful idea! I am sure your grandfather would enjoy that too. Let us plan to do that. All of you are growing up fast. Soon, you may even want to leave our home to start your own House. Is there any melf interested in courting you now?" The House great mother slyly inquired.

Je Leena replied, "Nana, I have no suitors now, but I do plan to stay in Torondell in our home. Whoever wins my heart will join our House and stay in our family stronghold where there is more than enough room. Besides, Kei can always design and build new additions onto our current stronghold. Afterall, he is the kingdom's second-best architect and builder, right?"

The House first great mother replied, "Yes, having Kei in our family has its advantages. Secondly, thank you for wanting to stay close to the family. At more than five centuries of age, I do not travel well like I used to. Also, your position may change about having your own addition to our current stronghold. Remember that all the land within the Toronwalein belongs to our family. So, your desired addition could be your very own stronghold on Je Luneefa land within the Toronwalein.

"By the way, why do you not have any suitors or are you choosing not to tell me of any? You are young, beautiful, the second daughter of a noble family, smart and you are a great battlemage in training. What more could young melfs want?"

"Nana," exclaimed Je Leena. "Most of the young melfs I know are basically idiots, wanting short-term romances to satisfy the longings of their bodies. Or they just seek short, romantic adventures of no consequence. I am not interested in shallow relationships either. I tell the fools to go to a brothel and not waste my time. I may need to look for someone who is more mature, perhaps at least fifty to eighty years older. Melfs about my age are not sufficient for me. Papa and father are such fine examples. And you and mother have instilled in all of us such high standards that most melfs I know do not meet."

"You are wise too beyond your years," said the proud House first great mother. "I do love you granddaughter. Tell everyone we will see them soon. Blessings upon you this night," Je Buel concluded.

"Goodnight Nana. I love you too," said an equally proud, young felf, grateful to have been born into a family led by strong, wise and loving females.

The next, fourth day's journey home was again uneventful except for the noisy bantering between Duenor Heartstone and Commander Djurdin Roerson. Heartstone is still quite anxious to get to the destination as quickly as possible, even desiring to start traveling just before dawn and continue just after sunset. There is no doubt that the kingdom's foremost architect and engineer is too excited to start exploring a new mountain. Heartstone wanted to even travel a bit faster with the Je Luneefa family who rode their horses while the slower dwarven contingent used their rugged, great mountain goats as their soldiers' mounts and miners' beasts of burden.

Roerson had to remind Duenor more than twice a day, it seemed, that "Me be de Commander in charge of de escort party!"

"And me be correctin' dat too de next time we go on an expedition!" the restless and excited Duenor declared.

After the party made camp for their evening meal, both House Je Luneefa great mothers would help cook for the entire group. Both Je Buel and Je Pagi had earned well-deserved reputations for being good trail cooks long ago; so, everyone wanted to judge their cooking skills for themselves. The dwarves were not disappointed at all. The House great mothers received more praise, especially when the escort party received fresh berry pies that night after passing a field of wild blue berries and strawberries earlier that day.

"How do ye do it? And why?" asked Annaei who would help the House great mothers prepare meals whenever and however she could.

"Sharing a meal with someone is a great opportunity to build friendships. My mother and I spent many days in our own kitchen preparing meals for our family. The kitchen and dining hall became our family's *center* meeting place. As a family, we talked about things, laughed, and cried. We even helped solve a few problems too.

"Through the stories we would tell, we tried to pass on our wisdom to help the young ones not make mistakes we had made earlier in our lives. It was also the place where we as parents and leaders of the family tried to teach our daughters and sons through those gatherings. As leaders, we had to make very difficult decisions at times; and we tried to explain our decisions when we could. For the times we could not, we wanted their unconditional obedience and trust which we got most of the time," Je Buel replied.

"Beggin' yer pardon House first great mother, me like to also reply to Annaei's question too," Jaso Ironfist of Clan Battle Hammer requested. Apparently, he was nearby when he heard Annaei's question. Je Buel nodded approvingly. "Little dings help us warriors fight harder. We have our own cooks whose duty be to cook fer us. But, when dis noble felf takes her important time to spend on us lowly warriors, it makes us feel special and shows us we be special too. We really appreciate dat. Dat be a little ding dat makes us fight harder. Lowly, common soldiers can become stronger, more fearless, braver, *uncommon warriors* when dey know der leader genuinely cares. She even fought wid us; ye know de stories. Soldiers' loyalty and respect be earned, not given. Good leaders, like dis House first great mother, know dat. Besides, she is a dern good cook too! Any more pie left?"

"For those gracious compliments, thank you Jaso Ironfist. And if you do not tell anyone else, I will get you another piece of pie from a secret stash," Je Buel remarked smiling at the young dwarf as she walked away. Moments later, she returned with her daughter, carrying a stack of *wood*. She handed the wood stack to Jaso Ironfist and told him quietly to add the wood to the pile on the camp's perimeter. Shortly after he walked away, the veil of disguise Je Buel conjured - the wood stack - disappeared to reveal a covered bowl with pie inside.

Looking at Je Pagi, Annaei said, "Yer mama is great. Me Clan loves ye both. If ye do not mind, me want to git to know ye better and me want ye to git to know me better too. So, just ask me any question ye want. Me tell ye de truth, me swear."

Chuckling, Je Pagi said, "It seems you may have many more questions than we have. Besides, time will most likely reveal our answers. So, we can be more patient. What do you wish to know?"

A fidgeting Annaei took a deep calming breath and released a barrage of questions, "How do me git to know ye better? Me be tryin' to show ye me be dutiful by helpin' ye when me can, but me do not want to be a nuisance; so, tell me if me be. What foods do Je Kei like most? Will ye teach me how to prepare dem? Will yer oder daughters and sons like me? If not, what can me do to show dem me intentions be true and heart-felt? What will me duties be after we git to yer stronghold? Can me even stay at..."

"Enough, young one," Je Buel said. "We still have plenty of leagues left on this journey to answer questions. You do not need to ask all of them tonight. In fact, let us join Commander Roerson's group over there and listen to their songs." With that announcement, Je Buel rose and started walking over to a roaring campfire where many dwarves were singing an old ballad started by Roerson himself. Even some of the House Je Luneefa escort soldiers were there drinking and singing with the dwarves. *"What a wonderful time and sight,"* Je Buel thought.

On the fifth iteration of the ballad, Je Kei started working his way through the crowd towards Annaei. He had finished making plans with Duenor Heartstone regarding the first four days of exploration once they reached the destination Taurus Mountain. Like his dwarf mentor, he too was excited about the expedition. The idea of developing an architectural and construction plan for a new dwarven stronghold was overwhelming. A stronghold's, especially a dwarven stronghold, requirements and specifications are complex and very demanding. He also wanted to get started as soon as possible. Je Kei and his mentor wrote, revised, and reviewed the expedition daily plans each night of their journey there. After four nights of examining the same details multiple times, he felt he was more than ready to start the exploration once there.

However now, after a certain felf had smiled and winked at him earlier this night, he put his work aside and now wanted to focus on another objective closer to his heart. After working his way through the crowd surrounding the main campfire, he touched Annaei on her shoulder and motioned to her to follow him. They left that group by the campfire and walked to the perimeter of their camp by the lake. Once there, Je Kei found a large tree they could hide behind, pulled Annaei close to him and kissed her very deeply.

"In case you did not remember, I am madly and deeply in love with you. You are my one and only, Annaei of Clan Battle Hammer. Do not ever doubt that," Je Kei softly said as he gazed into her moonlit eyes.

With labored breath, Annaei said, "Dere ye go, charmin' me again wid yer eyes. Yer kiss was just okay; me had better. Ye need to convince me more, me dinkin'."

Now challenged, Je Kei pressed himself close enough to Annaei to feel her excited heartbeat. He gazed at her for a few more moments and kissed her very deeply and passionately again.

"Kei, me love you so much too. Every day, will ye promise to make me feel like dis for de next few hundred years? What would ye say if me asked ye now to marry me? Would ye disappoint me wid some long, clever answer oder dan a simple 'Yes'?" Annaei asked panting.

Je Kei returned her determined gaze. He lovingly removed her hair that had blown onto her lovely face, and then he replied with a smile, "I promise to try and 'no'," Je Kei replied. "So, does this mean you will ask me or not?"

With joyous, tear-filled eyes and a devilish smile, Annaei pulled Je Kei closer and asked, "Will ye, Je Kei of House Je Luneefa, marry me?"

"Yes, Annaei of Clan Battle Hammer; I will marry you," he replied.

Just then, the camp horn sounded signaling all should return to the camp and the night watch should commence their rounds. After releasing her from his tight embrace, Annaei, still in a quiet trance from the last kiss after Je Kei's acceptance of her proposal, pushed Je Kei away and started running back towards the main camp.

Puzzled, Je Kei collected his thoughts and started walking back to camp to talk to his elders. After reaching the camp, he went straight to his elders' tents hoping they would all be awake or still sitting by the nearby campfire. To his surprise, all three elders were standing near the campfire looking angrily at him.

"What have you done?" asked a very displeased-looking Je Maron. Je Kei started to respond, but his father's hand gesture stopped him. Je Kei then started thinking about all his assignments and responsibilities given to him on the return journey home, *"I have dutifully finished all my assignments to-date. I am even ahead on some other assigned tasks. I am bewildered why Father would be angry with me."*

After several more uncomfortable moments, Je Maron started smiling at his youngest son, "Do you have any idea what your marriage proposal acceptance cost me? Why could you not wait just four more days after we got home?"

"What? I do not understand. Wait for..." a bewildered Je Kei said. After a few more moments of thought, Je Kei asked, "Ah... Father did you lose a bet?"

"Sadly, yes. I had thought you would be too absorbed with your mountain expedition planning to consider a proposal so soon," Je Maron confessed. "But evidently, you have proven again something I believe: 'males may choose; but females decide!' Your grandmother and mother's support and encouragement that night gave Annaei enough confidence to chance proposing to you much sooner than later. Your hasty proposal acceptance cost King

Joerson and me bottles of Napa brandy! And we are both happy to pay. We are both overjoyed with this great news!"

"Thank you, father. Grandmother and mother, are you pleased as well?" Je Kei asked.

"Yes, we surely are. We are both happy for you and Annaei," replied Je Buel. "I will still look good for a great grandmother!"

"Aye! And I will be an immensely proud and good-looking grandmother too," Je Pagi joyously added.

"By the way, where is my betrothed? She ran away from me after I answered her proposal question," a more puzzled Je Kei inquired.

"She is in my tent scrying with her grandmother. Good news spread quickly!" Je Buel replied.

Je Kei excused himself from his elders and went to his grandmother's tent. There on the side of the tent, Annaei was sitting at a table looking at a scrying bowl. Queen Marta, Urtha Dal, and Moira were at the other designated scrying bowl, one that is used for two-way communications for both visual and voice.

"Me queen, me have news," Urtha Dal said.

"Ye called me here in secret; said it be urgent. Has anydin' bad befallen our expedition team or Bueli's family? Did dat dern Roerson pick a fight already wid dem new neighbors?" an impatient Queen Marta asked.

"Nodin' bad happened, but somedin' good, really good. We won de bet! Annaei and Je Kei got officially engaged tonight!" exclaimed Urtha Dal.

"Me queen, Je Kei just walked in," Annaei announced.

"Your Majesty, future grandmother Dali and cousin 'Hello'," a beaming Je Kei said as he joined Annaei at the table and peered at the scrying bowl. There above the bowl, he could see the facial images of the three female dwarves at the Blood Tears Mountains stronghold. Their images were slowly revolving above the scrying bowl.

"Ye know, Kei will be de most handsome melf in our clan. Der be oder felf and dwarf maidens' hearts broken wid dis news too," Moira announced.

"Moira, please stop yer jokin' around. Soon, *me* Kei will be de only melf in our clan; so, he be de most handsome. Also, dose oder females will just have to cry and git over der loss. He be all mine!" an annoyed Annaei responded.

"Hello son of House Je Luneefa. So, dat rumor of long elf courtships be just not true den me suppose," Queen Marta said. "Congratulations. Please git yer grandmoder and moder; we elders got some more plannin' to do."

"Yes, Your Majesty," said Je Kei. "But first, before I, my father or King Joerson lose any more 'bets', just tell me your plans; and most likely, I will agree."

Queen Marta smiled and responded, "Me like de way ye dink, but der be no fun in dat!" The females at the Blood Tears Mountains laughed vigorously.

As Je Kei turned around to do as the queen commanded, his elders all came into the tent together. Je Kei directed Je Buel, Je Pagi and Je Maron towards the scrying bowl where the revolving images of Queen Marta, Urtha Dal and Moira were there, all bearing huge smiles.

"All of you planned this and bet against me, didn't you?" Je Kei asked. His question only evoked more victorious laughter from the scrying dwarves in response.

"Hah! We did not bet against ye at all. We just be bettin' more on Annaei's hard to resist, female powers!" Hail to us females!" Urtha Dal proudly proclaimed.

Both Queen Marta and Moira collectively responded with a loud, supporting "Aye!"

"Your Majesty, Dali and Moira, good evening. Before we start more planning, I need to send a few extra ears away," said Je Buel who just looked at her son-in-law and grandson with a warm smile. Both Je Luneefa males knew that was their signal to take their leave.

Before Je Maron and Je Kei left the tent, the consoling father looked at his son and said, "My son, this is a time when the females will gloat in their victory. We should leave; you do not want to hear what they will say. Trust me."

"Je Kei, wait please," Annaei said as she rushed over to Je Kei. "I do absolutely love ye. Dank ye for saying 'Yes'. Goodnight me love; I hope yer not angry. If ye be, me will definitely make it up to ye," Annaei said with a passion-igniting kiss and devilish smile.

After taking a moment to recover, a defeated looking Je Kei replied happily, "I did not even have a real, fair chance against you and your *team*, did I?"

"Of course not!" Annaei replied winking at her beloved. His House great mothers started laughing too.

Je Buel shooed away her son-in-law and grandson as Queen Marta declared, "Me be claimin' me victory bottle of brandy tonight!" These were the last words Je Kei heard since Je Buel quickly sealed her tent after the two male elves finally left.

Though "defeated," both House Je Luneefa melfs left with

spirits high.

Walking back to his parents' tent, Je Kei asked, "Father, how do I now calm the passion raging inside me now?"

After reflecting on his youth when he was courting Je Pagi, the elder melf replied, "In all honesty, why would you want to? Lust is sometimes an elusive feeling and even when it has hold of you, it can still be fleeting. You want and need both lust and love in a relationship. It is good that Annaei can ignite your passion for her. That feeling is part of a healthy relationship too. Males seem to thrive on their capacity for lust more so than females. Lust has caused many males to do very stupid things... 'Beware not to let your second head misguide you' is something I have told you and your brothers for centuries. Lust is more related to your physical being; whereas, love is based more upon emotions.

"On the other hand, females tend to be more emotional than males. Their dependence upon inherent lust factors seems to be less than that of males in general. But their emotional content is greater than that of males, in my opinion. Female emotional range varies from female to female, is complex and can be a source of great power. For example, if one had to fight either your grandmother or grandfather, I believe your grandmother would be more formidable and merciless. That normally kind, wonderful female can transform into hell's fury when required.

"If your passion continues to rage and sleep cannot find you, you will find that cold water may help to quench that fire. Lots and lots of cold water sometimes... You should sleep in Duenor's tent again tonight. I hope your mother will try to claim her victory bottle of brandy and more this night too."

"You know that, how?" asked Je Kei.

"No son; I am just hoping... I may even need to *coax* her some to play my game. Even in war's defeat, there may be small victories to be won," Je Maron said with a devilish grin.

"So, no late-night swim in the lake's cold water with me then?" inquired Je Kei.

"Absolutely not! I want my rage to remain blazing hot! Anyways, good night son. Congratulations again," a happy Je Maron said and departed to his tent where he had to prepare for his own private celebration with his wife using his very last bottle of Napa brandy.

It was the morning of the sixth day of the return journey. Annaei walked out of the Taurus Mountain cave's entrance towards the area where Duernor Heartstone had hitched his wagon. She was going to fetch a bag of tools and instruments the dwarf needed.

Duenor had left his wagon tethered to a small tree at the base of the mountain, about two hundred steps away. The mountain slope was steep; so, she had to walk carefully and slowly. Although her walk was a bit arduous, she knew this mountain's entrance also had good, inherent defensive qualities which Duenor Heartstone would fully exploit. Plus, with fifty to one hundred years of construction, this mountainside will be transformed into another fabulous monument of the famed dwarf's ingenuity.

She was greeted by the early morning sun and a cool early morning wind. Before dawn, Duenor Heartstone, a small troop escort, Je Kei, some miners and Annaei had left the main, returning House Je Luneefa party and went directly to this designated cave on the southern side of the Taurus Mountain. After making camp the night before, this mountain was in clear sight and Duenor Heartstone, was overly anxious and excited to start exploring the new, potential, second dwarven stronghold as quickly as possible. Roerson had to purposely assign three of his Mountain Wreckers to guard Duenor and keep him in the camp the day before. Otherwise, the renowned dwarf would have kept travelling through the night to get to the Taurus Mountain. Evidently, seeing a mountain Duenor Heartstone had not yet explored was like dangling food in front of a ravenous beast.

Fortunately, Roerson permitted Duenor and his small group to start the last trek of the journey a short time before dawn. Now, an exploration camp base was being set up just inside the mountain's southern entrance.

As Annaei got closer to the wagon, she started to hear low talking voices in the distance. Immediately, she became wary of her unknown surroundings. She instinctively pulled her beloved war hammer, forged by the greatest blacksmith of her clan and given to her by her adopted grandmother. She silently crept closer to the noises. There on the ground was a hooded figure, with hands tied, seemingly unconscious, and with three other elves standing over this prone, captive individual. The three standing elves were all dressed in dark clothes. From the sounds of their voices, Annaei surmised that two are male and one is female. They all carried swords on their sides, except the female also carried additional blades in her boots. They were in good spirits it seemed, perhaps because of their success in abducting the hooded figure.

Suddenly, Annaei recognized the boots of the hooded figure; they belonged to her Je Kei! Fear gripped her now, thinking these three standing over him were perhaps bandits or worse, assassins. Regardless of who these three were, she knew she would fight, even die, if need be, to save her beloved. Annaei summoned her inner strength and quickly drew upon battle lessons and stories. She quickly thought, *"Me wish me had my shield; den my upcoming fight would go better for me... Me must kill dat female first because she looks to be de most dangerous... Je Kei must be saved... If dey harmed him, dey will all die!"*

Annaei also drew her long knife. She finally calmed herself and let her battle rage grow inside her. In those few moments as Annaei silently moved closer to the bandits, she formulated her attack plan. She was determined to protect Je Kei at all costs. She picked up a rock and threw it into the brush away from the bandits. The ensuing rustling noise caught the attention of the male bandits who turned towards the sound; however, the female bandit turned in the opposite direction to watch Annaei emerge from tree line hiding her. All three bandits had quickly drawn weapons in their hands.

Now discovered, Annaei switched her tactics and said, "Good mornin'. Me would appreciate it if ye let me have dat elf ye got tied up dere. If need be, me will pay any ransom ye want for his safe return. Know dat if ye harm him in any way, me will hunt ye down and kill ye. If ye want to fight me for him, den so be it."

"Do you know who we are?" inquired one of the male bandits.

"Do not know and do not care. Let him go, now," demanded Annaei gripping her hammer and knife tighter.

"So, you would fight all of us just for him? What is he to you?" the second male and now curious bandit asked.

"And by the way, there are five of us. You are surrounded too," the female bandit disclosed with a sinister stare.

"It does not matter me dyin' to save me betrothed..." Annaei said returning the female bandit's stare with her own determined gaze.

"Hold, all of you!" said a commanding voice. From behind Annaei, Je Buel silently emerged with a much younger felf, an almost a mirror image of herself, and a black panther. The House Je Luneefa great mother walked over to Annaei, smiled at her and said, "Let me introduce you to my other granddaughters and grandsons. Apparently, they had some special plan for welcoming Kei home that included kidnapping him."

"Interestin' way to welcome kin folk home," Annaei said looking at the House great mother.

"Yes, but they all mean well. It is their way of showing affection to their brother whom they missed very much. Being so serious most of the time, Je Kei was often the target of their intended humor," Je Buel explained. "Leena, now revive your brother. While she is doing that, please greet Je Jero, the eldest and first son of House Je Luneefa. Next to him is Je Tero, the second eldest son. Je Danei is the House first daughter. Je Leena over there is the youngest daughter. And lastly is this magnificent beast, Je Onyxia Ryoshi, Je Danei's pet panther. Everyone, this is Annaei of Clan Battle Hammer. She is now the betrothed of our Je Kei."

"Hello everyone, good mornin'. Me look forward to talkin' wid each of ye, widout weapons in hands preferably," Annaei said.

"Hello. Well met grandmother. It is good to see you again. So, I did hear correctly when you and Annaei said 'betrothed'. Oh, today will be such a good day!" proclaimed Je Danei.

"Hello Grandmother. Hello Annaei. Apologies for our unorthodox first meeting; but had we not taken these steps to abduct him, he would forgo a homecoming event given in his honor. Seriously Annaei, would you had fought all of us had we continued with our abduction, or would you pay the ransom for the third best looking son of the Je Luneefa family?" asked Je Jero.

"Widout hesitation, me would have fought ye all... and died most likely. But, for dat melf layin' dere, me would fight for him anytime, anywhere and against all odds." After reflecting upon some inner thoughts for a few moments, Annaei continued, "And me dink Je Kei is *de* best-lookin' House Je Luneefa son; but, me be a bit biased."

"Well said, Annaei; she is correct. Je Kei is now our best-looking brother," agreed a supporting Je Leena.

"Hmmm... They are correct, and I agree too. Living in that mountain for these last many years has made Je Kei more attractive in subtle ways. Je Jero, you are now the third best looking son in our family. Even Je Tero is better looking than you now," Je Danei added. "So, Annaei, what was your plan if you had to fight us?"

"Try to kill ye first, because me dought ye be more dangerous dan yer brothers," replied Annaei.

Flattered by her complimentary answer, Je Danei smiled at Annaei, looked at her grandmother and said, "I like this Annaei of Clan Battle Hammer! She has good, discerning eyes."

Je Kei was now awake, but still sitting on the ground, still a bit groggy from the gas he was forced to inhale when he was abducted. "Good morning all," Je Kei finally managed to say after looking around. "How did you render me unconscious so quickly? And I do not remember how I got here at all."

"Our secret. But since I carried you all the way here, I can say you have added some weight since I saw you last. My shoulder still hurts," complained Je Tero.

"Grandmother, as you can see, I have again been victimized by my siblings who seem to enjoy their games at my expense. I will have my revenge," Je Kei pledged. "By the way, why did you abduct me?"

"Hush, all of you. We need to return to the cave, and Danei, why did all of you need to abduct your brother?" Je Buel asked. Annaei helped Je Kei to his feet, and they all started walking back to the cave.

"Why me? It was not even my idea," replied the woeful House first daughter.

"No, probably not; but you were the fastest to start walking back. Hoping to escape my questioning perhaps? So, your actions portrayed you as perhaps the *guiltiest* for the time being," reasoned the House great mother. "Be quick and confess."

Je Danei said, "Yes, Grandmother. On our return journey to Torondell, tonight in fact, a welcome home feast was planned for Je Kei by the three House Pi Zhou sisters. The youngest, Pi Lin, has been and still is interested in Je Kei. This youngest felf was also the first to show serious interest in any of our brothers too. The two older Pi Zhou sisters, Pi Ling and Pi Liu later targeted the elder Je Luneefa brothers and continued their pursuit for over ten years. This is just another step in their overall strategy to try to marry into our family to strengthen theirs.

"Jero thought Je Kei would not normally be interested in attending any feast hosted by the Pi Zhou sisters. However, with some additional *encouragement* which Jero and Tero parlayed into compensation for their participation in getting Kei to attend the feast, they thought an abduction would be necessary and humorous. Leena and I participated in the scheme because she wanted to try some new potions and spells and I could practice a few assassin stealth tactics."

"What say you Annaei now, after hearing this tale?" Je Buel asked.

"Me dink dose Pi Zhou sisters be disappointed, especially dat youngest one; she be not gettin' me Kei!" Annaei firmly responded.

After returning to the cave, Je Kei's head had cleared from the grogginess and being unconscious. He looked at Je Onyxia Ryoshi, Je Danei's pet panther, and spread his arms wide. The panther went to Je Kei, stood on her hind legs, and the youngest Je Luneefa son hugged the mighty beast affectionately. "Oh, I missed you too Ony," Je Kei said.

He then turned to his siblings. "Everyone, please listen to me. First, thank you for welcoming me home, as strange as it was. I do understand your pranks are intended to show affection. Secondly, I will attend the feast tonight and introduce my betrothed. In doing so, several objectives will be accomplished, one of which is to finally demonstrate to Pi Lin that I had and still have no interest in her. Besides, she now really likes you Je Jero, not me; Pi Ling really wants our sister, Je Danei; and Pi Liu still wants Je Tero. Is this clear enough for everyone? So, we should use this event to communicate honestly with one another. Hopefully, we can all still try to be friends with the Pi Zhou sisters. Lastly, no more pranks. We are too old for such childish behavior; plus, you would not enjoy the custom revenge I would plan for each of you. Do we all agree?"

"You have been away for years. How would you possibly know all that about the Pi Zhou sisters, especially that part you said about Pi Ling? I told her decades ago I was not interested in her at all," a bewildered Je Danei asked.

Je Kei just replied, "I have my ways; I have my ways. Let us do celebrate tonight my return home with the Pi Zhou sisters. Because very soon thereafter, we will see our home again."

On their morning arrival in Torondell, the House Je Luneefa great dining hall was decorated. The great hall is warm from the fires as the House Je Luneefa guests and family members walked in. They were greeted with a variety of delicious aromas of all the foods that Je Kei especially liked. After ten years of being away studying architecture, engineering and construction, he had finally returned home.

Je Kei was remarkably close to his grandfather, and he loved his family's first patriarch greatly. So, when he first saw his House first great father, Je Kei jumped off his horse and ran into his elder's arms with tears flowing. In return, the dignified and stately Je Taeliel, the tough Warden of the North, melted too with tears upon embracing his youngest grandson. To Je Taeliel, his family was now all together and safe, protected by his Toronwalein and stronghold. His fears of any harm befalling upon his grandson, while Je Kei was away, were finally alleviated. Now that his family were all physically close to him, the House Je Luneefa first father had tremendous confidence he could continue to protect them all from ever-looming dangerous threats, known and unknown.

After arriving at the House Je Luneefa stronghold, while Je Kei took his grandfather back inside the stronghold for private conversations, the others dismounted to let the House attendants care for the mounts and take away the baggage.

"House first great mother me would be pleased to stay in yer House army's barracks. No special privileges me be needin'. Please assign me some chores or oder duties to help too while here. Just tell me what ye want me to do fer yer House," Annaei requested of Je Buel.

"For the time being, you will stay in our stronghold as our honored guest," Je Buel responded.

All the other granddaughters and grandsons just snickered as they overheard Annaei's request. The House great mother Je Buel's stern look quickly ended their laughter. Annaei, a bit puzzled, pulled Je Danei away and privately asked, "Did me say somedin' wrong?"

Upon seeing how seriously concerned Annaei was, Je Danei had to take advantage of her brother's vulnerable betrothed. Je Danei said, "No, you said nothing wrong, but you are about to meet the toughest and meanest melf in the kingdom. Somehow you managed to penetrate his powerful defenses set around his beloved family. Somehow you managed to get his favorite grandson to love you without his blessing first. Our grandfather may not like you and may want to postpone or even cancel any marriage plans until he knows you. He is difficult and that could take many years, like twenty to thirty, to gain his trust."

Annaei was stunned to hear Je Danei's disheartening message. After observing Annaei's gloomy expression, Je Buel rescued the young felf from assumed potential mischief saying, "Annaei please first just follow me." As Je Buel and Annaei walked through the main entrance of the stronghold, the House first great mother greeted the welcoming staff warmly. Through her mental bond, Je Buel quickly located her husband and walked directly to a small sitting room off the main hallway. "Annaei, please disregard anything Je Danei told you about my husband; she, no doubt, was again hoping to have some fun at your expense," the House first great mother said to the obviously, now very nervous and apprehensive felf.

When Je Buel and Annaei walked into the room, the elder melf smiled at his beloved wife, embraced her, and kissed her for several moments. Je Taeliel deeply missed his wife of more than four centuries. "Welcome home, my love; I have greatly missed you," Je Taeliel said to his wife. Turning to Annaei, he said, "And you must be, the felf who captured my grandson's heart. Welcome Annaei of Clan Battle Hammer to our home." Like his wife, Je

Taeliel extended his hands to warmly greet the felf. Annaei met the gaze of the smiling elder melf and started crying. Annaei then ran into his waiting arms and embraced him warmly.

"Not quite the effect I expected to have upon our first meeting, but you are truly most welcome here. Ah... Danei must have said something to you about meeting me, right? Do not worry; I am only ruthless and evil to those who threatened or try to harm my family. So, dry your eyes; this is supposed to be a happy occasion," House Je Luneefa first great father said with warm and comforting encouragement.

For the next few hours, Je Kei and Annaei spent time with his grandparents answering questions and sharing some stories. During most of that time of touring some of the stronghold and listening to tales of Je Kei's childhood, Annaei was quiet and listened intently to the elders. Annaei held Je Kei's hand tightly as they walked. She wanted to learn as much as she could about her future family and Je Kei.

"Dis garden be beautiful. Me noticed dere be two ancient, great oak trees dere, two smaller ones, and five oder smaller ones. Do dey represent yer family?" Annaei quietly asked.

"How good of you to notice. Yes, those oak trees are symbols of this family. House first great father and I first planted those ancient oak trees shortly after moving into this stronghold. We planted more trees when grand our granddaughters and grandsons were born," Je Buel said.

"Some of the other trees represent our adopted daughters and sons," Je Taeliel remarked, pointing to another group of trees.

"House great father, how long ye been married to yer wife?" Annaei further inquired.

"Hmmm.... Four hundred twenty years, eight moons and six days, I believe," responded the House first great father. Looking at his wife and taking her hands in his, he continued, "Yes, she has been and still is my *one*. Please do not misinterpret my statement as there has been only happiness in our relationship for all this time. No, we have had our difficult times too, but we are committed enough to each other to face each challenge together and overcome them all. We promised to fiercely love each other one day at a time. Those many days have now turned into centuries. Je Buel is the only felf I have ever loved enough to call my wife." The House great father then smiled and kissed his wife.

While in the garden, the other four granddaughters and grandsons joined them. Even Je Danei's pet panther came too. Upon seeing Annaei again, Ony walked up to her and licked her hand. "Grandfather, can we please keep Annaei? She was going to fight the three of us after we had abducted Kei. Please grandfather, we need another sister to make things fair," Je Jero requested.

"Ha! Things have never been *fair* since Leena was born! Our female victories will even be greater with Annaei," Je Danei countered.

"Well, it does seem you have everyone's support, including Ony's, Annaei. And I agree with them too. So, welcome to our family. I too would be pleased and honored to have you as my granddaughter," Je Taeliel warmly remarked.

With that announcement, Annaei again embraced the House first elder and quietly cried, "Dank ye. Me will be a dutiful granddaughter and make ye proud."

"Oh, please stop crying. Now that you are in Torondell, we need to take you shopping for some new clothes," Je Danei said looking childishly at her grandfather and extending out her hand. Je Leena immediately copied her older sister's childish persona as well and extended her hand too.

Je Leena also pleaded, "Please, please, please Papa."

"Watch and learn, Annaei from your future sisters," Je Kei said as he leaned towards his betrothed.

The elder House great father looked at his granddaughters momentarily with his stern, cold gaze, but then he softened his facial expression, sighed, and placed a small bag of coins into each granddaughter's outstretched hand.

Both House Je Luneefa daughters smiled at their grandfather and kissed him on his cheeks after thanking him for their gifts.

Annaei also kissed the House elder on his cheek and remarked, "Dank ye, but House great fader, dat be too much coin. Me do not require fancy clothes, maybe just a few, new simple dings. How can me repay ye back? We will return de extra..."

"Sister, hush," Je Leena interrupted, taking Annaei's arm in hers and started pulling her away. "Grandfather is pleased to spend coins on his beloved granddaughters, especially a future granddaughter. You must not diminish that seldom displayed joy from him. He gladly wants us to spend all the coins given; so, none shall be returned. Goodbye everyone."

"Bye all. We will return this afternoon. Thank you, Papa; you are still the best grandfather in all the kingdom!" Je Danei declared running to catch Annaei by her other arm.

Je Jero looked at his grandfather and extended his hand. Both Je Tero and Je Kei followed suit. Je Taeliel responded with a frown and then walked away laughing.  Je Jero said, "Brothers, grandfather again demonstrates a double standard."

"Hah!  Just to you eldest brother perhaps.  Thank you, Nana," a smiling Je Kei said while extending his open hand towards his grandmother who gave him a bag of coins.  "Thank you, Nana; you are still the best grandmother in the entire kingdom too!"  Je Kei shouted as he started running towards the castle with his elder brothers yelling and giving chase.

Smiling to herself, Je Buel realized her ten-year peace within the stronghold was now over.  "Welcome home dear grandson.  Thank you, Kei for returning home safely," Je Buel said, laughing and followed her husband inside.

The next morning, the Je Luneefa family met in the great dining hall for their early morning meal.  Annaei rose prior to dawn to help the kitchen staff prepare the day's first meal.  She was also hoping to have another chance to meet with the House first elders and listen and learn from them.  Just after dawn, both Je Buel and Je Taeliel arrived at the kitchen to prepare meals for the entire family, especially the things Je Kei likes.  Annaei was rewarded by helping both elders when and where she could.  She performed all tasks assigned to her without challenge and as quickly as possible.  The elders smiled at her a few times and even asked her some questions about her life growing up in the Blood Tears Mountains.  Annaei gladly shared her stories and appreciated the elders taking such an interest in her.  Annaei was beginning to feel more and more comfortable with her future, new family.

After a short time, Annaei followed the House elders to the main hall where the rest of the family would gather for meals.  All the Je Luneefa granddaughters and grandsons were already there arguing over some topic.  Je Kei was seriously busy studying some scroll.  The House second elders were seated, holding hands, and lovingly gazing at each other.  As the House Je Luneefa first elders entered the hall, everyone became quiet.  Warm greetings were exchanged.

Suddenly, all the granddaughters and grandsons rose quickly, pushed their chairs back away from the table, and rushed to their grandparents.  The males rushed to their grandmother and the females rushed to their grandfather.  The granddaughters and grandsons wanted to personally escort their House first elders to the table.  Annaei just observed quietly.  The House first elders enjoyed the affectionate attention they were receiving, smiling at their small group of attendants as they walked to the dining table.  The House second elders did not seem to notice their younglings' performance. The second elders continued to keep their loving gaze locked upon the other. Occasionally, Je Maron would kiss the hand of his wife and say something to her which Annaei could not hear. After the House first elders were seated, the granddaughters and grandsons took their seats again.

House first great mother Je Buel sat at the head of the large, rectangular table. House first great father Je Taeliel sat to her right. House second great mother sat to Je Buel's left. The Je Luneefa grandsons sat on the same side as their grandfather, from oldest to youngest. House second great father, Je Maron, sat next to his wife followed by the Je Luneefa granddaughters, from oldest to youngest. Both Je Kei and Je Leena signaled to Annaei to take a seat next to him and her. With all eyes upon her, Annaei began to feel that all-too-familiar nervousness. Not sure, Annaei decided and took the empty chair next to Je Leena.

"Ha! Little brother, your charm and love have their limits it seems. Do not ever underestimate the bond the House Je Luneefa females share! You now owe us some coins," Je Danei announced.

"Do not be sad son; it was all in good fun. Besides, I thought you had already learned not to bet against the females who help and support Annaei," Je Maron said.

"Father, did you too bet against me?" Je Kei asked.

"Fortunately, yes; I finally won a bet," Je Maron proudly declared. Laughter started around the table as requests were made about the other Je Kei stories. During the meal, there was plenty of laughter. Questions were asked of Annaei too and she gladly told the family about her early meetings with youngest grandson of the Je Luneefa family.

"So, Annaei, did you sleep well last night? Is your room comfortable?" asked Je Pagi.

"Yes and yes, House great mother. Dank ye. Me room be very nice. But, if me be causin' any trouble by me stayin' here or if inappropriate, de House soldiers' barracks would be fine too," Annaei said.

"No, no, no, we have plenty of room here in our stronghold. You are our guest, and your staying here is no trouble at all," Je Pagi said.

"Annaei, I hear you had a bit of an altercation yesterday when you went to the market. Please explain," Je Buel requested. At that moment, all conversations around the table ceased immediately. Annaei stood and faced the House great mother who now had a cold, emotionless appearance.

Annaei took a deep quiet breath and explained, "Yes, House

great mother. Me wandered off a bit to look at some shops and noticed while lookin' at some various cloths, a group of noble females were harassin' some poor dwarves beggin' on de street. One of de females in dat group also attended de welcome home feast given by de Pi Zhou sisters. Me looked at dem and commented dat it be not very noble of dem to harass de poor and unfortunate. De main loud female looked at me and asked if me knew who she was. Me told her me did not and did not care. De oder female who attended de Pi Zhou sisters welcome home celebration told her friend me was Je Kei's betrothed. De main loud female den sneered at me and remarked dat 'Je Kei could do so much better'. Now, bein' annoyed, I responded, 'Perhaps, but he chose me and me him. So, dat matter be closed.' One of her oder friends asked if dey should teach me some manners in speakin' to me 'betters'. Me asked de main loud female if she just wanted to fight me or all four of dem. Me told dem it did not matter to me. Me asked dem if dey wanted to fight unarmed or wid weapons, first blood or to de death. 'Nobles should marry only nobles, not peasants', be all she den said.

"Dose females just laughed at me and de main loud female made some snide remark about ye House great mother not directin' yer grandson properly. Me drew me hammer and knife den and challenged dat main loud female again. Her eight escorts drew der weapons and started approachin' me.

"Me learned later, yer friends, House great father Nui Samu and his nephew, Ona Drachir, both came out of de seamstress shop and stood next to me. Dat loud female did not accept me challenge and told de escorts to stop. She did say dat der was some unfortunate 'misunderstandin'' and dey left. Me do not understand why dey just walked away when der insults be challenged. Also, dey clearly had de numbers on der side, twelve to just dree."

Je Buel smiled slightly and said, "My dear, thank you. As you found, nobles can be petty. Secondly, House great father Nui Samu is arguably the finest weapons master in the northern kingdom. His nephew is also a fierce, accomplished warrior. Despite their numbers, skill and experience greatly favored you and those melfs, I believe. They really did not want to fight you after Nui Samu and Ona Drachir joined you. Also, there were three other formidable warriors in the crowd whom you do not know yet. These three would surely have assisted you."

"That is quite impressive Annaei; you saved that young noble felf's life. And it is only your second day here in Torondell. Had Je Danei or Je Leena heard that remark against grandmother, either sister would have killed her," Je Jero remarked.

"This matter is then closed; let us now finish our after-meal tea," Je Taeliel said.

# A Dragon's Blessing

They finally made it to the designated meeting place atop Mountain Toron. It was just before sundown, and they were all exhausted from their three-day journey to this rendezvous point. At this height, the weather was quite cold, with strong blowing winds of ice and snow. Fortunately for this group of travelers, they were protected by their magically enhanced House capes which kept them warm and insulated from the violently harsh weather.

The trek up the mountain was dangerous and arduous; only very few knew the safest routes. Ona Drachir had carefully guided the group up the mountain. Despite severe unwelcoming weather, they endured over the past few days, they were all in good spirits; for today, they would finally reach their destination, the secret lair of the great dragon, Ona Kei Kuri Ryuu.

Ona Drachir had safely guided all the sons and daughters of Houses Je Luneefa and Nui Vent to the dragon's lair. After passing through a secret entrance and a few outer protective, magically enhanced, warded walls, the group entered a warm, comfortable inner sanctum of the dragon's lair. There, the group was welcomed by the great dragon herself, her rider, Ona Noirar and House Nui Vent great mother Nui Honei.

"*Well met Ona Drachir and daughters and sons of great Houses Je Luneefa and Nui Vent,*" said Keiku to her guests through Ona Noirar. "*Welcome to my home.*" The guests greeted the dragon and the elders after bowing respectfully to them.

After letting her guests rest a bit and eat a warm meal, Keiku stood and looked upon the new guests to her home. The group immediately became silent and gave their attention to the great dragon.

Keiku mentally communicated her words to Ona Noirar who, in turn, vocalized the dragon's words for the guests, *"Again, thank you for coming to my home. You are all most welcome here. I have known some of you for a truly short period of time, and others I have known for over centuries. Regardless of the time spans, I have come to consider you all my friends. As such, I now wish to honor each of you with some gifts as sincere tokens of my friendship. I believe troubled times are coming; so, these particular gifts will better prepare you for whatever the future holds."*

Ona Noirar and his nephew went to a side of the lair and got a cloth-covered table and placed it to the side of Keiku. Keiku then said through Ona Noirar, *"Please rise and stand before me. Daughters and sons of great noble Houses Je Luneefa and Nui Vent, I want to bless you all, starting with the gift of my blood."*

Ona Noirar then said, "House great mother Nui Honei, if you would please." At this time Nui Honei rose, walked to the table, and removed the cloth. There on the table was a large, golden bowl with handles of dragon images. Also, on the table was a knife with a golden handle carved in the same dragon's image. In addition, there were eight matching smaller bowls as well as eight vials. Nui Honei picked up the knife and large bowl. She then went to the front side of the dragon, carefully lifted a scale on Keiku's shoulder, and made a horizontal incision. Blood started to flow, and the House great mother collected the blood in the large golden bowl. After a few moments, Nui Honei magically sealed the small wound, returned the scale to its rightful place, and stepped in front of the dragon. Nui Honei then presented the bowl of precious dragon's blood to Keiku. The great dragon examined the bowl contents and barred her fangs as if to mimic a smile, very pleased to see another example of her power and majesty right in front of her. Keiku fully blessed her untainted, freely given blood three times, citing the Massicenae incantation in the ancient dragon's language which Ona Noirar translated for the group,

> *Blood of my ancestors, blood of mine.*
> *To these friends, I freely give.*
> *I beseech thee my ancestors; bless my gift.*
> *Let our dragon's blood be transformative.*

The dragon's blood glowed a soft red as Keiku's blessing evoked the magical properties of her blood.

House great mother Nui Honei looked upon the eight guests and called Je Jero, the oldest, to step forward. The first son of House Je Luneefa first bowed to Ona Kei Kuri Ryuu and then to House great mother Nui Honei. He then kneeled stretching out his arms with his palms facing the ceiling of the lair. Nui Honei dipped the knife into the bowl of the dragon's blood, raised it and translated a question Keiku wanted her to ask him, "*Do you accept my gift, Je Jero of House Je Luneefa?*"

"Yes, great dragon, Ona Kei Kuri Ryuu," the melf replied. Nui Honei then cut both palms of the kneeling melf. Nui Honei placed twelve drops of the mixed blood into Je Jero's small vial. Keiku's blood was absorbed into the wounds of his palms. His palms glowed for a few moments. The hands' wounds closed and healed immediately.

This blood-magic ritual was repeated for each of the remaining daughters and sons of great Houses Je Luneefa and Nui Vent. Afterwards, the guests stood in front of Ona Kei Kuri Ryuu. The great dragon looked down upon them and said, "*Dear friends, you are now of my blood. As such, each of you can now communicate with me and I with you, through mentally projecting our thoughts. Since our bond is new, the distance over which you can communicate with me is limited. This distance will become greater as time passes and our bond strengthens. Since you all share my blood, it is a common link that can help you also communicate mentally with each other should you wish to do so.*

"*As you know, dragons are blessed with the best vision and hearing abilities of any creature in this world. Dragons also have a very keen sense of smell, like no other creature. My blood that now runs through your veins can give you dragon eyes, ears, and nose through the magical properties of my blood. Je Leena is a mage and can use a spell to give her enhanced vision, hearing and sense of smell; but they are not equal to real dragon senses. With a new spell I will teach you, you will truly have the vision, hearing and sense of smell I have, albeit for a short period of time.*

"*You each will receive a vial of our mixed blood. Use this wisely. Your vial is dedicated and bonded solely to its designated recipient; so, only that recipient can unlock its full blood-magic properties. You may or may not yet have seen what dragon's blood can do to your blood-magic weapons. If not, know that dragon's blood greatly increases the weapon's power.*

"*Taking a single drop of my blood will enhance your health, stamina, endurance, speed, and strength. It also can serve as a powerful healing potion. As before, I will teach you the spell you will need to unlock my blood's full potency. Remember to use my blood sparingly and wisely."*

"Again, thank you all for your friendship," Keiku said after describing the gift she had just bestowed upon the daughters and sons of Houses Je Luneefa and Nui Vent. Each daughter and son eventually regained her/his voice and thanked the great dragon for the gifts.

Keiku then taught them the incantations they would need to evoke the dragon's senses. She then taught them another incantation to evoke the magical properties of the vial's blood. Ona Noirar then instructed the group on how to mentally communicate their thoughts to just a single individual or to a group.

Before leaving the dragon's lair the next morning, Keiku recommended to the daughters and sons of Houses Je Luneefa and Nui Vent that each should place a drop of the mixed blood from their vials into their morning tea. On the return trip, Ona Drachir again led the daughters and sons of Houses Je Luneefa and Nui Vent home. They all practiced using their dragon blood-enhanced senses. They even practiced their ability to mentally communicate with each other. With their newly received blessings, the group returned safely in two days in incredibly good spirits and very thankful they were friends with a generous and mighty dragon.

# Meeting Death

It has now been two moons since the House Je Luneefa elders returned to their home in Torondell. Now that Je Kei has returned, the stronghold witnessed a variety of new, welcomed sounds. Some sounds were familiar, like the Je Luneefa granddaughters and grandsons arguing over some trivial matters or the Je Danei preemptively claiming victory again during battle or martial arts training. Even Annaei has fallen into a routine of helping the House elders when she could, training alongside the House Je Luneefa granddaughters and grandsons and spending time with her future siblings. Though quite noisy and chaotic at times, the House Je Luneefa first elders were overjoyed with the entire family being together again.

Je Buel and Je Taeliel found that they even liked the "new" sounds from Annaei when she participated in heated discussions or competed against others while training. All the House Je Luneefa elders were pleased with Je Kei's choice of the Clan Battle Hammer felf.

Well after sundown, a lone, invisibly cloaked figure silently walks towards the House Nui Vent stronghold. Earlier that evening, he had noticed that the House Je Luneefa first great mother and father, Je Buel and Je Taeliel, had visited this stronghold and had not yet left. The cloaked figure is a dark mage who had transformed himself into a small insect and clung to the cape of Je Taeliel to secretly gain entrance into the House Nui Vent stronghold, a stronghold expected to have magical wards of protection. The dark magic this mage adeptly practiced again helped him get closer to achieving yet another significant objective.

After transforming back to his human form, beads of sweat formed on this silent figure's forehead although it was a cool fall evening. His magic takes a high cost. A high fever had overtaken him; another symptom of his desperate situation. He is now truly dying, again... This man needs to secure a small amount of dragon's blood, ideally a black dragon's blood, to prolong his wretched life. Majeejp, a human dark mage, has lived well beyond a normal human's lifetime using dark magic whose main ingredient is blood. Since the murder of his elf wife and mixed blood belf, vengeance against his former sect gave him a reason to live. He reminded himself, time and time again, that he can join his loved ones in death only after he had utterly destroyed the dark mage sect, Night Wind.

Now quietly hiding in the empty great dining hall, the dark mage waits patiently, plotting his next actions. Majeejp laments silently to himself, *"I have now lived well over two hundred years even though I look like a well-fit man in my forties. However, this is only a temporary disguise. The dark magic is waning; my body and mind will revert to their true forms very soon unless I can perform the dark, blood-magic Sihirkan spell. Now, with each new day without performing that ritual, I feel the torturous pain of aging, my high price of using dark magic.* "*My true age hastens to claim me, to rightfully transform me back; so, I can be finally delivered into Death's waiting hands."*

The dark mage also reminds himself, *"I must not die yet; my revenge is still incomplete! Yet, without obtaining some dragon's blood soon required to incant the dark magic Sihirkan spell, I will continue to age quickly by forty years with each new sunrise. I will revert to an increasingly decrepit soul since the dark magic maintaining my youth wanes. Only dragon's blood, the most powerful blood, enhanced with my dark magic, can delay this aging process. I have cheated death before and I dare to again rob Death yet of another victory these next few days! I am just not yet ready to die!*

*"Such is my desperation, that I will take blood from a dragon whether alive or still unborn. Beyond prudence, I even dare to invade the House Nui Vent stronghold where I knew the famed dragon rider, Ona Noirar, visited often to see his beloved House Nui Vent great mother, Nui Honei, an acquaintance of mine from many years past."*

The dark mage further recalled, *"After escaping captivity*

*from the House Si Moina's stronghold long ago, Ona Noirar and his then pregnant dragon returned to Torondell. Had the eggs been laid? Where were they hidden? Ona Noirar led another attack against House Si Moina that left him terminally poisoned. This warrior died; and as such is the bond with his dragon, his dragon followed him in death. But before his great dragon died, Ona Kei Kuri Ryuu destroyed her secret lair in the Taurus Mountain. But did Ona Noirar share any secrets with his beloved Nui Honei regarding the location of any dragon eggs? Did Nui Honei even have them secretly hidden away? Dragon eggs, especially those of a black dragon like Ona Kei Kuri Ryuu, would be prized even more than a small kingdom. Surely, Nui Honei must know."*

Majeejp is jolted again with shooting pain throughout his body, again feeling the repercussive effect of his waning dark magic. This reminds him that Death still happily waits... Given the severe torment his mind and body would face over the next few days, Majeejp knew his best chance of obtaining any black dragon's blood soon would be from extracting some, regardless of the small quantity, from a dragon's egg.

*"I am literally betting my life on the existence of such eggs or a secret cache of dragon's blood that Nui Honei might have. Ona Noirar and his dragon would have only entrusted any of those precious eggs to Nui Honei. Hence, I must force her to give me that information of their location. Being a renowned battlemage herself, I know extracting the information from her will be quite difficult; because she would die before willingly sharing that well-guarded secret. But that is a chance I had to take. I have no other options but to die a painful death which I do not want now. All of Night Wind had not yet been destroyed; so, I must still live a while longer,"* he thought. *"However, there may be others, ones very close to Nui Honei, I can use for my benefit..."*

"Your grandfather is being attacked!" yelled House great mother Je Buel. Immediately, she, her granddaughters and Nui Honei rose from the dinner table and dashed out of the small dining room. Je Buel, always having a mental bond with her husband, directed the group's path to her husband. "He is now in the great hall fighting some unknown assailant!"

"*Ony, to me now!*" Je Danei mentally called to her pet panther who was also enjoying a meal in the Nui Vent stronghold kitchen. Je Onyxia Ryoshi, Je Danei's twenty stones, pet black panther, quickly transformed herself into fighting fury given the tone of Je Danei's mental voice. She knew death was coming for someone this night. The great cat darted out of the room and headed towards her master as a dark blur of light.

Before opening the doors to the great hall, House great mother Je Buel said, "Noisa!' to the group. This was the House Je Luneefa secret battle language command that informed her group that they would soon encounter a battlemage. Je Buel, being a proficient battlemage herself, opened one door of the great hall, and encased her group with a protected shield of magic. As the group entered the room, they spread out to make each of them less of a target. There on the floor, in a pool of his own blood, lay House first great father Je Taeliel.

"You are indeed a desperate fool to come here and attack my father Majeejp," said Nui Honei. Know that you will surely die this night! Are you still looking for dragon's blood to prolong your terrible life?" As she expected, each member of her group instinctively called upon their dragon eyes magic to locate the invisibly hidden mage who was standing in one of the room's darkest corners.

Using a magically enhanced voice he could cast from afar, a tactic to distract opponents, Majeejp, deliberately disrespectful, responded, "Honei, give me a dragon's egg or any of the dragon's blood I know you must have. Do so quickly and I will let the old melf live."

Je Buel then mentally communicated to the group, "*Attack!*" From that moment, Je Danei threw deadly shuriken; Je Leena summoned lightning and hurled it; Nui Honei cast a spell to immobilize the intruder; and Je Buel, not fearing for her own life, just walked slowly towards their adversary with deadly intent. The dark mage stood about one hundred steps before her. Her shield of magic was projected in front of her, protecting her from the assassin's attacks. There would be no retreat; this mage or she will die tonight. From her cape, the House great mother had retrieved two blood-magically enhanced sai swords which she planned to use to extract her revenge personally. The usually kind-hearted and warm grandmother had now transformed into a hell's death angel. Her walk was steady and deliberate as she approached the dark mage who was busy countering attacks from her group.

When she was just two steps away from Majeejp, an almost invisible black blur of light darted past her and into the dark mage. Ony had received another command from Je Danei to kill the dark mage. As such, the panther immediately located her victim and began ferociously raking away at the mage's protective wards with blinding speed and fury. Now, Majeejp began to weaken even more quickly from the numerous powerful, rapid attacks of Je Danei's panther.

Prolonging any defense against the panther and the small group would be hopeless and end with his death, especially with House great mother Je Buel one step away from striking him. Magically, Majeejp greatly enhanced his hands' size, grabbed Ony and threw her at Je Buel who was then knocked off her feet several more steps away. He then quickly siphoned what remaining life force the dying Je Taeliel had to himself. This supplemental energy, he hoped, would help him then escape after he carefully aimed a bolt of deadly dark magic at the youngest felf, Je Leena who had foolishly discarded her protective magical shield to increase her attack speed.

"No!" Je Buel screamed, somehow sensing Majeejp's plan; and she threw both of her enchanted swords at the dark mage. Both penetrated his multi-layered, protective wards, but not deep enough to kill him immediately. He still managed to release his dark magic bolt as he fell to his knees in greater pain. Je Buel too continued to act quickly intercepting his magic bolt and absorbing it into her body away from the less-protected Je Leena.

Now that the small Je Luneefa and Nui Vent group was momentarily distracted by the fallen House elders, the wounded Majeejp broke one of the great hall's windows and made his escape with the use of his cape's levitation power.

Pointing to the broken window, Je Danei commanded her panther to go after the dark mage, "Kill!" Without hesitation, Ony hurled herself through the broken window to track and kill the dark mage.

Meanwhile, Nui Honei bent down and gently raised the dying Je Buel, propping her against the wall.

"I do not have much time left; so, listen carefully and dutifully obey my last wishes without questions," Je Buel slowly said in a dry voice. She grabbed her granddaughters' hands, looked at them and smiled. "Granddaughters, I am so proud of each of you. I have and will always love you both. Continue to honor our House. Be strong, noble, brave, honest, and kind. Fight and love fearlessly. May you both find happiness and become great leaders of House Je Luneefa. Make your own destiny. Look after each other.

"Nui Honei, you were closer to me than my own sister. I have always considered you to be one of my closet friends and another precious daughter. I love you too. Please look after my family," continued Je Buel.

Moments later, the dying House first great mother opened

her eyes and told Je Leena, "Quickly, get my sai swords." Je Buel then presented her hands to Nui Honei who cut both palms of the House great mother. Je Leena returned with her grandmother's sai swords and placed one in each of her grandmother's bloody palms. Looking at Je Danei, Je Buel said, "I bequeath to you granddaughter these noble swords which befits you, warrior." She then spoke the blood-magic incantation ending with, "Canela voi drago Je Mosai and Je Mosii Wei. I release you both now to my granddaughter Je Danei. Serve her well." Nui Honei then cut the outstretched palms of Je Danei, with tears flowing from her eyes, who took the swords from her grandmother. Each sword began to glow, as well as absorb Je Danei's spilled blood from her hands. Both weapons, Je Mosai Wei and Je Mosii Wei, ceased glowing after absorbing the blood of Je Danei.

Je Buel next said, "Leena, I must now pass on to you my last gift. As the last living mage in our family, please accept my magic essence."

House first great mother Je Buel next looked at her old friend and just said, "Again, please." With tears flowing down her face, Nui Honei again cut the outstretched hands of Je Buel again and then the hands of Je Leena. Je Buel clasped her granddaughter's bloodied hands and started another blood-magic incantation. Their hands glowed red as Je Buel's blood and her magic flowed into her granddaughter. This ritual also transferred the House great mother's magic knowledge. Smiling, the dying elder felt, "Now take me to your grandfather because I wish to die in his arms."

The House Je Luneefa daughters lifted their grandmother and carried her to the deceased House Je Luneefa first great father, her beloved husband. Je Buel was gently placed next to Je Taeliel. Je Danei and Je Leena then wrapped their grandfather's arms around their grandmother. House great mother Je Buel opened her eyes one last time, looked upon her deceased husband, and proclaimed "I will meet death with a peaceful heart; I have lived a good life. Welcome me beloved, for I am now joining you." House Je Luneefa first great mother Je Buel then died with both her heart and mind at peace.

Je Danei released a loud yell. Je Leena quietly cried to herself. Nui Honei had already mentally cried out to Ona Noirar, Nui Samu, Ona Drachir, and her sons. All six seemingly reached the great hall at the same time. All were battle-ready looking for signs of any foe to slay.

"Jooba. Go; get my armor, weapons and cape and return

quickly," commanded Je Danei, now engulfed with blood lust. Silently obedient, he turned and ran away to fulfil the command.

Je Pagi now entered the hall with the rest of her family and Alleina. The House Je Luneefa second great mother surveyed the death scene quickly and asked, "Who dared attack my mother and father?"

"The dark mage, Majeejp who was still looking for dragon's blood. He killed your father first; your mother sacrificed herself to save Je Leena from a dark magic bolt he launched at Je Leena," a greatly saddened Nui Honei reported. "He is gravely wounded and left through that broken window. Ony is tracking him now."

"Speak to no one about what has happened this night to anyone outside of our family," ordered House great mother Je Pagi.

"I will give chase too this night and kill him myself!" Je Danei promised.

Je Pagi noticed that her daughter now held her mother's favorite weapons; no doubt she received those treasured swords just before she died. The House second great mother also looked at her other daughter, Je Leena who was still crying quietly. She gestured to both daughters and embraced them both. Je Pagi started crying along with her daughters. The others joined the House Je Luneefa females in quiet, respectful mourning.

Shortly thereafter, Nui Jooba returned carrying Je Danei's requested items. Upon seeing him entering the hall, Je Danei turned and ran towards him. At the door, she turned, looked at her mother and said, "I now go seeking blood revenge on those who attacked the Je Luneefa family! If I should die, do not mourn me; I have lived well. And I promise, I will die well, spilling the blood of our enemies." She turned again, leaving the hall with Nui Jooba close behind.

After reaching the hallway, she took her House cape from Nui Jooba and put it on. She then uttered a magic spell which removed her outer clothes. Her light armor then went from her hands onto her body. She then called upon another incantation and hair fell from her head, leaving only two strips of hair, one red and the other black, running from the front to the back of her head. The sides of her head were magically shaven clean. She placed the sai swords she received in her boots and donned her sword belt, taken from Nui Jooba. She now had a scimitar on each of her sides. She last put on her helmet and took her spear from Nui Jooba who marveled at the transformation. "Now, let us go to war!" she said. She and Nui Jooba left the stronghold immediately.

"*Ony, where are you now?*" Je Danei asked mentally.

"*North pier docks,*" was the returned message from her pet. "*He boarded a boat, but I do not see him. I believe he collapsed on the deck.*"

Both she and Nui Jooba left the Nui Vent stronghold, mounted their waiting horses, and headed quickly towards the docks. Before she left the stronghold, she mentally communicated her destination, "*the south pier docks,*" to her mother, aunt, and sister. Her mother and daughter simply relied, "*Hunt well.*" Tonight, Je Danei is consumed with blood-rage and intended to kill all the enemies herself without any additional assistance.

Moments later, Nui Honei looked at her sons and the sons of House Je Luneefa and ordered them to follow Danei and Jooba to the south pier docks and help them on their quest.

When they reached the north pier docks, Je Danei and Nui Jooba could see one ship had just cast off from the pier. A fierce battle raged as loud noises erupted from that ship's deck as a black panther fought against the crew. The panther's prey was still lying on the deck, not yet dead. Those who dared get in her way, Ony made them pay dearly with each swipe of her deadly claws. With the hoisting of the ship's sail, Je Danei could see the sigil of House Si Moina on it. They halted their horses close to the end of the pier, dismounted, and ran to the pier's edge. Both jumped towards the ship, using the magic of their capes to levitate onto the fleeing ship. "*There are only about twelve sailors left on-board,*" an enraged Je Danei quickly discerned. "*That is nearly not enough to kill this night!*"

When the panther got within six steps of the still mage, she leapt towards him. Somehow sensing eminent danger, the mage opened his eyes to cast another spell at the leaping panther, paralyzing it in the air. Ony fell immediately onto the deck. It was then completely helpless as three sailors mercilessly stabbed the panther repeatedly.

"No!" screamed Je Danei as she finally landed onto the ship's deck. She was now engulfed in Hell's maddening fury. "*All aboard that ship will surely die this night without any mercy!*" she thought. In a matter of moments, the enraged Je Danei and Nui Jooba killed all the remaining sailors. Je Danei plunged her sai swords into the mage's eyes as he gasped his last dying breath.

After she removed her blades, Nui Jooba beheaded him with one swing. He then went over to the beloved panther and lifted Ony off the deck. They both then called upon the magic of their House capes which lifted them easily off the boat and carried them back to the pier where they gently landed.

"What do we do about the boat?" asked Nui Jooba.

*"You need not worry; I will take care of that,"* came the voice of Nui Honei mentally transmitted. In the next moment, a large, red flame-spear was hurled from an invisible source high above them. When the flame-spear struck the ship, that was now out in the middle of the bay, the ship was completely incinerated with such force and heat that a nearby fishing boat also caught on fire. A short while later, the obliterated Si Moina ship sank.

Nui Jooba gently placed Ony across the saddle of his horse. He and Je Danei turned and walked slowly back to the Je Luneefa stronghold. Neither spoke knowing no words would give either comfort from their first, real meeting with death.

Although it was now close to midnight, Houses Je Luneefa and Nui Vent were on full alert when they reached the western gates of the Toronwalein. House soldiers were now in full battle armor along the wall and at the gate. As Je Danei and Nui Jooba walked through, there was an eerie silence that seemed to grip everyone. The normal sounds of the night seemed mournfully extinguished, out of respect to those who had fallen this night.

After crossing into the Je Luneefa stronghold, House servants met the House first daughter and Nui Jooba. "Clean my pet and prepare her for burial," ordered Je Danei. Upon seeing her personal maid, Tess who had also come out to meet the House first daughter, Je Danei ordered harshly, "Have my horse cleaned and clean my weapons and armor. Prepare my bath first." She then turned to Nui Jooba and said seething with anger, "At dawn, the day after my grandparents' funeral, I leave to go to repay a blood debt. Will you join me?"

Nui Jooba looked at Je Danei and knew that she sought revenge upon House Si Moina and wanted to now go straight there to kill all in that House. For the deaths of her beloved grandparents and pet, Je Danei sought the blood of all within the enemy House. Nothing else would sate her thirst for revenge. Anything or anyone not supporting her current objective would be quickly disregarded, he knew. She intended to be an angel of death and wanted to start her journey as soon as she could.

"Yes," I will join you on your quest," Nui Jooba answered. "Let us meet later today to plan our journey. "To the end!"

"To the end," Je Danei replied solemnly.

# Gambit Answered

Later that morning, Nui Honei observed that the bodies of her fallen, dear friends, her only beloved "real parents" had been removed. No doubt they had been returned to the House Je Luneefa stronghold for funeral preparations. She was grieving quietly through tear-filled eyes as she watched the servants clean the hall, stained and damaged from the previous night's battle.

Other than her brother, Ona Noirar and Alleina, the House Je Luneefa first elders were her oldest and dearest friends. In fact, she considered them more like family. Her real family, the few that were still alive, disowned and abandoned her long ago. She and her brother joined the banished princess Rho Chele and Ona Noirar in their exile to the northern kingdom. Then, House Je Luneefa welcomed her and her brother not caring about their clouded pasts nor the circumstances by which they had come to this forsaken part of the kingdom at that time so long ago.

With time, Nui Honei and Nui Samu proved themselves to be true, good friends of House Je Luneefa. She and her brother were both "adopted" into the Je Luneefa family which gave them more protection, being members of one of the kingdom's great noble Houses.

Both House Je Luneefa first great mother and father, Je Buel and Je Taeliel, considered Nui Honei and Nui Samu to be the great mother and father of House Nui Vent. The Canae queen and king, still bitter and angry with the betrayal of their daughter to go into exile with Ona Noirar, would not recognize House Nui Vent because of Nui Honei and Nui Samu's support for Rho Chele and Ona Noirar's relationship. Despite their differences with the kingdom's rulers, House Je Luneefa afforded both Nui Honei and Nui Samu all the respect, honor, and courtesy of being leaders of their House.

"I must do something. Blood must be answered in kind," Nui Honei thought.

Later, she walked into the small dining hall where her sons were eating their midday meal. Unlike so many other times, she did not greet them warmly. From the moment they first noticed her after she entered the hall, they all knew something was quite different about their adoptive mother. The new House Nui Vent brothers immediately stopped eating and became very still and just watched their mother who was approaching them with a grave look upon her face. Her anger, from the previous night's attack upon the House Je Luneefa elders, was still visible to those who knew her. Further, the Nui Vent House great mother was attired in their House colors of red and black. She wore her full, protective armor and carried her helmet adorned with dragon wings. Nui Honei also wore her House cape clasped with the innocent-looking, Manriki-gusari chain. She carried a small shield, as well as long and short swords. What the sons noticed first too was the most striking feature, her shaved head with two bands of three-fingers high, red and black hair from the front to the back of her head. Her eyes foretold her message: death comes this day.

Nui Honei said, "My sons, I bid you 'goodbye' should fate have it so. I leave now to kill all House Si Moina soldiers I find within this city. Their audacious murder of a dear loved one within my House demands my immediate response. Remember me as your mother who absolutely loves you. Avenge me should I fall."

"Mother, please wait just a short while till we return," Nui Danka said. Without any further words, the three House Nui Vent sons then immediately rose from their table and left the hall. Shortly thereafter, Nui Danka, Nui Jooba and Nui Rei all returned, clad in their armor and ready for battle. Nui Danka carried shield and javelin; Nui Jooba held his battleaxes and Nui Rei carried his shield with short swords on his sides.

"We shall join you on your quest to inflict death upon the enemies of our Houses," Nui Danka said to his mother after he and his brothers returned to the hall. The Nui Vent sons all extended a weapon and declared together, "To the end!"

Looking proudly at her sons, Nui Honei repeated the same vow, "To the end!" She then sternly issued an order, "None of you die this day!"

"The Nui Vent House soldiers replied as one, "Yes House great mother, we understand."

"Where should we first begin?" Nui Danka asked.

"The place where I can kill many of them," the vengeful Nui Honei responded. She turned and left the hall with her dutiful sons following her.

When they arrived at the Red Horse Inn, a well-known gathering place for House Si Moina soldiers, it was loud inside with numerous and varied patrons meeting there in the early afternoon. Most of the inn's guests were there drinking in the large, main room. This room accommodated over twenty tables, most of which were already occupied with patrons. After Nui Honei and her sons arrived, they quietly walked in and stood by the door. Very few took serious notice of the deadly four elves who moved a bit more into the main room of the inn after a few moments when their eyes adjusted to the room's light. The noise emanating from the many patrons ranged from loud stories being told or retold to quiet debates over the best armorers in the kingdom. Lies and truths were all intermixed well together again.

Finally, an impatient Nui Honei said, "Jooba, get their attention." Nui Jooba responded by raising and swinging an axe, ending with the shattering a large, unoccupied table. The thunderous noise from the destroyed table immediately demanded and received obedient silence from everyone. The House Nui Vent great mother looked around the room and then announced, "Anyone not associated with House Si Moina, I strongly suggest you leave now; those remaining will be killed." Whether shocked and/or too drunk, many patrons just stared momentarily at the House Nui Vent elves. Reality then hit them that death for some had just entered the room and for those not part of House Si Moina, death could maybe pass them by today. The next moment, many patrons started to leave quickly.

Upon first entering the room, the House Nui Vent foursome instinctively scanned the room and recognized those bearing the sigil of House Si Moina, a great brown bear on a background of light bluish grey. In total, there were sixteen House Si Moina soldiers there sitting at six different tables around the room.

The clear four-to-one odds or his drink may have emboldened one Si Moina soldier who threw a knife at Nui Honei as he rose from his table. This Si Moina soldier's knife missed; Nui Rei's knife thrown in a fast, deliberate response, just after the Si Moina soldier started to rise from his chair, did not. Nui Rei's dagger was completely buried in his enemy's neck.

"Soldiers of misled, deceived, and now doomed, House Si Moina, I am House Nui Vent great mother Nui..." Nui Honei started.

"Peasant blood bitch..." another Si Moina soldier started to say but could not finish for Nui Rei killed him instantly with another well-thrown dagger to his neck.

Nui Rei said, "Please continue House great mother."

"As I was saying, soldiers of misled, deceived, and now doomed, House Si Moina, I am House Nui Vent great mother Nui Honei. You are just pawns sacrificed in a game you do not know well at all. Your House's gambit of secretly attacking mine has failed! Where are more of you in Torondell? I wish to kill you all," Nui Honei continued. The only response she received was the drawing of blades from the remaining House Si Moina soldiers as they stood.

Much blood was spilled thereafter in the ensuing mayhem. The House Nui Vent warriors were victorious in the small battle, and no one was seriously injured except those soldiers of House Si Moina. All the Nui Vent sons gave silent thanks to their weapons masters, both Nui Samu and Ona Noirar, for their many days of close quarters combat training.

A short while later, Nui Honei and her sons opened the door to the inn and emerged into the afternoon autumn sun. When she saw the innkeeper standing in the street, she reached inside her cape and retrieved a small bag of silver. She threw the bag of coins to the innkeeper and said, "This is again recompense for the damages and inconvenience. Do let me know if the amount is insufficient." The innkeeper knew from the bag's weight that there was too much compensation judging from the time she paid him for his inn's damages last caused by her sons and their friends. Still, he was quite grateful for the House great mother's generosity.

Nui Honei and her sons made their way to other inns known for entertaining House Si Moina soldiers. Just before sundown, Nui Honei and her sons were leaving a third inn where they had left more dead House Si Moina soldiers. The House great mother extended a bag of gold to the innkeeper before entering the street to stand next to her sons.

Down the street, clad in full battle armor was a squad of Brown Bears, the elite fighting unit of House Si Moina soldiers. Like the House mascot, the great bear, these soldiers were supposed to be ferocious and the finest of the House Si Moina army. There were twenty-four soldiers facing them in a six-by-four formation.

They all were armed with spears and shields except the squad commander who carried a single-bladed axe and long sword.

Tredan, the Brown Bears commander, looked at the House Nui Vent group and pointed to Nui Jooba. The squad commander then leaned forward and roared his battle cry while hitting his weapons together. This was an invitation for single combat to the death. No mercy is wanted nor would be given.

"I wanted to first kill that little, scrawny son of yours, but I think that would be too easy," boasted a confident Tredan who pointed at Nui Rei. Smiling and unafraid, Nui Rei started to move forward smiling, but his brother stopped him.

"He challenged me first brother, not you. Let us see if he is any good. All his other comrades died too easily," Nui Jooba said. Looking at the House Si Moina squad, Nui Jooba continued, "Thank you for finding us; you saved us time by not searching for you. Are there any more of you left in Torondell? We plan to kill you all. So, it is good that you sought us out first; for death awaits you."

"Death awaits us all, peasants; but you shall be first to lead our way," responded Tredan. Now enraged by the House Nui Vent soldier's arrogance, Tredan screamed his battle cry again and charged at Nui Jooba. Nui Jooba, after taking four long strides forward, threw both of his axes at Tredan which struck with such force that both of his axes shattered Tredan's meager defense and buried themselves deep in his chest. Tredan died instantly. The dead Brown Bear leader was also propelled backwards and crashed into his squad.

Two spears, from the squad of Brown Bears, were then launched at Nui Jooba who had already magically recalled his axes and blocked the hurled missiles. In that same moment that the spears were thrown, two arrows went screaming down into the squad of Brown Bears killing the would-be, cowardly assassins. From a building's rooftop, Ona Drachir descended to the streets. He laid down his bow and quiver; he then next removed his House cape. The last son of House Ona Feiir then drew his twin scimitars and scoffed at the remaining squad of Brown Bears while joining his friends of House Nui Vent.

"The numbers still favor us!" shouted another House Si Moina soldier.

"That is what the other House Si Moina soldiers thought too, and they are now all dead, including your famed leader who is also now worm food," shouted Nui Jooba in response.

"Hold House Nui Vent," came an order from a familiar voice behind the Nui Vent group. Without turning around, House great mother knew that her brother, the ever so deadly Nui Samu, armed with his twin battleaxes, had just joined their ranks. To the House great mother's surprise, Je Kei and his loved one, Annaei, were there too ready for battle.

"Can we please fight now before any more unwanted help arrives?" Nui Danka asked.

With that, Nui Honei issued a command, "Axei fourei," which told Nui Samu and Nui Jooba to advance forward from their group and hurl their axes into the Brown Bears who were now marching towards them in standard spear-shield formation. As expected, the enchanted, dragon blood-enhanced, Nui Vent weapons easily cleaved through the shields of the front soldiers who had false hopes of relying upon those shields and armor for protection. Their faith was misplaced as the four more soldiers now lay dead in the streets. A moment later, all the battleaxes magically returned to their owners' outstretched hands.

Both groups clashed ferociously thereafter. The small House battle waged on for a while. No Brown Bear remained alive at the end and no House Nui Vent soldier nor friend was seriously injured. "Now, let us go home," House great mother Nui Honei said to her group.

"Not yet, you peasant bitch!" screamed a female voice from down the street. Walking from one of the street front stores' shadows was a lone soldier wearing armor and a House cape bearing the sigil of a great brown bear against a background of light bluish grey. This House Si Moina soldier's face was painted with a scary red pattern indicating she was ready to meet her death should fate have it so. "I owe you a debt of blood Honei; come fight me now." This lone House Si Moina soldier removed her cape and started walking slowing to the middle of the street. She then drew her long and short swords from her sides.

All the House Nui Vent sons regripped their weapons and turned to face the lone Si Moina soldier upon hearing their mother being challenged. All three sons requested to kill the Si Moina soldier on their mother's behalf.

"Who are these three fools rising in response to a challenge directed at you? Or are they your mongrels perhaps? None of them even look like you; so, they cannot be yours. Oh, that is right; my mother closed your womb. You could not bear any offspring with your dead lover. Ha, Ha, ha," laughed the Si Moina soldier mocking the House Nui Vent great mother.

"Who are you, one so ready to die?" Nui Honei asked.

"I am the third daughter of House great mother Si Cairyn, Si

Caili. I am here to die after first killing you and any other of your House. Though I stand alone, I am honored and proud to die for my House. So, Coa vae coa!" Si Caili demanded. She desired single, individual combat of House versus House, just she versus Nui Honei first and then any other afterwards. House honor, valued more than one's individual honor, was at stake. "Enough talking now; come meet my blades."

Nui Honei calmly removed her House cape and helmet. She then grasped her Manriki-gusari. This innocent-looking adornment is very much another deadly weapon. At one end of the black steel-linked chain was a blade. A weight was attached at the other end of the eight-fah length chain. After removing the sheath covering the dull black, diachrom Kyoketsu-Shoge blade, Nui Honei walked to the middle of the street facing her opponent. The House Nui Vent great mother held the bladed end of her Manriki-gusari in her left hand. She dropped the weighted end and started slowly spinning the chain with her right hand while walking slowly towards Si Caili.

"*Good choice of weapon sister,*" Ona Kei Kuri Ryuu's voice echoed in the House Nui Vent great mother's mind as she approached Si Caili. "*You expected treachery and this House Si Moina soldier's blades are covered in poison I see. Again, this House chooses to fight without honor. Beware. I could spear her, even from this height, and just spare you the trouble.*"

"No, thank you. Just remain high in the sky cloaked invisible. I will give this hag her last life's lesson. I did expect poisoned blades given that House's reputation. Have Ona Drachir be ready with his bow should other Si Moina cowardice soldiers be lurking in the shadows," Nui Honei replied to her sister.

"Before you die, Si Caili, answer this question: is it true that you and your four, five, maybe even six sisters all have different fathers?" Nui Honei requested.

Not enraged, Si Caili screamed her war cry at Nui Honei and started charging towards the House Nui Vent great mother. At that same moment, Nui Honei started spinning the weighted end of the chain faster and faster until the chain seemingly disappeared. Given the chain's color and the remaining low light from the day's sun last rays, Nui Honei's weapon was rendered practically invisible. Her Manriki-gusari was also an excellent defensive weapon against an opponent wielding a weapon in each hand. Nui Honei also knew she could keep Si Caili's poisoned blades at a safe distance with her Manriki-gusari, her chosen weapon of death.

Nui Honei spun her weighted-end chain horizontally above

her head as Si Caili charged. When Si Caili was within three steps of Nui Honei, the House Si Moina daughter lunged with her long sword hand. At that same moment, Nui Honei quickly side-stepped, started spinning her weighted-end chain vertically and hurled that end towards Si Caili. Si Caili attempted to block the missile with her short sword, but it was invisible to her eyes. The weight of the Manriki-gusari hit Si Caili in the chest just below her chin.

Each of Si Caili's attacks thereafter was blocked either by chain or by Nui Honei's blade. In response, Nui Honei countered with other weighted-end attacks, heavily hitting the Si Moina soldier four more times in her head, chest, and arm areas. While Si Caili's armor protected her from Nui Honei attacks' deathblows, each blow inflicted severe pain.

"Your lesson is now about over," Nui Honei coldly declared to her opponent. With this announcement, Nui Honei started spinning both ends of her Manriki-gusari vertically while gripping the center positions of her chain. This was the first time Nui Honei used this tactic and it confused the doomed House Si Moina soldier. Si Caili hesitated.

Given that Nui Honei could alter the effective length of her weapon and effectively use either end for deadly purpose, Nui Honei would alternate the speed and attacking end of her Manriki-gusari. Perhaps, out of frustration being unable to launch any successful attack or defense, effectively counter any Nui Honei's attacks, and being mercilessly pummeled, Si Caili made one last desperate, low charge at Nui Honei with both her blades. This time, Nui Honei spun her weighted-end Manriki-gusari around the attacker's arms locking them. Nui Honei then spun into her opponent hitting Si Caili's chin upwards with an elbow attack that then exposed the neck of Si Caili. With her blade hand, Nui Honei viciously cut Si Caili's exposed neck with a mighty downward slash. The Si Moina soldier fell to the ground gripped firmly in death's hand.

With no remorse for the fallen Si Moina soldier, Nui Honei silently recovered her weapons and cape and started quietly leading the House Nui Vent soldiers home. *"Well done sister, well done!"* Keiku said to the House Nui Vent great mother as she departed.

Although still sad and grieving over the loss of her dear friends, she was now less angry. Battle and killing enemies lessened her pain.

After arriving at the eastern Toronwalein gate, the Houses Nui Vent and Je Luneefa party passed through and went to their respective stronghold. Nui Honei had also reached out mentally to Alleina and asked her to attend to any minor wounds they had. Other than bruises, Nui Jooba had also suffered a few small cuts. Alleina met Nui Honei and her sons after they entered the stronghold. She pulled Nui Jooba aside into a small sitting room to clean and dress the small wounds he had.

"Where is he?" came a shout moments later from a familiar voice outside the room. Je Danei stormed into the room and looked at Nui Jooba angrily. "Why did you go to battle with House Si Moina soldiers without me?"

"Hello Danei; bye Danei," an annoyed Alleina said, then stood and turned to leave the room. Just as she reached the door, Alleina turned and scowled at Je Danei saying. "He is fine by the way with no serious injuries." Alleina left the room.

"Thank you Alleina," Nui Jooba called out loudly and then turned to enraged Je Danei and replied, "There was no time."

"How many House Si Moina soldiers died? Are there more left in the city?" Je Danei asked quickly.

"Fifty-two House Si Moina soldiers fell this day. We believe there are no more soldiers remaining here in the city," responded Nui Jooba.

"Argh!" she exclaimed, swinging her axe and destroying a small table in the room. "How many did you kill?" she asked, continuing her angry and frustrated rant.

"Twelve died by my hand," Nui Jooba replied.

"Brother, how is your wound? Will you need help getting to your room and removing your armor?" Nui Danka asked after he and Nui Rei poked their heads into the room. "We were both hurt too; so Je Danei, would you please help our brother?" Nui Danka requested.

Nui Jooba stood and feinted he had an injured leg and needed support by stretching out his arm towards the House Je Luneefa first daughter. She then went to him and let him lean on her while he started propping up his imagined hurt leg.

"I nearly died tonight," he said whispering in her ear after she leaned towards him for support.

"You may still," she replied quickly as they started walking slowly out of the sitting room.

"As I was nearing death a few times, I only thought of you first daughter of House Je Luneefa," Nui Jooba whispered undeterred into the ear of his attending felf.

As the two of them walked and limped towards Nui Jooba's bedchamber, Nui Samu saw them making their slow progress. He walked up to them and said, "Well met niece. Danei, my nephew fought brilliantly tonight. I only joined them for the last battle. We/they were outnumbered in all four battles as much as four-to-one. We honored your grandparents very well on this night with the ultimate offering of our enemies' blood. May they continue to rest peacefully. And may you continue to honor them by living well."

"Thank you, Uncle; I shall try," Je Danei pledged. The pair respectfully bowed to the House great father and continued their slow walk-limp to Nui Jooba's bedchamber.

"Lastly, please do not kill my nephew this night; I am quite fond of him, and it would be so embarrassing too," Nui Samu requested as he left.

"I shall not tonight," Je Danei promised. Then looking at Nui Jooba, she said, "You are indeed a fortunate melf; I do love your House great father and will honor his request. You will not die by my hand this night." Nui Jooba smiled in response.

After a few more steps walking towards his bedchamber, Nui Jooba said, "Then kiss me now so that I may heal faster," the embolden Nui Jooba whispered in Je Danei's ear. Instead, she punched him in his side in response. Nui Jooba responded with fake sound of pain.

When Je Danei and Nui Jooba finally reached his bedchamber, the persistent Nui Jooba, unshaken by her earlier threat and punch, looked at the felf and asked, "Will you help me remove my armor and garments?"

"I can," she replied, now with a bit of a shaky voice.

"Are you not afraid that I may try to kiss you again? Battle ignites my passion for you I have learned. Facing death earlier tonight emboldens me now, first daughter of House Je Luneefa. And, most importantly, you promised our uncle you would not kill me this night," reminded Nui Jooba.

"You are such a foolish male! Are you not afraid of meeting one of my eight hidden blades, wielded by a much more skillful hand than those you fought tonight? Yes, I will not kill you this night, but I may remove certain parts from your body. So, beware; you have been warned," Je Danei quickly retorted. "Your insurance is quite limited and can expire in a moment."

Nui Jooba limped to the middle of his bedchamber and raised his arms inviting Je Danei to now remove his outer garments and armor. Je Danei quietly stood motionless thinking to herself. After a few quiet moments, the felf walked seductively over to him looking deeply into his eyes while removing her jacket. "Close your eyes," she whispered when she stood next to him. Je Danei removed his house cape with fingers caressing his neck and threw it aside. She could feel Nui Jooba's intense body heat emanating from him. Nui Jooba was even slightly shaking nervously.

"You seem to have a fever; are you not well?" she asked.

"No and yes. When you are this close to me, dangerously close, my blood boils. I want... eh. I do want to discover all your hidden blades," Nui Jooba said as sweat started to form on his brow.

How many blades have you counted?" she asked while biting his ear.

"Only the two in your boots and the two on your arms," he replied after a long thoughtful sigh. He then moved his head closer to kiss her. He missed his intended target since he could not aim properly with closed eyes.

"Good observation," she again whispered into his ear. "I still carry four more deadly blades and can use any of them with either hand for deadly purpose. Beware melf. Speak and act carefully. This will be your only warning," Je Danei said. She then moved again silently behind Nui Jooba, and purposely "threw" her voice into his right ear while she moved to his left.

Nui Jooba feinted movement to his right but turned quickly to his left to kiss a surprised Je Danei who then pushed him away and silently drew two blades from sheaths on her back. Still with closed eyes, Nui Jooba smiled and said, "I claimed your second kiss too! My gambit was worth it. Today is indeed a good day," he proclaimed.

"Your faking injury you mean in hopes of getting me alone in your room? For what purpose? I noticed too your switched "injured" leg when you walked to the middle of your room. The ruse is over, foolish, foolish male," declared Je Danei.

"My love for you is no ruse. I willingly faced death earlier tonight with no fear but am far more excited and fearful to face you and to kiss you again," Nui Jooba said as he opened his eyes to face Je Danei several steps away. "I do not fear your long knives either. Why is that?"

"You are clearly now thinking with your other, smaller head, foolish male. Do not be misguided," Je Danei noted. She then put her knives back into their sheaths and started to unbutton her vest and shirt. "Now, close your eyes and keep them closed."

"Do you plan to harm me?" Nui Jooba asked.

"Yes fool, in a way you cannot imagine," Je Danei replied again using her soft, seductive voice. She walked over to Nui Jooba, kissed him deeply and whispered in his ear, "Go and clean yourself, because you stink." After a few moments needed to recover from his emotional shock and paralysis, Nui Jooba walked to a door on the side of his room, opened the door to his private water room and went in. He quickly cleaned himself. Moments later, he emerged from his private water room clothed only in a robe to find his bedchamber now empty and almost silent. He only heard his loud, beating heart.

After laughing hard about his failed last gambit, he recaptured some victory from knowing that she willingly and passionately kissed him last! Her third kiss was his too! Today was surely a good day, he thought and laughed again despite his distinct, stiff frustration...

Thinking now of the beautiful Je Danei and *her* third kiss, Nui Jooba reached out to her mentally, "Oh *first daughter of House Je Luneefa, you indeed harmed me like no other tonight. I will seek revenge!*"

"*Ha, ha, ha. You are such a foolish male,*" Je Danei replied mentally. "*Plan well then since you will not sleep well this night, I imagine...*" she laughed as she ended their mental communications.

Upon reaching the entrance to the Je Luneefa stronghold, Je Danei started to again feel the immense grief of losing her beloved grandparents and family elders. Her precious Je Onyxia Ryoshi is gone too. The weight of losing close loved ones engulfed her as tears began to form again in her eyes. She imagined Ony was there, just inside the stronghold's entrance like so many times in the past, waiting for her. Upon Je Danei's entrance, the panther would open her eyes and stand by the felf's side.

Instead of going directly to her bedchamber, Je Danei silently checked to ensure her parents and siblings were all there. She knew the magically warded stronghold offered a variety of secret, protective defenses; but the first daughter felt compelled this night to personally verify each one's presence and safety.

When Je Danei arrived at her sister's room, she noticed the bed chamber's door was partially open. Je Danei softly knocked and opened the door wide. There she saw Je Leena standing in the middle of the partially dark bedchamber staring back at her. A small fire in the room's fireplace radiated some warmth, as well as illuminated the bedchamber with some light. "All is well, sister? Did you kill Jooba?" Je Leena asked.

Je Danei closed her door and then replied, "Everyone is here safe, including an extra guest. No, I did not kill Jooba this night despite his not contacting me for battle."

"Annaei is no guest; she will soon be our sister. She is our dear brother's chosen beloved one; please welcome her. Both she and Kei were in a deadly battle this night with House Nui Vent against House Si Moina. I am sure that blood-rage ignited and multiplied their passion for each other. Being close to death will make them want to cherish life and each other more. Understandably, Annaei will be in his arms tonight. She will most likely make him hers completely. Similarly, Jooba's passion for you was also ignited after his battles. I am even a bit surprised you returned home tonight. Is that hard to understand? Are you still uncertain about yourself?" Je Leena asked.

With tears forming in her eyes, Je Danei replied, "Leena, again your words both amaze and frighten me. Though you are my younger sister, you are most wise for someone so young. You are more like Nana in this way. I understand Jooba's feelings, but I am still not ready to return his feelings since I truly do not understand mine. More time is required."

"Take your time then; he is patient and will wait for you if and when you are ready," Je Leena said opening her arms to embrace her sister. "I love you Danei and will support you."

"Thank you, sister. I love you too Leena." Je Danei responded and hugged her sister tightly. She then turned and left Je Leena's room.

After finally reaching her bedchamber, Je Danei remembered walking with her pet panther so many times. After closing the door, she walked to the east wall of her room and started putting away all her blades except for the sai swords she had received from her grandmother. Those she will always keep close to her. Je Danei went to the center of her cold, lightless room, sat down on the floor, and started shedding new tears with the now overwhelming grief of her deceased, dearly beloved grandparents and pet.

*"I am also very confused and overwhelmed with the burden of Nui Jooba's unrequited love. How do I remain strong in this situation?"* she asked herself, desperately hoping that the wisdom of her grandparents would be recalled and help her. After a while, an old memory of her Ony came to mind. Ony then had mentally communicated an answer to that same question many moons ago after she imagined the loss of her grandmother who was terribly ill then. Ony then answered, *"By living well; this is what your noble grandparents would want you to do. They both told you that, 'The only certainty in life is death. We all must die someday. So, live well, bravely and with honor till then.'"*

*Ony also added then, "Should you even need the comfort of*

a melf's touch to just hold you, Nui Jooba would immediately come."

"Why would you think of him?" Je Danei had asked.

"Foolish felf! His scent is on you. Evidently, you wrestle with him again after he disarmed you in battle training, did you not? His heart is completely yours. Did you really think I would not notice? Why do you seem to 'try harder' during training exercises especially against him?" Ony mentally communicated as she made a low guttural sound which was the panther's way of mimicking laughter. "Did you enjoy his company this evening? Did his presence provide you any comfort? If so, maybe you should thank him.?"

"Yes, he did, in his own way," Je Danei had replied. She had looked at her pet and said, "I am so grateful you are my best friend. Thank you." Ony then began licking Je Danei's hand in response.

After a few more moments of careful inner-reflection, Je Danei mentally reached out, "Jooba, are you there? Answer me quickly fool; I know you are not asleep. Uncomfortable and frustrated now perhaps; but trying to deceive me again by feinting sleep gains you no advantage."

"Yes, I am here. Do you miss me already?" An embarrassed and frustrated Nui Jooba responded hoping his question would deflect Je Danei away from furthering his aggravation and discomfort.

Je Danei then continued, "Thank you for taking away my grief, but for only a short time."

"You are most welcome. I do not know the pain you feel, but I will try to comfort you as best as I can. You do not need to grieve alone. Your family is there too to support you, to cry with you, to comfort you and to listen to you. Please do not feel you need to be 'strong' all the time. Even the strongest are weak sometimes; such is life. Should you ever need me to listen to you, cry with you or just hold you close, I will come to you. Just ask," Nui Jooba said.

"Thank you again, Nui Jooba. Good night," Je Danei said concluding their mental communications.

# Subtle Messages

It is early morning, shortly after dawn. House great mother Nui Honei is sipping tea in front of the fireplace in the small dining hall. She is deep in thought, going over all the events occurring in the last few days. Since the attack on the Je Luneefa family elders, both Houses were on alert, fully prepared to repel a single intruder or stand against an entire army. No outside visitors were to be permitted inside of the Toronwalein. Fortunately, only House Je Luneefa, its private army and House Nui Vent resided behind this wall. The Je Luneefa private army, now at four hundred eighty strong, is well trained and ready for any possible conflict. Je Taeliel's vision, executed by Duenor Heartstone's ingenuity, made the center of Torondell a very well-designed and mighty fortress from its inception. Nui Honei again quietly acknowledged the foresight of the House first great father. She knew if any enemy ever attacked them there, they would pay dearly with their blood, as well as their tears.

"What were the true intentions of House Si Moina by attacking the Je Luneefa elders? What did they hope to gain? The fifty-two Si Moina troops she encountered within Torondell were not in itself significant since Torondell attracted many types of visitors. Was the mage's attack a diversion or the beginning of another attack upon her House and/or the Je Luneefa family? Did Majeejp, by accident, encounter the Je Luneefa elder or was it preplanned?" the House Nui Vent great mother thought quietly to herself reviewing many unanswered questions after returning from yesterday's quest of purging Torondell of any remaining Si Moina soldiers.

Later this morning, she would meet with the troops of the House Je Luneefa along with House great mother Je Pagi and father Je Maron. This afternoon they would also speak to the northern army and inform them of recent events. Nui Honei took comfort in knowing that these House soldiers were extremely loyal to Houses Je Luneefa and Nui Vent, just like most of the northern army. Je Taeliel had built strong forces, treated all his troops well, earned their respect and trust, and became a much-loved commander. Throughout his time as the Commander of the northern army, he himself would lead charges and fought during some of the greatest battles. As a warrior himself, Je Taeliel inspired his troops and gained devoted loyalty.

The House Je Luneefa first great father, an accomplished military leader, though did not practice kingdom politics well in Rhodell and had been perhaps "banished" to the northern kingdom for his honest, straightforward, but unpopular manner. As the first appointed Commander of Canae's Kuze Karkazanae, "lands conquering" northern army, he was expected to die fulfilling his duty. Canae's history had proven such in the past when kingdom expansion became a priority for the Crown. Through Je Luneefa's leadership, the northern frontier did become Canae's lands; law, order and peace were firmly established in the once lawless territory; and the once vast unproductive land expanse was transformed into a fertile, productive and the most highly valued territory of the kingdom.

Commander Je Taeliel founded the North's first city, Torondell. After initially defeating Canae's enemies opposing the kingdom's expansion, Torondell grew from that first military bastion the Commander founded. Settlers from the capital, as well as other parts of the kingdom, slowly migrated to the North. For his near-impossible accomplishments, Commander Je Luneefa Taeliel was appointed to the position of Canae's Warden of the North. With time, Torondell not only expanded, but it also greatly flourished, like the northern realm.

The citizens of Torondell loved the North's Warden for his fairness and just administration. Even during the early hard times, when many citizens could not pay their taxes, taxes rightfully due to the Crown were always paid on time even if the Je Luneefa family would secretly pay the shortfall and collect the delinquent taxes later. Je Taeliel and Je Buel had said that was a small price to pay for keeping the evil of Rhodell in Rhodell and being left alone in peace.

Yet the Canae king and queen's jealousy of the House Je Luneefa's unequaled success and Torondell's growing popularity greatly annoyed House Rho who envisioned themselves to be the greatest and most powerful family in the kingdom. Even the glory of Rhodell, the capital of Canae, seemed to be waning in favor of Torondell.

The queen and king loved power, sought more of it, and continued to plot to establish their family as the kingdom's rulers for generations to come. Queen Rho Jiedae and King Rho John, covertly and overtly, accumulated and maintained current knowledge of the all the great noble Houses within and around Canae. Whenever House Rho anticipated or encountered a threat to their House or its power, Rho Jiedae and Rho John, the first elders of House Rho, either boldly seized or ruthlessly destroyed that threat. Either resulting action was quite acceptable to the House Rho ruling elders who placed their House and attainment of more power above all else.

Even after several centuries, Je Buel and Je Taeliel kept the many secrets of the Je Luneefa family just to themselves. No Crown spy could ever successfully infiltrate Je Buel and Je Taeliel's formidable defenses. Like House Rho, the House Je Luneefa first elders addressed threats to their Houses with merciless deadly force. Despite the numerous attempts by the queen and king to assess the true strength and wealth of House Je Luneefa, the Je Luneefa first elders would not ever disclose true, detailed information.

Along with jealousy, ever-mounting fear had also plagued Queen Rho Jiedae and King Rho John for House Je Luneefa also controlled the powerful dragon, Ona Kei Kui Ryuu whose rider, Ona Noirar, was an adopted son of House Je Luneefa. Even though Ona Noirar had faithfully served the Canae kingdom and was extremely successful, he still committed a grave unforgivable crime against House Rho by returning the love of Princess Rho Chele. So, his death and more importantly, the death of his famed dragon were not mourned at all by the Majesties.

Several nights ago, Queen Rho Jiedae and King Rho John received the news of Je Taeliel's death. Queen Rho Jiedae was awakened when her special scrying bowl's magical alarm was activated. Upon hearing the news, the queen smiled evilly, awoke her husband and shared the secret communication. She said, "Husband, Commander Je Luneefa served Canae extremely well; he and his son-in-law accomplished several impossible feats in the

North. House Je Luneefa, through its other adopted daughters and sons, provided distinguished and exemplary services, deserving of our great appreciation, as well as our recognition. Still, House Je Luneefa, unlike all the other great noble Houses within Canae, has never requested a favor of me. I believe they never feared House Rho unlike the other noble Houses."

"We know Je Buel and Je Taeliel were very capable leaders; they quietly resolved their issues and threats to their family without our involvement," King Rho John remarked. "House je Luneefa never involved itself in petty squabbles with other Houses either. Both Commanders Je Luneefa even returned all the recovered stolen treasure on three occasions! No other Commander has ever done that before. Further, all of the North's taxes were always paid in full and before or on time. How? How was he able to do that and not the other Wardens, current and before? Were and aer the others just fools? Incompetent? Or was he again covertly making us look foolish? My best spies could not ever tempt, seduce nor wrest family secrets from him; he was beyond reproach. I hated Je Taeliel for that too."

"Yes, they never embarrassed the Crown. House Je Luneefa proved its loyalty and provided distinguished service to Canae repeatedly. They did so without ever expecting or requesting a reward too. In fact, their actions greatly benefitted the Crown and exalted the Canae's Majesties. Je Buel promised me that she and her family would solidify our places in Canae's history as its greatest rulers. Surely, she and Taeliel have accomplished that too. Je Buel told me directly, on several occasions, she just wanted peace and to her help raise her young ones... That wretched hag even threatened me in her own subtle way... Damn Taeliel! Damn Buel! And damn that so-called noble House full of adopted mongrels, especially that Noirar whose dragon protected their Houses from my wrath more than once. I agree; I too believed they never feared House Rho unlike the other noble Houses. But now is another day and very different circumstances... So, my king, my dear beloved husband, how should we now reap benefits from this new chaos? Also, our vengeance can finally be unleashed upon Houses Je Luneefa and Nui Vent!" Queen Rho Jiedae proclaimed.

"There will be some turmoil stemming from Je Taeliel's death. The next Warden of the North and First Commander of the kingdom's northern army will be a true prize with many competing for that coveted position. Alas, shall we wager upon who will first seek this open position and know to pay us handsomely for it?" the king asked, contemplating greater riches for House Rho. The queen soon also rejoiced, joining her husband in quiet evil laughter.

Nui Honei was awakened from her reverie after her brother entered the hall. Nui Samu joined her at the fireplace after pouring himself some tea. He knew his sister well and greeted her warmly, "Good morning, dear sister. You have been here for a while it seems thinking. What troubles you?"

Nui Honei returned to staring at the fire and replied, "All of these recent events created many unanswered questions. I want answers, not more questions."

A few moments later, the peace of the dining hall was disturbed when two of the three Nui Vent sons entered the room in a not too quiet manner. Nui Danka and Nui Rei were both excited, not for escaping death multiple times the day before, but for something else it seems. The sons greeted their elders respectfully with a bow and a warm, "Good morning." Nui Rei then went to his mother, kissed her on her cheek and gave her a slight hug to cap his greeting.

"Has anyone yet seen Jooba this morning? Did he survive his final battle last night?" Nui Danka asked jokingly.

Nui Rei snickered quietly to himself. "I just hope he is alive," Nui Rei said.

Nui Samu looked at his nephews sternly and said, "I would suggest you do not tease your brother when you see him. He may be in an unpleasant mood this morning."

"Why is that?" Nui Honei asked puzzled by the previous statements.

Nui Samu explained, "The House Je Luneefa first daughter came to visit last night shortly after you returned. She was angry that we went to battle against House Si Moina soldiers without her. She helped Jooba to his room since he was limping from some fake wound and requested assistance. Fortunately, when I saw them, I asked her not to kill him, but that was more for not inviting her on our previous day's mission."

After sighing, Nui Honei stated "Foolish male! She may have done so anyways or at least injured him; because she does not like being duped in any way."

"So, Jooba might be dead or hurt now?" Nui Rei quietly asked not wanting to really know the answer.

At that moment, the third son, a "happy" Nui Jooba, entered the room carrying two bouquets of pretty flowers. After first greeting his elders and brothers, he went to his mother and presented her a bouquet of flowers saying, "These are for you dearly beloved Mother. I again want to thank you for adopting me and my brothers. Since I am your favorite son, I would like..."

"Ha! No, you are not!" Nui Rei scoffed.

"Please, do not start that argument again. You both are so tiresome. Mother, could you please consider un-adopting those two?" Nui Danka asked.

Nui Jooba continued, "Mother, I may need your assistance this day. Would you please give these other flowers to the House Je Luneefa first daughter when you visit there House later this morning? I made some progress in my war with Je Danei last night; but she uncovered my ruse. I wish to apologize, but she will not try to kill or injure me if you present this peace offering."

Nui Danka just shook his head in disbelief and Nui Rei just quietly said, "Coward. Yesterday, you so easily faced the House Si Moina soldiers who surely would have killed you; but now, you are so afraid of this felf? I do not understand."

Nui Honei looked at her brother in frustration and he shook his head, acknowledging her same thought. The House Nui Vent great father looked at his nephews. "Let me please use this time as another teaching moment," the House great father started.

*"Of course, dear brother, please,"* the House great mother's eyes requested.

Nui Samu looked at Nui Jooba and continued, "Your mother is currently preoccupied with immense grief and other important thoughts over recent events. Further, this is a matter best handled by you, Jooba, since you are the one who tried to deceive Je Danei to gain some romantic advantage presumably. My experience has shown me that females appreciate a 'foolish male' more when he acknowledges his mistakes in a timely manner. So, make haste and sincerely apologize yourself while bearing your own peace offering. Consider escorting your mother to the Je Luneefa stronghold when she goes there."

"Thank you, Uncle. That is good advice, as always," responded Nui Jooba after a long sigh.

"Still, do wear your armor," Nui Honei added.

Both Nui Danka and Nui Rei laughed.

"More good advice. Thank you, Mother," said Nui Jooba.

Late morning, Nui Honei, accompanied by Nui Jooba, went to the House Je Luneefa stronghold. After entering the stronghold and walking to the designated meeting room, they met Je Danei in the hallway. "Well met, House great mother; good morning Jooba. Is that a peace offering for me for your failed ruse?" Je Danei said pointing to the bouquet of flowers Nui Jooba carried.

"Well met, Danei," responded Nui Honei who kept walking

towards the meeting room, giving the two young elves some privacy.

"Good morning, Je Danei," responded Nui Jooba. "These flowers are not for you. Why would you think that? There are other wonderful members of the House Je Luneefa family I do care about besides you. Ah Alleina, good morning; I have a small token of appreciation for your saving me from more serious harm last night. Thank you again," Nui Jooba said to the passing healer as he quickly handed her the bouquet of flowers.

"Good morning Danei; good morning Jooba. Thank you, but do you not think these flowers would be better served giving them to the rightful person you tried to deceive last night along with a sincere apology? Besides, you are not wearing your armor and standing dangerously close to your victim who is carrying six deadly blades, foolish male," Alleina warned and walked away.

"How does she know how many blades you now carry?" a puzzled Nui Jooba asked.

"Is that really important now?" an annoyed Je Danei replied.

After releasing a deep sigh, a baffled Nui Jooba replied, "You are correct; I do wish to apologize for my attempted ruse. I wanted to spend more time with you and the right words were lost. I..."

Je Leena, now walking by, interrupted, "Good morning Jooba. Why are you standing so close to my sister without wearing your armor? She is carrying six blades and you foolishly tried to deceive her last night. She does not like being tricked. Foolish, foolish male. Why do you seem so surprised? The bond between the females of this House is unbreakable and so very special, unlike any other. I strongly urge you to be completely honest henceforth. You have been forewarned."

"Thank you; I apologized just before you arrived," Nui Jooba explained.

"I know; but I still enjoyed watching your nervous reaction," said Je Leena who then walked away.

Turning to Je Danei, an uncomfortable and confused Nui Jooba quietly asked, "How did she know..." He stopped, cleared his thoughts, and decided to ask a different unrelated question to deflect the House first daughter away from his confused state. "And where might I find your brother Je Kei? I need to ask him a question regarding the mathematics of tunneling..."

"Shhh... Again, is that really important right now or would you rather spend your time alone with me showing me how to better use the blades you gifted me?" Je Danei whispered in his ear and then walked away.

Now less confused and a bit wiser, Nui Jooba just stopped talking and followed her.

Later, Nui Honei met with Je Pagi and Je Maron. Nui Honei again expressed her feelings of condolences and shared her feelings of rage against House Si Moina and the follow-on battles against the Si Moina soldiers. The House Je Luneefa elders thanked Nui Honei for her condolences and response to the killing of their House's elders.

"Have you completed the funeral arrangements?" asked Nui Honei. "Is there anything my House can do for you?"

"The funeral arrangements are still being finalized. We will hold a public memorial service by the Warden's castle in two days. Afterwards, we will return to our stronghold where my parents' bodies will be burned and their ashes entombed," Je Pagi said. "Today, we should scry a message to the Crown and we would like your assistance.

"Also, my mother transferred her magical essence to Je Leena before she died. I am uncertain how much power our daughter now has, but we fear she does not yet have the wisdom to manage all the new knowledge and power she received. So, please help her with the transition to rapidly becoming a more powerful battlemage. We know you have worked with her for a long time; please continue to do so."

"Yes, of course. I will spend even more time with her if she wants," replied the House Nui Vent first great mother and battlemage.

"Je Danei is another concern; she is filled with much grief and rage due to the loss of her grandparents and pet panther. She wants to lead a preemptive strike against the enemy House right after the funeral," Je Pagi said. "I fear her need for revenge is clouding her good judgement. Let us all help her through her grief and protect her as best we can."

"Yes, I understand and will help her too. Fortunately, Jooba, in his own, awkward way, tries to comfort her. I believe he is helping and regardless, he will be by her side should she try to leave by herself," Nui Honei said.

"Has Noirar returned yet?" Je Maron asked.

"No, but he is due back tonight," replied Nui Honei. "Shall we again meet at midnight here?"

"Yes, agreed," Je Pagi responded. "And let us postpone contacting the Canae queen and king then till tomorrow."

"By the way, I had a chance to watch Annaei in battle last night. She fights well and she compliments Je Kei too. Their dance reminded me of you two," Nui Honei added, wanting to hopefully uplift the Je Luneefa elders' sorrowful moods.

Je Pagi said, "We do like her and feel she fits Kei well. On the night we first formally met her, she declared that our Kei was her 'one'! She asked for our blessings to court him! I admire her strength and determination. I could not help but smile, knowing that our Kei finally met someone who could distract him from all his books and scrolls. He truly seems happy. He wants to keep her close to him too. Ah… First love is so awkward.

"Maron and I were told Kei seemed to enjoy life more since he first became serious about Annaei. The near-death experiences they shared last night during the battle just amplified their feelings for each other. I saw the passion and lust in their eyes after they returned here. I am sure Kei kept her close in his arms throughout the night…"

Je Maron continued, saying, "Even when they are just here, walking in the garden, he holds her hand. In fact, he is quite protective of her. He was only that way before with his sisters, especially Leena. By the way, Annaei even proposed to our Kei on our return journey after his graduation. So, there will be a Spring wedding we will need to plan."

Conversation shifted away from the funeral and other sad topics to the Je Luneefa daughters and sons, much more pleasant and spirit-lifting topics.

Later that night, Nui Honei met with Ona Noirar who had returned from a reconnaissance mission in Rhodell, the kingdom's capital. Nui Honei and Ona Noirar had a late evening meal together well after sundown. Ona Noirar started recapping his recent visit with the most relevant information, "The news of the Je Luneefa family elders' deaths had reached the ears of the king and queen. No doubt, Majeejp communicated news of his successful attacks to someone before he died, most likely another mage aboard that Si Moina ship. I can only assume that news was communicated back to the Si Moina stronghold and maybe to the capital, as well. Regardless, the news has caused quite a bit of unrest in the capital. Political maneuvering for the vacant Warden of the North post has already started.

"Although there may be five candidates vying for that position, the two assumed lead contenders are the king's General Yun Huang of family Ni Beitu and Pi Deahn of the Pi Zhou family. Both are greedy, anxious to increase their family's wealth and status; and they are very loyal to the Crown. Pi Deahn, a former ambassador to the kingdom's eastern frontier, is no friend since he failed to woo you, dear Honei, to his political ambitions when you both attended the Academy. He does not like to lose at anything.

"Pi Deahn is still bitter and has also developed more dislike for our Houses. Je Taeliel won the appointment of Warden of the North over him. His nephew lost the opportunity to court the first daughter of House Je Luneefa and his House has lost the last three Kilecfla events to House Nui Vent. Pi Deahn mistakenly feels the success that Je Taeliel created here for House Je Luneefa should have been his. He refuses to accept the fact that he was first to decline the opportunity when the king offered the Warden of the North position to him. He lacked foresight then and was unwilling to utilize the genius of Duenor Heartstone since he was a presumed commoner and a dwarf.

"The Crown has also dispatched troops to Torondell. Rhodell is sending two thousand troops here supposedly to honor the fallen Warden of the North. The Crown's emissary, General Yun Huang, journeys to Torondell for the funeral. Pi Deahn accompanies him. I suspect both are using this opportunity to spy and assess the Je Luneefa family strength and holdings here in Torondell. We must maintain constant vigilance for the time being and trust no one outside our families and House armies."

Later that evening, just before midnight, Nui Honei and Nui Samu, went to the House Je Luneefa stronghold. They were also accompanied by Ona Noirar. Despite the sorrow weighing heavily upon the House Je Luneefa elders, they were eager to hear what Ona Noirar had learned from his clandestine reconnaissance mission. Ona Noirar repeated what he had learned on his recent trip. He also noted that it was "unusual" that the king and queen would send such a large force to someone's funeral. This display of honor was a ruse in his opinion. If there is an ulterior motive for the deception, it was not readily clear. Ona Noirar urged caution and to maintain battle-ready alert and status.

"When do you plan to communicate with the queen and king? And have you given any thought to a recommendation for the Warden of the North position?" Ona Noirar asked. "Also, what is the status of the Canae northern army?"

Je Pagi replied, "We plan to speak with the Canae queen and king later this morning. We will have a public memorial service in two days. Afterwards, we will bring the bodies of my parents here where they will be cremated and entombed in the family crypt.

"Two days ago, we informed Queen Marta, King Joerson, Prince Dajald and Urtha Dal of the recent tragedy. King Joerson and Queen Marta, along with their escort, will first journey to their Taurus Mountain site and then come here for both memorial services. Before you ask, I do not know how they will be able to travel so quickly; however, Urtha Dal did say 'much magic be involved!'"

Nui Samu said, "I have recently spoken with the Canae northern army's three commanders. They are all deeply saddened and wanted me to express their sincere condolences to the House Je Luneefa family. They are also overly concerned about the appointment of the new Warden of the North. Many of the soldiers whose military service duties will end this year, plan not to reenlist should they not approve of the new Warden. Many of these same soldiers would like to join the ranks of our House soldiers."

"That, at least, is some good news," remarked Je Maron. "How many soldiers might want to join our Houses? And how much gold is required to purchase the early release of those soldiers whose military service terminates this year? There may be a need to have them join our ranks much sooner than later."

"This is the year when a full third of the northern army soldiers' service duties will end; and of that number, there is an estimated two hundred twenty that would want to enlist into our House armies. Five hundred gold should be more than adequate to acquire their early release, if need be," Nui Samu remarked. "Maron, the commanders would all favor your appointment to the vacant Warden's position."

"That may be so, but the Crown would not, I believe. I suspect the Canae Majesties would want to appoint someone here who would be loyal to and controlled by House Rho," Je Pagi said.

"What about you Brother taking that position?" Nui Honei asked.

"To preserve our Houses' relative peace and isolation here, I would gladly; however, I am neither loyal to nor can be controlled by House Rho," Nui Samu replied.

"Samu, you are much more qualified than me and your ability and patience to deal with the Crown exceed mine. The Canae northern army commanders would gladly endorse your appointment too, being a former commander in the northern army. I strongly suspect you would be most welcome returning from your 'retirement'," Je Maron said. "My role as the Ambassador to the five great orc tribes of the North could continue without any disruption, as well."

"I agree as well; we will just need to now convince the Canae queen and king to support our choice for the appointment. Could we possibly 'purchase' the appointment? Afterall, House Rho does like gold," Ona Noirar said. "Maybe if we sent the queen a secret message weighted with gold, she and the king would be inclined to accept our proposal."

Nui Honei said, "Giving that fool gold may just ignite King Rho John and Queen Rho Jiedae's passionate greed for more. I believe she will seek to establish some control over our Houses by insisting upon a marriage with their nephew and Je Danei. He will even agree to their living here in Torondell hoping his spies would be living inside the Toronwalein."

Je Maron then added, "Or maybe, the Canae queen and king plan to appoint one of their nephews as the Warden of the North and the other would become the Crowned Prince of the kingdom. House Rho would continue their royal line and a devoted spy would be firmly planted here in Torondell, the real jewel of Canae."

"Wait," Je Pagi interjected. "I thought it was strange when the king dispatched many troops the day after my parents were killed. How could he have learned of that tragedy so quickly? It would take days for so many troops to start a march. Is Rhodell truly responding to King Joerson's expedition? Or has something significant occurred in the northern frontier and Rhodell is responding to that?"

"Here we are again with more questions and not enough answers," a frustrated Nui Samu declared. "We should plan for the worst scenario, like Rhodell's preemptive attack upon our Houses."

"That is a bit extreme, do you not think?" Nui Honei asked.

"Maybe, but the king's troops will be here in three days. We need to be ready," responded Nui Samu.

"I will contact my spies again and see what more I can learn about the Crown's troops true destination and objectives," Ona Noirar added.

"Maron and I will contact Queen Rho Jiedae and King Rho John later today and formally inform them of my parents' deaths and our recommendation for the new Warden of the North. I will also contact Prince Dajald at Taurus Mountain. The dwarves' queen and king should arrive there later today," Je Pagi said.

After a knock on the door, Je Leena entered carrying some refreshments. After bowing, the young felf said, "I had thought you might like some additional wine, fruit and cheese. By the way, would it not be appropriate to thank Commander Roerson and his brigade for personally escorting you back home by inviting him and his brigade here, inside the Toronwalein, for a feast?" she asked. "It seems a potential issue may go away if we do have a feast for them.

With the Mountain Wreckers inside the Toronwalein for training purposes and another three thousand warriors nearby, I would hope any Rhodell force would seriously think twice before potentially attacking us here."

"Daughter, that is an excellent suggestion," Je Pagi remarked. "I and your father will speak with Prince Dajald, Urtha Dal and Commander Roerson later today then."

"Father, are you weeping?" Je Leena asked.

"Daughter, you again remind me you look so much like your grandmother and your suggestion is another reminder of her great wisdom. Thank you," Je Maron said.

"And my father, being ever so pragmatic would ask, "How will we possibly feed two hundred dwarves indefinitely? Do you realize how much they can eat and drink?" a tearful Je Pagi jokingly laughed.

About midday, Je Pagi and Je Maron planned to magically scry to formally communicate the deaths of the House Je Luneefa first elders to the Canae queen and king in Rhodell. The Canae Majesties expressed their sincere, heart-felt condolences for the famed nobles and true, "founding pillars" of the kingdom. The queen and king spent several moments praising both deceased elders for their many significant contributions to Canae over the centuries.

The queen also mentioned that two divisions of troops had recently been dispatched to the northern frontier for "training" exercises. These training exercises in the northern frontier are supposed to thwart a large tribe of renegade orcs who have been gathering on the northern frontier's western border. Considering the recent tragedy, the king would divert an emissary to Torondell who would personally attend the memorial services as a representative of the Crown.

"Your Majesties, we really appreciate this honor you will give us; so, please know that we will warmly greet your emissary. However, the memorial services had already been planned and will take place tomorrow. For my family's wellbeing, I want to bring closure to this tragedy quickly," Je Maron said just as his wife started to cry. "Please understand that losing the first elders of our House has been very difficult for us and we need to put recent events behind us as soon as possible."

"Your Majesties, please forgive me; but the grief I now bear is very heavy," Je Pagi interjected. "Husband, let us wait another day before we hold the memorial services to allow the Crown's emissary a chance to attend."

"We understand the pain of losing family's elders; we can sympathize and do mourn with you. Thank you for your kind consideration; it is also important for us to let the citizens of Torondell know that that Canae Crown is also mourning with them too and share their great grief. We will inform our emissary to be in Torondell by the day after tomorrow," Queen Rho Jiedae said.

"Thank you, Your Majesties, for your kind words and considerations," Je Maron said, "My wife, do leave if you wish. I only have one short matter to discuss with our Majesties." Je Pagi, crying softly, bowed to the images of the queen and king above the scrying bowl and went to the far side of the room, away from the communications device.

"Your Majesties, I would like to share with you our recommendation for the now vacant Warden of the North post," Je Maron continued.

"By all means, please do," the king said dryly.

"For a variety of good reasons ranging from in-depth knowledge of the territory and the northern army itself to maintaining the successful high standards already set by Je Taeliel, please strongly consider Nui Samu of House Nui Vent. He also has other golden advantages like no other candidate may have," Je Maron suggested.

With the mention of the term "golden", Je Maron could discern that both Queen Rho Jiedae and King Rho John's interests were aroused...

"Thank you for your input; but let us discuss this matter later after the funeral services. Thank you again," the king responded and ended the scrying communications.

"My dear wife, you never cease to amaze me; your acting skills are superb. Your 'crying' was a nice component of your deception," Je Maron said, complimenting his wife with a bow and the elegant gesturing of his hand.

That same evening, the House Je Luneefa elders contacted Queen Marta and King Joerson of Clan Battle Hammer. "Wat do ye need? Just please ask," a sorrowful King Joerson and Queen Marta implored.

Je Pagi replied, "First of all, thank you again for all your kindness and condolences in these sad, sad days. Your Majesties, we have learned that Rhodell has dispatched two legions of soldiers supposedly going to the northern frontier for 'training' purposes. Of those two thousand troops, some are now in route here for my parents' funeral services. One strange thing is that those troops left Rhodell two days ago, but we only informed the crown of my parents' deaths today. Those troops should arrive here in three more days."

"The crown did say that their troops dispatched to the northern frontier were going there for 'training purposes'; however, we really believe, according to our spies, they are going there in response to a large tribe of renegade orcs amassed in the western side of the northern frontier," Je Maron added.

"Dat king already has another plan fer dose troops headin' yer way, me dinkin. He cannot be trusted; he be too much like his father. Me Queen?" King Joerson remarked.

"Pagi and Mari, we could send ye some more warriors to yer House if ye want. We got three dousand here and two dousand more on de way. Apparently, word got around about yer and Bueli's good trail cookin; so, more warriors quickly volunteered to do some 'trainin'' wid yer House soldiers. How many do ye dink ye can feed indefinitely; cause good trainin' takes time and lots of good food?" Queen Marta asked.

"Ha, ha, ha. Well, Your Majesties, thank you. Could you please first send the rest of Roerson's brigade here tomorrow?" Je Maron's asked.

"Beggin yer pardon Pagi and Mari, me oder boys be already here, just outside yer city wall," Commander Roerson announced. "Me king and queen, when me told me boys and de oder warriors what happened to House first great moder Buel and fader Taeliel, dey all wanted to march here to guard de family. But me only wanted me oder boys here. Me did not want to cause any problems or have oders git de wrong idea about seein' dousands of dwarf warriors. Me also figured me King and Queen would need a large escort to git here safely in two days fer de funeral services."

"Dat be smart. Very good Roeri," King Joerson said.

"Please have them quietly join us here tomorrow morning inside the Toronwalein. I will send House Commander Lefohng to coordinate preparations with you," said Je Maron.

The next day, the fourth day after the deaths of the House Je Luneefa first elders, House great fathers Je Maron and Nui Samu walked into the House Je Luneefa great hall to address the commanders of their respective House armies, the commanders of the Canae northern army and the commander of the Dwarven host.

Je Maron first welcomed all the military leaders and said, "Commanders Somai, Lefohng and Devron of Houses Je Luneefa and Nui Vent, these are troubled times. Our Houses are under new attacks by unknown and unclear forces. Further, with the death of my father-in-law, the Warden of the North, new conspiracies against this House and Nui Vent have risen. We must remain on full alert indefinitely.

"We are only expecting Queen Djurdin Marta, King Djurdin Joerson and their immediate entourage inside the Toronwalein. No others are to be permitted without explicit orders from either Houses' great mothers or fathers. Should anyone attempt unauthorize entry, consider them a threat to our Houses and eliminate the threat immediately. I want extra guards posted along the Toronwalein and to accompany members of our Houses should anyone go out." Je Maron then looked at Nui Samu and slightly nodded.

Nui Samu continued, "Commanders Baka, Fini, and Sochae, you are the leaders of the Canae northern army. I fear your loyalty to the kingdom will be tested. Your priority has been and will be safeguarding the wellbeing of the Torondell citizens. Should either House Je Luneefa and/or Nui Vent come under attack, stand-down until House great father Je Maron or myself ask you to do otherwise."

"You all know both Commanders Je Luneefa were exemplary warriors and outstanding leaders whose soldiers would gladly fight beside them anytime, anywhere and against all odds. Fini, Sochae and I all served with the Commanders for many years. We loved them too and we are proud to say we called them friends. Their repeated, selfless generosity, dedication and loyalty shown to the northern army will not ever be forgotten. Know that Canae's northern army will continue to do its sacred duty of protecting the kingdom's northern realm and all its citizens," declared Baka, a harden soldier, born and raised in the army and a still very humble, having survived many battles.

"What would cause Rhodell to attack either noble House?" Commander Sochae questioned.

Nui Samu replied, "All the facts are not yet known, but this is what we do know. One: House Je Luneefa first elders were killed on House Nui Vent property. Two: Their killer fled to and boarded a vessel bearing the flag of House Si Moina. The killer and ship's crew were all killed later by our Houses' members. Three: Two divisions of troops left Rhodell the morning after the House elders were killed three days ago and were originally bound to the kingdom's northwestern frontier for supposedly training exercises. These troops include the Crown's emissary who now plans to attend the funeral services. However, no one here had communicated the news of my House elders' deaths to Rhodell until yesterday. Rhodell's troops should arrive here in two more days. Another two divisions left Rhodell today. Four: General Yun Huang is the Crown's designated emissary. As you probably already know, this general is ruthless and desperately wants the Warden of the North position.

"Commander Baka, I know about your brother's issues with this general and his unfortunate death. After Yun arrives, he will be the highest ranking Canae army officer here and most likely will provoke you intentionally as he did your brother. Would it be better for you not to be here when he arrives?"

"Thank you for your concern, but I will meet him as a dutiful and honorable soldier of the Canae army. Hopefully, fate will favor me," Commander Baka remarked.

Je Maron said, "House great father Je Taeliel never trusted Rhodell nor House Rho. I will continue to maintain that distrust and the family safeguards House great mother Je Buel and he established. Lastly, know that I have recommended to the Crown that House Nui Vent great father Nui Samu be appointed to the Warden of the North position. He has served with all of you in the past, knows and advocates for Torondell and will maintain leadership continuity here. Let us hope the Crown will support the advantages of his appointment."

"Aye, we too agree and support his appointment as well. That will have a significantly positive impact on the northern army's morale too," Commander Baka said. Nui Samu nodded his head to the northern army's commanders in gratitude.

Nui Samu looked at the northern army's commanders, sighed and solemnly remarked, "I know there are a number of soldiers whose military service ends this year and may want to join our Houses' army, assuming I do not receive the Warden's appointment. For those who wish to do so, please let it be known quietly that I will purchase their early release, as well as offer an enlistment bonus upon acceptance into our House army." Commanders Baka, Fini, and Sochae all smiled, seemingly quite pleased with the last announcement.

"Lastly, we are also very privileged and honored to have Commander Djurdin Roerson, leader of the famed Mountain Wreckers Brigade of Clan Battle Hammer, here with us. As you all know, House Je Luneefa has a long relationship with the clans of Blood Tears Mountains. That relationship was forged in battle, sanctified with the blood of enemies..."

Commander Djurdin interjected, "Aye! And wid many, very good meals and drink too!" The group laughed heartily.

Je Maron then resumed saying, "This mighty relationship

continues to grow stronger as each century passes. Commander Djurdin Roerson and his brigade arrived this day for 'training purposes' as well; and fortunately, we also started stockpiling needed provisions a few days ago." Je Maron concluded the meeting as smiles and laughter erupted again across the small group.

# Taken

Crowds had started forming during the early morning. For the last four days, the City of Torondell has been in deep mourning. Today is the fifth day since the House Je Luneefa first elders' deaths and the day of the public memorial service for Torondell's first, esteemed dignitaries.

It was now midmorning. Zhen Laehua, accompanied by two flute players, started playing a sorrowful dirge on her koto. This was an original composition of the koto prodigy and one that the House Je Luneefa elders had selected for such an occasion. The song of sorrow was to be a reminder of the elders' early life growing up in a rural area of Rhodell. Although those early years were filled with sadness, the orphaned Taeliel found his "one" in Je Buel whose family eventually did accept the persistent, roguish melf when he married into the Je Luneefa family.

Both-elders lay close to each other with Je Buel's hand in Je Taeliel's hand. They each displayed not smiles, but expressions of pleasant peace. The final peace they had at last was earned after centuries of uneasiness, guarded joy, periodic evil and sorrow. They were now at their final rest with the one each loved most in the world. Next to Je Taeliel lay Je Onyxia Ryoshi, the pet panther of Je Danei. The great, noble panther too looked peaceful with closed eyes, glistening black coat and raised head. The elves were dressed in their finest robes. The elves and panther were also covered with his or her House cape.

The bodies had been placed on a tiered table which the

House great mother on the highest level followed by the House great father and then the panther. This table was decorated with flowers and rocks from the Blood Tears Mountains. The rocks were a dwarf tradition used to honor their dead. These stones were incredibly special; they were all from Queen Marta and King Joerson's family stone collection, a most sacred gift usually reserved for immediate family members and/or royalty. One large, magic-imbued bloodstone, a House Je Luneefa family symbol, was also placed on the table in the center of the lowest tier. The "blood" in this stone would move and glow, randomly changing the stone's pattern.

A large tent had been erected outside of the Warden's castle, east of the main center gate. This tent was against the wall of the castle. Je Luneefa House soldiers, clad in their finest uniforms and armor, were above on the castle's wall. This was the main tent for the memorial service and covered the main center table upon which the deceased bodies lay upon. Soldiers of the northern army were there too, surrounding this tent. These soldiers were guards of honor, many of whom had fought beside the fallen Warden and had been handpicked by the Canae northern army's commanders.

To the left of the center, main table were two tables. Je Pagi and Je Maron sat with King Joerson, Queen Marta, Prince Dajald, Urtha Dal, Commander Roerson and Duenor Heartstone. House Nui Vent elders great mother Nui Honei and great father Nui Samu and Ona Noirar sat at the other table with Alleina, the Canae northern army and the Houses Je Luneefa and Nui Vent army commanders. Je Taeliel had carefully handpicked all five commanders and had served with all of them for at least a century, centuries in a few cases. They were trusted, competent and completely loyal to him and his family.

To the right of the main table sat the House Je Luneefa daughters and sons along with Ona Drachir and the House Nui Vent sons. Family members and dear friends were all shrouded in black and solemnly mourned the deaths of the House Je Luneefa first elders.

House Je Luneefa first great mother and father had lived good lives for over six centuries. Now, they were both at their final peace as they would want, together. The final peace the first elders displayed was well justified.

Though unexpectedly taken away from the realm of the living, the House Je Luneefa first elders' memories and legacy would live on. The House Je Luneefa first mother and father were extremely proud of their family and all that they had accomplished through the centuries in Torondell. Je Buel and Je Taeliel left the realm of the living a better place than what they first encountered. For this accomplishment, they were pleased. Their daughter was now the first great mother of House Je Luneefa. They had no doubt that Je Pagi and Je Maron would continue to honor her parents' legacy of family values and administer fair and just policies over Torondell. Je Buel and Je Taeliel were equally proud of all their granddaughters and grandsons. Je Buel and Je Taeliel believed strongly that the five of them would also be a notable legacy of the family's first elders.

All Torondell's citizens, nobles, and commoners, rich and poor, came to pay their last respects to the city's first House nobles. The procession of mourners lasted all morning and well into the afternoon.

Further away from the main funeral tent, about a thousand steps, other tents had been erected to serve food and water to those in need.

Late in the afternoon, a wagon carrying the bodies of the House Je Luneefa first elders proceeded back to the western courtyard of the Je Luneefa stronghold. Here, a private memorial service would be held just for the family and closest friends, only those seated at the tables of honor. Two stone pyres had been erected, one for the House Je Luneefa first elders and the second was for Je Onyxia Ryoshi.

Now, Je Pagi officiated and said her last goodbye to her parents and the great panther along with the other members of the family. She then signaled to Ona Kei Kuri Ryuu that walked over to the pyres. After bowing to the elders and to the attendees, the great dragon emitted a burst of hot dragon flame upon each pyre instantly cremating the bodies. Attendants carefully gathered the ashes of the House elders and placed them in a black burial urn bearing the heraldic sigil of House Je Luneefa. This urn was presented to Je Pagi and Je Maron. Another similar urn was prepared, and it contained the ashes of Je Onyxia Ryoshi. This urn was presented to Je Danei.

With teary eyes, House great mother Je Pagi ended the memorial service by reading a letter Je Buel had written for her memorial service:

*Beloved Je Luneefa, Nui Vent and Ona Feiir family and dearest friends,*
    *Though my life was taken and is over, I am now at my final glorious peace. I lived a long, good, and*

*honorable life. I found my life's one true love and shared a good life with Je Taeliel for over four centuries. We were blessed with a wonderful daughter and son-in-law. They, in turn, blessed our family with five wonderful granddaughters and grandsons.*

*Through adoption, I was further blessed with four other amazing and wonderful daughters and sons whom I also loved dearly and unconditionally, like they were of my very own blood.*

*In my own way, I loved you all. Though difficult and hard to understand at times, please appreciate our wisdom; my husband and I placed the well-being of our family as an extremely high priority. Please forgive us for any unpleasant pain or discomfort we may have caused.*

*Death comes to take us all at some time. Do not mourn me for too long. Live your life well and with honor. Love those you care about bravely and honestly. Cherish your loved ones with unconditional love. Fiercely protect and guard the love you share.*

*All my love,*
*Je Buel, House Je Luneefa First Great Mother*

"My parents loved their family dearly. Living under their rule was hard at times, but they had their reasons for their decisions and for the actions they took. In most cases, their decisions and actions aimed to protect and preserve all the Je Luneefa family members, our values, and our peace. I will deeply miss them. But I am fortunate in that I have not completely lost them. When I look at my daughters and sons, I can see my parents in them. For this, I am most grateful to be so blessed in many ways.

"Our family flourished not only directly through my daughters and sons, but my wise parents blessed us too with the adoption of Nui Honei, Nui Samu, Diazae Alleina and Ona Noirar. Time proved that their decision to do so, through frowned upon by many other nobles, was again a very wise decision. Personally, I could not ask for better sisters or brothers. My parents, my family and I love you all dearly.

"Lastly, my mother befriended a renowned battlemage of Clan Battle Hammer. That friendship flourished as well by blood and time. She and Urtha Dal, comrades in arms, became blood-sisters. My parents both loved this Clan, we all became close friends and will even become real family when my Je Kei marries Annaei of

Clan Battle Hammer. My parents loved all of you too dearly.

"Thank you all again for this great honor given by your presence. It is very much appreciated." At this point, Je Pagi started crying as all the weeping attendees rose to gather around the House Je Luneefa great mother for support and consolation.

Early the next day, at pre-dawn, Commander Baka left his quarters at the northern army barracks and went to a section of Torondell famous for its numerous, high-quality inns. In particular, he sought the comfort of a familiar inn owned and operated by an old friend, Master Katsu.

As usual, the inn hardly ever closed. At this time of day, Commander Baka was able to easily get an empty table in the main hall, away from entrance. Very few patrons were there; so, it was also quiet which suited the Commander as he welcomed the solitude to review his many life's thoughts. As he continued to mull over numerous memories, some good and some bad, the silence of his morning peace abruptly changed.

"Why are you here so early in the morning?" questioned an ancient looking melf who had silently approached the Commander's table unnoticed.

"Today, I believe will be my last. I will meet an old enemy later this day and one of us will surely die. So, I am here for my 'last meal'. Legend has it that any soldier can die bravely and happily after eating such a meal prepared by you, old friend.

"Your cooking is truly infamous and well known throughout the kingdom of Canae's army. Whether you are cooking for First Commanders or foot soldiers, no one prepares a meal better than you. Your cooking goes beyond just supplying nutrition; your cooking also inspires troops. You have fed countless number of soldiers throughout your military career. I am honored and privileged to have served with you for many of those years. Thank you for all the times you listened to me and shared your wisdom with me. I will be forever grateful.

"Even at your age, you still work, managing others, directing your kitchen's operations, and sharing your many, many memories with your patrons. I hope you live another hundred years! You still have much wisdom and knowledge to share," Commander Baka explained.

"If today is truly your last day, may you die well Commander," requested Master Katsu. The ancient melf then turned and walked back into the kitchen to personally prepare another one of his 'final meals'.

Six days have now passed since the deaths of the House Je

Luneefa first elders. Shortly after the rising of the morning sun, more than a division of Canae troops from Rhodell arrived at the outer gates of Torondell. The one thousand-plus soldiers are supposedly there to pay homage to the fallen Warden of the North on behalf of the king and queen of Canae. Rhodell's chief emissary and commander of these troops is the infamous General Yun Huang. Few officers ever held such a highly prestigious rank. Such officers commanded multiple divisions of Canae land military sources. Many thousands of troops ultimately reported to this highest-ranking, army officer who reported only to the Canae queen and king.

General Yun Huang of House Yun Beitu is a seasoned military veteran with more than three centuries worth of service to the realm. He has distinguished himself as a key military strategist with dozens of large, successful campaigns. For him, the "end results justified the means"; so, Yun Huang could be ruthless, evil, and even sacrifice his own soldiers to achieve more glory and fame for himself. At this stage in his career, before he retires from the military, Yun Huang craves a position of prestige that he could use to covertly add more wealth to his personal coffers. Becoming Warden of the North would be that position of opportunity according to the king and queen. Yun Huang needed first to demonstrate to the Crown that he could accomplish a few clandestine tasks for the Crown.

General Yun Huang and his immediate direct reports were first through the central gates of the Toronwalzwei. All the northern army commanders, Baka, Fini, and Sochae were there with their attendants to formally greet the general.

After saluting the general, Commander Baka, the most senior commander said, "General, welcome to Torondell. The Warden's residence has been prepared..."

"Why are you not in your formal uniforms? Aren't the funeral services for the House Je Luneefa elders today?" scoffed the general after rudely cutting off Commander Baka's announcement.

"No. The memorial services were conducted yesterday," replied Commander Baka.

Although the general's officers grumbled a bit, the general himself only displayed a small sigh of frustration. "Show me my quarters now," commanded the general.

Commander Baka said, "Please follow me." The northern army commanders Baka and Sochae then led the general and his immediate officers to the Warden's castle. Northern army Commander Fini led the general's Fourth Commander to an area next to the Warden's castle where tents could be erected to house the visiting soldiers.

After entering the Warden's castle, Commander Baka led the general and his staff to the large main hall where refreshments had been prepared and placed on several tables for the visiting Rhodell emissary and his immediate staff. Also, in the hall were the Warden's castle staff, including the head steward, Edroc, a dwarf who had served Je Taeliel for over a century.

Commander Baka said, "General, I would like to introduce to you the Warden's castle staff…"

"There will be no need for that," interrupted the general. "They can all go, effective immediately, they are all relieved of their castle responsibilities. I have my own staff who know my detailed requirements. My staff will take over all their duties as of now. Thank you." The general then sat at the main table in the hall followed by his officers. Several of Yun's attendants started serving food and drink to him and his staff. Meanwhile, Edroc and his staff quietly left the hall.

After a short time, General Yun stopped eating and looked at a painting of Je Taeliel on the wall. Looking at Commander Baka, he ordered, "Remove that painting. I will not need any reminders of my predecessor. Today is the first day of a new beginning."

"Shall I have it returned to the family?" a considerate Commander Baka asked.

"That or burn it; I do not care. Just remove it now," responded the General scornfully.

Commander Baka nodded to Commander Sochae who went to retrieve the painting of the former Warden of the North. As Commander Sochae started to pull the painting down, a dagger hit the portrait's left eye of the former Warden.

"Well thrown, Commander Sena, well thrown indeed," General Yun said complimenting his commander whose dagger hit the small mark from a distance of about fifteen steps. "Who now owes you coins?"

"Wang Meixiu, of course. She continues to doubt my abilities," replied Sena.

To not further damage the painting, Commander Sochae drew his sword and knocked Sena's dagger out of the painting. The dagger fell to the floor and Sochae returned his sword to its scabbard. As Sochae was about to take the painting down and place it aside, Sena threw another dagger, and this dagger pierced the right eye of the former Warden's portrait.

"It was double or nothing," Sena quickly said justifying his action. With that remark all the Rhodell officers started laughing. Commanders Baka and Sochae, on the other hand, were angry with the display of gross disrespect. However, both northern army commanders maintained their composure refusing to allow the Rhodell army officers to intimidate them or lure them into some trap.

"Enough Sena. We know you are the best at throwing knives. Besides, your game is delaying the removal of that annoying painting although it cannot stare at me any longer," General Yun remarked jokingly. Another burst of laughter erupted from the Rhodell officers.

Commander Sochae removed the dagger, letting it fall to the floor, and carefully removed the painting from the wall. He then started walking away.

"Return my daggers to me since you are right there too," Sena requested.

"I think not. If you want them, get them yourself. I am not your attendant, nor do you outrank me," Commander Sochae responded defiantly.

"I do outrank you. Now, retrieve and return his daggers," General Yun commanded.

"Yes sir; as you command," Commander Sochae said. Sochae placed the painting down, retrieved the daggers and started walking towards Commander Sena. Sochae held both daggers in his left hand and had his right hand on the hilt of his short sword on his right side. When he reached the table where Sena was sitting, Sochae placed the daggers on the table, handles first, instead of placing them in Sena's outstretched hand. "Your daggers Third Commander," Sochae said as he calmly backed away.

"See, we can cooperate well and get along," General Yun said. Looking at Commander Sochae, General Yun continued, "Convey a message to the Je Luneefa elders that I would like to meet with them at their stronghold tomorrow night for dinner. Tell them to expect me and six officers at their castle at sundown. You are dismissed." Sochae saluted the general, picked up the damaged painting and left. The general nodded to one of his attendants and the hall's doors were closed.

"Now Baka, have a seat, make yourself comfortable and let us discuss some things. First, what details can you tell me about the Je Luneefa stronghold's defenses and how many House soldiers do they command?" General Yun quickly asked.

Annoyed and hesitant, Commander Baka replied, "General, forgive my hesitance; I am a bit surprised by your questions."

"Annoyed and/or surprised, I do not care as long as you answer my questions quickly now," the General said in an overbearing tone.

Commander Baka then said, "The Je Luneefa stronghold is a formidable fortress. It is built on a steep hill and into a mountain. Fast-moving water surrounds the fortress on three sides and there are only two bridges that can be used to cross over this water. The banks of the river are also steep. There is no direct path from either bridge to the stronghold's single gate. The fortress walls are thick with high parapets. Surrounding the fortress is a great wall, the Toronwalein, with two protected gates. Taking such a fortress would be very costly if not impossible. Lastly, I believe there are only four to five hundred House soldiers under the family's command."

"Is that all the details you can share? You do not truly know, or you are not telling me all that I wish to know?" the General asked.

"General, the Je Luneefa family has always been secretive and guarded. No northern army soldier knows any intimate details of the House soldiers or the interior of that stronghold. Your mage there can test me to verify I am telling you the truth."

"Your value to me then is decreasing more and more as you speak, Commander," the general remarked.

"Given your reputation General, I am not surprised that is your assessment," Commander Baka responded. He then stood, backed away from the table and drew his two short swords. "You will not get any useful information from me about the Je Luneefa family; so, let us end this meaningless discussion now. Take my life if you can!"

"This is the second time you have drawn your blades against me; it will be your last!" General Yun looked at his Commanders and continued, "So, who among you would like the honor of ending this fool's life?" All five of the general's officers rose and drew their weapons. Sena rose and quickly threw the two returned daggers at Baka who swatted both away from him.

"You are still a hard one to kill Baka I see, just like your brother," General Yun remarked.

"It is a family trait your niece learned too well. And I see, you are still a coward, commanding someone else to do something you cannot or will not risk your dishonorable life to do. At least my brother lived and died honorably; you have and will not," Baka retorted. "Whatever your Crown-appointed objectives are, you will fail. I suggest you leave Torondell while you can," Commander Baka warned.

"Kill him now!" an infuriated General Yun yelled.

Just before sundown, General Yun and four of his commanders arrived at the closed gates of the western Toronwalein. The general was displeased; one of his commanders, Sena, had been killed by Baka before the remaining four commanders could kill the old melf. Another of his commanders also bore serious wounds inflicted by the old soldier. Like his older brother, Commander Baka indeed proved again he was a hard one to kill. After the battle at the Warden's castle, General Yun berated the surviving commanders threatening to replace them all.

A lone House Je Luneefa soldier, atop a horse, was in front of the gate and greeted the general and his party. One of the general's commanders addressed the soldier, "Why are you blocking our path and this gate is closed? House Je Luneefa is expecting General Yun and staff for dinner. Clear our way now and open the gate."

"No. You will not cross beyond the Toronwalein nor will you be having dinner with the Je Luneefa elders this night," said the House soldier.

"And who are you to communicate with us on behalf of the Je Luneefa family?" asked the same Canae army commander, Ming Shen.

"I am Baka Jose, son of Commander Baka of the Canae northern army. I am also this gate's commander. You are not authorized guests of House Je Luneefa for the elders are still deep in mourning and will not entertain anyone tonight. Upon receiving the General's request yesterday, the House elders' response indicated the dinner needed to be postponed indefinitely. My orders are to treat anyone who tries to gain entry beyond this wall as a threat to the family. You will be considered a threat, we will fulfill our duty and we will kill any of you without a second thought," young Baka said coldly.

"Lowly House soldier, do you know who I am?" General Yun questioned with seething anger.

"Yes. You are General Yun, General of the Canae army, master military strategist, hero of many campaigns and second elder of House Ni Beitu," replied Baka Jose.

"Impressive that a lowly House soldier would know of me," General Yun remarked arrogantly with much condescension.

"Yes, I am just a lowly House soldier, but a learned and dutiful one. I can assure you I will perform my duty, protect my post, and stop any unauthorized persons from entering through these gates. I suggest you leave," Commander Baka warned calmly.

"So, you would order your soldiers to fire upon a General of the Canae army? Are you mad?" Wang Meixiu asked.

"No order need be given, the soldiers protecting this gate all know their duty; and without hesitation, they will kill you if you try to cross through these gates without authorization," Gate Commander Baka reaffirmed.

As General Yun then started waging a staring war with the gate commander, young Baka remained calm while the General was clearly agitated from the verbal exchange he and his officers just had with a common House soldier who had the gall to defy them. Filled with rage, the General made a mental note to find this soldier later and torture him. *"For that matter, I now want to kill any other soldier or sailor, belonging to the Baka family, wherever he or she may be. I will end this family's defiance to me once and for all!"* General Yun further thought.

Before General Yun could finish his thoughts of eradicating all the Baka soldiers or sailors throughout the kingdom, the gates of the Toronwalein opened. Two hooded individuals rode from inside the Toronwalein to stand beside Gate Commander Baka. After removing their hoods, one rider was female bearing the Je Luneefa sigil on her House cape and the other rider was a dwarf whose cape bore the sigil of Clan Battle Hammer. Je Leena and Commander Djurdin Roerson now joined the gate commander.

"General Yun, good evening. I am the second daughter of House Je Luneefa, Je Leena, and I am here to express..." Je Leena said before being rudely interrupted by an impatient and irritated Ming Shen.

Ming Shen interjected defiantly, "Apologies for this poor gate commander's behavior, apologies for not properly welcoming a Canae general and apologies for delaying us."

"Gate Commander Baka, please return to your post now," ordered Je Leena. Now looking at General Yun, Je Leena boldly continued, "No, I am not here to offer any apologies. Quite the contrary, I am here to inform you again my parents will not see you this evening nor anytime soon. They are still too grief-stricken. They would advise you to leave Torondell. By the way, where is First Commander Baka? Why is he not with you? He would have been your authorization to safely enter through these gates. My eldest brother would have then formally greeted you before delivering the same message.

"First Commander Baka left us claiming he had another urgent matter to attend to," Commander Wang Meixu said.

Je Leena frowned and said, "You do not lie well at all.

Commander Baka would not do that. Is he dead?"

"De Je Luneefa elders' message be clear. Dey be not seein' ye or any outsider fer a long time. Just go," suggested Roerson.

"Or on the other hand, maybe I will visit again tomorrow with my entire legions and take this fortress," General Yun warned angrily.

"You could try General Yun, but you will find that objective most difficult, if not impossible," responded Je Leena. "How many dragons do you have?"

Roerson just smiled from ear to ear and remarked, "Dat be not smart at all, but try if ye must. Me, Djurdin Roerson of Clan Battle Hammer and Commander of de Mountain Wreckers, be waitin' fer ye all! Or ye General and me could meet in single combat too if ye want; me be preferrin' dat. No need fer yer troops to die fer yer bad decision. What say ye General?"

General Yun glared at Je Leena and Roerson one last time, turned his horse around and left.

After watching the Yun leave, Roerson said, "Second daughter of House Je Luneefa let us go now and meet wid yer parents. Me have just stirred up trouble me fear."

Within the House Je Luneefa stronghold, Roerson immediately met with the House Je Luneefa and Nui Vent elders, sons, and daughters, along with King Joerson, Queen Marta, Prince Dajald, Urtha Dal, Ona Noirar, Alleina and Ona Drachir.

"First, me like to extend me apologies. Me anger got de best of me; me saw de Gate Commander talkin' to dat savage General Yun..." Roerson started. King Joerson pounded his chair once upon hearing the name of General Yun, breaking both arms of his chair. The suddenly splintered chair startled most to confusion and silence.

A tearful Queen Marta explained, "Over a century ago, dere be a land dispute between de Battle Hammer clan and Rhodell. De Canae Crown claimed dat de mountain where we found gold be in Canae land; we disagreed. Disputes followed, sometimes wid violence. To end furder hostilities, de dwarves ended der minin' operations after gettin' most of de gold out it seemed and returned to de Blood Tears Mountains.

"Yun be no general den, but a high-rankin' commander who hungered for more fame and glory. He be wantin' recognition by de Crown fer his abilities to 'solve Canae's problems'. It be his idea to set fire to dat great forest soud of our mountains. Dat forest was our prime source fer much of our food. We could hunt plenty of good game dere and de rivers gave us good fish too. Land been cleared too for many farms. It be Yun's idea to set de forest afire. De Blood Tears river, south of de forest protected oder Canae lands. It be late Autumn; winds blew from south to north. Dat great fire spread quickly, killin' all in its path. We lost many dwarves includin' me moder and fader in-laws. Dat fire burned for many days destroyin' dat land. Wid so much death and loss, we even renamed our mountains to Blood Tears. It be taken over a hundred years fer dat land to recover. We rebuilt de farms; game animals returned. But, we be not fergettin' what happened and never fergivin' Yun…"

"Me King, me Queen, House elders, daughters and sons, please fergive me. Me challenge may provoke him to attack yer Houses here," Roerson added.

"I do not think so," Nui Samu said. "From what I know about General Yun, he craves victories to add to his reputation. Attempting to attack our Houses would not yield him any victory. He and his legions could not breech the Toronwalein."

"Your Majesties, if I may speak on Roerson's behalf, no apologies are needed. I know firsthand what the General and Crown did to your kingdom," Nui Honei said. "Though I am surprised Commander Roerson you did not try to provoke him more. He demonstrated great restraint."

The Houses' Je Luneefa elders, daughters sons, Nui Samu, Ona Noirar, Alleina and Ona Drachir all responded with a loud "Aye!" in support of Commander Djurdin Roerson's actions.

Je Pagi quickly added, "Also, not only are we good friends, but we are soon to become family too. My mother was blood-sister to Urtha Dal! Je Kei will marry Annaei of Clan Battle Hammer. And our family fights together regardless of odds and enemy! So, let General Yun bring his legions here if he dares; we will gladly stand by you!"

"Aye!" Je Maron exclaimed again, fully supporting his wife's declaration.

"Roeri, I agree wid House great mother; no apologies be needed nor said. Ye just owe her a new chair to replace de chair me broke," King Joerson said smiling and then grabbing his dear brother in a hug.

Most everyone laughed then; their sad spirits had been lifted. Alleina though was still grieving and angry. Je Leena noticed her adopted aunt and felt her pain. This young felf remembered and recalled a story her grandmother had told her. Evidently, this General Yun was the one who sent the rogues who attacked her grandparents' food supply train destined to Blood Tears Mountains so many years ago.

Je Leena also conveyed to the assembled group her conversation with the General's party at the gate. She strongly suspected that General Yun had Commander Baka killed. Je Leena too now wanted revenge and later proposed a plan to just the elders there.

It was late in the same evening, well past midnight. After knocking softly on her parents' bedchamber door, Je Leena entered the room. Both her parents were sitting by the hearth anxiously waiting for their daughter's safe return to the Je Luneefa family stronghold. Despite how Je Leena's secret mission objectives were achieved, her countenance did not reflect any outward despair. Both parents rose and welcomed their daughter with open arms. After they lovingly hugged Je Leena, Je Pagi asked, "Did all go well?"

"Yes. But before I begin, let me first thank you for sending the protective 'shadows' to watch over me on my mission tonight," Je Leena said.

Smiling, Je Maron responded, "You are most welcomed; but please forgive an overprotective father who wanted to ensure his daughter's safety. I know you are capable, but having some insurance increased the odds of your safe return. The streets of Torondell late at night, especially in these times, are not safe. Rei and Drachir both gladly accepted the duty."

"Let us all sit now and then, Leena, please explain what happened," a concerned Je Pagi requested. They all again sat by the bedchamber's hearth where a small, crackling fire kept the room's temperature comfortably warm and broke the occasional silence of the small group.

After pouring herself a glass of wine, Je Leena sat by her parents and recalled the night's events, "This tale actually begins years ago. It was the year that House Nui Vent first competed in the Autumn Festival Kilecfla's final event. At the Kilecfla grand banquet that night, I first met Commander Wang Meixiu. Her cousin is the infamous archer of House Tsau Chu, Mei Ling who had invited Wang Meixiu to attend the festival's grand banquet.

"Although all the House Je Luneefa and House Nui Vent females had shaved heads with a single shock of black and red hair from front to back, Commander Wang Meixiu thought I was the most 'striking'. She then claimed to be attracted to me. We had much wine and we talked for a long time that night. I learned she was a distinguished officer in the Canae army. She fascinated me with her adventurous stories, and she intently listened to my boring tales. I was greatly intrigued with the attention she paid to me.

"We went for a walk later and eventually found ourselves alone in the House Tsau Chu horse stables where she kissed me again and again. Her kisses were passionate and lustful. That was the first time I had ever experienced such intense physical feelings. Somehow Wang Meixiu found my undiscovered sexual lust and ignited my cravings. I then became obsessed with this female.

"She said, 'She wanted me'. I, in kind, somehow desperately wanted her. So, we agreed to secretly meet the next night at an inn. That next night, Wang Meixiu became my first sexual experience. I freely gave her my 'innocence' and she gladly devoured it, ravishing me till I thought I was 'in love' with her. I left then feeling I was just another one of Wang Meixiu's many 'conquests'. But I did not care; I foolishly thought I could win her heart. We met two other times since then just for her to have sex; my love was still unrequited. My intended/wanted love was sadly mistaken and woefully misplaced. It has been over two years since I last saw her till tonight when she came to the Toronwalein gate. I signaled to her I wanted to meet. She agreed.

"So, we met again this evening in secret. What she did not know was that I was now a more mature and wiser felf, thanks to my elders' blessings of their wisdom. She thought I was still a foolish young felf. I feinted my lust for her; we drank much wine; we had sex again; but I extracted information from her without her knowledge. This time too, I first left her while she slept." Je Leena paused letting her tumultuous feelings subside.

"How do you feel now?" Je Pagi inquired.

"Wang Meixiu is a distant, unimportant memory of my past. As my first love, she will be remembered. She will not be my future nor will any other female. Wang Meixiu will die as planned for her part in killing our beloved Commander Baka," Je Leena coldly responded.

"Does this mean you now like a male?" Je Maron then asked.

"Yes Father. There is someone I have liked for some time now," Je Leena replied trying to hide a slight smile.

Moments later, Je Leena quietly continued, "General Yun's secret objectives are to lay siege to the House Je Luneefa stronghold only if he could take it, kill all within the Toronwalein, and seize our family's wealth. Only Yun and his immediate direct reports know his secret objectives. This task, if successfully completed, would secure him the Warden of the North position.

"With his appointment as Warden of the North, many of the northern army soldiers would exercise their option to purchase their immediate resignation, being in the last few moons of their military service. Knowing that over a third of the current northern army could and most likely would immediately resign their military assignment and join our House army gave him serious pause, I suspect. Having three divisions of ally warrior dwarves so close by also affected his plans. General Yun would not want to be caught between our House soldiers and that dwarven army. He is also terrified of the fact that our family may still control a dragon which we could bring to bear against his forces. Given the very unfavorable odds, he, most likely, will retreat. It is still uncertain exactly where he may go next. Chances are General Yun plans to retreat to the west northern frontier. General Yun and his soldiers plan to depart the day after tomorrow."

Je Pagi said, "Leena, thank you. Now go and rest. Your father and I have more things to discuss."

The next morning, Je Danei rose early and prepared for another dawn morning ride she enjoys. Her escort of six House soldiers met her at the westernmost gate of the Toronwalein. After passing through, they quickly made their way to the second great wall of Torondell, the Toronwalzwei.

Je Danei and her escort passed through the center gate heading south towards the forest just about two leagues away. As in the past, she would ride just to the edge of the forest, turn around and race back to the center gate. Je Danei rode her new "gift" horse, the famed Starjai, supposedly a very swift horse and wanted to see her horse run. Racing against her escort seemed like a good challenge, especially when she even offered to give them a quarter-league lead. After reaching the edge of the forest, they dismounted, finalized the terms of the wager which the loser(s) will buy the morning's meal for the winner(s) and remounted their horses.

Je Danei's escort then started riding back to Torondell, taking their agreed-to lead. After reaching their designated spot, the escort stopped, turned to watch Je Danei start their race. Je Danei raised her arm and waved it twice signaling to start.

At that same moment, the first daughter of House Je Luneefa felt the sharp sting of a dart hit her exposed, bare neck. The horse became disquieted and started prancing about, reacting to the sudden unconscious rider's slump into the saddle.

"Gui stolera Starjai," a voice familiar to Je Danei's horse said from the forest. Pi Rhem came from behind a tree and the horse stopped nervously prancing about. Starjai started walking towards her former master. Pi Rhem, a former would-be suitor of Je Danei, took the horse's reins. He quickly transferred the now sleeping Je

Danei to a waiting wagon while other brigands emerged from the forest. All, even the noble Pi Rhem, wore plain, commoner clothes. Their disguises reflected the colors of the forest, nothing that would distinguish his House nor allegiance in this kidnapping scheme.

Looking at the leader of the brigands, Pi Rhem threw a bag of coins to her and said, "Do your last duty and kill anyone who tries to follow me," Pi Rhem commanded. Pi Rhem and a small escort of six soldiers rode away, deeper into the forest. The other ten brigands waited for the House Je Luneefa first daughter's escort who now realized something was amiss and were returning to the edge of the forest.

All six House Je Luneefa soldiers galloped at full speed heading towards the spot at the edge of the forest where they had last seen the House first daughter. Je Danei's escorts, like any other House soldier assigned to escort a family member, were distinguished, and considered elite given their very important duties. They were all highly skilled in hand-to-hand combat and weaponry. Their fighting skills were exemplary and their loyalty and dedication to the Je Luneefa family were profound.

Commander Sochae Soni, whose brother was a second commander in the northern army, knew today would most likely be his last day of life. Thanks to House great father Je Taeliel, he and his brother had been rescued from an abandoned Rhodell orphanage when the Je Luneefa family left Rhodell. The Sochae brothers were only young belfs then, but they both pledged fealty to Je Taeliel if they could accompany his family to the northern kingdom. The wise House elder saw something special in the young belfs and agreed to their joining his House army. These brothers were his first personal recruits. Sochae Soni was ready to die to save the House Je Luneefa first daughter. He would not disappoint the House first great father who had been so kind and generous to him and his brother.

The escorts galloped abreast from each other with ample space between the riders to fit four riders. This tactic was designed to present a more difficult target to any would-be archers in the forest. Each escort also carried short shields which they all deployed forward to provide some additional protection. Sochae Soni gave a hand signal and the riders at each end of the escort group broke away and took a wider path to the forest. The remaining four escorts expected an ambush and would engage anyone who tried to stop them. The other two needed to go into the forest and find the missing House first daughter without encountering the expected, forthcoming delay. In response two brigands were ordered to attack each of the House escorts trying to circumvent the Pi Rhem's rear defense of brigands.

Sochae's main escort soldier group now faced six brigands immediately in front of them. Two of the brigands pulled bows out and started firing arrows hastily at the charging escorts. Fortunately, one of the House escorts was also a battlemage who conjured a forward protective shield. No escort nor horse would be harmed for a brief time.

When Sochae and the other three escorts were less than a quarter league away from the brigand party, Sochae gave another signal to his group, the battlemage removed his magical shield, and they quickly pulled their own short bows and starting firing arrows into the group of brigands. Two arrows hit brigands as Sochae and his three escorts continued charging towards the forest.

Moments later, Sochae and his three escorts battled the remaining four brigands. As expected, the routine practice of fighting from horseback was an advantage for the House Je Luneefa escorts. Although assigned primarily to escort duties, the escorts still had to train regularly with the House soldiers to maintain all their fine fighting skills. After a few moments of combat, Sochae broke free of his group and continued pursuing the kidnappers who took the House first daughter deeper into the forest.

The road through the forest displayed fresh wagon and horse trails which were easy for him to follow. He could maintain his fast pace given the good, well-travelled road conditions. Soon, he saw riders and a wagon about a league ahead of him. Sochae pulled his short bow again and notched an arrow. A few moments later, five brigands turned to face the charging Sochae while one brigand, carrying the unconscious Je Danei, boarded a waiting boat at a dock. Several sailors thereafter pushed the boat away from the dock. Other sailors, four on the opposite boat side, positioned oars into the water and started rowing the boat towards the middle of the river.

Sochae had time to fire three arrows as he quickly closed the distance to the brigands, aiming to intercept him. His arrows hit two of the enemies. The remaining three brigands engaged Sochae determined to cover the escape of their comrade and the kidnapped House Je Luneefa first daughter.

To limit his disadvantage of fighting three foes, Sochae would press battle against one brigand, attacking and defending with his sword and shield. He constantly moved using his legs and feet only to command his battle-experienced horse which way to go. This would allow him then to use both hands for offense and defense. After vanquishing one foe, Sochae now had to defeat the remaining two brigands who seemed more committed to stopping him as opposed to escaping. Being an experienced warrior, Sochae kept both opponents on just one of his sides. He could not afford to let the enemies attack him from two sides.

At this point, the rescue boat was in the middle of the river, with an unmarked and unfurled sail, and heading westward with the flow of the strong river current.

Pfft! A dull-sounding arrow from the forest struck one of the two remaining brigands fighting Sochae. Though not immediately killed, the brigand was now wounded with an arrow protruding from the back shoulder of his sword arm. At about this same time, four other brigands now charged towards the dock. The last brigand fighting Sochae was momentarily distracted seeing her comrades and that was time enough for the escort commander to pull a knife and throw it at the enemy, killing her instantly.

Emerging from the forest came Renari, a skilled, House Je Luneefa army battlemage and archer. Renari rode up to his commander and stopped. Both House soldiers used their bows to down two of the charging brigands. Renari then hit the last two brigands with a paralysis spell. Both enemy riders collapsed and fell from their horses. One fell and rolled hard against a tree and a loud cracking sound could be heard. The other brigand just fell hard onto the road.

Sochae and Renari first went to the brigand who had fallen onto the road. They tied his hands and feet together after removing the brigand's weapons. After inspecting the other brigand who had fallen hard against a tree, Sochae and Renari discovered this bandit sustained several broken ribs from his fall and was now spewing blood from the internal injuries.

"My fellow soldier here is a battlemage who is also skilled in the healing arts. Do you wish to be healed or die painfully?" Sochae asked. Before the wounded enemy could answer, an arrow shot from the forest hit the wounded brigand. Instinctively, both House Je Luneefa soldiers rolled away quickly. Sochae used his shield to cover his retreat till he was able to hide behind a tree. Renari immediately created a shield of protective magic to cover himself. Moments later, another arrow was fired at the brigand who had fallen onto the road. The last two brigands now lay very still; mostly likely, they were now both dead. This last assailant was eliminating potential "loose ends" by killing any surviving brigands.

Sochae uttered a command to Renari, "Nesta uinen" which meant for him to drink from the precious dragon's blood potion they both carried. Sochae being an escort commander and Renari being a battlemage, are positions highly valued by House Je Luneefa's dedicated army. As such, both were of a select few given a small vial of the blessed, precious elixir. In addition to its healing powers, Sochae and Denari's senses were greatly enhanced, as well as their abilities to communicate mentally since the primary component of the elixir is the blood of the great dragon, Ona Kei Kuri Ryuu. After speaking the appropriate individual incantation, both House Je Luneefa soldiers drank their respective elixirs.

Sochae ordered mentally, *"Find that assassin quickly and throw me your bow and four arrows. We need to also protect our horses which should be the assassin's next targets."*

With his dragon's eyes, Denari confirmed that the archer was still hiding behind a thicket of bushes and small trees. After telling Sochae the location of the assassin, Denari moved further away from his commander. Denari also kept his shield between him and the assassin as the battlemage moved. Now, Denari moved from around a large tree and started slowly walking towards the thicket where the assassin was still hiding. While maintaining his large magical, full-body shield with his left hand, Denari conjured a flame spear which he held in his right hand. This spear could pierce through the thicket with its dragon-flame heat and hit the hidden assassin. Sochae, in the meantime, had also moved away from his fellow soldier, but in the opposite direction. Moments later, the assassin was now effectively between the two House Je Luneefa soldiers.

Suddenly, Denari dissolved his shield and hurled his spear into the thicket. At that same moment, the assassin leaped into the air away from the thicket in time to avoid the spear. The assassin also managed to fire an arrow and hit Denari in his unarmored portion of his leg. Sochae also fired two arrows at the assassin at the same time, one directly at the assassin's current position and the other at his next, anticipated position when falling. The assassin flipped over in mid-air, effectively moving his target area and then levitated for a few moments in the air. Both of Sochae's arrows missed the intended target. When the assassin returned fire at Sochae, the escort commander was also hit in an area of his unarmored leg. Both House Je Luneefa soldiers succumbed to the deadly, poisoned-tipped arrows quickly.

The assassin floated back to the ground and started running westward into the forest laughing. A few moments later, Sochae reached out to Renari mentally, *"Did you get the needed information?"*

"Yes, you can rise now. She is gone. As you suspected Commander, the assassin was Mei Ling, the famed archer of House Tsau. She is now in a hurry to return to her husband Si Tadejo of House Si Moina and boast about her most recent successful assassinations," Denari said.

"After we return, you too can boast about your great skills of mind manipulation and illusion. Thank you. Well done. Now, let us return quickly to Torondell after retrieving our fallen comrades," an appreciative Commander Sochae remarked to Denari.

Canae troops from Rhodell were still within the second wall of Torondell. These troops, commanded by General Yun, came there originally as emissaries of the Crown to honor the recently deceased House Je Luneefa first elders at their funeral services. However, days have passed since the memorial services and the Rhodell troops remained. An uneasy calm draped over the city.

Je Maron, distrustful of the Crown's superficial intentions with those troops maintained constant vigilance. He and his wife were still in deep mourning over the passing of the House first elders and refused any visits by the Crown's chief emissary, General Yun. Je Maron's standing orders were still, "No unauthorized person was allowed inside the Toronwalein. Anyone attempting to gain unauthorized entrance was to be treated as a threat to the Houses Je Luneefa and Nui Vent. All threats were to be eliminated without mercy."

This message and his treatment as anything less than a noble dignitary of the kingdom greatly angered the general. Further, General Yun was not patient; he knew he needed to take some actions to achieve his secret objectives to secure his appointment as the new Warden of the northern realm.

News of the newly arrived northern frontier messengers quickly spread throughout the Je Luneefa stronghold. Three messengers from the northern frontier had journeyed there to bring news of the kidnapped House Je Luneefa first daughter, Je Danei. Je Maron called a meeting and the House Je Luneefa family members assembled in the great hall.

House great mother Je Pagi and great father Je Maron sat at center table on a dais. On their right-were now empty chairs, still respectfully reserved for the fallen House first elders, Je Buel and Je Taeliel. Next to these elders was honored, adopted family member, Nui Samu, Alleina, and an empty chair. The expected occupant of this empty chair was Nui Honei who was currently absent from the meeting. To the left of Je Maron were five chairs, four of which were occupied by their daughters and sons. The empty fifth chair was for the missing first daughter, Je Danei. Bordering the great dais table on the main floor were two other tables, each placed perpendicularly to the great table. These two tables were intended for honored guests and currently, a few House military officers sat there. For security reasons, Je Maron limited this meeting to just immediate family members, trusted advisors, and individuals vital to any follow-on action plan.

After a short while, after all who had assembled there took their place at the appropriate table, Je Maron nodded to two soldiers standing at the rear of the room in front of the hall's great doors. This was the signal for them to now admit the messengers. After entering the hall, the hall's doors were again closed.

Je Pagi mentally reached out to her daughter Je Leena, and commanded, "*Stay alert for any treachery!*" House great mother Je Pagi knew full well that "honor" meant little to House Si Moina and had quickly remembered a loss her mother suffered centuries ago at a similar type of "peace" meeting... For a moment, Je Pagi gave thanks to her friend the great dragon, Ona Kei Kuri Ryuu, who had shared her blood and magic with the House Je Luneefa family, Nui Honei, Nui Samu, Ona Drachir and Alleina many years ago to allow them to mentally communicate to each other.

Two House Si Moina soldiers walked confidently into the hall and stood before Je Pagi and Je Maron. The House Si Moina soldiers then formally greeted the now House Je Luneefa first great mother and father. They then greeted the rest of the assembly members. The messengers, two female elves, were to bring news about the status of the House Je Luneefa missing daughter and expected conditions for her release and safe return.

The second messenger, a fearsome looking rock elf, then spoke, "First, know that your daughter, Je Danei, is well cared for while living under the protection of our great House. Secondly, we bring a message of peace from the northern frontier great House Si Moina. Although our House has allied with several renegade orc tribes, fear not. We have no plans of invading your lands since that would only provoke another war. We wish only peace and prosperity between our two lands. (Cough)

"To solidify our peaceful intentions, we want to propose an alliance between your great House and ours through marriage. We would like you to consider honoring the prince of our House, Si Tadejo, with giving your daughter Je Danei's hand in marriage."

At this declaration, some Je Luneefa family members released their frustration and anger through disciplined, low groans. House great mother and father sat where they were quietly and stoically. Before anyone spoke, Je Pagi raised her hand for silence.

"How many of your soldiers has our daughter killed so far?" asked Je Pagi.

Je Maron said, "What else does your House want through this so called 'alliance'? How would we profit? What do we gain since we have had our differences for centuries? Lastly, if we reject your proposal, what then happens to our daughter?"

The second Si Moina soldier continued, "As your daughter's dowry and a further sign of good faith, please consider gifting her with the forest lands just below our border and north of the Blue Rock river. House Je Luneefa owns this land, and you could bequeath it to the House first daughter." (Cough, cough)

This particular large parcel of land is now quite valuable for both farming and hunting. Even though long ago, it was just part of another desolate wasteland. But through some brilliant engineering and hard work, the vision Je Taeliel had then finally come to fruition. Je Taeliel's faith in his friend Duenor Heartstone, a prolific engineer, yielded an amazing return for the entire northern realm of Canae. Hearthstone was able to build a river wall and a series of water tributaries off the Toron river and redirect the water flow to the once wasteland.

"Lastly, we would want your personal endorsement to the Crown for the appointment of our House great mother Si Caila to the king's high council," concluded the messenger.

Je Pagi then spoke, "You ignored answering my question. Je Maron, did this messenger answer any of your questions? I think not. From your uniform, I see you are a soldier. Do your commanders also have to repeat themselves to get their questions answered too? Please be quick with your answers. My patience is limited."

The first Si Moina messenger then replied, "Our great House offers nothing in return except peace between our great Houses and the benefits of the strongest alliance in the North. The daughters and sons born from this marriage would only continue to enrich our heritages..."

The doors to the great hall flew open suddenly and in walked Nui Honei, leading a group comprised of Ona Drachir and Nui Danka. These melfs carried a box between them.

"Please forgive this interruption, but I too have some news you will want to hear during this meeting," announced Nui Honei. "*Has either of the messengers been coughing?*" she asked Je Pagi mentally as she walked towards the dais. "*If so, remember to kill that one first when the time comes."*

"She *would be the one on your left,*" Je Pagi mentally responded.

Nui Honei's party stopped a respectable distance from the dais, and she advanced alone to the right and in front of the two messengers from House Si Moina. She stopped about ten steps away from the dais and spoke, "Did they ever tell you what benefits House Je Luneefa would receive from a marriage with the son of House Si Moina and your daughter? Quickly speak messenger. No, wait, before you do, let me first show *you* something. Gaze upon your missing third companion." The box Ona Drachir and Nui Danka carried was opened and there lay the severed head of the House Si Moina third messenger.

The other House Si Moina messengers, now enraged, turned towards the dais, and started to rush at the House Je Luneefa family members even though they were both unarmed. Before either messenger had taken one step, three well-thrown knives protruded from the head and neck of the second Si House Moina messenger who had been coughing. The first messenger collapsed where she had stood encased and incapacitated by magic, a spell that Je Leena had casted moments earlier.

"What did you discover?" asked Je Maron.

Nui Honei looked at the dais and around; she saw that all Je Luneefa family members were not harmed. She released a sigh of relief and said, "These three House Si Moina soldiers did bring a deadly message. First, they do want to wed Si Tadejo to your daughter, but for other reasons I suspect. When that third messenger started coughing last night at dinner after secretly giving him lilac juice, I suspected then there would be attempted treachery at this meeting.

"The third messenger had several teeth replaced with false teeth containing an airborne poison. They wanted to charge the dais, crack their false teeth, and blow the poison at as many Je Luneefa family members as possible. In killing any family member, an alliance with Si Moina through marriage would give them an excuse to wage war on House Ai Morai, the House that borders the northern frontier territory to the east of Si Moina's land. This dead messenger has the secret brand of House Ai Morai. So, these would-be assassins would provide the initial justification needed for House Si Moina to wage war to expand its territory more into the northern frontier.

"And let us not forget House great father Je Maron that you may also have a direct claim to the throne of this kingdom through your obscure lineage. So, who really knows what House Si Moina's end game might truly be? By the way, if the current House Si Moina great mother is anything like her grandmother, she was watching this meeting too through her messengers. Let us find out, shall we?"

Je Leena lifted her paralyzing magic from the first House Si Moina messenger. Nui Honei awakened the messenger while she was still encased within her protective, magical wards which also limited her vision and hearing to just Nui Honei. Yet the other individuals in the hall could still see and hear everything that transpired between the messenger and Nui Honei. Nui Honei then cast a scrying spell and called out to the messenger's House Si Moina controller. Before long, the messenger's eyes turned bright yellow signifying a catatonic state.

Nui Honei started the communication with provocation, "Your suicide assassins completely failed."

"Who are you, meddling old felf?" inquired the Si Moina controller through the messenger.

"The alive and well Nui Honei of House Nui Vent," responded Nui Honei. "And you are?"

At this announcement, the messenger echoed his controller's frustration, "Damn you to hell. I will take your head..."

Nui Honei quickly interjected, "Silence, stupid young one! Other members of your wretched family tried and failed. Know that I am coming for my niece and will take *your* head should you get in my way, just like I did your grandmother's. And yes, I will NOT lead the northern army there to provoke any war with any other Houses or orc tribes in the northern territory either." Now with a sinister smile, Nui Honei continued, "By not doing so, I can then kill as many of your House Si Moina members as I please without any kingdom repercussion. You made a seriously grave mistake by kidnapping my niece. I failed before to exterminate the pestilence your House is some years ago. I will not fail again, I promise you. Know that I am coming and will be there soon bringing Hell's fury with me. Let us finally end this feud. I challenge you Coa vae Coa! Let us meet at the western plains of Borauec Mountain. Do you accept stupid gelf?"

The captive messenger's face contorted into a seemingly smile and replied, "Yes." With this last statement, Nui Honei broke the captive messenger's neck with a spell and then watched the messenger collapse in death.

Now turning towards the dais, Nui Honei said, "Let us now talk about House war!"

# Unrequited Love's Call

"Why are you here? Surely you did not come to *save* me. I do not need you or anyone else to save me. I can save myself!" exclaimed an angry Je Danei. "Do not speak; just hand me my belongings quickly and turn around."

Before turning Nui Jooba could see the guards lying on the floor of the dungeon. Evidently, they misunderstood and overestimated whatever advantages they thought they had. The House Je Luneefa first daughter made them pay the ultimate price for their serious errors in judgement. *"They are dead most likely, killed by Je Danei. You are truly a marvel,"* he thought. *"She managed somehow to escape from her cell. And she was in relatively good spirits given the greeting I had just received,"* Nui Jooba thought.

Handing her the potion vial, he said, "This is a gift from my mother and the great dragon, Ona Kei Kuri Ryuu. Mother wants you to drink all of it. This potion is enriched and enhanced with dragon's blood and should counteract any poison the Si Moina vermin gave you."

Je Danei took the vial and recited the incantation Keiku had taught her. She drank the entire contents and immediately started feeling better, no longer affected by the debilitating drugs Si Moina had forced her to take.

Nui Jooba next gave her the bag he was carrying. In it were her clothes, armor, House cape and another vial of special potion received from his mother. He also carried her sword belt which he gave her. After removing the clothes, the Si Moina guards had given her, Je Danei quickly dressed into her own clothes. She then cited an incantation, and her armor was magically placed onto her body.

After attaching her sword belt, she donned her precious House cape bearing her family's heraldic sigil, three red and black roses on a black field. Je Danei wanted her enemies to know full well that she was a warrior of House Je Luneefa. Should death take her this day, her House would be glorified. She planned to kill all House Si Moina warriors who stood before her. She cited another incantation and started removing certain blades from her cape's magically hidden compartments and placing a few in sheaths on her arms and back. Lastly, she placed her grandmother's bequeathed sai swords into her boots. When Je Danei was finished, she stepped forward to stand next to Nui Jooba. After stretching her muscles for a few moments, Je Danei drew her scimitars and solemnly pledged while extending a blade forward, "To the end."

"To the end," Nui Jooba responded, touching her extended blade with his battleaxe.

"*Why are you wearing your death mask, a horrific face painting acknowledging one's acceptance that death may be encountered and welcomed? Do not die tonight; we still have more 'firsts' to discover together,*" Je Danei mentally commanded.

"*As you command, Je Danei, as you command. What is the plan?*" Nui Jooba asked, knowing full well the enraged, revengeful House Je Luneefa first daughter's expected answer.

"*Kill them all!*" Je Danei said with quiet rage. They then both started silently walking towards the entrance to the dungeon ready to bravely greet death should that be their fates.

Fortunately, when Je Danei and Nui Jooba arrived at the dungeon's entrance, only three guards were posted there. Je Danei killed two guards with well-aimed sword thrusts and Nui Jooba killed the third with a well thrown knife taken from Je Danei's belt. When the House first daughter looked at him with questioning eyes, he just answered mentally, "*That blade was the closest to my hand. With enemies all around us and the threat of death hanging over us, I wanted you to know I still love you.*"

"*But that blade was on my back, not on my ass, fool. Touch me like that again uninvited, I will treat you like an enemy,*" Je Danei angrily told her bold companion who was caught smiling at her.

Je Danei and Nui Jooba silently made their way up two flights of steps and through a hallway of the stronghold leading to a courtyard. To their surprise, Je Danei and Nui Jooba found a few more House Si Moina soldiers' dead bodies. The three dead bodies they passed seemed to have died in a similar fashion: by well-thrown knives to their exposed, unarmored necks. The last Si Moina soldier corpse they encountered had a knife protruding from an eye even though this dead soldier was wearing a full helmet covering her face.

"Did you kill these enemy soldiers?" Je Danei inquired, looking sternly at Nui Jooba.

"No," Nui Jooba replied.

"Rei is here too?" Je Danei asked.

"Judging by the dead soldiers we just saw, 'Yes'. This is indeed Rei's work," replied Nui Jooba.

After more tense moments, Je Danei and Nui Jooba finally made their way to an enclosed courtyard on the side of the stronghold. As they continued to move silently under the veil of invisibility provided by their House capes, Nui Jooba reminded himself again to thank the great dragon Keiku for the wonderous gift of her blood. The amazing, magical properties of her blood once again proved invaluable as the two of them avoided hidden traps with their dragon's eyes, ears, and noses as they continued their escape.

"Well met Je Danei and brother," Nui Rei's familiar voice echoed in their minds.

"Speak quickly; why are you here?" an apparently annoyed Je Danei inquired.

"Only to save my brother of course should he need my help," Nui Rei quickly replied nonchalantly. "We must make haste and leave here quickly. Danei, you must return to Torondell. Jooba and I must go to Borauec Mountain. I will tell you more after we leave."

Moments later, an alarm sounded most likely signifying someone had finally found the dead guards' bodies. They heard shouting in the distance and the clanging of armor as soldiers rushed around. Across the courtyard, a lone figure stood in front of the gates defiantly blocking the assumed exit of the escapees. This figure shrouded in dark clothing that matched the night's darkness, issued a command and the courtyard's gates swung outward. Many House Si Moina soldiers marched in formation before the gates and behind the lone figure.

"Well met first daughter of House Je Luneefa," said a soft voice originating from the dark-clothed, House Si Moina figure. After pulling back the hood, it was revealed that the lone figure was indeed a young felf, a truly angry young felf. "I am Si Caidyn, the second granddaughter of House first great mother Si Cairyn. Like my grandmother, I too am a skilled battlemage and can clearly see you both despite your veils of invisibility. There is also an impenetrable shield of magic around this courtyard; so, you will not escape.

"Wait, there is a third here. I can feel your presence too melf. There is no need for you to hide any longer either.

"House Je Luneefa first daughter, know that there will be no more negotiating with your House by my older brother, Si Tadejo. My older sister and I now rule this House alone! She has killed him, and you too shall die this night by my hand as well. You killed my teacher, Majeejp, and for that, I owe you a debt of blood. But your death will not come easy nor fast. After we beat you, my soldiers and I will ravage you. I will heal you thereafter and we will do it again and again. When I finally tire of you, I will take your precious sai swords and plunge those into your eyes just like you did to my teacher.

"Soldiers of House Si Moina kill that fool who is with her; but do not kill the felf. Attack!"

"*Danei, do you trust me?*" Nui Jooba mentally communicated to the House first daughter.

"*Yes,*" Je Danei replied.

"*Quickly, stand close behind and touch me. Rei, you too,*" Nui Jooba mentally ordered. Puzzled, but compliant, Je Danei stepped behind her companion and stood very close to him like Nui Rei. Nui Jooba then started spinning his battleaxes around them. After reciting an incantation, a shield of magic formed around them. In seeing this, Si Caidyn started bombarding his shield with magic bolts with one hand while maintaining the shield of enclosure around the courtyard with her other hand.

When the advancing Si Moina soldiers were just about thirty steps away, Nui Jooba ended his blades spinning with pointing both battleaxes at the enemy soldiers and citing another incantation, "Eitl aithorn Nui Teinori und Zeinori Wei." A raging storm's thunderous sound boomed loudly, and the stored lightning bolts shot forth from his axes into the charging soldiers. The lightning bolts, crooked white fingers of death, arched through and around the enemy soldiers in front to the soldiers in the rear. These bolts killed all in its path and finally settled upon the lone Si Caidyn, initially caressing the shield she had placed around herself. With determined, relentless fury, the lightning bolts did slowly penetrate her shield eventually and mercilessly stabbed the young felf. After a few moments, the bolts disappeared being fully spent.

Now, greatly weakened by Nui Jooba's powerful counterattack, Si Caidyn fell to her knees, now gravely wounded. She could now no longer maintain power to the shield she used to encapsulate the courtyard. Blood freely flowed from her nose and other wounds. The battlemage looked up to see her enemies now approaching.

"Majeejp was more than your teacher; was he not?" Nui Jooba asked.

"Yes. He was also my first love, an unrequited love," Si Caidyn replied. With all her remaining rage, she then started to lift a hand to cast her final, magical bolt. Before she completely raised her hand and uttered another word, a red flame-spear screamed down from the sky and pierced her body, killing the mage instantly. The great dragon, Keiku, landed in the courtyard shortly thereafter.

"*Young ones, when it is time to kill, do not hesitate; slay your foes before they have any chance for retaliation. We are long past discussions with this foul House,*" Keiku advised.

"*Where is Rei?*" Nui Jooba asked as he looked around.

"*While you hesitated to kill the mage, Rei fell killing a hidden archer over by that large tree. He is wounded,*" Keiku replied. "*Quickly see to him. I will carry all of you away from here.*"

Keiku applied healing magic to an unconscious Nui Rei. After carefully wrapping Nui Rei in his House cape, Nui Jooba placed him in an open area in the courtyard. Je Danei purposely mounted the rear saddle while Nui Jooba mounted the front saddle on Keiku's back. The great dragon picked up Nui Rei and flew high into the dark night sky and magically rendered herself and riders invisible. Instead of flying back directly eastward, Keiku first took a southeastern route before heading north to the Borauec Mountain. In doing so, they hoped to avoid any direct conflict with any remaining House Si Moina forces.

After flying for a while, Je Danei mentally asked Nui Jooba, "*How did you know that Majeejp was more to Si Caidyn than just her teacher?*"

"I recognized the pain in her voice and look of unrequited love all too well as I gazed upon her face before she fell to her knees. That cursed pain I know well," Nui Jooba replied. Je Danei then released her hands from the saddle grip in front of her and tightly wrapped her arms around Nui Jooba.

Je Danei then asked, "*Why did you choose to chance death to find me? I do not want you or anyone else to die for me. I am not worthy.*"

After some thought, Nui Jooba replied, "*Despite your contrary actions and words, your 'heart' called to me and said, 'I do not want to die alone'. My intent was not to die for you, but with you, should fate have it so. My heart and person were compelled to answer your true call.*"

With that response, Je Danei gripped him tighter and simply said, "*Thank you.*" She started crying, quietly touched by his committed devotion.

"*Excuse me, but I have news of great importance,*" Nui Rei mentally hurriedly communicated to all. "*While saving my brother, I moved silently through the Si Moina stronghold searching for him. I encountered several enemy House members and killed as many as I could. Pi Rhem was boasting of his part in kidnapping the House Je Luneefa first daughter. Apparently, his 'reward' was to be first to ravage Je Danei.*

"*Later, I overheard a conversation between a severely burned felf, a Si Cailae, another House Si Moina granddaughter, I presumed, and her brother. They were arguing over their strategy in the next negotiating meeting with House Je Luneefa. They mentioned the 'treasure' that Majeejp had stolen from them and hid in the Borauec Mountain. Si Cailae killed her brother, and I killed Si Cailae. Afterwards, I claimed their treasure map. This map will supposedly lead us to a stolen dragon's egg. This egg belongs to our friend, Keiku.*

"*I also discovered the location of the House Si Moina treasure. Make sure Mother gets this map written in an ancient elvish language. The location is protected by magical wards, but she can most likely defeat the locks.*"

"*So, it is true then. The dark mage stole an egg from my womb for his own foul purpose,*" Keiku said. With that said, the dragon's rage compelled her to fly even faster to her next destination.

For the remainder of the flight to the designated rendezvous place at Borauec Mountain, no one "spoke" and Je Danei fell asleep. During this peaceful time, Nui Jooba did thank Ona Kei Kuri Ryuu several times for her assistance and for the gifts of her wondrous blood with which she had blessed him and his friends. He shared with her what had happened while he and Je Danei made their escape. Her blood, once again, proved to be invaluable. In response, Keiku gladly accepted his future gift of two scrubbings, welcomed pampering she had come to greatly enjoy.

# Last Stand at Borauec Mountain

The sun is shining, high above the mountains. A lone soldier of House Nui Vent stands guard at the entrance of a secret passageway into the Borauec Mountain. Just before dawn, the great dragon, Ona Kei Kuri Ryuu, landed with her passengers. Only Nui Jooba and Nui Rei dismounted. Keiku immediately took flight again returning to Torondell. Once there, the House Je Luneefa elders and Keiku hoped her presence would greatly discourage an ambitious and greedy General Yun from attacking Houses Je Luneefa and Nui Vent.

     Nui Danka was pleased to see his brothers again, as well as the first daughter of House Je Luneefa. With the rescue of Je Danei the night before from the House Si Moina stronghold, Nui Danka stands guard at the very narrow entranceway to protect his comrades' escape path as well as preventing the enemy House from entering Borauec Mountain secret passageway.

     "Danei, why did you not return to the greater safety of Torondell and your family?" Nui Danka asked the House Je Luneefa first daughter.

     Je Danei replied vehemently, "I do not seek safety. House Nui Vent goes to war against House Si Moina. I am the goddaughter and niece of the House Nui Vent great mother Nui Honei. Through that beloved bond and relationship, I am a member of House Nui Vent, and I shall repay House Si Moina a debt of blood for the grievous wounds they inflicted upon Houses Nui Vent and Je Luneefa."

Tomorrow is the day that House Nui Vent is to engage in war against House Si Moina. This House war, Coa vae Coa, was to be a conclusion of a long-time feud House Si Moina has waged against House Nui Vent. At the end, only one House will remain; the other will be erased from the kingdom's *Chronicles of Noble Houses*. Per the rules of Coa vae Coa, the members of each House will fight the other till only one House's forces remain. Only immediate family members, through bloodline, adoption, and marriage, can participate. Blood-brothers and blood-sisters can also participate. Any weapon and magic can be used. Animals bred and trained for battle can also be utilized if these animals only fight on the ground.

In a House war, the Crown provides an official and soldiers to ensure the rules of engagement are enforced with deadly intent, if need be.

As of now, House Nui Vent will field House great mother Nui Honei and great father Nui Samu, Ona Noirar, Ona Drachir, and the sons of House Nui Vent, Nui Danka, Nui Jooba and Nui Rei, along with Je Danei who will also fight for House Nui Vent. The House Si Moina force is unknown. In addition, several of the House Si Moina daughters and sons had married members of House Tou Ahn. So, some unknown force from House Tou Ahn would likely join House Si Moina in this battle. The leaders of House Tou Ahn still harbored old grudges against the House Nui Vent great mother as well.

Nui Danka knew he might not survive any upcoming fight; yet his newfound love for his adopted family and extended family bolstered his inner courage, strength and duty. He is young, brave and filled with the committed spirit of unwavering loyalty to his House. Although a skilled and proficient soldier, Nui Danka had not yet mastered his weapons, but he would gladly follow his Commander's orders even at the likelihood of losing his life. His love, loyalty and duty to Houses Nui Vent and Je Luneefa, his soldiers in arms and House great mother Nui Honei were unbreakable.

Nui Danka watched over his sleeping, wounded younger brother while Je Danei and Nui Jooba had gone into the mountain. He recalled laughing at the pair as they hurriedly ran into Boreauec Mountain, hand in hand. He jokingly yelled, "Yes, go on you two. Make a precious memory; and have no regrets; for tomorrow, we could all die in battle!"

Nui Rei immediately scolded his eldest brother, "Fool, they go in search of Keiku's stolen egg, not to make love. Guard your words." Nui Rei then conveyed the night's previous events.

Midmorning, Nui Danka perhaps heard approaching horses, before he saw the enemy. No doubt these were just a small band of scouts. A small smile came upon his death mask-painted face. He had already accepted the fact that today could be his last. Yet, he had no regrets being such a young melf. More importantly, he had summoned enough courage to tell Zhen Laehua that he even liked her and wanted to formally court her three nights before. So, he felt he would not die with so much now to live for...

The enemy soldiers stopped about two hundred steps away. The stone bridge connecting the valley to the Borauec mountain's hidden entrance was narrow only supporting a possible two-person-across path. The enemy unhorsed and only two approached the bridge slowly, wary of any potential archers protecting the mountain guard. Nui Danka stood at attention and greeted the two enemy soldiers when they approached the front of the one hundred steps bridge, "Soldiers of House Si Moina, your journey may very well end here should you try to cross over this bridge."

One enemy soldier shouted, "I am Joam Bram and my comrade-in-arms here is Nadd Dois. We are both First Spears of the House Si Moina army. Clearly, you must not even be a simple soldier of the falling House Nui Vent given your poor looking armor. So, stand aside quickly, for we shall pass. Whether you live or die is of no concern to us. Choose carefully now!"

Nui Danka, without fear, immediately replied, "Soldiers of the falling House Si Moina, come then and try to pass. By the way, I was told I look quite handsome in my custom-made armor." A smiling Nui Danka then moved into a defensive posture with his spear and shield, blocking the end of the bridge, and awaited his destiny.

Nadd Dois started moving forward with drawn sword and setting his shield in the normal, first position. Nadd Dois shouted, "Who are you young, foolish melf that you would defy superior rank and force? Fortunately, I see you have prepared yourself by wearing your death mask. Tell me your name fool so I can inform your mother and father of their son's foolish, pitiful death."

"I am Nui Danka, a newly appointed, proud soldier and adopted first son of House Nui Vent, and a former homeless thief. Try to cross this bridge and I will show you how costly my death will be," Nui Danka defiantly replied.

Both Si Moina soldiers were amused with the fact that a former thief had enlisted into the enemy House army. With this declaration, Nadd Dois felt some remorse that he was about to take the life of such an assumed poorly equipped and seemingly ill-prepared conscript of the enemy House. Laughter arose from his small party while bets were made about how many strikes Nadd Dois would need to dispatch the House Nui Vent bridge guard.

Nadd Dois thereafter approached and engaged Nui Danka quickly. He wanted to seize the opportunity of getting inside his enemy spear's reach. Although quite skilled with his sword and shield, Nadd Dois was kept at bay by Nui Danka who would not press any attack, but just maintained his defensive position with a flurry of parries countering his enemy's many different attacks.

"You have been trained well," the frustrated Nadd Dois then said. "Remarkably, you are still alive former thief. Is that why you even still smile?"

Without hesitation, an undisturbed Nui Danka responded, "No, disgraced and humiliated enemy House First Spear. You have failed to kill me, and your comrades have to place their bets again. Also, I will continue to smile because I finally realize that my House weapons master battle lessons prepared me quite well. Finally, if I die by your sword, I die by the hand of a ranked First Spear soldier, but if you die today, you will die by the hands of a lowly, former thief. Whose reputation will be greater then? So, come; let us both meet our fates joyfully."

Now, filled with frustration and anger, Nadd Dois pressed an undisciplined attack. Nui Danka continued to maintain his stringent fighting discipline amidst his enemy's rash onslaught. Nadd Dois' attack speed dramatically increased; yet Nui Danka's death was postponed. Laughter arises from the other enemy soldiers as new bets are wagered. In response, an enraged and embarrassed Nadd Dois yelled a battle cry and continued pressing his House Nui Vent adversary with renewed fury.

Suddenly, Nui Danka dropped his shield and took his spear into both hands. A sinister smile then filled the bridge guard elf's face. He now begins to reply to Nadd Dois' attacks with his own vicious counterattacks taught to him by Nui Samu. Nui Danka's battle cry was deafening. There were few outside of House Nui Vent that knew of these specialized spear attack combinations and how to even counter them. With his last parry, Nui Danka spun behind Nadd Dois' defenses landing a vicious deadly kick to his Nadd Dois' neck. Nadd Dois gasped and then died instantly from a broken neck.

Now utterly outraged, Joam Bram attacked quickly screaming his battle-cry. Joam Bram's weapons of choice were the night stars, pointed steel balls connected by chains to shafts. Fortunately, Danka had quickly regained his shield by this time. As before, Nui Danka took only defensive measures as Joam Bram pressed on with his attacks. In the span of eight short heartbeats, Nui Danka nearly lost his head and leg from the ferocious attacks of his enemy wielding weapons unfamiliar to him.

The enemy's blows upon his shielded arm became numerous and painful to the point that Nui Danka again decided to drop his shield and again take up his spear in both hands. After cutting his finger on his spear's blood-point, he whispered magical words that then transformed his long spear into two shorter javelins. Nui Danka then decided to attack himself now and stay inside the full range of his enemy's night stars. This sudden shift in strategy surprised Joam Bram. He was now unable to take advantage of the full might of his deadly weapons. Even when he tried to retreat to gain more distance between him and the House Nui Vent soldier would counter by advancing to maintain some advantage. The narrow bridge also limited his maneuvering capabilities. So, Joam Bram suddenly found himself having to use his weapons' shafts defensively.

Unfortunately for Joam Bram who needed to block a vicious attack by Nui Danka with both shafts, allowed Nui Danka an opportunity. Nui Danka was able to pin both shafts momentarily against Joam Bram's body with only one hand. He then was able to use his free hand to fatally stab Joam Bram using his other hand's short spear.

The remaining scouting party now quickly crossed the bridge. No longer interested in granting their enemy an honorable death through one-on-one combat, they now wanted to end this annoying House Nui Vent soldier's life without further delays. All four House Si Moina soldiers, brandishing spears and shields, marched in an orderly and disciplined fashion towards Nui Danka.

Yet, true to his nature and despite his weary condition, Danka, now armed with his long spear and shield, steeled himself and awaited his upcoming glorious death vowing to himself to take at least one more enemy life. So, he again smiled.

The enemy leader gave a command, and his battle unit quickly formed a battle shield wall consisting of two-by-two overlapping shields with four protruding spears. Given this formidable formation, Nui Danka slowly retreated till he was beyond the end of the bridge. When the enemy reached the end of the bridge, the unit leader again issued another battle command, ordering his battle unit to now spread out against their lone enemy soldier.

At this time, Nui Danka final target was made clear. He

aimed to attack and kill this enemy battle unit's leader if he could. As Nui Danka lunged at the leader of the enemy soldiers, the other enemy soldiers on his sides intercepted the House Nui Vent soldier's attack. One enemy pinned and neutralized Nui Danka's spear, while the other immobilized Nui Danka's shield. Both shield and spear were ripped from Danka's grasp as the enemy unit leader dealt him a vicious blow across his face with the shaft of his spear. The blow was not fatal, meant only to perhaps "teach" a harsh lesson and not kill. The commander's blow did launch Nui Danka into the air several steps away.

With blood dripping from his mouth, Nui Danka slowly rose grabbing two rocks as he stood vowing to himself to continue to fight until he drew his last breath. He must follow his orders; he must still defend the mountain's passageway, giving his brother and Je Danei as much time as possible to continue their quest.

"Brother, you are not alone; I, another former thief, will join you," a wounded Nui Rei called as he approached and stood by Nui Danka. Nui Rei faced his enemies with shield and sword. Looking at his brother, Rei inquired mentally, *"Rocks? What part of our training ever included rocks? Fool, call to your weapons."*

*"I cannot; my jaw is broken I believe,"* Nui Danka replied mentally.

"Your courage is without question, and you have trained well. However, you are just lowly thieves soon to be slaughtered like an animal by superior mighty beasts," said the enemy leader. Arrogantly, this enemy soldier started approaching Nui Danka and Nui Rei alone, without his squad.

Nui Rei then defiantly shouted, "Yes, we are of peasant blood and heritage, yet transformed to be much more than low-born. Although we are both newly appointed soldiers of House Nui Vent, we now possess our House noble warrior's spirit. So come, kill us if you surely can. By my count, two of your comrades, First Spears even, are now worm food by my brother's hand. Yet, he still lives and continues to smile."

Before the other three enemy House soldiers could form-up again in their previous two by two formation, Nui Danka called upon his remaining energy, yelled his last battle cry, and attacked the enemy battle unit leader.

From the corner of his eye, Nui Rei noticed a lone archer across the bridge shoot an arrow aimed at his brother's exposed head. A heartbeat later, Nui Rei pushed his brother aside to avoid getting hit, but Nui Rei missed blocking the arrow with his shield and was hit in the stomach. Since his armor had been removed earlier so his previously received wound could be cleaned and dressed, he had not placed the armor back on. Excruciating pain overtook him, and Nui Rei immediately fell to the ground. The arrow was tipped with a paralyzing poison, a known specialty of House Si Moina.

Nui Rei collapsed to his knees and mentally called out to his brothers one last time, "*Brothers, I believe this is my death blow. I will die this day. Do not mourn too long for me. Think of me sometimes. Live well. Jooba, if you can, capture Je Danei's heart. Danka, you capture Zhen Laehua's heart too. Love them fearlessly, faithfully, and mightily. Name your firstborn after me.*" The dying Nui Rei requested lastly. "*Tell all the elders 'Thank you' again. Hug them all too for me. Thank you too. You and Jooba were the best brothers I could ever have. Know that I loved you in life and will love you, my dear brothers, in death too.*" Nui Rei then started chanting, "I am going to die with the blood of enemies on my hands. I die knowing I was protecting our House and our lands. I joyfully greet the sun knowing that today is my last stand. May our black dragons fly me home. May our ancestors welcome me home."

Nui Danka through his tear-filled eyes responded, moaning, "Yes, my brother, you died with the blood of enemies on your hands. I know this day you will find your final peace. I know this ground will mark your final stand. You died well my brother for our black dragons to carry you home."

Nui Rei then closed his eyes and took his last breath, smiling and at peace.

Seeing his fallen brother, blood-rage completely overwhelmed Nui Danka. Even though the surprised enemy squad leader immediately got into a defensive position with his spear pointed at Nui Danka. Nui Danka still managed to beat the spear away and then crash both rock-filled hands against the sides of the enemy's helmet, fatally crushing the enemy unit leader's head.

With his slow rise, the remaining enemy soldiers now ferociously charged Nui Danka. Still armed with the two rocks, he prepared again for combat be his knowing this fight would truly be his last. He threw both rocks simultaneously at one enemy soldier. The second thrown rock landed hard upon the knee of that one enemy soldier.

"Bartoo!" This House Nui Vent battle command came from behind him, and Nui Danka obeyed, "falling immediately to the ground." Out of the dark passageway, two spears and an arrow flew over Nui Danka's head; each weapon finding a target in the charging enemy soldiers who died upon the deadly missiles' impact. Out of the dark, misty hidden cave passageway walked Nui Honei, House Nui Vent's great mother. Beside her walked her brother, the equally dreaded Nui Samu. With great pain, Nui Danka slowly stood, saluted his superiors and fell back to his knees dying knowing he had fulfilled his last given command to protect the passageway with honor. The third elf emerging from the cave's shadows was Ona Noirar.

Another enemy scouting party, a band of eight soldiers had also arrived and crossed over the narrow bridge. Nui Danka slowly looked up, saw the enemies approaching and tried to rise as blood flows freely from his head wound. "Rest, you have battled enough today. Drink this," said Nui Honei quietly as she handed her son a bottle of potion. She then helped him lay against a large rock.

"*Please grant me one last wish,*" said Nui Danka. "*Give me my beloved spear and shield; I wish to die with them in my hands!*" Nui Samu recovered his adopted nephew's gifted, beloved weapons and placed them in Nui Danka's hands."

"I order you not to die this day! *Next time just call to them; both Nui Benoiti and Nui Breici Wei know your voice, even when you call them with your mind,*" Nui Samu said mentally and recognizing his nephew's broken jaw. Mentally, Nui Danka called his beloved weapons and they both magically returned to his waiting hands.

Meanwhile, the last wounded enemy soldier, unable to stand due to his crushed knee, started crawling towards his comrades. The leader of this squad mercilessly killed the wounded soldier, shouting "Useless male!" as she passed. She then continued approaching the House Nui Vent soldiers.

"So, is that how your House continues to show loyalty to your soldiers?" greeted Nui Honei.

"He was of no longer use to our House and he let a miserable, low soldier dispatch him. He deserved to die," responded the presumed, newly arrived enemy soldiers' leader. "Who are you old, soon to die fools? Shall history even remember you?"

"So young and arrogant you are," replied Nui Honei. "Know that as your *old* elders, we have had chances and created history; whereas, you probably have not and most certainly will not. All of you will die this day.

"Secondly, be more respectful one last time and introduce yourselves first. I can see from your fine armor, weapons, and capes, you may be high-ranking soldiers or at least from a high noble House perhaps. Social courtesy dictates you introduce yourselves first. So, may we know your names?"

"I am Tou Crysei of House Tou Ahn, the first daughter of that House and these are my personal guards, the Seven Demons, all blood-sisters. I was a wife of Si Tadejo, now deceased first son of House Si Moina," said Tou Crysei. "Fear not, your end will come swiftly and without mercy. But first, what are your names and House?"

A sinister smile came upon Nui Honei's face as she replied, "My brother's name is Nui Samu, the great patriarch and weapons master of House Nui Vent; and I am the great mother, Nui Honei of that House. That melf is my love and Nui Samu's blood-brother, Ona Noirar." With that proud declaration, Nui Samu unleashed his deadly weapons from underneath his cape. His chosen weapons were his exquisitely crafted, double-bladed battleaxes, Jeiru and Teiru. Nui Honei retained her great bow, Nui Jaei Wei. Ona Noirar chose spear and shield this day.

"It is a shame your mother and grandmother are not here. I would greatly enjoy ending the lives of all House Tou Ahn's mothers today," Nui Honei said.

Then, Nui Samu remarked saying, "Are you sure, they are not here dear sister?"

"Ah.... Dear brother, you are correct. There is a certain, feint stench on the wind; maybe that cowardly grandmother and mother of hers are truly here," remarked Nui Honei. She then uttered a few words of magic and the enemy's veil of concealment lifted. There, hiding by the bridge, stood the House Tou Ahn's first and second House great mothers in their fine battle attire. They were also accompanied by all the granddaughters of House Tou Ahn, five in total. The remaining sons and daughters of House Si Moina were there too. "This is indeed a most welcomed gift brother. Kee and Maree welcome," Nui Honei disdainfully greeted.

"Still, after all this time, you show no respect to me, you great whore of a ruined house," the ancient, first great mother, Tou Kee, of House Tou Ahn said. "Well, it matters not. For you will not see the sun rise tomorrow."

Nui Honei replied, "That may be true; but I still doubt it though. And I certainly did not need to hide my approach like you and your cowardly litter of bitches did. Will you try to again demonstrate your *leadership and courage*, by first fighting me alone? If so, you will be the first to die."

All eyes of the House Tou Ahn soldiers scrutinized their House first great mother. Another time, long ago, she had failed to answer a challenge of single combat offered by Nui Honei. That refusal had brought disgrace upon her and her House when she did not answer the call. Thereafter, several unsuccessful attempts were made to try to kill Tou Kee by members of her own House. House respect and public image were viciously protected.

After a few more moments, like before, Tou Kee did not engage Nui Honei in single combat, but vehemently yelled a battle command to Tou Crysei and her Seven Demons, "Soshoo!" which means to "attack by four formation."

"Demons hold!" shouted Tou Crysei angrily. "You, Grandmother, do not command my guard! You again show your cowardice and disgrace our House!" Turning to Nui Honei, she yelled, "I do not fear you, old bitch Honei; I will answer your challenge gladly."

"Think first, young bitch House mother; your chances were a bit better when eight of you were going to attack me. But you by yourself will truly have little chance of defeating me. So, this will be your final battle lesson rapist," remarked Nui Honei. "Do not look so shocked. My House knows your reputation of torturing and raping prisoners. So, come and meet my blades, Sun and Moon."

"Wait you disrespectful, disobedient daughter!" Tou Kee shouted. Then turning to Nui Honei, she said, "Where are the daughters of your House? We mean to kill you all this day and finally eradicate your House from memory and eliminate your chance to be ever reentered into the kingdom's *Chronicles.*"

Moments later, a shout emanated from the cave, "I am here Auntie," Je Danei shouted walking towards the House Nui Vent soldiers.

"Me here too, House great mother and me new aunt," Annaei of Clan Battle Hammer also shouted walking side by side with Je Danei.

Along with Je Kei, Nui Jooba was the last to emerge from the cave carrying a new member of House Nui Vent on his shoulder, an infant black dragon. Nui Jooba handed his dragon to Nui Danka first before joining his other House members. Je Kei, brandishing a battle hammer and shield, and Nui Jooba, carrying his deadly double-bladed battleaxes, joined the other members of House Nui Vent. Je Danei held her twin scimitars; Annaei of Clan Battle Hammer carried her shield and battle hammer.

"I see Honei you are still a peasant and now mother of mongrels too. You are indeed disgraceful; you are no noble," House great mother Tou Kee shouted disdainfully.

"Argh!" a death-scream sounded in the distance behind the

Tou Ahn soldiers.

"Ah, my nephew, I believe, just beheaded the famed archer, Tsau Mei Ling. She was the wife too of House Si Moina first son Si Tadejo, was she not? Your nephew was such a whore it seems," Nui Honei remarked. Just then the severed head of the famed House Tsau archer, Tsau Mei Ling, was thrown and landed in front of the House Tou Ahn soldiers.

The soldiers of Houses Tou Ahn and Si Moina now totaled thirty-two and were facing the Houses Nui Vent and Je Luneefa soldiers.

"Do you still wish to answer my challenge first or do you now also decline, little bitch House mother?" Nui Honei challenged Tou Crysei. "I will even give you honor of naming the weapon I will use to end your miserable life. Speak quickly; it is time to battle."

"Enough! Attack!" screamed House great mother Tou Maree who then pulled her blades, long and short swords, and charged at Nui Honei.

Nui Honei and the House Nui Vent soldiers were about forty steps away from their enemies. The soldiers of Houses Tou Ahn and Si Moina recklessly charged in without using any formation hoping, it would seem, to just overpower the House Nui Vent soldiers with their far superior numbers. Little did the Houses Tou Ahn and Si Moina soldiers know that House Nui Vent soldiers were comfortable fighting against unfavorable odds.

Invisible arrows from Nui Honei's bow screamed quickly into the pack of enemy soldiers. Her targets were the four battlemages in that group. The House Nui Vent great mother quickly killed two, because they could not prepare an adequate defense in time against her dragon's blood-enhanced, deadly arrows. Ona Drachir, still invisible and behind the enemy soldiers, had detected the other two battlemages and killed them quickly too with screaming invisible arrows that became visible only after hitting the intended mark. Keiku's blood again proved it was invaluable as his enhanced arrows penetrated the magical shields the two, now dead battlemages had conjured. Now, the soldiers of Houses Tou Ahn and Si Moina totaled just twenty-eight against House Nui Vent's eight.

Nui Honei dropped her bow when she felt her eldest son find his final peace in death. She screamed and summoned her twin scimitars, Sun and Moon, to her hands and charged into the enemies closely followed by Nui Samu and Ona Noirar. Completely engulfed in battle-rage, Nui Honei battled like a demon possessed with no fear. She was Hell's fury unleashed, killing all who stood before her. Even when the last four Demons, including Tou Crysei, surrounded and attacked her, Nui Honei killed them all. Death was the House great mother's closest friend and she lived unafraid of its final mercy.

Nui Samu and Ona Noirar fought together, killing many of the enemy. Their experience of fighting together many times in the past overwhelmed the Houses Tou Ahn and Si Moina soldiers.

Several enemy soldiers were bashed to death between Annaei and Je Kei who now carried his own battle hammer bearing the sigil of Clan Battle Hammer. This new husband and wife "danced" very well together.

Like in the Kilecfla, Je Danei and Nui Jooba "danced" their ever-deadly battle dance together well too. The felf would throw knives or use her twin scimitars to deliver death. Nui Jooba battleaxes both killed quickly and mercilessly.

Death's quiet, ominous warrior, Ona Drachir, too chose to wield his spear and shield this day, but he replaced those with his twin scimitars which he could deliver death with greater speed.

By morning's end, the Coa vae Coa was over; the long-time feud finally ended. With the death of all her family members, House great mother Tou Kee dropped her weapons, fell to her knees, and begged for mercy. The defeated House first great mother even pleaded to join the victorious House Nui Vent, a custom seldom practiced.

A blood-drenched Nui Honei walked towards Tou Kee and shouted, "I would not ever stain the honor of my House by accepting you or any other member of your treacherous House or House Si Moina. However, I will grant you your final mercy!" Nui Honei then swiftly beheaded the last member of House Tou Ahn.

Nui Honei looked around at her House members and commanded, "Make sure there is no enemy left alive. Display their heads for the Crown to witness that all the great mothers and fathers of those most heinous Houses are dead." Thereafter, each enemy soldier's head was taken and placed on an enemy's discarded spear or sword to mark the final, last stand of the eradicated Houses Tou Ahn and Si Moina.

Now finally overcome with devastating grief, Nui Honei wept openly as she knelt beside her fallen sons.

# Angel of Death

It was long after sundown. The military camp was relatively quiet and peaceful. Most soldiers had retired for the night; some soldiers were still talking of past or future adventures. A lone soldier of the Canae army walked with purpose towards the center of the camp, specifically towards the commanding general's tent.

General Yun and his troops had left Torondell two days earlier. He failed his mission of uncovering any House Je Luneefa family secrets, killing all within the Toronwalein and claiming the Je Luneefa wealth. Nor could he possibly take the family stronghold without incurring heavy losses and even a potential profound defeat. Though he had only lost just two soldiers in trying to first kill Commander Baka, he felt no comfort from his overall unsuccessful mission. General Yun no longer had a strong position to contend for the vacant Warden of the North position. He loathed defeat; so, he quietly contemplated how he could regain favor with the Crown. He desperately wanted to secure the Warden of the North position to conclude his military career.

General Yun and his legions were now on their way to a secret rendezvous point at Borauec Mountain in the northern frontier. This mountain is far west and north of Torondell, about eight days' ride away. Yun had carefully planned his new mission, thinking, *"I can rejoin with my other legion and eliminate the surviving members of the anticipated House war between Houses Nui Vent, Tou Ahn, and Si Moina. The Crown would gain riches from Houses Tou Ahn and Si Moina that recently started recovering gold from their local mountain mines and destroying House Nui Vent would be removing a long-time source of great annoying pain to the Crown. Eliminating an important ally of House Je Luneefa too would be an additional benefit. Despite his failed mission in Torondell, completing these secondary objectives should still greatly aid me in bolstering my chances to claim the Warden of the North position."*

After reaching about two hundred steps from the center of the camp, the lone soldier walked about surveying the center. Magical wards were now in place around several tents, as well as the extra guards. Banners also marked the location of distinguished, key officers. These tents, no doubt, were those of the general and his senior officers. After completing the reconnaissance, the lone figure simply vanished behind a tent without anyone noticing.

Moments later, the lone figure rose from the ground inside the general's tent, veiled invisible and surmising, given the way General Yun was snoring, he had finished whetting his appetite with the female lying next to him. The silent visitor recited an incantation and blew some fine powder upon General Yun who inhaled the powder. Any powder that was not inhaled was quickly absorbed into the General's skin leaving no surface traces of the substance. Immediately thereafter, this lone figure disappeared underground again and visited each of the senior officer's tents.

The next day at their evening meal, General Yun presented another bottle of stolen Napa brandy to his senior officers. As was his custom, General Yun would share a glass with them after their evening meal. For him and those senior officers who had shared in the killing of the northern army's Commander Baka, it would be their last meal...

Je Leena had met the Je Luneefa elders, Nui Honei, Urtha Dal, Alleina, Ona Noirar, Roerson and Nui Samu late evening five days earlier. They had all gathered to commemorate the passing of Commander Baka. Warden castle servants had found his dead body behind bushes in the courtyard shortly after General Yun and his staff vacated the premises and Torondell.

When Je Leena first told her elders what had happened that fateful day, they first planned a memorial service for the dedicated commander. They then planned his revenge. His service was meant to be small and simple, but the entire House Je Luneefa and northern armies attended and participated in the procession. First Commander Baka was mourned greatly, not only for being a wise, dedicated and highly capable military leader, but also for being a loyal friend for centuries to the elders of Houses Je Luneefa and Nui

Vent. He received the highest honor being buried inside the Toronwalein in the House Je Luneefa private cemetery.

No one mourned Commander's Baka's death more than Alleina, his oldest living friend. After Baka was placed into the ground, the kind-hearted healer transformed due to her rage and anger. She wielded neither sword nor axe; her weapons of choice were poisons. Being a gifted healer who practiced the medical arts for centuries allowed her to gain much knowledge. So, it came as no surprise when Alleina convened a meeting with the Houses Je Luneefa and Nui Vent elders to present her role in a plan for revenge.

Alleina would prepare a special poison that is undetectable and only activated by a planned agent. A special ingredient placed in Napa brandy was one of the selected components. Nui Honei and Urtha Dal supplied certain magic spells that would enhance the designated assassin's ability to move throughout the army camp underground. This secret tactic was sometimes used by experienced, powerful dwarf battlemages and could give an assassin an ability to bypass certain magical wards which are typically established above ground.

Alleina's custom-designed poison is also part powder administered through the target victim's inhalation. The assassin need only applied the powder to those commanders who shared in the killing of Commander Baka. When the powder is mixed with the tainted Napa brandy stolen from the Warden's castle, an extremely violent chemical reaction will result, causing severe internal burns when the targeted victim next drank water, the poison's triggering agent. The intended victim will die from excruciating pain caused by severe internal organ damage, as if from an internal, uncontrollable inferno is raging inside the victim's body.

In the morning, the lone assassin heard from afar all the victims' screams as each began to die in horrific pain. The assassin watched each targeted victim die and thought that death by fire was an appropriate method for killing General Yun. His long moments of screaming and uncontrollable writhing from the pain were a fitting end of the evil general's life. In the turmoil caused by the deaths of General Yun and his senior officers, the assassin quickly fled from the chaos of the camp undetected to an awaiting dragon. Along the way, she met with another friend, her "shadow," who was there to protect the assassin's retreat with his deadly, great bow.

The great dragon, Ona Kei Kuri Ryuu, invisible and well hidden away behind some hills, awoke immediately when she detected the two assassins, still veiled invisible, approaching her. The assassins mounted the dragon, and she immediately took flight, returning to Torondell.

Since all the targeted victims were far away from Torondell when they died, all the suspected Houses Je Luneefa and Nui Vent elders were still in Torondell, and other officers who drank the same Napa brandy were unaffected, Rhodell could not logically suspect either House Je Luneefa or House Nui Vent elders as the perpetrators.

Je Leena was especially proud of her role in the clandestine mission; she found she enjoyed being an assassin, an angel of Death.

# New and Old Good Friends

On the plains south of Borauec Mountain, Commander Roerson and Urtha Dal, both of Clan Battle Hammer, led three thousand dwarf warriors into a potential battle with the troops of Rhodell. The Rhodell legions were supposedly sent to the northern frontier for training purposes. In addition to training, the commanding officer, now Second Commander Somai, was to oversee the Coa vae Coa battle between Houses Tou Ahn, Si Moina and Nui Vent.

Commander Somai received his appointment as the new commanding officer after he had learned of the deaths of General Yun and his command staff two days before. The mysterious deaths were found to all be "random and accidental. No foul play was suspected." Commander Somai also suspected that General Yun's true secret objectives in Torondell and the northern frontier were truly more than just "training" too. Unknown to most, Commander Somai also distrusted the Crown. He strongly suspected that General Yun's true objectives were aimed to benefit him, his House, and the Crown. Commander Somai, on the other hand, was honorable and would do his duty properly.

So, when Commander Somai encountered the dwarven army who was also there for "training" purposes, he met and greeted the dwarven commanders professionally and with courtesy. They all found they had much in common and had many stories they could share. Army commanding officers learned too that they had a very dear friend in common, the House Je Luneefa first great mother Je Buel.

The day before the Coa vae Coa, Commander Somai was honored when asked to officiate the marriage of Je Kei and Annaei of Clan Battle Hammer since they were closest to the Canae kingdom, and Somai is the senior commander. This marriage also formally related Je Kei to Clan Battle Hammer and in so doing, he now had an extended family that included over two thousand dwarf warriors who happened to be "training" there in the northern frontier. His kin, according to the realm's Coa vae Coa rules, could also fight in the House war if need be, since Je Kei was a nephew of his adopted aunt, House Nui Vent great mother Nui Honei.

On the day of the Coa vae Coa, Commander Somai and Commander Roerson spent the day fishing at a nearby river. Later sharing a good meal of fresh fish, drinking fine ale with new friends encountered in the frontier was a much better use of their time instead of meddling in a House feud as Commander Somai suspected his predecessor had planned.

Commander Somai had decided he could inspect the battle site the next day and later go to the Houses Si Moina and Tou Ahn fortresses. While fishing and later during dinner, Commander Somai received valuable information regarding the location of the hidden House Si Moina treasure. Nui Honei, an invited dinner guest, presented the treasure map to Commander Somai. She and Urtha Dal deciphered the House Si Moina treasure map's secrets and instructed Somai's battlemages how to defeat the magical locks protecting the treasure.

Lastly, Nui Honei said privately, "Unlike most victors who would pillage the defeated Houses and keep any recovered treasure, please fairly distribute some to your troops. Give the other half to the Crown; I know they desperately need the coin."

"Why would you do this? I do not understand," a bewildered Commander Somai questioned.

With a small smile, reflecting some deep, past memories, Nui Honei quietly responded, "It is what my very beloved and wise mother and father, Je Buel and Je Taeliel, would want." The House Nui Vent great mother then left the Canae army camp that night to return home.

The next day, Commander Somai and Commander Roerson said their goodbyes. Commander Roerson even invited Commander Somai to visit him at the Blood Tears Mountains stronghold. Commander Somai reciprocated in kind.

Afterwards, Commander Somai carefully surveyed the Coa vae Coa battle site and witnessed that Houses Tou Ahn and Si Moina were no more. All known family members were now dead as their heads were ghastly displays upon the plains of Borauec Mountain. The Canae army then went westward to recover the valuables from the fallen Houses' strongholds. Commander Somai's army discovered and loaded the well-hidden and magically warded treasure found at House Si Moina.

The Commander chuckled to himself as he watched his soldiers load the last chest of discovered gold. His day of fishing yielded a surprisingly great reward. The Crown would be incredibly pleased, he thought. Commander Somai had also learned that House Rho was nearly bankrupt and desperately needed gold. The Crown had secretly "encouraged" House wars; so, House Rho could share the spoils of the defeated House. Commander Somai reminded himself to again thank Commander Roerson and Urtha Dal for all their valuable information. It was good to find other "old" honorable soldiers like himself. He felt strongly that his new friends would indeed become his good friends.

After their "training" exercises ended, the dwarven army returned to Torondell and Taurus Mountain. Commander Roerson and Urtha Dal were still guests of Houses Je Luneefa and Nui Vent along with Roerson's brigade of Mountain Wreckers. "Training", especially good training, as the wise Queen Marta predicted, did require time. The quiet entry of the famed Mountain Wreckers brigade inside the Toronwalein, along with other factors, such as the periodic flights of the great dragon, Ona Kei Kuri Ryuu, over the Canae troops, were key deterrents of any hostilities possibly planned by Rhodell through General Yun.

Even when the General would ride near the Toron River to view and perhaps assess the Toronwalein, an invisibly cloaked Keiku hurled a flame-spear in front of the Rhodell commanding officer. On each of his three visits, Keiku's spear got closer to hitting its target, the last hitting the ground two steps away from the General. After being thrown from his frightened horse, General Yun quickly followed his wise horse's retreat. This last action proved to be the final deterrent needed to encourage General Yun's cessation of considering taking the strongholds beyond the indomitable Toronwalein and departure from Torondell.

After the funeral services of the House Je Luneefa first elders, Je Buel and Je Taeliel, Queen Marta and King Joerson extended their stay near Torondell for two moons to safeguard the peace of Houses Je Luneefa and Nui Vent during that time.

The day after General Yun left Torondell, King Joerson commanded his brother to take three thousand warriors from the Taurus Mountain stronghold to the Borauec Mountain for more rigorous "training". His mission was to safeguard the House Nui Vent soldiers and ensure there was no Canae kingdom interference. Fortunately, there was no Canae interference, and all the dwarf warriors returned safely to their new Taurus Mountain stronghold or Torondell.

Before returning home with their escort of two thousand warriors, Queen Marta and King Joerson held a great feast. Je Pagi and Je Maron attended the feast at the Taurus Mountain, the new second, future stronghold of the Clan Battle Hammer dwarves. A variety of gifts were exchanged. The Houses Je Luneefa and Nui Vent elders gifted the queen and king with four large bottles of powerful, untainted, fully blessed dragon's blood and one thousand berry pies. The precious dragon's blood, as the most powerful magical energy source component, was given to the queen and king and could be used to help the dwarves in many ways. The latter gift of pies was just enough to serve to all five thousand dwarf soldiers.

And of course, King Joerson was overjoyed when he received his very own, personal "magic cape" that hid three more bottles of the infamous Napa brandy liquor. When he received the gift chest and found the cape, King Joerson looked at his wife and devilishly hugged his gift remembering his request and yelled, "Mine!"

"Ha! Me be stealin' dat der magic cape of yers if ye do not share yer private stash wid me!" promised Queen Marta.

After the laughing had subsided, Queen Marta and King Joerson spoke privately with the House Je Luneefa elders. King Joerson said, "Pagi and Mari, our time here be at an end; we enjoyed our visit. But we be headin' home tomorrow. We want to git home befer the first snows fall. But befer we left, me Queen and me wanted to first personally honor our agreement made wid yer ma, Bueli back at our stronghold. Minin' at Taurus Mountain gone and continues to go well. Dat tent over there, covers yer family's twenty-five percent of de gold and diachrom we mined in dat new mountain dis first year so far. When ye return home tomorrow, two extra wagons be goin' back wid ye. Dank ye again for helpin' me clan."

Queen Marta added, "We be seein' ye again soon in de Spring at de youngins' second wedding ceremony on the third day of the fifth moon. By de way Pagi, we got more bets to win!"

After many warm hugs and goodbyes, the next day, Queen Marta and King Joerson, along with Prince Dajald, Commander Roerson and Urtha Dal started their return journey to their home in the Blood Tears Mountains.

Je Pagi and Je Maron returned to their home in Torondell.

On their trip home, the House Je Luneefa elders reflected upon the House Je Luneefa first elders' blessings of having good, old friends. They indeed felt truly fortunate.

# New Life and Revelations

Shortly after returning from the House war with Houses Si Moina and Tou Ahn, Nui Honei destroyed five great oak trees in the garden. The enraged battle mage hurled devastating fire bolts at each tree, completing obliterating the once sacred symbol of her family. With the destruction of each tree, a horrific cracking sound erupted, startling all within the Toronwalein and those close by... After letting the ensuing fire rage for a few moments, the House Nui Vent great mother quickly extinguished the fire. In doing so, her rage also subsided.

Nui Honei walked amongst the charred remains of the trees, fell upon the scorched earth and wept.

It has now been eight moons since the House battle at Borauec Mountain. Welcomed peace once again shrouded Houses Je Luneefa and Nui Vent. Like many nights in the past, House great mother Nui Honei is spending time alone with the great dragon, Ona Kei Kuri Ryuu. The two of them share an incredibly special bond even though Nui Honei is not dragon-kind, nor is Ona Kei Kuri Ryuu elf-kind. They considered themselves sisters; they share like minds, values and even one Ona Noirar, the now legendary, great warrior and dragon rider. Since Keiku has been alone in the world without any parents or siblings, the dragon decided long ago that Nui Honei could be her "sister."

However today, Keiku is no longer alone, for one of her precious eggs, stolen from her womb long ago, was found, and hatched. This baby dragon, now standing eight hands tall, was bonded to Nui Jooba. To honor his brothers fallen at the recent House war, he named his female baby dragon, Nui Kei Dan-Rei Ryuu. Since her daughter's birth, Keiku too spends time with her young one, teaching her the ways of a dragon. Nui Jooba and Dan-Rei would journey to Keiku's lair many times to visit the great dragon. Ona Noirar also teaches Nui Jooba and Dan-Rei the ways of a dragon rider. Lessons from both the elder dragon and dragon rider are welcomed by the young ones who expected their training to continue for many, many years.

Tonight, after completing the documentation of Keiku's personal battle at the Zehthyme Mountain in her dragon's *Chronicles*, Nui Honei retired for the night. The felf became unusually tired and especially quiet this evening only after reading a few chapters of the book *Architecture of the Blood Tears Mountains* by Duenor Heartstone. Nui Honei could not ever find sleep easily since their return from the House battle. She had lost two precious sons and is still grieving. Although the enemy Houses had been completely destroyed this time, she would gladly kill more members of Houses Tou Ahn and Si Moina if any existed.

Losing one's child, even adopted as Nui Danka and Nui Rei were, unleashed such fury and rage like she had never felt before. It is good she thought to isolate herself for a while, away from others. In doing so, she would not feel she had to converse or interact with anyone. *"Being alone and isolated with my sister is good therapy,"* she thought. Unlike others, Keiku and she could not converse for days and still be quite comfortable in their silence and shared solitude. *"Keiku's lair is an ideal place for me to heal in peace."*

Nui Honei reclined in her usual place on a bedding pallet near the great dragon. Keiku would then cover the felf with one of her wings. This is another demonstration of the great affection the dragon has for this felf. Now, past midnight, Keiku was shaken from her sleep.

"Honei, wake up!" she called out mentally. *"Wake up, sister. We must talk now!"*

"What... What is it that you cannot wait till morning to disturb me?" asked Nui Honei. Still half asleep, Nui Honei rose from her short slumber and stood before the dragon. *"What now troubles you sister? We already agreed that your daughter is very pretty and looks very much like you."*

"New *voices called out to me, not one you can hear; but one I can only feel in my mind!"* an excited Keiku said.

"Who called out to you? What was the message?" a half-asleep Nui Honei asked.

"*Your young ones!*" replied Keiku.

"With tears forming in her eyes, Nui Honei rose and affectionately hugged Keiku around the neck and said with a grieving voice, "I see and hear them too in my dreams. I miss them so much. I..."

"*No, your unborn young ones. Sister, you are pregnant!*" Keiku declared joyously.

"*What? I am in no mood for any jokes at this time of night. How can you be so sure?*" When have you studied medical journals?" a surprised and now fully awake Nui Honei asked.

"*I completed studying all the elf biology and anatomy books Alleina authored over a century ago. Ona Noirar had an annoying infection on his leg then; so, I started learning more about the medical arts. But that is not important now. What is important is that the blood flowing in the veins of your unborn is partly mine; so, I must share a unique, magical connection with them. You are indeed pregnant. I know the signs well even at your early stage. That also explains your moodiness, restlessness, and other conditions I have recently observed.*

"*And 'Yes' before you even ask, you are carrying twins! Dear Sister, your fame will continue to grow! We will be the most famous sisters in history!*

"I do hope they both look like you and not Ona Noirar," Keiku jested. "*By the way, you must give birth to our young ones here and not in that castle. I want to be the first, maybe the second to see them. I can bless them immediately too.*" After looking around her lair, Keiku continued, "*Hmmm, I will also need to redecorate.*"

"*Keiku, how can this be after all the time that has passed? Why now? Female elves are only supposedly fertile between one hundred eighty and three hundred sixty years of age. Within that time, ovulation is supposed to occur once only every ten years. I am now well beyond three hundred sixty years in age; so, how can this be?*" the baffled Nui Honei asked.

"*Damn the rules! The fact cannot be refuted, and the fact is you are surely pregnant! Oh, my dear sister, you have again proven you are so incredibly special!*" Keiku proudly proclaimed, releasing a short burst of flame.

Extremely shocked, Nui Honei started pondering the possibility of motherhood, a very distant and long-lost dream... "*I have told Ona Noirar 'No' so many times to his marriage proposals; he may no longer wish to marry me,*" Nui Honei sadly stated.

"Most importantly, do you want to marry him now?" Keiku immediately countered. "Stop! Do not fret. If he does not marry you now, I will surely kill him. Besides, he has already made his contribution; we do not need him anymore. We can both raise our young ones by ourselves! We are smart, strong, independent females! We are warriors and will be great mothers too!" declared the great dragon. "Je Pagi and Alleina will surely help us. Do not fear, we have no need for that great warrior."

"Keiku, I need to sleep; I am overwhelmed now and weary from this news," Nui Honei confessed.

Keiku responded, "How can you possibly sleep now? We have much to discuss, but first..."

"First, I need to contact Alleina and ask her to examine me. Afterwards, I need to speak with Ona Noirar and share this news with him," Nui Honei interjected. "In the meantime, please do not speak to anyone about this." Nui Honei then returned to her pallet bed where the great dragon gladly welcomed her with uplifted wing. "Let us sleep now and talk more in the morning."

"Surely. Rest well, Sister. I love you and my... Oh! Do you want to know the sex of our unborn young ones now?" Keiku asked after lowering her wing over Nui Honei and snuggling closer to the felf.

"Ha, oh no! No more discussion. Let me sleep. You think, you plan then, but with yourself; do not try to lure me into any more discussions!" Nui Honei replied. After a few moments of silence, Nui Honei said, "Sister, I love you too. Good night."

Both felf and dragon slept well for the remainder of the night in quiet peace.

In the morning, Keiku requested a meeting with Nui Honei and Ona Noirar to discuss a matter of great importance. They all met in the House Nui Vent stronghold courtyard midafternoon. Nui Kei Dan-Rei Ryuu was there too with Nui Jooba. The young dragon was hoping to play again with her mother. Although a bit disappointed when Keiku told her she needed to leave, Dan-Rei joyfully played with Nui Jooba who distracted her with some fresh fish.

Shortly after her passengers arrived, Keiku took flight with Nui Honei and Ona Noirar and flew south from Torondell. After climbing high above the ground, Keiku leveled-off and glided effortlessly, riding the air currents. "Great warrior Ona Noirar, please say the words; just the three little words," Keiku urged through her mental communications. "What more needs to be

*proven? Is it really that hard for you to just admit it!"*
"Why must we again have this discussion? Why are dragons so vain and persistent? I have seen you bask in your beauty and glory as your attendees 'pampered' you. I will say again, you are magnificent, unlike any other creature in this world. Is it not better to let others praise you; rightfully so I might add?" Ona Noirar reluctantly remarked.
"I am much more than just beautiful and magnificent. I can communicate in twelve different languages, including ancient Elvish. I have learned Canae law. I am knowledgeable in the medical arts. I have even started learning architectural engineering too. I am very learned.
"Great warrior Ona Noirar, can you fly? Can your blood heal wounds or enhance the power of your weapons? Can you hurl flame-spears? Can you defeat not two or three, but four mighty great bears by yourself? I think not! So, just admit it to me just this once. This will stay between the three of us, I promise," vowed Keiku.
"My love, you are awfully quiet. You have not uttered a word since we took flight. Is something troubling you? If so, I am sure my so-called 'perfect' dragon can create and deliver a 'perfect' solution for you," remarked a sarcastic Ona Noirar.
"*I want a Spring wedding,*" Nui Honei surprisingly and suddenly announced.
"What?" Ona Noirar reflexively responded. "*I do not understand. Wait. You rejected all my many marriage proposals in the past. Why now? And you said you would not marry me since you could not conceive baby elves. What has now changed?*"
"*Fool, I am pregnant now!*" Nui Honei declared emphatically.
"*What? How did this miracle happen? Has Alleina confirmed your condition? When did you know?*" questioned the awestricken warrior.
"*I calculated it was four moons ago, on that night before...*" Keiku started responding.
Nui Honei immediately interrupted, "*Keiku, please hush. I am pregnant because of our love making during a time when I could finally conceive. Your genitalia have been presumably repaired to produce the necessary quantity of balinayagi and enhanced by Keiku's blood, the very miraculous blood that healed your body evidently in more ways than one. 'Yes', Alleina has confirmed my pregnancy. 'Yes', it was about four moons ago after my estrus cycle began. Now, close your mouth; you look*

undignified," replied an irritated Nui Honei.

"Finally, we will have an infant of our own. How can that be? Am I ready? How do I prepare? How do I train for this?" Ona Noirar thought. He then shouted, "Spring wedding. Yes, of course, I will be there!"

"Our young one will also be of my blood too! The first in history of truly mixed elf and dragon blood, I believe. So, famed warriors of the Canae, I again have achieved another historical first!" declared Keiku.

"Wait, four moons ago? So, who else knew before me besides you two and Alleina, the elf's father, your beloved future husband? We should have a celebration soon after we return and make an announcement. I must find Je Pagi and learn about infants. Je Maron can help train me too. Let us have fish tonight for dinner; we have not had fish in a long while. We can all eat in the garden," Ona Noirar rambled incessantly.

"How can such a renowned and dignified warrior turn into a babbling idiot?" Nui Honei asked, quietly laughing at the famed warrior.

"Keiku, please land. I need to think; so, walking back to our stronghold will help me clear my mind of so many thoughts," Ona Noirar requested.

Before sundown, Ona Noirar returned to the same garden from which his day's journey started. He had washed away the dust from his return walk and had changed his clothes. Upon seeing all those he deeply cared about, his heart and mood were uplifted greatly. Although he is about to embark upon another perilous journey, he is committed to his success with the same dedication he always had on previous dangerous missions. He reminded himself that becoming a good father to his infant is a most important duty that will not defeat him; it will just be another difficult challenge. "Afterall, I am a renowned warrior of the kingdom. I just need to stay strong and committed for the next two hundred ten years to raise our young one to adulthood. Yes, I know I can do this. It will perhaps be difficult at times, but I am determined to succeed!" he thought.

The House Je Luneefa elders, sons, and daughters, including Je Kei's new wife, Annaei, had all gathered there. Alleina and the Ladies Zhen, Mother Lae and her daughter Laehua, were there too. Also in the garden, House Nui Vent great father Samu seem to be debating the pros and cons of certain weaponry again with Ona Drachir. The Canae northern army and House armies' commanders were all there too.

House great mother Nui Honei was there standing near the great dragon, Keiku, who seemed more protective of his beloved future wife given her posture and physical closeness to the felf. Nui Jooba was standing near them with Dan-Rei. Although he was still grieving over the loss of his brothers, he now appeared to be in better spirits.

After pouring himself a glass of chilled wine, Ona Noirar walked slowly towards his future bride, warmly greeting his friends individually and thanking them for joining him on this great day. After making his way to Nui Honei, he took her hand and kissed it. Ona Noirar looked at his beloved felf and said, "Thank you, thank you, thank you. You have made me incredibly happy by finally accepting my marriage proposal. Your young one and mine will..."

"*Our young one!*" Keiku quickly and emphatically corrected the great warrior. Her private communications to Ona Noirar and Nui Honei caused Nui Honei to chuckle to herself.

"*Keiku intends to play an integral role in raising our offspring,*" Nui Honei thought. "*That is good; this is very good. Another great battle will be waged against my future husband and famed dragon rider. And of course, like most of our battles, Keiku and I will surely win!*"

Ona Noirar started to mumble something, but Keiku immediately countered, "*I can converse in all twelve different languages spoken in this kingdom and throughout the known world, but 'mumbling' is not one I have yet learned, great warrior. So, please try a more popular tongue spoken.*"

Ignoring his dragon's annoying remarks, Ona Noirar pulled his dagger and hit his wine glass several times to get his guests' attention. After clearing his voice, he said, "Thank you all family and dear friends for meeting me here on such short notice. I have some unbelievable, great news I wish to share with all of you. I..."

"My sister finally deemed you worthy enough now to accept your marriage proposal after about a hundred years plus of your asking. Why would that be 'unbelievable great news'?" Je Pagi jokingly asked.

"We have already started planning your Spring wedding too. Do you really have any other 'unbelievable great news' to share?" Je Leena added.

"I see now that you have become much more like your grandmother, young one. Your mother and you now will continue to tease me it seems," Ona Noirar announced.

"We do love you Uncle; so, some family traditions must be honored and maintained!" Je Leena declared raising her glass to

Ona Noirar in acknowledgement.

After some laughter from the guests, Ona Noirar continued, "I really do wish to share more great news with all of you. What I am about to tell you is truly a miracle and could not have happened without my very *perfect* dragon, the Ona Kei Kuri Ryuu." With this declaration, Keiku rose to full height, spread her wings, and released a mighty roar and fire stream.

*"Finally, you have admitted it! You need to take more long walks by yourself it seems. You finally now have greater clarity of thought and reasoning,"* Keiku proclaimed just to Ona Noirar and Nui Honei.

Alleina interrupted, "We already know that Keiku is perfect and have acknowledged that fact moons ago. Thankfully, you have finally recognized and accepted that well-known fact. But what 'unbelievable great news' are you going to share? We still wait."

"Such an impatient crowd," a smiling Nui Honei said as she joined Ona Noirar and took his hands. She looked at the guests and exclaimed with a big smile, "I am pregnant!"

"Yes, so? We already figured that out too Sister. And do not even ask me how I would know; after all, I have been pregnant myself multiple times. I know the signs all too well. So, is that his 'unbelievable great news'?" Je Pagi said.

*"Quickly Jooba, please stand next to Ona Noirar,"* Keiku privately communicated to the young melf who did as the great dragon requested.

"I think that is 'unbelievable great news'; my body is fully repaired, and..." Ona Noirar started saying.

But Nui Honei gently placed her hand over his lips and said, "Beloved, I am pregnant with twins!"

Fortunately, Keiku's instincts were correct in directing Nui Jooba to stand next to Ona Noirar whose knees buckled upon hearing Nui Honei's announcement. Nui Jooba caught the shocked great warrior as he began to fall and assisted Ona Noirar to the waiting chair, placed nearby.

All the females immediately then gathered around Nui Honei and engaged in loud conversations to congratulate her and pledge their assistance throughout her pregnancy and the birth of her infants. Female elf biology is such that a mature felf supposedly can only conceive every ten years and that period of possible conception only lasts about ten days. Conception is indeed a rare occurrence. Birthing multiple elves is an exceedingly rare occurrence, a near miracle.

The assembled males relegated themselves to congregate by

the recovering Ona Noirar. They too became loud in their congratulating Ona Noirar and pledged their support. Soon, it became a shouting match between the females and males.

"Thank you all for your hearty congratulations. I really appreciate your support. Forgive my near fall; I was completely overwhelmed with that last bit of very surprising news. I had no idea. Also, please forgive my barrage of future questions. I will need support and assistance from all of you, especially you House great father Je Maron. You are an expert in this area of raising fine sons and daughters. Wait, son(s) and/or daughter(s) do we have?" Ona Noirar now questioned. After a few more moments of quiet thought, he immediately stood and walked back over to the group of females followed by his all-male entourage who were laughing.

"Sisters and daughters, I believe a great warrior, one of the kingdom's most feared warriors, a renowned victor of many death-filled battles, and now a soon to-be father of *two* baby elves has something else important to say. Before you speak mighty warrior, know that we all love you, but we must love our dear Honei more now during this time since she has the joy and burden of carrying *two* unborn elves, your *two* unborn elves," Je Pagi announced adding special emphasis on the word "two" just to observe another small cringe reaction from Ona Noirar.

Je Pagi smiled and mentally communicated to Nui Honei, her daughters and Alleina, *"Oh my, we certainly have a new, highly vulnerable target for our future jests!"* The others snickered in acknowledgement.

"Yes, I do. Thank you," said Ona Noirar. "It seems some of you may have received and/or deduced some privileged and confidential information before I did. Be that as it may, I do have a question I want answered truthfully by all here. Who knows the sex of my unborn young ones?"

*"Our unborn young ones!"* loudly declared Keiku who mentally communicated her thought to all.

"Apologies all. I am again reminded that the blood of Keiku also runs through the veins of these unborn elves. So, Nui Honei, Keiku and I share progeny," Ona Noirar thought out loud for all to hear. "Does this mean Keiku will expect to play a role in our parenting decisions too?"

Je Leena quickly inquired with quiet laughter, "Uncle, need you even ask such a question?" Keiku snorted. The others laughed except Ona Noirar who responded with a scowl.

"Never mind; please just ignore my last question for now," Ona Noirar continued. "Before I am distracted again, please answer my question: Who knows the sex of *our* unborn elves?"

Most eyes turned towards Alleina, but she nor anyone else responded.

Finally, Keiku answered telling all, "*I do!*" Keiku exclaimed, seemingly quite proud of knowing those exclusive facts.

"Beloved Honei, you do not know either?" Ona Noirar asked.

"No, nor does it matter. I will love them unconditionally and equally, female and/or male," Nui Honei said.

After a sigh of relief, Ona Noirar looked lovingly at Nui Honei and said, "Then like you dearest future wife, I will love them too unconditionally and equally. Although I am a bit frightened, I am committed to becoming a great father like the ones gathered here."

"However, I do want female cousins, future battlemages like my aunt. You Uncle will be so much fun to watch at their Day of Adulthood celebration!" Je Leena jested.

"Maybe when they are both three hundred years old!" declared the soon to be over-protective father, Ona Noirar.

After the laughter subsided, Alleina then offered some serious advice, "Ona Noirar, your beloved is now four moons pregnant. If her pregnancy is normal, she will give birth in about another eight moons' time. The remainder of her pregnancy may be difficult for her. Her moodiness and discomfort will increase over time till the time after she gives birth. Honei will need her rest; so, do not overtax her. She must eat good, healthy food too. She should walk every day as well."

Je Pagi added, "This is also very important for you to know: whatever and whenever she may request, provide it. Even in the middle of the night, she may make a request. Do not question the rationale of the request, just fulfill the request obediently and quickly. Pregnancy with one elf can be difficult. Our dear Honei is pregnant with two, your *two* elves; the potential harmful risks are multiplied and far greater now. Support her tirelessly with unconditional love, dedication and commitment."

"For your future peace of mind and body," heed my wife's invaluable wisdom," advised Je Maron.

"That is right Uncle. Remember, Auntie is a very accomplished and renowned battlemage; she could do a variety of unspeakable, evil things to you. Be forewarned," Je Danei said.

"And I can poison you again without any chance of recovery too. So, be an exemplary father-to-be," Alleina added smiling.

"And I can now hide a dead body never to be found," Je

Leena stated matter-of-factly while changing her eye color to dragon green slits.

"You females can be quite terrifying at times... Why do your threats always seem much more danger-filled and ominous than the enemies I faced?" wondered Ona Noirar. "Let us all be joyous this day, please."

Commander Sochae too offered a fatherly suggestion, "I am the father of three, all sons. My experience has shown me that complete obedience and dedication to my wife's whims, big and small, during her pregnancies were crucial to maintaining peace at my house. Their advice is absolutely true, my friend."

More congratulations and pledges of support were made; more stories of pregnancy and child births were shared. Ona Noirar was teased often being such as easy target. The merriment continued well into the night. The joy of new life coming is great reason to celebrate.

After a while, House great mother Je Pagi pulled her husband away to walk hand-in hand to the distant side of the garden. At an old tree there, Je Pagi pulled Je Maron behind the great, old oak tree and kissed him passionately. After a few long moments, she released him and said, "Husband, do you still have any of that special Napa brandy left? Why don't we try to make another infant elf tonight!" The House Je Luneefa elders smiled at each other, quietly laughed, and returned to the gathering arm in arm.

Nui Honei pulled her son aside to talk to him privately. As usual, Dan-Rei dutifully followed her bonded rider. "Do you still love me, my son?" she asked.

"Yes, of course I do. More in fact today than when you adopted me," Nui Jooba replied.

"That is good to know. Thank you. As you know, I am new to this condition; I have no personal experience with my condition. So, please be patient with me. Help me when I ask. Know that I may not always have good reasons for my requests or moods, but please bear with me. My explanations may not always make good logical sense either. I too will need your support to get through this time period of my pregnancy and birth of your little brother(s) and/or sister(s)," Nui Honei said.

"Are you frightened mother?" Nui Jooba asked and starting to appreciate his normally fearless mother is now fearing the one thing she has wanted for so long.

"Yes, I am. I have been in many battles. I could rely on my training, experience, skills, weapons, and even my fellow soldiers.

But pregnancy is very foreign to me; it is completely unknown to me. Handling fear of the unknown is difficult for me; so, I will need your great strength too for support," Nui Honei quietly admitted.

"Mother, of course I will support you, as well as my little sister(s) and/or brother(s). I love you all greatly," Nui Jooba said.

"Thank you, my son. I and we love you too," Nui Honei said. She and her son, now in higher spirits, rejoined the group.

After congratulating their aunt and listening to more pregnancy tales, the young felfs, Je Danei, Je Leena, Annaei and Laehua, walked away from the larger group of females. "Sister, you have been unusually quiet this evening. What troubles you?" Je Leena asked her older sister.

"I believe Jooba may be losing interest in me, and I do not understand why," Je Danei responded sadly.

"Ye do threatened to kill him quite often and me think dat will not charm him much," Annaei offered in a shy manner.

"Or you threatened to dismember him," Je Leena added. "If you want more of his attention, I believe you need to give him more attention too, preferably without a blade in your hand or on your tongue."

"Or if ye must have a blade in yer hand, use it to cut away his shirt befer ye..." Annaei started to reflect before being interrupted by a coughing Zhen Laehua.

Je Leena then interjected, "Or is it that those three felfs paid Jooba an extraordinary amount of attention at the Warden's castle's training ground yesterday? Jooba gave a martial arts demonstration for Uncle Samu to the some young felfs and melfs. These three older felfs apparently really liked the instructor's *style* perhaps... They even invited him to visit their home for some private lessons. Hmmm... Sister, are you jealous?"

Before Je Danei could respond, brothers Je Jero, Je Tero and Je Kei joined the four felfs. Je Jero remarked, "Brothers, I will say it again; do we not have the finest looking sisters in all the kingdom? We are so honored to be related to you all."

"Well, we had just decided Jero that you are no longer the third best looking melf we know. You have fallen further down our list. Your rank is now number seven. But we are still deliberating; so, please go away before you fall further," Je Danei announced. Laughter erupted amongst the other sons and daughters of House Je Luneefa. Je Jero looked on in sheer puzzlement of disbelief.

"Before I take my leave with my brothers, I did bring you felfs all more wine," Je Kei said.

"See how thoughtful Kei is? That is one of the reasons why

he is the most handsome melf we know," Je Leena proclaimed. "Now, all of you males, please go away."

Before leaving, Je Kei offered his wife the last refill wine glass.

Je Jero pulled Je Kei away jokingly scolding him for being disloyal to the House Je Luneefa sons while amid the House daughters! "Kei, must you be so attentive? Why must you be so considerate to our sisters all the time? You make Tero and I seem so inconsiderate," Je Jero said annoyed with his youngest brother.

Je Kei quickly defended himself, "Eldest brother, did you not ever discuss male-female relationships with grandfather and father? They both have loved their wives for *centuries* and their wives, as best as I could and can tell, love them equally and deeply. Why is that? Grandfather and father have both told me, 'It is easy to get a female; but it is most difficult to keep her wanting to stay faithfully and dutifully by your side.' So, we males need to learn and *master* the little things our females like and want to nurture and enhance our relationship." Je Kei then turned to his wife and said, "I am committed to loving only Annaei this lifetime. So, I must do the things she likes to keep her happy with me. Because I want her to love only me. I will not ever take her love for granted. So, like grandfather and father, I will follow their lessons and master the *little things* she likes. Being considerate is just one simple requirement of our relationship." With a devilish smile, he pulled Annaei close and kissed her softly and whispered, "Beloved, me be charmin' ye more later dis night too!"

"Our youngest brother is so wise. Jero, take heed to his words. Your *charm* is quite limited and does not always impress every female as much as you think," Je Danei reminded.

Je Leena then said, "Yes Jero, Kei is very wise to have learned such lessons from Grandfather and Father. Further, Kei successfully and routinely practices those lessons. Annaei seems to be incredibly happy; Kei obviously is. So, take heed all of you males and learn from the elder melfs who have been in or are in centuries-old relationships. The relationship standards of these felfs here are quite high and daunting."

A frustrated Je Jero said, "Brothers, let us take our leave now." Je Jero turned and walked towards the courtyard gate. He was soon followed by his two brothers.

After the melfs left, Annaei turned back to Je Danei and continued, "Me dink Jooba be still a bit grievin'. But me dink ye can help him recover more by first lettin' him find all de blades ye carry, drink some brandy, cuttin' away his shirt, spill some brandy on ye and have him clean it up slowly, and... Oh, fergive me; me mind be dinkin' too fast... Let me end by sayin' somedin' House great moder Je Bueli told me, 'Go git yer elf!'" And with those sage words said, Annaei left the young felfs in search of her husband.

After catching up to Je Kei, Annaei took Je Kei's hand and pulled him to a large tree just inside the garden, away from his brothers. She positioned her husband behind the tree to be out of sight of the others and pressed him against the tree. Annaei kissed Je Kei passionately for several long moments. She then stepped back, looked lovingly at her stunned husband, and said, "Me want us to make an infant elf tonight!"

Soon thereafter, the shy and quiet Zhen Laehua left the group, saying, "I too will now take my leave. I now have much to think about."

Je Leena turned to Je Danei and with candor remarked, "Sister, also understand that Nui Jooba, now has bonded with a dragon, a black dragon, and has now become one of the most wanted melfs in the kingdom. Females from all over the kingdom will want him; so, take heed and make him yours now if you genuinely want him. Those words from our incredibly wise grandmother are very profound and timely. Let us heed them and take charge of our destiny tonight. I too will leave you now to 'go and git my elf!'"

"What? And whom might that be?" inquired a very curious and surprised Je Danei who did not know any details of her sister's secret, romantic interests.

"None other than the most mysterious melf we know...," replied a smiling Je Leena who too walked away going towards the Nui Vent stronghold. Moments later, the young felf was followed by the ever-watchful Ona Drachir...

As expected, Ona Drachir found Je Leena in his bedchamber, standing in the middle of his dark room. He walked silently to the felf and placed his arms around her, hugging her close. The felf pushed him back and asked, "What do you want of me, my mysterious melf? Tell me. I now want what my brother, Je Kei, has: real love as best as I can tell. If you are not serious about me, tell me now. I will then know that this night is just filled with our lust meant to fulfil our physical desires. I can then treat it as so afterwards and not place any importance upon tonight. Lie not to me! If you do, I will make you experience excruciating pain that you have never felt. So, tell me true; what do you want of me?" Je Leena asked with tearful eyes.

"Come, let us share a bath as I try to answer your question,"

Ona Drachir replied leading the felf to his private water room.

Now alone, Je Danei sipped her wine and thought to herself. After reexamining her feelings, she had indeed become jealous yesterday of the attention Nui Jooba had received from those other felfs. She also realized she wanted his romantic attention exclusively... With that revelation, she reached out to Nui Jooba mentally in private, *"Can Dan-Rei go to her mother's lair this night?"*

*"She can, but why?"* replied Nui Jooba.

*"Well, I... I... I want you to tell me about the book you were reading today..."* Je Danei nervously responded.

*"You mean the 'Mathematics of Tunneling'? You know that book was written by your brother and that subject is now taught during the first year of study at the Heartstone Architectural and Engineering Academy. Je Kei is truly brilliant.... Wait. Are you genuinely interested in that topic or just seeking to be alone with me? Please be honest,"* a nervous Nui Jooba requested.

After a few long moments of silence, Je Danei honestly confessed, *"Please forgive me. Although a bit confused and afraid, I will not hide behind shields of threats. I do want to be with you tonight. I want you to comfort me and I you. I want to feel your passion and heat for me again. Though my heart trembles, please do not be afraid because I am."*

Nui Jooba walked over to Dan-Rei and told her to go with her mother this night and he would see her tomorrow for more lessons and training. The young dragon, when standing on her four legs, was now as tall as Nui Jooba. Nui Kei Dan-Rei Ryuu looked at her rider with her big inquisitive eyes and tried to discern if her rider might be upset with her at all. Nui Jooba returned the dragon's thoughtful gaze with a smile and hugged her tightly saying, "Good night. I love you." He then walked around the group of elders, saying his goodbyes for the evening. When he finished, Nui Jooba walked towards the closest door to the stronghold. Just before he left the courtyard, he reached out to Je Danei again mentally, *"Follow me then to my bedchamber where I will attempt to discover all the hidden blades you now carry."*

After some time, Je Danei found herself to be the only young one left at the gathering; so, she too started walking around the group of elders saying her goodbyes for the evening. At an opportune time, she inconspicuously left the courtyard and went into the Nui Vent stronghold. Je Danei quickly and silently made her way to Nui Jooba's bedchamber whose door was partially open. After entering the room, she closed and locked the door.

Instinctively, Je Danei called upon her dragon senses to survey the dark and silent room. A few moments later, Nui Jooba walked into his main bedchamber from his private water room.

After lighting two candles on the fireplace mantle, he turned his attention to the first daughter of House Je Luneefa who was still standing quietly in the middle of the room. Nui Jooba walked slowly towards her still wary of the felf's potential, hostile nature. He smiled at her, and she returned his smile. When he was finally close enough to her, Nui Jooba first removed her House cape. Even in the low light, he gave pause to allow his eyes to again feast upon the felf's subtle beauty as he slowly walked around her. While gently undressing her, he discovered that Je Danei was carrying four hidden blades beside the two sai swords in her boots. Finally, Nui Jooba quietly said, "Come, your bath awaits you." He then took her hand and led her to his private water room which was illuminated by numerous scented candles.

After helping Je Danei into the large tub, Nui Jooba offered her a glass of brandy and began to wash her. Eventually succumbing to the warmth of the water, the effects of the brandy and his gentle and devoted touch, Je Danei relaxed. She closed her eyes and leaned back. She splashed water upon her dutiful attendant and even tried, unsuccessfully, to pull Nui Jooba into the tub with her.

Soon, he helped her out of the tub and started to dry her body glistening in the soft candlelight. With closed eyes, the young felf quietly panted with each deliberate, slow touch of Nui Jooba. Without any forewarning, an annoyed Je Danei asked, "Why have you not kiss me yet?"

"Perhaps for the same reason you have not kissed me yet," Nui Jooba quickly replied. "Go now to my bed and wait for me."

Je Danei looked longingly at Nui Jooba, grabbed his shirt with both hands and pulled him close to her before kissing him deeply. She released him and whispered, "But, I have nothing to sleep in."

"Exactly!" Nui Jooba responded with a sly smile.

After the felf left his water room, Nui Jooba undressed and used the waterfall there to quickly clean himself. Shortly afterwards, he emerged from his water room dried and naked. Surprisingly, Je Danei had not escaped his room this time, but was now in his bed lounging against the head of his bed looking at him. The upper part of the felf's body was not covered and Nui Jooba again marveled at her beauty. Though his room was now completely dark, both she and he utilized the magic of dragon eyes to see each other clearly. His dragon ear sense also reminded him of his pounding heart which emphasized his insecurities and fears of being a lowly melf. As he walked slowly towards her, he also began to realize that the cold water used to clean himself was not sufficient to calm the growing passion beginning to rage inside him. More fear started to grip him again.

"Do you plan to harm me?" Je Danei asked.

"Unlike you, I have no intentions of ever harming you like you harmed me the last time you were here. Quite the contrary, I plan to love you," responded Nui Jooba.

Upon reaching the bed, Nui Jooba got in and pulled the trembling felf close to him. He gazed at her, looking deeply into her eyes; he slowly stroked her long hair many times trying to calm both her and him. He placed her hand upon his chest so she too could feel the intense pounding of his heart. After a few quiet moments, Nui Jooba detected that Je Danei's heart was pounding with great intensity as well. He continued to hold her close to him, tightly wrapped in his powerful arms. In response, Je Danei nestled even closer to the melf.

Eventually, nervousness slowly ebbed away. The overwhelming fear they both have loosened its grip. After smiling at her, Nui Jooba kissed Je Danei's forehead, each closed eye, and mouth. He then whispered, "Go to sleep now knowing that you are much loved." They slept soundly in each other's loving embrace.

Je Danei awoke first just after dawn and gazed upon the melf's face. She still was nestled close to Nui Jooba's body such that she could feel his heat and quietly pounding heart. She also recognized that her own heart was pounding in a similar manner. After slowly tracing his facial features with her hand a few times, Je Danei kissed him and whispered softly, "Jooba, I think I am beginning to love you."

Nui Jooba opened one eye, smiled, and said, "Yes, I know."

Je Leena was especially proud of her role in the clandestine mission; she found she enjoyed being an assassin, an angel of Death.

# Epilogue

It is shortly after midnight. Queen Rho Jiedae and King Rho John lay quietly in their royal bedchamber. Both Majesties had succumbed to sleep long before. Their bedchamber was dark after the fire had burned down to just quiet, glowing embers. Even the few candles that normally burned through the night had also gone out. Outside, the storm's winds howled as heavy rain fell. Light did briefly illuminate the darken room momentarily as lightning flashed and thunder gloriously raged during the heavy rainstorm.

From the darkest corner in the ceiling, an invisibly cloaked figure silently descended from the room's rafters and approached the foot of the bed. With the next crash of thunder, the cloaked figure pulled the covers away from the queen and king who then woke up. Neither could speak since the cloaked figure had cast a spell upon them to prevent their communicating with anyone outside their bedchamber. Similarly, their limbs were also magically bound. The Canae queen and king could discern that someone else was in their bedchamber; however, they could only see the outline of the small, ancient-looking, cloaked figure standing at the foot of their bed by the glowing embers of the fire. The royal couple also knew they had been immobilized by magic; they could neither speak nor use their hands for any possible signaling for help. After Queen Rho Jiedae and King Rho John sat up, the cloaked figure gestured with a small, ancient, crooked finger for them to remain still.

"Listen to me carefully and heed my words," said the aged,

cloaked figure with an eerie voice, dripping with much evil and whose facial features were still partially hidden from view. "Your meddling with the Houses Nui Vent and Je Luneefa, whether directly or indirectly, will no longer be tolerated. Your malicious schemes and plots against these Houses must cease immediately. These Houses pose no threat to yours. Leave them alone. Both Houses' elders know your House is nearly bankrupt and that you secretly schemed and manipulated noble Houses to engage in House wars to control their power, as well as to share in the spoils of those wars. The treasure recently taken from the fallen House Si Moina will help you restore House Rho's financial stability. So, cease your actions of deceit and jealousy.

"Secondly, formally re-enter House Nui Vent into the kingdom's *Chronicles of Noble Houses*.

"I do not wish to visit you or any member of your family here or wherever again; but I will if I must. And if there is ever a next time, your entire family's blood will be spilled without mercy. I will utterly eradicate House Rho. No House Rho progeny will be left alive." With these last words, lightning flashed; and thunder crashed loudly to accent the message.

"Do not mislead yourselves either thinking that your two red dragons will help you. They will not; because the Houses Nui Vent and Je Luneefa now have three more dragons, all gloriously black too." With that announcement, both rulers disclosed more shock, surprise and annoyance with their faces that their "secret weapons" were no longer a secret. Knowing that Houses Nui Vent and Je Luneefa now have four powerful, black dragons completely terrified the king and queen.

"Thirdly, within three days, you will also appoint and announce that Nui Samu of House Nui Vent will be the next Warden of the North.

"Lastly, I left a reminder, a bloodstone, of my message on your table. A similar stone has been placed in each room of your family members too, including those three bastard young ones you two sired. Surprised again, I see... King Rho John, did you not know your wife also gave birth to a bastard? You are foolish to think all of House Rho's secrets would remain secret forever... Regardless, heed this warning; there will be no other. Now, return to your sleep," said the cloaked figure disappearing as thunder crashed loudly and lightning flashed brilliantly again.

The invisible, cloaked figure silently left the royal bedchamber, passing through a hidden door. After a short while, the ghostlike assassin reached a designated courtyard where her escort, another invisibly cloaked individual, met her. They both then silently made their way and mounted the invisibly cloaked dragon waiting for them in the rear of the stronghold's courtyard.

"*Mission accomplished?*" asked Ona Kei Kuri Ryuu, the great dragon, mentally.

"*Yes, of course and thank you for those special, ominous lightning and thunder sound effects. They clearly emphasized the import of my warning judging by how much both queen and king jumped,*" responded a proud Je Leena. "*And thank you too my love for shadowing me on this mission. I am again in your debt.*"

"*Then repay me after we return with your giving me a hot bath,*" Ona Drachir said just as the great dragon took flight.

"It will be my pleasure, beloved," Je Leena whispered into the ear of her companion as she hugged him tighter.

Later that day, the queen and king learned that similar red and black bloodstones had been found in all sixteen of their sisters, brothers, nieces, nephews, grandnieces, grandnephews, and extended family's rooms. Later, three other similar stones were also found in the rooms of the king and queen's bastard daughters and son, located outside the castle stronghold, in remote parts of Rhodell.

Five nights later, Ona Drachir made the trek to Keiku's secret lair. *Passing through several protective warded walls of magic, he made his way silently to the dragon's inner sanctum. Ona Drachir greeted the great dragon and removed his outer clothing. He then gathered the necessary writing materials.* "Do you need or want anything before we begin?" asked Keiku mentally.

"*I think not; I am ready. Please begin,*" responded Ona Drachir. Now that Nui Honei is ten moons pregnant with twin elves, she can no longer easily make the trek to Keiku's lair to record the great dragon's historical moments. Those duties have now fallen to another trusted friend, the young melf, Ona Drachir of House Ona Feiir, the nephew of the dragon's rider.

"*This year has had many noteworthy moments of great import. We have much to capture in my Chronicles; so, do let me know when you grow tired little one. We can stop and resume our recording later,*" Keiku remarked.

"*Thank you for your kind consideration. Though young and strong, I still do not have the strength nor stamina of a dragon. But I have made a list before coming here of some topics you may wish to consider for recording into your Chronicles,*" Ona Drachir remarked.

"That is very thoughtful of you. I knew you would be a good choice for assuming my Chronicles' scribe duties from Nui Honei. Thank you again for agreeing to capture my history. I greatly appreciate your time and efforts. What suggested topics do you have?" Keiku asked.

Ona Drachir unfolded a small scroll containing his list of suggestions and said, "These topics are in no particular order of assumed importance to you, but I thought you would want to record your thoughts about the following:

> Closing the final chapter of pain when Houses Si Moina and Tou Ahn were finally eradicated. With the final destruction of those two Houses, full recovery from being held captive has been completed I suspect.
>
> Three days ago, the Canae queen and king formally announced the reentry of House Nui Vent into the realm's Chronicles of Noble Houses. They also announced that Uncle Nui Samu is the new Warden of the North.
>
> Participating in your first funeral of our dear friends, the House Je Luneefa first great mother and father, Je Buel and Je Taeliel and Je Onyxia Ryoshi. Your dragon-flame instantly cremated their bodies. Though your action was brief; it was of great importance to the Je Luneefa family.
>
> Sharing your great sorrow of losing the House Je Luneefa elders, Ony and the House Nui Vent sons, Nui Danka and Nui Rei. We all felt great sorrow with their deaths too. They were your good friends; so, I imagine you also experienced great sorrow. Your flame also cremated the bodies of Nui Danka and Nui Rei. For the second time, your flame performed a most holy and sacred act.
>
> Learning of the birth and raising your first infant dragon and daughter, Nui Kei Dan-Rei Ryuu. When Jooba presented your daughter, I imagine you must have felt overwhelming and immense joy seeing your new progeny and legacy. She too looks very much like her 'perfect' mother.
>
> Preparing for your first wedding. I believe you will achieve another 'first' to add to your infamous list. I suspect you will be the first dragon to be part of a bridal party. That will indeed be a rare accomplishment.
>
> 'Hearing' the first sounds of your, Nui Honei and Ona Noirar's unborn progeny. Again, you have achieved

another 'first' since your blood also flows through these unborn elves. You must share a rare connection with them. We are all extremely excited to welcome them both into this world.

Watching the birth and bonding of your sons, Ona Tae Kuri Ryuu and Je Ri Kuri Ryuu. You now have three magnificent offspring! Your excitement of having two more young dragons has greatly multiplied; has it not? Your parenting duties will dramatically increase too.

Instructing your young ones and the new dragon riders about Dragonosophy. This is an important topic which you, Auntie Honei and Uncle Noirar will teach your offspring and the new dragon riders. What does it mean to be a dragon, a great dragon? An offspring of the greatest dragon, Ona Kei Kuri Ryuu? What are the responsibilities of the dragon and dragon rider? Though you have just started teaching this subject and training your offspring and their riders, this instruction will hopefully continue for centuries.

Watching Je Leena's first duel with another battlemage. Though I could not see you, I too 'felt' your presence high above that field. That was her very first 'death' battle – one that results in the death of one and/or both combatants. She did not yield to her foe's on-going taunts; she stayed focused like a good warrior should. Dariel's repeated disrespectful jeers did not unnerve her. It is ironic that Dariel's description of how he planned to ravage a defeated Je Leena became his death's reality with his limbs and head being pulled taut till he was finally decapitated... Well done, Leena, well done indeed. I watched her duel with great pride, as well as great sadness...

"Why sadness?" asked Je Leena who was sitting across the lair.

"Had you lost that duel and then forcefully taken away, I was duty-bound to fulfill my pledge and kill you. Mariel would have died next and all in his family and anyone else who attempted to interfere with our revenge upon Houses Tou Ahn and Si Moina," Ona Drachir mournfully replied.

"Let me remind you little one that my words are to be captured in my Chronicles," an annoyed Keiku remarked. "Hmmm... you do though have a talent with words."

Je Leena was sitting by the fire in the great dragon's lair. Sitting next to her was her bonded dragon who was sleeping peacefully. After rising to join Ona Drachir at the writing table, Riku immediately rose too and followed her. Although still considered to be an infant, this young dragon and his older brother, Taeku, were both four fahs tall. They were both now four moons old.

When Riku saw his brother lying next to Ona Drachir, he pounced upon him, initiating playful wrestling. The jostling between the two young dragons soon led to their flying around the lair chasing one another. They also made screeching sounds at each other in their early attempts at making dragon roars. Their current screeches were now more annoying and woefully short of a mighty dragon's roar. Still, Keiku proudly admired her sons' attempts. From time to time, either of them would bump into things since they still had not yet mastered their flying abilities. Even so, their mother would look upon them with immense pride for they were her very handsome offspring. And no one would even dare attempt to convince the great dragon otherwise. All Keiku's offspring are "perfect" too like their mother.

Je Leena wrapped her arms around the melf's neck and commented, "Do not forget Keiku, you also observed the beginnings of my love relationship with your new scribe too. And even though he tried to keep his relationship a secret, Uncle Samu fell for Zhen Lae. And did you not also observe the challenges and joys of love between Je Danei and Nui Jooba, Annaei and Je Kei, Pi Liu and Je Tero, and Pi Lin and Je Jero?"

"And, perhaps last, but not least, Uncle Noirar finally proclaimed that you are 'perfect', o great Ona Kei Kuri Ryuu!" concluded Ona Drachir.

*"Yes, indeed he finally did. With this year's great sorrows, we all experienced great joys also. We shall cherish our memories of dear friends who are no longer with us. We shall also rejoice in our new joys and look forward to making more good memories. Let us now begin,"* Keiku remarked.

# About The Author

M. R. Lucas is a former business management consultant, legal project manager, and legal electronic discovery consultant. His professional work experience has spanned over three decades.

Although he formally studied mathematics in college, he then began to develop deep interests in information technology and computer programming. While in college, Lucas was also a four-year varsity athlete on the college fencing team. He also was an active member in the college's gospel choir and volleyball club.

After college, Lucas started working full-time with a leading information technology and services corporation. He later married and raised a family with his wife of over three decades. His current hobbies mostly include playing strategy games, especially trading card games, and reading a wide range of fantasy books. After transitioning into semi-retirement, Lucas started devoting more efforts to his newly developed hobby: authoring sword and sorcery fantasy stories.

www.ingramcontent.com/pod-product-compliance
Lightning Source LLC
LaVergne TN
LVHW041747060526
838201LV00046B/929